HIDDEN
SINS

By Stacey Abrams *writing as* Selena Montgomery

Hidden Sins
Secrets and Lies
Reckless
Deception

HIDDEN SINS

A NOVEL

STACEY ABRAMS

WRITING AS

SELENA MONTGOMERY

AVON

An Imprint of HarperCollinsPublishers

HIDDEN SINS. Copyright © 2006 by Stacey Abrams. All rights reserved. Printed in the United States of America. No part of this book may be used or reproduced in any manner whatsoever without written permission except in the case of brief quotations embodied in critical articles and reviews. For information, address HarperCollins Publishers, 195 Broadway, New York, NY 10007.

HarperCollins books may be purchased for educational, business, or sales promotional use. For information, please email the Special Markets Department at SPsales@harpercollins.com.

A mass market edition of this book was published in 2006 by HarperTorch, an imprint of HarperCollins Publishers.

FIRST AVON PAPERBACK EDITION PUBLISHED 2021.

Designed by Diahann Sturge

Library of Congress Cataloging-in-Publication Data has been applied for.

ISBN 978-0-06-314451-4

21 22 23 24 25 BRR 10 9 8 7 6 5 4 3 2 1

For Mom, Dad,
Andrea, Leslie,
Richard, Walter
and Jeanine—
my beloved muses.

HIDDEN SINS

August 7, 1937
Austin, Texas

AIKO WIELDED THE GUN WITH AN ARTIST'S PRECISION. AGAIN and again she pierced her victim's flesh, leaving behind a permanent stain, one so indelible she'd never be forgotten. Sweat beaded at her high, unlined forehead and trickled along her skin, but she refused to be distracted. Around her the air grew thick and heavy with curses, as each victim succumbed to her craft. Occasionally she had to check her aim, to angle it so she could be certain of her target. Her work was precise, delicate, and true.

"How much longer, honey? We've got a train to catch." Reese, lying on his stomach, turned his head to the side and flashed his wide, gapped grin at the young woman. The teeth that had gone missing had been lost to fistfights and barroom brawls, but Reese still liked to think he was a handsome devil. Even with his bare ass hanging out. "Wanna come with us?"

"Stop pestering the young lady," came the quiet caution from the front of the circus tent. "You don't want the needle to slip and hit bone, now do you?"

When he spoke, Aiko lifted her head from the third man she'd been asked to tattoo that night. The drawings had been onto the men's hips, dangerously close to their posteriors, but she knew better than to ask questions. Her boss had ushered them into her tented work space nearly two hours ago, plopped a stack of bills in front of her and a series of strange pictures at her elbow. Mr. Hadley had shooed her other customers away with the guttural growl he called a voice. It worked for taming lions and had a similar effect on nervous humans.

Aiko had an ear for sound and a fascination for the human voice. In her travels, she'd heard accents and tones and pitches that could swirl the mind. And Hadley's rumble was the exact opposite of the intoxicating timbre that came from the man in the corner. He sounded like an angel sipping honey, all sweet, smooth, and soft. The tones drifted over her, wound inside her.

Blushing at her own thoughts, she sent a shy smile over her shoulder to the tall, stunning man who leaned negligently against the tent frame. Once again her breath stuttered as she took in the mahogany skin and piercing brown eyes that seemed to see inside her. He reminded her of a statue she'd seen once, where a warrior stood poised to kill. Like the marble sculpture, he had a ruggedly carved face and a powerful build. He looked like a prince or maybe a president.

Not like a preacher.

"Reverend Reed?" She spoke softly. Normally, Aiko was always being told to lower her voice, but there was no need in his presence. Somehow, her booming tones grew naturally muted, dulcet even. Her mama would have been proud. She nodded to the pictures on her worktable. They were nice-looking and all, but odd. She'd never seen anything like it before. "I don't understand these symbols, Reverend. What did you say they meant?"

Micah Reed smiled slightly. "They're in Greek, Ms. Bethea. One of the Lord's languages."

"You know Greek?"

"I've studied many things. Ignorance steals the soul. But a woman of your talents obviously understands this."

Her creamy skin flushed a becoming rose, and her ivory smile grew wider. "We don't get such educated men here at our little circus very often."

"Micah's a regular re-nay-sans man," scoffed an irritated Reese. No matter where they went, all the ladies swooned over the preacher. And the men followed Reed like he was Moses. He was getting damned sick of playing second fiddle to a cut-rate holy man. "Thinks he knows everything God does and a little extra."

"That's blasphemy!" Aiko gasped, and she drew the tattoo gun away. "No man knows more than God."

"He's just teasing you, Ms. Bethea." Micah pushed away from the billowing blue canvas and joined her at her work station. His strides were soundless on the saw-wood floor. "He enjoys tormenting lovely young women. A bit of the devil in him, I reckon." Micah dropped a warning hand on Reese's shoulder, his fingers biting deep. "As I explained to Mr. Hadley, we're a religious sect traveling across Texas to spread the good word. I heard about Ms. Betty Broadbent's tattooing machine, and the Lord directed me to you. He wants his acolytes to wear his symbols."

Aiko nodded, but a worried crease appeared between her eyebrows. "No disrespect, preacher, but why would you put the mark of the Lord on a man's buttocks?"

Reese startled, but Micah kept his gentle smile in place. He had already thought about the question and what they'd have to do if it—or others—were asked. "The symbols are merely that, Ms. Bethea. Symbols. Like a crucifix worn beneath a dress." As he spoke, he snaked a quick hand along Aiko's nape and drew out the thin, gold chain. "Our symbols are for the Lord's eyes, not man's. Isn't that right?"

Aiko touched the tiny gold cross that gleamed in Micah's strong, wide hand. "Observant one, aren't you?"

"When there's something worth looking at," Micah murmured, closing his hand around the plump fingers. If he had more time, he thought, he'd explore the enticing mix of curiosity and innocence that watched him so closely. "You have the look of a daughter of God, Ms. Bethea."

Fed up with the flirting over his prone form, Reese snorted. "Look, missy. My ass is getting cold here. You gonna finish or not?"

Micah gave a short nod, and Aiko reluctantly returned to her drawing. The needle plunged again and again, swooping and circling into one of the symbols on the parchment.

As he watched her work, Micah congratulated himself. When he'd planned the heist of Saul Schultz's gold two months ago, he'd worked out every detail to the letter. Except for the most important part. But Ms. Aiko Bethea had solved that last problem, and he had to admit, hiring the tattoo artist was a stroke of genius. For weeks he'd wondered about this final part of the plan—how to hide six bags of stolen Spanish gold until it was safe to spend the money.

Stealing the gold had been easy. Reese had procured the porter uniforms and the train timetables. Bailey's wicked hand with chemicals had sent the regular crew off to early slumber. With Poncho and Guerva, the troupe of five located the secret compartment Schultz finagled on the government train and snuck the gold off as easy as you'd please.

As soon as the train arrived in Dallas, all hell would break loose. Which was why Micah had decided they'd have to lay low and hide the money and other booty until it was safe. Going through the bags, counting the gold, he had discovered a bound manuscript that piqued his interest—and a figurine carved of the hardest wood he'd ever touched. He hadn't recognized the language or the statuette, but the intellectual in him was curious about its origins. Reluctantly, though, he'd left them tucked in their pouch for later. He knew if he tried to remove anything, the men would begin to squabble about pinching a taste of the gold now.

With Roosevelt's embargo on gold, trading Spanish coins would look mighty suspicious, especially among colored men during a depression. In a couple of years, Micah was convinced it would be a different story. The trick was waiting. And while patience was a virtue, virtue among thieves was as elusive as honor.

He could have killed them all, but he had a code. And he didn't renege on promises. So the only solution was hiding the gold and creating a system that required all five of their contributions to get it back. Aiko had been the answer to an illicit prayer. Watching her work, he wondered about God's sense of humor and admired the deft movements of the needle, oddly eager for his turn under her ministrations.

HOURS LATER THE band of five stood in the woods not a mile from the train depot. Each man limped a bit, the painful legacy of having a cheek full of needle marks and ink. Night had fallen, indigo dotted with dazzling white. The air smelled of juniper and jasmine laced with the perfume of crude oil.

Micah stood before his men, eyes gleaming with pride. "A short wait, men, and we'll all be richer than Midas."

"Who?" Poncho whispered the question sotto voce. "He ain't on our team."

Stifling a sigh at his illiterate company, Micah corrected mildly, "He's a figure in Greek mythology, Poncho. Everything he touched turned to gold."

"Oh."

"Yes, oh." Sighing, Micah continued. "Only one man knows where the gold is hidden, and the four of us have hidden our keys to the safe. Bailey kindly rigged the safe to douse the gold with aqua regia if anyone tries to open it without the keys."

"Water of kings?" Poncho wrinkled his brow in confusion. "What will that do?"

"Try to open the safe or blow it up and it'll melt the gold and any fool dumb enough to touch it." Bailey shrugged. "Hydrochloric acid and nitric acid. Micah cast the keys to be used in order. Try the wrong sequence and the acid starts to flow. Plus, I've added a surprise ingredient that will make it mighty hard to live to spend the dough."

Satisfied the men would be too scared to break their pact, Micah added, "We've seen your handiwork, Bailey. We're believers."

"Explain again why we've got these cursed pictures painted on our asses," demanded Reese. "I look like a circus freak."

"Each of you gave me the rough coordinates for your hiding place and a hint to the location. August seventh, 1939, we meet here with our keys and unlock the gold. But just in case something happens, I understand that the tattoos will last forever." Micah fixed Reese with a solicitous smile that masked the growing doubt building inside him. One too many rumors of saloon girls and accidents trailed the team when Reese was around. He'd have preferred to kick him out of the group, but Reese had been his partner for too long and he knew too much. "Should poor luck happen to befall one of us before that date, we'll still have to rely on your ass to find the key."

"You're the only one who can read Greek."

"Insurance, Reese. However, I'm happy to tutor anyone who'd like to learn. However, only you know exactly where the key is, and if you've been smart, we'll need you alive to find it. If we're not that lucky, there's a lot of Texas to cover to find the keys." Micah met each man's eye, his dark gaze penetrating and level. "We're in this together. We have the secret in our skin and blood now. We're marked."

"He ain't." Reese slanted a furious look at Guerva. The silent bastard hid the safe. All the other men thought shoving their own key into a hole in the ground would protect their interests, but he knew better. Guerva could be in cahoots with Micah and have another way of getting at the gold. He surely would have. Which is why his key was nice and safe in his bag, and not in the desert like he told Micah. Instead, he'd trailed Guerva for nearly ten hours until his stolen wagon threw a wheel. Nevertheless, he knew enough to figure out where the man had headed. He'd figure the rest out all by himself.

If Micah had trusted him, they could have worked together.

But Micah, the silver-tongued devil, favored Guerva instead, like he always did. But Reese trusted no one, especially not a deaf-mute loyal to Micah Reed. "How do we know he put the money where he says he did? Or that you didn't conspire with him to cheat us all?"

"Because I'm a man of God, Reese. I don't lie."

"Bullshit." Reese spit a plug of tobacco onto the red clay beneath his feet. "You're crookeder than a whore on Saturday night, Reverend Reed." He sneered the title. "I don't trust you no more than one of them."

Micah felt disgust curl in his belly, but he kept his face bland. Reese had been an instrumental part of the team. He knew the train routes better than anyone, and had gotten them the porter uniforms. "You all watched me cast the keys in East Austin. We all tried them out in the safe. Together. When could I have cheated you?"

Reese hadn't figured that part out, but he reckoned there was a way. "Mebbe there's just the one key needed. Mebbe you've already got the right one."

For all that he was a thief, Micah was rarely a liar, and he never reneged on promises. Except today. However, the itch at his neck had never failed him before, and God would be as likely to forgive the lie as he would the theft. He was willing to gamble. "Be that as it may, Reese, you don't have much of a choice. The keys are hidden and the safe is buried. Guerva fulfilled his part of the bargain, and now we've got to fulfill ours."

"I gots to disagree." In the next instant, Guerva lay flat on his back, a hole ripped through his chest. With a roar of anguish, Poncho launched himself at his brother's killer. Reese tried to fend off the crazed man and angled the gun to fire at Micah.

"No," screamed Aiko, rushing pell-mell into the campsite. "Don't you hurt him!"

"Aiko, get away from here!" Micah reached for her, but she eluded his grasp.

She launched herself at the grappling men and, handily avoiding the flying fists from Poncho, pinched the gun from Reese. With a dazzling sleight of hand, the Colt disappeared. Seconds later Aiko vaulted away in a series of tumbles and turns that landed her by Micah's side.

She shoved the gun into his hand, and he cut a bewildered look at the shockingly spry young woman who watched him out of exotic chocolate eyes that seemed to see into his soul. "Aiko, what are you doing here?"

Breathing heavily, she gasped, "I don't know. I think I'm supposed to be with you." She watched Bailey tackle Reese and urged, "Let's go!"

"I can't leave my men," Micah countered. "Go hide in the woods. I'll come and get you!"

"You ain't goin' nowhere, you son of a bitch!" Reese threw off Poncho and Bailey and snagged Bailey's Colt. Rolling to his side, he bellowed, "I'll see you in hell!"

Micah spun Aiko behind him as the shot rang out. A flash of light. A deafening boom. And the world fell dark.

August 14, 2006
Detroit, Michigan

Mara Reed perched on the edge of the bar stool, nursing a martini. The snug red dress slid cunningly up her silk-stockinged thigh, and the man on the seat next to hers hadn't taken his eyes off its journey. To toy with him, to amuse herself while she waited, she delicately slid her finger along the embroidered hem, where reality gave way to imagination. She could hear the man gulp, his breaths shortened. When she recrossed her legs and the edge moved up higher, the reverent sigh almost made her laugh.

But she knew better. Tonight she was regal and aloof, a woman encased in ice. Men would see her and want her, but she would not let herself be taken. Only one man would be able to break through. The man with the answers she'd searched for most of her life.

She knew the instant her mark stepped into the hotel bar. An amateur would have turned to double check or begun to fidget. She was no amateur. She didn't glance over her shoulder to verify her senses. Instead, she slid a quick glance into the mirrored panel behind the bar. The look was imperceptible, but thorough. As she thought, he'd come alone. According to her source, when in Detroit, Arthur Rabbe played poker in the backroom of the Hardin Hotel. He paused in the entryway and scanned the room.

You couldn't tell by looking at him that he'd murdered a young woman in cold blood last night.

Ice coursed through her as she recalled opening the apartment door that had been left ajar. Mary Kay Ross-Harper, a ninth grade history teacher, lay in the center of the living room, whimpering and dying. Body torn and violated, she'd managed to whisper a single name while Mara waited by her side for the ambulance to arrive.

Arthur Rabbe.

Mara sipped at her drink, the cold liquid trailing fire down her throat. She would have preferred a glass of wine or a Diet Coke, but she appreciated the burn as it seared through the memory of the bruised face going slack with death.

Taking another bracing gulp, she reminded herself of the goal. And the reward. For this con, her character drank dry martinis because her mark did. He would appreciate her taste for the man's drink and her ability to stomach its harsh tones. She welcomed the liquid courage. She needed it.

As Rabbe moved closer, she ran a light hand over her hair, accenting the flash of sparkle on her wrist. Her own short cap of curls was snugged beneath a wig that swung ebony hair at her chin. The sleek bob accented her almond-shaped eyes and drew attention to the beauty mark she'd added to the corner of her mouth.

A creamy strand of pearls circled her long, elegant neck, their restrained luster screaming wealth, and the single diamond drop at their center drew attention downward. The bustier she wore beneath the sheath of red pushed her breasts up to her ears, a fitting frame for the diamond. Only a jeweler's eye would have known that the one carat stone was counterfeit. Since she'd gotten the necklace from one of L.A.'s finest craftsmen, she wasn't worried about discovery.

After tonight she'd have more pressing problems.

Rabbe had killed Mary Kay in order to secure a journal. One that could lead him to millions in gold stolen by her grandfather and his cronies and hidden in the desert of the West. Mary Kay's great-uncle Bailey had been a part of the band of thieves. Bailey, Poncho, Guerva, Reese, and her grandfather Micah. Names she knew by heart.

In her hotel room, Mara had filled a notebook with all the data she'd collected over the years. The leather-bound volume sat on the nightstand with a fresh entry. Before a few nights ago, the last time she'd picked it up was in Sierra, Nevada, where she learned about Bailey's only remaining relative. She'd finished up a job and headed for Detroit.

Too late to get to Mary Kay before Rabbe did.

The lock had been intact when she arrived, and she could see now how he might have gotten himself invited inside the lady's apartment. Nearly six feet tall, Rabbe was muscular and broad-shouldered, but not so overwhelming that he scared off customers. The clear green eyes and thin mustache added char-acter to a banally handsome face that could be forgotten in a crowd but could also be fondly remembered. He reminded her of the high school quarterback, with a Luger tucked in his back pocket.

"Ms. Malko?"

The name she had chosen whispered over bare skin as Rabbe spoke from behind her. Taking her time, she lifted her head to meet his eyes in the mirror. "Yes?"

Rabbe waited for her to turn to face him, but she continued to watch him steadily. "Ms. Jennie Malko? I'm Arthur Rabbe."

She quirked her red-painted lips into a mildly confused smile. Deliberately, she allowed her eyes to warm, skimming over his mirror image, but she remained in place. "Do I know you? I'm certain I would remember if I did."

Rabbe was irritated by her refusal to turn to meet him, but when he caught her checking him out in the mirror, he relaxed. He angled himself to stand beside her, which forced her to turn to him. Bracing a hand on the bar, he extended the other to her. "No, we haven't been formally introduced. But we have acquaintances in common. Cassandra Coley mentioned to me that you were staying here this week."

Nice job, Cassandra, she thought. The cocktail waitress at the MGM had done her job well. "You enjoy gambling, Mr. Rabbe?" To draw attention to her mouth, she took another small taste of her martini, trying not to grimace. She really hated vodka.

"I enjoy games of chance, yes. And please call me Arthur." Rabbe could feel himself hardening, especially when Jennie

Malko shifted on her stool and her skirt slid up her thigh another precious inch. He could have her stripped naked in seconds, he imagined wildly, and his hands curled with anticipation. If she had a sense of adventure, it would be even better. "I'd like to invite you to join me in a game of poker. We're about to start the game in the club room, and I thought you might enjoy a hand or two."

Mara gathered her designer handbag and slid off the stool, lightly brushing against Rabbe as she stood in the cramped space between her seat and his body. "Scamming rubes has its charms, but I prefer longer odds. And bigger payoffs."

Rabbe froze, taken aback. "I'm not sure I know what you mean."

With a half smile, she took a final sip of her drink and placed a fifty beneath the glass, generous for a single drink. "I mean you've been running this little operation for a few years now. You've probably netted enough to have your Cavalier detailed."

"Bitch." He balled his fists and crowded her against the bar.

Mara didn't flinch. "You can pummel me if you'd like, but I doubt your marks would take too kindly to you hitting a defenseless woman."

"They won't know if I drag your skinny ass into the alley." A solid, iron grip closed around her upper arm, bruising flesh. "Give me one good reason not to."

Five points of agony pulsed beneath his hold. She smiled. "I know about Mary Kay and the journal. Why don't we retire to your room and you can tell me why I shouldn't call the police."

Rabbe thought about killing her then, but knew his new boss wouldn't approve. Public displays offended Davis Conroy's sensibilities. The man had peeled a strip off him when he reported that Mary Kay had died—not because he had killed her, but because the cops found her so quickly. Apparently, he had Jennie Malko to thank for the tip to the police. The anger humming through him would make the pleasure of revenge sweeter.

But the lady was right about the lobby. Instead, he'd take her upstairs and first he'd do her, then do her in. Might be worth it to Conroy to find out how the hell the lady knew what he'd been up to last night.

"Follow me." Without giving her much choice in the matter, he dragged her to the elevator. At his suite, he shoved her inside the spacious room. Before she could speak, his gun found her throat. "Who are you?"

Mara lifted a hand and lightly pushed the barrel away, proud that her fingers didn't shake. "I'm an interested party." Feigning nonchalance, she turned and set her handbag on the low coffee table, slipping the vial into her palm. "I had a meeting with Mary Kay last night, but you appear to have met with her first."

Caressing the barrel lovingly, Rabbe remembered the shocked eyes going blank when he popped her. It made the last time even better. "Little Mary Kay. Tried to tell me she didn't have my merchandise."

"So you did find the journal?" Mara slowly released the top

with her thumb, not removing her eyes from his. He would do the same to her, if she gave him a chance. She wouldn't. "I've been looking for it myself."

"Don't know why." He had tried to read the pansy writing last night, to find out what inside was worth the $50,000 he'd been authorized to pay. "Just a bunch of rambling about nothing. And crazy pictures."

"Pictures?" She advanced slowly. "Show me."

Abruptly suspicious, Rabbe lifted the gun. "What's your game, honey?"

"No game. I'm ready to retire, and I think you can help." Whipping her hand around, she tossed the contents of the vial into his face. Simultaneously, she lashed out with her heel and felled the screaming man. The concoction, a recipe from her pal Sebastian, took quick effect.

Seconds later Rabbe was sprawled on the blue carpet, unconscious. Wasting no time, Mara jumped over the body and headed to the closet safe. She'd been a guest of Hardin's before, and luckily, the Detroit branch offered the same shoddy protection as the others. Cracking safes was a skill she'd honed with years of practice.

With a whir, the lock released and she seized the black journal and a briefcase. She flipped the latch and swiftly determined that the case contained close to fifty grand. Glancing at Rabbe, she slammed the case closed and decided to help herself. He had.

She stepped gingerly over the prone body. Moving quickly,

she headed out to her hotel, since the drugs would hold for a couple of hours.

She knew she should take off immediately, but she couldn't help herself. In her tiny motel room, Mara curled onto the bed and started to read. And dream. Bailey had indeed been one of the five who helped her grandfather. He'd kept copious notes, careful descriptions of his life since then. Time slipped away as she read, engrossed.

When the first bullet lodged into the plywood door, she realized Rabbe had recovered. She scrambled from beneath the meager comforter provided by the motel and splayed herself flat on her stomach between the double beds. Tendrils of first pink light crept through the heavy crimson drapes, dancing dust motes on the air. In the hallways, she could hear the sounds of patrons screaming and the thud of feet rushing to safety.

"Damnit, bitch! I know you're in there!" The introduction was punctuated by another volley of gunfire.

Mara easily recognized Rabbe's drunken voice, the insults to her parentage slurring under the influence. *How the hell had he found her so quickly?* she wondered with mild curiosity as she cased the room for an alternative exit.

"Your friend took some convincing, but she told me where I could find you!" Rabbe yelled. He rammed his shoulder against the door, determined to batter it from its moorings. He'd save his bullets until he got inside, he thought balefully, cursing himself for rushing out without reloading. But at the time, he'd been good and pissed.

Even now, with each collision, his shoulder ached and his temper grew. Once he'd stopped vomiting in his bathroom, he'd been on a tear, fueled by a bottle of tequila and bruised male ego. However, he had managed to salvage of bit of his dignity when he figured out he'd been played by two women—not just the one he was about to kill. Taking another swig from the bottle in his hand, Rabbe growled, "She may never walk straight again. But we had a hell of a time coming to terms."

Rabbe sniggered at his double entendre, and inside the motel room, Mara closed her eyes over a guilty grief. Cassandra hadn't been her bosom buddy, but they were friendly. They'd worked together before, selecting marks who deserved to be taken. No one deserved the type of punishment Rabbe had meted out, and as she crouched on the floor, she decided she had no intention of becoming his next victim.

Forcing her breath to steady, she considered her options. From the sound of the creaking wood, she only had a minute, at most. Her choice of abode, the Starburst, wasn't known for its high-level security team. The clientele were mainly hourly customers, ones who would find it in their best interest not to summon the authorities. She'd chosen it, as she always did, because the proprietor accepted cash and a murmured claim of a missing ID.

As she should have done before, Mara swiftly surveyed the terrain. Two beige and green double beds made of prefabricated wood were bolted to the floor. The single lamp had been welded to the wall, its twin bulbs covered by a nearly transparent shade.

The air conditioner lay below a window that seemed to also be made for decoration but not removal. No handle, no sliding apparatus. The doorway to the bathroom was ajar, letting the light seep into the room as she read. No help there, she recalled. The only other furniture in the room was the massive bureau/entertainment unit that sat squarely in the center of the room.

Against a white metal door that joined her room to the next.

Praying that the frugality of the furniture included a cheap unit, Mara moved stealthily to the thirteen-inch set and set it on the floor. She yanked out the plug and unhooked the cable. Then bracing her feet on the air conditioner, she pressed her back to the unit and shoved with all her might. Slowly, it scraped along the carpet, tearing at the mottled blue nap.

Hearing the sound, Rabbe shouted, "You ain't goin' nowhere, bitch!" To accentuate his threat, he shot another one of his precious bullets. The projectile sailed through an earlier hole and punctured the pane of glass. A web of cracks quickly spread along the window, and Mara fairly sagged with relief. She abandoned her moving project and snatched the comforter from the nearest bed.

Swathing her hand and ducking her head beneath its protective cover, she cocked her hand and punched through the hole. The fine cracks exploded into shards of glass. In the hallway, Rabbe roared as he realized his prey might escape. He hurried for the glass doors to circle around to the outside.

As Mara expected.

Taking advantage, she grabbed her duffel bag and backpack

and rushed for the door. With slippery palms she yanked open the nearly broken sheet of wood and checked the hallway for Rabbe. Coast clear, she raced for the fire exit and took the stairs two at a time. By the time Rabbe made it to the rear of the building and her shattered window, Mara was on the roof of the Starburst, huddled near a turbine, with nowhere to go but down.

Returning to Hollywood wasn't an option. Not Chicago either, she presumed, given her limited engagement as a psychic who helped solve a crime her partner had committed. The television coverage had been phenomenal, but fatal for a grifter. Paula and Bill were still miffed about the rout in Atlanta, and the Gordon-Russells had become legendary for their creative expressions of temper. Stefanie Grant would probably take a call from her, but hiding out in Liberty, Missouri, had about as much appeal as Rabbe's plans for her.

She had to face facts, Mara decided, crawling along the ground to peer over the edge of the roof. She'd burned nearly every bridge between San Francisco and Atlantic City. Not that she cared much. Relationships inevitably led to annoying habits like honesty and loyalty. She preferred to keep her life commitment-free. No ties, no responsibilities to anyone but herself. No urge to mold a person into her image or to try to control his every thought. Love was an alchemist's mockery. She'd succumbed once, and learned her lesson well. For all she knew, he had forgotten her by now.

Mara pulled herself to her knees and watched as Rabbe circled the building, banging on doors. When one opened, she saw her chance. She slithered down the fire escape into the night and quickly gained entry into a Ford Crown Victoria that had to be on its third decade. With the ease of practice, she connected the wires and fired the engine. Sliding down against the cracked green leather, she eased the car into gear and slowly rolled out of the parking lot.

At the freeway exit, she shot up in her seat, gunned the motor and shot onto the ramp. The sign indicated that she was heading south, heading toward home, but she really had nowhere else to go. So she'd drive for Texas, praying for a better idea along the way.

And anything would be better.

CHAPTER 1

RAGGED BREATH SCUTTLED THROUGH HEAVING LUNGS AS Mara dodged the rusted bumper that jutted out from the nearly deserted parking lot stall. The edge nicked her skin, ripping through thin black cotton pants. Pain zinged along nerve endings made raw by terror, but she ignored the ache and the fear. There would be time to check her wounds later, when monsters weren't nipping at her heels.

To distract herself, she concentrated on other sounds, other sensations. She could hear the blood pounding through her veins, could hear the wind whipping past her hollowed cheeks. Both told her that she was alive, though not for long if she didn't find shelter soon.

Muscles burned as she sprinted along the broken, empty sidewalk, her pale brown eyes checking for and discarding possible routes of escape. Above her, the dawn sun shone down with unnerving ferocity, as though daring her to evade its punishing rays. The Sunday sky was cloudless and blue, a lovely and lethal combination. Even at daybreak the temperature had already reached above ninety, with nowhere to go but up. Old and young alike died in these conditions, even faster if they had spent the past twenty minutes running flat out as she had.

In wet testimony, sweat ran rivulets down her back, soaking the skintight black tank top she'd been wearing for three days. She had no choice. She'd been forced to ditch her duffel bag and nearly all her worldly belongings back in Baton Rouge, when her alarm system—a hostile trailer park owner who didn't like squatters—threw her out in the middle of the night. Luckily, she'd decided to sleep in her favorite shirt and the loose-fitting pants that breathed in the dank heat of what passed for a southern summer. She'd snagged her backpack with its frayed wallet containing thirty-six bucks and the lumpy, crude quilt called "Fool's Paradise," which Grandma Reed gave her when she was five and too young to sin.

That was a long time ago.

The streets flew past in rapid succession, each stretching longer than the last. It was a trick of the mind, Mara knew, because the town had been laid out by stodgy city planners with every avenue and boulevard a uniform length. The very sameness of the place had always galled her, but she welcomed the homogeny today. She would only have to rely on stubborn memory for shortcuts and hideaways.

If she survived this, Mara thought wistfully, and things worked out as she planned, in a few weeks she'd check into the finest hotel in Dubai and soak for days in a tub of cool water that smelled of rose hips and lavender. She'd buy a stack of paperbacks and wouldn't emerge until every page had been read. But the pleasant image ended abruptly when she heard the squeal of tires signaling that her pursuers were catching up. And then flakes of dried mud bricks spattered as a bullet lodged in a wall inches from her ear.

She ran faster.

Old adobe buildings, constructed at the turn of the century, flew past in a blur of burnt umber. Names once as familiar to her as her own faded on wooden placards or blinked out neon signs. When the corpulent pink pig of Lorraine's Bar-B-Q winked its false lashes at her, Mara knew she was close to her destination.

The grand problem lay in getting there. She sprinted around the corner of the restaurant, riffling through her mental map. It had been more than a decade since her last visit, but certain places were destined to remain the same. Like Kiev, Texas. Some called the changeless, eternal nature of aging western towns like Kiev charming. She called it hell. But even hell would be better than what chased her.

The Franklin Pharmacy sat squat on the lot it had occupied since the first Mrs. Franklin opened it in the late 1800s. A hurried glance showed that the latest owners had recently spruced up the whitewash. The layout of downtown flashed in her mind's eye. Franklin's then the Shop-N-Save and then salvation. One hundred yards, she thought. A hundred yards between her and salvation. If karma didn't catch up with her first.

As quickly as the bleak thought surfaced, Mara forced it back down with a silent oath. Kiev was a way station on the road to a fortune. Pop in and out was the plan. Find the map Bailey mentioned in his diary, check on her grandmother, and keep moving.

The thought of visiting the woman she'd abandoned brought a lump to her throat and a hitch to her stride. But now was not the time to consider whether wounds stayed fresh past a reasonable expiration date. And twelve years was a long damned time. Heaven only knew what mess she'd left behind and whether her grandmother cared enough to forgive. She'd spent Rabbe's $50,000 on atonement, but that may not have evened the score.

Of course, in her world there never was such a time to contemplate the consequences of a decision made. Or unmade. *Think. Act. Deal.* That was her mantra. No recriminations allowed. As a corollary, Mara had a strict rule against looking too far into the future. You might see something you don't like and never take a chance. *Or see something even better and stay put just to have it.* She ignored the punch of sorrow at the traitorous thought, as she always did.

An engine revved behind her, and she could hear the hiss of a power window sliding down its pane of glass. With instinct born of experience, she dodged between two buildings as the pop of a silencer registered its fury. Glass shattered and sprayed the ground, shards tinkling in the quiet morning. A second shot was fired, and she could feel the bullet pierce skin, singe flesh.

Mara stumbled, her knees nearly giving way. The bullet had torn through her left arm. An anguished cry escaped her, and she felt the warm rush of blood along the aching limb. Her blurred glance told her that the fragment of metal had nicked the back of her arm and ripped skin and tissue on its way past. It hurt like hell on fire, but she'd survive. She stumbled forward, forced herself to breathe in short, shallow bursts, and picked up speed again.

Behind her, the vehicle veered closer, but the narrow trail between buildings was too small for the SUV. The passage, however, was wide enough for someone to take careful aim and hunt her from the passenger seat. In confirmation, she heard the next shot strike a Dumpster just ahead of her. That gave her an idea through the hazy fog of pained panic. Struggling, she jogged behind the heavy green container and shoved the metal bin on its casters to block the path. The movement stretched her wounded arm and hot crimson trickled onto her hand.

"I'm gonna kill you, bitch! Just wait till I get you in one of these alleys!" The furious threat followed her down the alleyway and out the other side onto Cooley Avenue. She heard the slam of a door and the sudden sprint of tires, and realized they had decided to split up. It made good sense, if you were tracking prey. Send one down the alley to catch her and bring the SUV around to trap her on the other end. But if your prey was smarter, she'd do something altogether different.

Grinning despite the wicked throbbing of her arm, Mara considered her options. Instead of emerging onto Custer, she angled down the short back driveway of the clothing store, coming out on a half street that abutted the main thoroughfare in Kiev.

How had they caught up so quickly? she wondered as she continued to run toward her only hope of refuge. Just yesterday she'd had a safe two- maybe three-day lead. When she slipped out of the bar in Alston, tipped to their pursuit by a nice young man with perfect teeth, she figured she had enough time to make it to Kiev before they found her trail. But as it had been for the past three weeks, they were right behind her, tracking every move, every decision.

Part of her wanted to stop running. To turn around, surrender, and face what came next. Yet, in sharp flashes, Mara remembered the sleek barrel of the .22 tucked into her pursuer's waistband and the cruel edge of his partner's razor blade. Given their last encounter, she had no doubt that both would be used to exact their revenge.

So they would have to catch her first.

Instinct screamed for her to check her trail, but she dismissed the shrill command. Rule number three in the world of Mara Reed was to never look back. Not at your questionable decisions, not at your mangled life, not at the angry, pistol-wielding lunatic who just wanted to get close enough to actually shoot you in the heart and spit in your eye at the same time.

She nearly smiled then, despite the thud of thick-soled boots that sounded frighteningly close and the hitch that signaled she was running out of air. Somehow, they'd realized she'd gone sideways instead of forward, which meant she had only seconds on them. But she pushed on, swinging into another alleyway that would cut the hundred yards down to fifty.

When she cleared a stack of discarded paper boxes that leaned drunkenly against the Catacomb Bar and Grill, she could feel the tension ease a notch. She'd make it, she thought. One more alleyway and two streets and she'd be home free.

For the time being.

Mara didn't delude herself. Rabbe wouldn't take too kindly to having his prey elude him for a third time. He'd chased her from Detroit to Nashville to Baton Rouge and now to an eminently forgettable town on the outskirts of East Texas. In all likelihood he would eventually catch up to her and she would rue the day she met him and stole from him. But that day would wait. Because she knew the sleepy border town he was chasing her through, and he didn't have a clue.

She was sure that neither Rabbe nor his new barrel-necked partner, Guffin, had ever been to Kiev, Texas, before. They hadn't spent long, humid weekends running breakneck through its unpaved streets, leaping over bramble bushes that had been replaced in recent years with corrugated steel pipes to carry the dregs of oil that had been discovered there.

Arthur Rabbe, the product of a misbegotten conception somewhere north of Atlanta, had no doubt never careened along Route 7 in a stolen car, blasting the radio loud enough to drown out tomorrow. And she had it on good authority that Seth Guffin believed the world began and ended just south of the Bronx.

Mara was certainly partial to Manhattan, where a night's work had once netted her enough for a scenic vacation to sunny Puerto Rico. But Puerto Rico and Manhattan were the past. The present was closing in with a vengeance, loudly huffing its imprecations at her disappearing back. If she survived long enough, the future might be worth something, but she had to get there first.

With a confident though painful leap, she sailed over a couple of overturned trash barrels in a hurdle worthy of Olympic fame. However, when she heard Rabbe curse as he smashed into the same barrels, she churned her legs harder.

"Stop, bitch!" he gasped, not more than thirty feet behind her. "When I get my hands on you, I'm going to rip your worthless heart out through your—"

The rest of his threat was lost in the sudden blast of an angry car horn as she shot across two lanes of moving traffic to the other side of the main thoroughfare in Kiev. Though it was just past dawn, truckers on their way to Oklahoma would be winding through town to reach the interstate. Those trucks had blocked Guffin and ruined Rabbe's plan to box her in. Curses and shouts from Guffin echoed Rabbe's threats, and Mara lifted her hand in a nasty middle-fingered reply.

Close, she thought, so damned close. According to memory, salvation lay one block away. Once inside, Rabbe could scream and threaten all he liked, but he wouldn't be able to touch her.

Mara rounded the corner, skidded down the final alleyway, and stopped dead in her tracks.

The shortcut across Shahar to Gaul used to be a narrow strip of land wide enough for two skinny teenagers sneaking back home after curfew. Now, a brick wall rose out of the ground, cutting off her only exit. More blaring horns signaled Rabbe and Guffin's imminent arrival. She had ten, maybe fifteen seconds at most.

Adrenaline mixed with slippery terror as she spun around wildly, looking for escape. All that greeted her was more of the smooth-surfaced concrete, a metal door that seemed to open from the inside, and the devastating realization that she would finally do what she'd spent the past twelve godforsaken years avoiding by breaking every rule, law, and commandment known to man.

Damn it all to hell, she thought grimly. She was about to die in Texas.

CHAPTER 2

WITH A SUDDEN CREAK OF METAL THE KNOBLESS DOOR swung open and hard hands jerked Mara inside. Before she could emit even a yelp, the heavy sheet of solid steel slammed into its frame. A minute later—maybe less, maybe more—in the corridor, she could hear the report of bullets as they hit the concrete wall. More bullets careened into the metal door and fell useless to the ground. Muffled shouts from Rabbe and Guffin were punctuated by more random shots.

Through the panels she could hear them arguing about where she could have gone. Guffin, always the rocket scientist, suggested that she had somehow scaled the concrete wall. To his credit, Rabbe thought about the metal door, but he couldn't find an opening. Finally, Rabbe commanded Guffin to check the other alleys, since they'd obviously chosen the wrong one.

Her pulse pounding in her throat, Mara turned in the darkness to thank her savior. But the words stalled in her head, and her hands, lifted in gratitude, froze at her waist. A twist of emotion, fierce and plaintive, ripped at a heart she imagined numbed to feeling. In that instant she wished with all her might that Rabbe and Guffin had accomplished their mission.

"You never learn, do you, Mara?"

The subtle Texas drawl had once been as familiar to her as her own voice. But the cadence had deepened, the tone had roughened. Like the man himself. Ethan Stuart had been a beautiful, gangly boy when she'd last seen him. Time had filled out the once shyly hunched shoulders that now ranged broad and straight. Muscle had been layered over his naturally lean frame, resulting in a wide chest, corded thighs, and sculpted biceps.

But it was the face that told the full story. The long-lidded eyes that had always reminded her of the darkest, most bitter chocolate were now shadowed. Thick ebony lashes fanned down to shade their expression and drew attention to the fine lines etched along the corners. His fancy, full-lipped mouth had grown more sensual with age, but with a harder edge than she remembered. The aristocratic nose had been broken at least once since they'd last spoken, and high cheekbones were stretched tight with burnished copper skin that held no expression.

Mara looked her fill, trying to reconcile the nineteen-year-old orphan to the impassive, powerful man who stared down at her. Silently, she ran her hungry eyes over him again, this time taking in other details. Like the white T-shirt that bore a University of Texas logo and indeterminate stains. Like the faded blue jeans that were zipped but not buttoned. Like the stained scalpel that he gripped in his hand as it flashed in the half-light. And what lay behind him in the darkness.

"Crapadapolus," she muttered, edging back to the door. "Am I dead?"

"Not yet." Ethan stepped closer, crowding her against the cold metal, taunting her. "Where are you going? Out to the men trying to kill you? But I have my own reasons to hate you, don't I?"

Guilt, its smear terribly familiar, coated her gut. "I'm sorry. So sorry."

"Too late, Mara. Too goddamned late."

Again the scalpel flashed in the tepid light that seeped from the opposite side of the vast warehouse. Again her eyes were drawn to the specter that stretched along the wall at the far end of the space. Shrouds seemed to drift in the white light, covering rows of bodies. Human bodies. And Ethan loomed out of the shadows wielding a tool of death.

"Did you kill them?" Mara panted out the question, fighting off the panic that threatened to wring the last of the air from her lungs. She had nowhere to run. Rabbe and Guffin were idiots, but they would eventually return to find her. Her arm was numb from the gunshot and her leg burned from the scrape at the car lot. Yet if she remained inside, the man with every reason to despise her might do to her what he'd done to the sheet-draped bodies behind him. Either way, she was about to die. The question was how soon.

Adrenaline shot through her. Behind her, her slick hands scrambled for the door handle. She found the bar to release the latch, but a silent, deadly Ethan reached out a long arm to stop her. His hand closed around her left shoulder and squeezed, and the agony was too much. Mara collapsed to the floor, the moan of terror shifting into a cry of anguish.

Ethan quickly dropped to his knees beside her, cupping her arms to lift her to face him. "Mara? What the hell is wrong with you?" When his hand slipped lower, he lifted it and saw the stain of blood on his palm. His eyes shot back to her, limp in his grasp. "My God. You've been shot?"

Mara didn't answer, concentrating solely on staying awake. Blackness summoned her, begging her to rest. The ache in her leg throbbed mercilessly, in counterpoint to the burning waves cascading along her arm. She wanted to run, to hide from Ethan's eyes and Rabbe's gun and Guffin's razor.

She wanted to escape from haunting memories and lost paradise and a future that seemed bleaker than she could imagine. She wanted more than she ever deserved, and the futility of wishing sliced through her like the scalpel she'd seen in the beloved hands that used to hold her close.

That held her now.

Through the mists clouding her brain, Mara felt herself being lifted and carried. With remarkable ease Ethan cradled her body to him, tucking her head into his shoulder. Wordlessly, he climbed a set of metal stairs and nudged open a door that led to a room filled with light.

"Ethan, love?" She mumbled the phrase, forgetting and remembering who they were to each other. "Don't let them get me."

"Who could get close enough?" came his whispered reply.

Gently, Ethan laid Mara's exhausted, slack body on a futon in the far corner of the improvised studio apartment. With quick, unsteady motions he dragged the tangled blue sheets crumpled at her feet up and over the body he once knew as well as his own.

Mara Reed.

The love of his life and his most devastating mistake.

Ethan moved to the kitchenette to fill a bowl with warm water, then he gathered up the first aid kit he kept below the sink. He moved confidently, quickly gathering supplies. Grimly, he recalled his stint as a paramedic during college. Too may GSW patients changed his mind about medical school.

Still, he knew what had to be done. The bullet wound was a through and through, ripping through flesh but missing bone, arteries, and nerves. Nasty and painful, but nothing that required hospitalization. Besides, he doubted Mara would appreciate a trip to the emergency room. He figured the hole in her arm was the least of her troubles.

He returned to her side to treat the obscene injury, taking a second to switch on the swing-armed lamp plugged in near the bed. The sight of the wound, framed by the lamplight, clutched his gut. Against Mara's caramel skin, the blood was a discolored streak that ran down the sleekly muscled arm to the curled palm resting on the sheets.

It struck him then how she might have died, so close to him but without either of them knowing. A part of him had always expected it to be so, had mourned for her thinking it was already true.

Yet Fate had intervened once again. It was batting two for two.

The studio had two massive bay windows that overlooked the northeastern vista of Kiev. Ethan relied on the streams of natural light to wake him, and this morning had been no exception. The only difference was that while he stood at the treated glass, sipping the coffee that would rush needed caffeine to his sluggish brain, he saw a young woman darting across traffic and between buildings. Kiev was not a town for joggers, and in his month-long stay in the warehouse, he hadn't seen the runner before.

Curiosity and an uncanny sense of recognition had compelled him to follow her flight. There was something memorable in the loping gait, the determined speed. As the figure had drawn closer, he noticed the black Expedition trailing behind her, steadily closing in on its prey. It wasn't until the window slid down and a gloved hand aimed a gun at the fleeing body that he reached two conclusions.

The familiar form chased down Kiev's deserted streets was that of the woman who'd snuck out of his bed and his life more than a decade ago. She drew nearer to his street and he recognized the tight curls that framed a gamine face, screwed fierce with determination. Memory slammed into him as he noticed how the long, lovely limbs, once wrapped around him in ecstasy, now churned with a feral speed. He watched in horror as the SUV chased her down an alley, hiding her from his view, and silently cheered when she emerged onto the main street, running even faster, if more unsteadily.

He realized then where she was headed. Inside her mind, he could see her sifting through options, reading a map of town. He knew instantly that she would aim for Shahar Avenue as a way over to Gaul and the one place she'd ever truly called home.

Yes, he'd thought, her natural choice would be the path they'd taken more than once as young lovers who stayed out past the town's curfew. What she didn't know, couldn't know, was that the new owners of the row of warehouses and office towers had built a solid, unscalable wall to block cut-throughs. In seconds Mara would be trapped in a passage with no way out.

So Ethan had drawn the drapes over the open windows and hurried down the stairwell to the main floor of the warehouse. Through a one-way viewer he waited for her to arrive, timing her steps. When he heard her skid to a stop, trapped by the wall, he opened the massive steel door and dragged her inside.

Now, as he cleaned the flesh seared by the bullet's exit, Mara grimaced in her sleep.

"Shh, everything will be fine, just rest," he crooned. "I won't let them get you." She turned toward him, toward the comfort in his voice. Ethan stroked his hand across her forehead, which had grown clammy. "Ah, love. What happened to you?"

When she murmured unintelligibly, he returned to his ministrations. After dousing the wound with iodine, he tilted her limp body to reach the entry point. There, the flesh was red and livid. He treated it with iodine and antiseptic and taped a bandage over the hole. It would leave the wound clean but not stitched closed, since closing it would increase the chance of infection.

Ethan decided to wait until she awoke again to offer her medication. Her almost painfully gaunt form could have been the result of poor eating habits or a drug addiction, and he wouldn't risk compounding a problem. Instead, he busied himself with cleaning up his nursing station and trying to ignore the woman sprawled across his bed. He had plenty of work to do, he reminded himself as he sank down onto his chair. Chi Development was expecting a preliminary report from him soon, and it had to be good if he wanted his funding to continue.

And if he wanted to find the Yorba manuscript and statue that would make the need for funding irrelevant.

He turned his head toward Mara again, wondering if she had any idea. Brow furrowed at the thought, Ethan retraced his plan, examined every conversation that had led him back to Kiev. He'd been careful to keep his own counsel, and had shared nothing of his pursuit with his colleagues or his employers. If he had to come back to Kiev, he was determined to look for the Reed gold—and the more important treasure that lay within one of the satchels, while he was at it.

A search that was inextricably linked to the woman lying unconscious in his bed. It seemed too coincidental that she would reappear now.

And damned inconvenient. Lesley was coming up on Friday. He'd returned to Kiev to lay ghosts to rest, and the most haunting one had made a surprise appearance. Then again, Mara always had damnable timing.

As though she heard his thoughts, Mara cried out. Ethan shoved back from the desk and crossed the short distance to the bed. "Mara? Sweetheart, what's wrong? What hurts?" Furious at himself for not conducting a more thorough exam, he whipped the blue sheet away from her restless form, which was now sheened with sweat.

Trying to distance himself from the woman, Ethan focused on the body itself. He grabbed his shears from the desk and summarily cut away the frayed jogging pants, leaving only a pair of boy-cut briefs the color of ripe strawberries. The nicely rounded hips they covered tapered into strong, trim thighs and firmly molded calves. He leaned over her and ran careful hands along the sweat-dampened limbs. Finding nothing, he moved to check her other leg. When he angled the lamp toward her shin, he found a jagged tear.

"What's going on, Mara?" Moving the lamp closer, he knelt beside the wound, trying to figure out what had caused it. Unable to see much, he fumbled in his desk drawer for a magnifying glass. An examination of the cut revealed flecks of rust. Cursing beneath his breath, he carefully cleaned and bandaged the tear. Then he returned to the cabinet and removed an empty syringe. From the refrigerator, he collected a vial filled with a clear liquid. He filled the syringe with the fluid and gripped Mara's arm.

Pale brown eyes, nearly amber, fluttered open. Her sleepy gaze locked on the syringe in his hand. Ethan saw confusion change to shock and then to fear. Releasing her arm, he lifted his hands in a silent demonstration that he meant no harm.

"It's a tetanus shot, Mara. You've got a bullet wound and a cut on your leg. I think you may be at risk, so I want to give you a preventive dose." With careful movements he raised the vial for her review. "Read the label. Tetanus antitoxin. That's all it is, honey, I swear."

Mara's eyes locked with his and he returned her appraisal steadily, without blinking. Finally, she nodded imperceptibly and her eyes shut once more. Before she reawakened, Ethan injected her with the tetanus shot.

Finished with his doctoring, he unlaced the sneakers on her long legs. The sight of the incongruous Smurf socks, given the situation, brought a chuckle. He freed both feet and then restudied the unveiled flesh. Ostensibly, he checked only for other hidden injuries, but his breath shortened as he ran suddenly hypersensitive fingers over the smooth planes of her legs, under the supple curves of her thighs and hips. He felt a ridge of scar tissue but refused to look. What she did to her body didn't matter to him. Not anymore.

"You deal with naked bodies everyday, man. Get on with it," he chided himself as his hands halted at the edge of the top now stained with her blood. He didn't remind himself that those bodies were cold and frozen, not warm and soft under his touch.

Beneath the worn fabric there was nothing but skin. Still, a second groan from Mara urged him into action. He lifted the hem of the top and drew it slowly up, revealing in tormenting inches the flat, nearly concave stomach. The long torso stretched up to taper into a slender waist. More rich brown skin was revealed to his mesmerized eyes, the surface unblemished by her adventures.

He realized then that moving her arm farther was out of the question. Instead, he grabbed the shears from the table and sliced through the fabric. He peeled it away from her damp skin and the pert breasts she left unbound. Abruptly, Mara turned toward him. The movement pressed her nipple into the palm of his hand, and for a shattering instant he cupped the taut flesh in instinctive reaction. Appalled, Ethan released her and surged to his feet, chased by questions.

She'd sleep for hours, he calculated as he moved across the room. At the door to the stairs, he glanced at her supine form. Lovely, he thought. And so dangerous to the life he was terribly close to having. Ethan paused, waiting for the spear of agony that had dimmed to an ache of betrayal over the years. The flutter of delight had him rushing down to his workshop.

Surrounded by corpses, he restively searched for something to do—to take his mind off the hazard lying in his bed. When he lit upon the phone near his workstation, he released a breath of relief. He could check in with Davis Conroy. A conversation with the man chilled his blood every time, and he could do with a dose.

He lifted the phone and quickly dialed his benefactor. "Ethan Stuart for Mr. Conroy."

On the other end a soothing soprano advised him to hold.

Propping himself on the edge of the metal slab, Ethan shifted through his notes, preparing his report. He felt the tightening at his shoulders that accompanied every conversation he had with Conroy. As usual, he chalked it up to nerves and his feeling of duplicity. After all, he was using Conroy's generosity to pursue his own interests.

"Dr. Stuart? Davis Conroy. What have you got for me?"

"I've completed my preliminary report." Ethan scanned his precise writing. "I've reviewed the medical examiner reports and most of the bodies. With few exceptions, everyone buried on the site you uncovered died of natural causes in the last twenty-five years. I found no evidence of historical significance."

"What about the marks? I saw a few of them myself, Dr. Stuart, and I must say they gave me the willies. Do you know who made them?"

Ethan demurred. "Not yet. With your permission, I'd like to stay on a few more weeks to research their origins. I might have a lead."

"Who?"

"No one specific yet, Mr. Conroy, but in a town this size,

fifty dead bodies would draw attention. Particularly given the ritual attached to burial. I should know more by the end of the week." Ethan looked at the room. Fifty bodies that lay within a stone's throw of Mara's old homestead. He shuffled the papers into order and returned them to their appropriate, color-coded folder. "With your permission, of course."

"Certainly, Dr. Stuart." A pause stretched over the line, then Conroy spoke again. "And you haven't found a body that might have been buried more than twenty-five years ago?"

Startled, Ethan nearly dropped the phone. He had found two bodies that he couldn't reconcile, but he was reluctant to share that information with Conroy just yet. The tightness knotted into a throb of tension, and Ethan replied, "Are you expecting someone?"

"No. But I thought I recalled from one of the city council resolutions that if the bodies were older than twenty-five years, we'd have to request more legislation. I would prefer to not involve the politicians more than necessary, Dr. Stuart."

Ethan didn't quite buy the explanation, but his project benefited from the flimsy excuse. "I understand. But I don't have anything conclusive yet. I'll let you know as soon as I do."

"Fine. Thanks for the update." The call disconnected abruptly, and Ethan rubbed at his nape. He'd bought himself a week. Probably should get to work. Rising, he moved to the pile of bones he'd arranged the night before. A man, late seventies, healthy. With a shadow of black on the edge of his hip. A tattoo unlike any he'd ever seen before, until he'd gotten this assignment.

Now he was surrounded by the dead and a set of symbols that had to mean something. If only he could figure out what. Perhaps the woman upstairs could offer a clue. Which, he decided balefully, dusting a solution onto the length of femur, was the most she had to give him. As he prepared for the examination, he firmly put Mara's reappearance out of his mind and focused on the task before him. Step by step, he reminded himself. The simplest solution to a problem was uncovered step by step.

When he nudged open the loft door in late afternoon, Mara was sprawled across the futon, sleeping fitfully. She'd kicked the blanket onto the floor, and the pillows were damp with sweat.

"Damn it, you've gotten a fever," he muttered as he pressed a hand to her forehead. Fevered heat seeped into his cool skin. He shouldn't have left her alone, he chided himself. Quickly, he checked her bandages and drew the covers over her gaunt, restless form. She'd never been able to keep much weight on her, he remembered darkly.

Out at the Reed compound, food had always been in short supply. Maybe that was why she'd learned to steal. Bitterness resurfaced, unbidden. If she'd ever bothered to trust him, he would have taken care of her. Of them.

She hadn't.

Instead, she'd chosen to cheat. Years later, he still didn't understand her choices. Between foster homes and trips to the orphanage, Ethan had gone his share of nights without dinner. But he'd never become a thief. He'd worked hard, driving himself in order to escape Kiev. It had been his heart's only desire. Until Mara.

He allowed himself to look at her again. By God, she was stunning. The time between them had sharpened once softer features, had turned gamine into striking. She'd cut her hair so that the mass of black coiled wildly around her face. Reaching out, he stroked the soaked curls away from her damp forehead.

"Where have you been?" he whispered. "Why did you come back?" He lowered himself lightly to sit beside her on the narrow bed.

Mara turned over in her sleep, body restless and anxious. Ethan watched the agitated motions, heard the garbled mumblings, but he did not move from his seat at her hip. He realized he must have been at work longer than he thought as twilight approached and cast an ethereal glow over Mara's fidgety body, elongating and gilding her restive form. Nightmare or dream? he wondered.

It doesn't matter, Ethan reminded himself sternly. Using the instruments he'd left at her side, he slid the thermometer under her parched tongue. The readout hovered high, but not hospitalization level. Yet. Tipping her head up to give her water, he murmured, "Open up, Mara. You're thirsty. It's just water."

"Don't come in here." She pulled away from his supporting hand, eyes jerking wide. "Don't let him find me. Call the Starburst. Tell them not to let him in."

Ethan lifted the cup away from her. "Not to let who in, Mara? Who are you hiding from?"

"He'll do it to me." Suddenly, she focused on him, amber glittering wildly. "I saw what he did to her. He found Cassandra at the Lucky Lake. Made her take him. Don't let him do me too."

The ferocity in her voice held Ethan immobile. Just as abruptly as she'd awakened, she drifted out again. "Mara? Mara?"

At a loss, he slowly fed her the contents of the cup, careful not to let her choke. "Who's after you, honey? What is the Lucky Lake? The Starburst?" He murmured the questions, knowing he wouldn't get an answer until the fever broke.

In her uneasy sleep, her hand sought out the warmth of his leg, then slipped terrifically lower. Ethan reared away and sprang to his feet. He wandered around the room, shifting books and CDs until they lined up perfectly along the edge of their shelves. The cracked plastic covers and steam-bloated pages didn't disturb him.

The contradiction made sense to him. Straight lines were a sign of order, of structure. But the contents were meant to be devoured hungrily, consumed by a ravenous mind. He crossed to his desk and sat heavily.

Yes, he possessed a ravenous mind stubbornly bound to the earth. Learn about the world from the safety of a book. Disgusted, he booted up the computer. On the screen, a totem appeared, a replica of a twelve-inch figure composed of a priest at the base, holding a traditional sword and axe. Atop the priest a miniature figure of a bata drummer beat his instrument in the center panel, and a woman rose above the drummer, lifting Shango's sacred stone axe above her head.

"What's that?" The question drifted from the bed, and Ethan turned.

"You should sleep." He resisted the urge to shut off the screen, but she probably wouldn't remember seeing it. "You're not well."

"I've seen that before. Somewhere." On the bed, Mara struggled to sit up. "Where have I seen that?"

Ethan rushed to her side and pressed her firmly down. "Mara, honey, you've been shot. You've got a slight fever and you seem to be exhausted. Please, sleep."

"You won't let them get me?" The tremulous question carried an undercurrent of demand.

As if anyone could, he thought. "I'll take care of you. Sleep."

"Yes, you always do."

Ethan waited until her lids drifted down, then he returned to the image on the screen. This, as much as anything, had drawn him back to Kiev. A Shango priest in Benin whose writings on medicine and the preservation of the dead had made its way to America a century ago.

A set of writings and a totem that had become part of an easterner's prized collection—along with hundreds of gold coins cast under the reign of Queen Isabella. A chance for Ethan the pedestrian, he thought, to undertake a quest. First, though, he had to determine where to look.

It was getting dark now, and he occupied himself by organizing his notes and transcribing his findings. Hands cramped from typing, he stood, turned on the light, moved into the kitchenette and snagged his abandoned cup of coffee. Pouring leftovers into the ceramic mug, he heated the tepid brew and took up post at the kitchen island. Watching his patient, Ethan brooded over the unlikely coincidence of Mara's return at the precise moment he came close to finding the manuscript. Interrupted only by the murmured litany coming from the bed.

Over and over again, the same refrain. Names he didn't recognize and a fear he could fairly touch. Where had she been all these years? What had she done? How had she stayed alive, when her livelihood seemed to include armed gunmen eager for her blood? He drained the bitter dregs and stared into the empty recesses. Too tired to sleep, afraid to go downstairs and leave Mara, he decided he needed another cup. He straightened and turned to the coffeemaker.

"Ethan?" Mara mumbled his name. Dropping the cup, he circled the island and hurried to her side.

"I'm here. What is it?" He drew closer, bending over the prone body. With a lean hand he brushed damp tendrils back from her forehead, testing automatically for fever. Beneath his touch the skin was clammy but cool. "What do you need?"

"Don't let him get me." The anxious plea tumbled out and she struggled to sit up. "Don't let him touch me."

"Who, honey? The men in the truck?" Ethan leaned in. "Who wants to hurt you?"

"Him. I took his money. Can't give him what he wants. Won't."

She thrashed her head, and he caught her chin to hold her still. "What does he want, Mara?"

"Me. Don't let him have me." She held his stricken look then faded into sleep. The blanket had fallen and the stark white bandage mocked his feeble efforts to protect her.

After a quick check, he was certain there was no infection. No sinister poison to gnaw at the smooth cinnamon flesh. He rested his hand at her shoulder, stroking her into calm. *Don't let him have me.*

Her plea reverberated, and his traitorous brain quickly settled on a possibility. He rubbed at the permanent knot of pressure at his neck. Why hadn't it occurred to him before? The woman asleep in his bed was probably a prostitute.

Flesh that she peddled to the highest bidder, mocked a bitter voice. *Anyone but you.*

Ethan snatched his hand away. Still, the feel of her lingered on his fingertips. Faithless memory taunted him, but he couldn't look away. Questions he'd sworn never to ask redoubled and burned in his brain.

How had she been reduced to selling herself? Didn't she know that he'd have come for her? That every night, in his dreams, he came for her? Saved her. Loved her so much better each time that she never ran away.

No, he thought angrily. Not again. He'd spent more than a

decade wallowing in recriminations and regret. No more. His life was nearly his own again. This trip back to Kiev was step one in the final stage. Soon he'd be rid of harsh memory and would no longer be tied to a place he loathed. In a month, maybe less, he would finally be free.

So, he reminded himself, forcing his eyes to Mara's once beloved face, he would give her until Friday to recoup, and then she would be gone again. This time, though, he swore, he would be ready for good-bye.

Mara rolled closer to him, and when she bumped against his thigh, she twisted to rest her head against the hard length of it, her hand curling over tensed muscle. Immediately, his body betrayed him in reaction.

How could it be that years later, in spite of everything, he could taste her, remember the way she fit against him? How could it be that he wanted her nonetheless, when he hated her? When he had finally found another woman he could care for?

Ethan attempted to summon the fierce pain that had been his talisman against love for so long, but the picture morphed into an impish Mara on their last night together.

A million stars had flickered above them as they lay on the roof of his apartment. She had wanted a midnight picnic, so they brought crackers and cheese and cheap red wine to the only place they could be alone. A few hours later Mara would climb down the fire escape and make her way back to the ramshackle two-story house on the outskirts of town, where her father would be waiting. He hated that Mara continued to put herself in danger to see him, but he couldn't make her stay away. He didn't want to.

"I love you, Mara." He said the words quietly. Simply.

She turned her face up to him then, her smile dazzling, and had he bothered to see it, edged with an eloquent sadness. "I know." She lifted his hand to her mouth, pressed a fervent kiss to his palm. "I don't understand why, but I know you do."

He tried not to notice that she hadn't responded with her own declaration, but he was willing to wait. Although she refused to give him the words, she'd given him everything else. Her body, her mind, her trust. It was evident in the way she curled against him on the blanket, her head tucked beneath his chin.

"Tell me about the future," Mara whispered.

Ethan smiled. It was a favorite game of theirs. Two changelings who dreamed of escape. "We'll live in New York. You'll be an artist, with showings in every gallery in the city. In the mornings, you'll paint whatever your eyes see. And at night we'll see plays and eat dinner in the best restaurants."

"Yes," she added, "and you'll spend the mornings with your patients. You'll be the most famous doctor in the country. Presidents and movie stars will want you as their personal physician, but you'll politely decline."

"Why?"

"Because you have to save all the children, of course. Dr. Ethan Stuart will spend his afternoons running a free clinic for the poor and downtrodden." Mara laughed lightly, the sound haunted. "I'll be your first patient."

Pulling her closer, Ethan played along with the fantasy, eager to banish the shadows. "And how are we funding this haven of medical good?"

"With the Reed treasure, of course. I'll find the gold my grandfather stole, and we'll use it to save lives."

Ethan sighed so lightly it barely escaped. The legend of Micah Reed and his stolen bounty had fueled a thousand fantasies for Mara, and Ethan never had the heart to disagree. Satchels of Spanish gold, hidden somewhere in the Texas Hill Country, had been only one of the scandals tied to the Reed name.

To Ethan's mind, an impossible treasure had been more palatable than the darker, less romantic stories told of the Reed men who lived on the edge of Kiev. Men like Obadiah Reed, Mara's bastard of a father. Evangelist and asshole, to Ethan's way of thinking. The hollow-eyed parishioners who stayed on the Reed compound gave him the shivers, and he hated the fact that Mara had to return to their fold every night. But this would be the last time, he had sworn silently. If all went well tomorrow, she'd never have to go back to those lunatics.

He hadn't told her about his plans then, or the letter he was expecting in the mail soon. Their ticket out of Kiev and to that dream Mara loved to spin.

He'd pressed a kiss to her temple. "Will you live with me, angel?" he had asked.

"Where else would I be?" Mara answered quietly.

In the years since, Ethan had realized she hadn't answered him at all.

Instead, she'd turned in his arms and lifted her mouth to his. They'd sunk down onto the bright picnic blanket and loved each other under the stars. Afterward, they finished the bottle of wine, with him drinking the lion's share because the next day was Sunday and he didn't have to work at the plant. They'd dozed off beneath the September night, their bodies sated, their limbs entwined.

And in the morning the clothes she'd left in his place had been tucked inside his army duffel bag, and the $2,854 they'd saved had vanished from the bureau drawer.

Mara had loved him and left him, and now, when his life was finally his own and he was about to have everything he'd ever dreamed of, she had come home.

CHAPTER 3

MARA AWOKE WITH A START.

In a rush, memory returned, bringing a febrile apprehension. Rabbe and Guffin had chased her down a passageway, and Ethan appeared out of nowhere to pull her to safety. Images of a scalpel and dead bodies danced in her still fuzzy mind. She couldn't make sense of the pictures, could recall only the clasp of Ethan's strong hand to her arm and sinking into unconsciousness from the pain and adrenaline. The sensation of floating and being cared for.

She should have known that she'd finally get her one wish—to be in Ethan's arms again—only to faint dead away when it happened. In her dreams, her lovely, impossible dreams, Ethan embraced her and told her all was forgiven. He didn't save her from an angry thug and patch up her bullet wound.

Awake and aching, Mara lifted a tentative hand to her upper arm and felt the delicate gauze that covered her wound. Her hand dropped lower and she abruptly realized that her top was gone.

She'd missed that part of the treatment.

A quick peek beneath the single sheet draped over her revealed that her pants had vanished too. Man, she had been really out, to have not noticed being stripped naked by the only man she'd ever loved. But there was no denying the evidence. Like her arm, her scarred leg sported a strip of gauze and neatly squared tape that bound the cut. At her feet, the ruined clothes had been folded neatly. Out of habit, she touched the pattern scarred into her hip. A reminder of who she was and who she could never become.

Not that she had to worry about Ethan ever trying to take advantage of her, not in this lifetime. Heck, she had to admit she was surprised he deigned to touch her at all. She wouldn't have blamed him if he'd left her crumpled on the floor of the warehouse, which she assumed was below her. Vaguely, she remembered a syringe and soft words of comfort, and she grudgingly relaxed. Though she'd never been shot before, she knew the drill. Bed rest for a couple of days, then she'd be on her way. Out of Ethan's life again.

Still, she thought, there was nothing to prevent her from taking a peek at what she'd given up. From her half-sprawled position, Mara scanned the area. Her first discovery was that Ethan lived in a spacious studio with one way out. The door, she noted with a grim laugh, had been bolted shut with a second lock, and it was on the opposite end of the wide area. She wondered whether the locks were to keep intruders out or her inside.

Between her and the doorway were a series of obstacles, but nothing insurmountable. Gingerly, she angled her head to look around. A nickel-plated nightstand with glass shelves was stacked high with books, each with a bookmark trailing from some midpoint. Titles she didn't recognize mixed indiscriminately with pulp fiction. Other than books, the remaining items were obviously for her. A glass of water, two orange pills and a large ivory pill sat on a napkin. Recognizing the pain reliever and the antibiotic, she propped herself up using her good arm and downed the pills.

Beyond the nightstand, Roman shades blocked tall windows that flanked the bed. Glancing down, Mara corrected herself. She was on a futon, not a bed. She firmly believed there was a difference. No one who could afford a good box-spring mattress and feather top would ever voluntarily choose to sleep on an anemic padding of foam and cotton tossed onto a platform of sticks.

Continuing her survey, she noted that the closed door directly opposite the bed had to be the bathroom. Good to know, she decided, shifting a bit. Along the same wall was another table, this one holding a thirteen-inch television and a slightly larger stereo system. Like the books on the nightstand, compact discs stood in precise, military order. Straight and true, like her Ethan.

No, Mara chided herself. Not her Ethan. Not anymore. The sooner she remembered that, the better.

She skimmed over the makeshift entertainment center and took in the second largest piece of furniture in the studio. A black laminate bookcase leaned almost drunkenly against the far wall, its shelves laden with heavy tomes and inches-thick binders. In the center of the structure, suspended between the two columns, a desktop jutted out into the room. The laptop computer on its surface whirred almost silently as colored lines danced and bounced across a darkened screen. Next to the silver casing of the computer, Mara noticed a pair of wire-rimmed glasses.

"Told him he'd go blind," she murmured. She used to chide him about reading in the dim light of the single lamp in his apartment. Ethan would respond simply by kissing her into silence, pulling her close and reading to her from his book of the moment.

When she found her hand drifting to her mouth, Mara snatched her fingers away and lightly touched her arm above the bandage. Ethan's kisses were part of the past. A bullet hole and two very angry men had to have her attention now. All of it. In fact, if she cared about Ethan at all, she'd get out of his house before Rabbe returned with reinforcements.

Her plans hadn't included a reunion with her former lover, and she'd made her choices a long time ago. To her, the past was a four letter word, and about as helpful.

Time to move. Levering out of bed, she swayed drunkenly,

then righted herself. Okay, she accepted, easier said than done. Determinedly, she wrapped the sheet more tightly around her and stumbled over to the bathroom. The door opened easily. Later she would blame her reaction on trauma and lowered resistance. There could be no other reason that the smell of soap and sandalwood would nearly buckle her knees. Looking around, she cursed the familiar longing. A bathroom littered with books bloated from steam shouldn't tug at her jaded heart.

"Always ruined perfectly good books," she muttered. Ethan had a penchant for returning books that had fallen into the creek or been stained with some mysterious substance. Then, the poor victims had been hard-boiled spy novels or slim collections of poetry. Not, she thought, reading the title engraved along the glossy spine, *Symbology and Modern Man: A Quest to Understand Nature's Dimensions.*

Like the dead bodies she'd imagined downstairs, Ethan's new reading material had nothing to do with her. She was grateful for the rescue, but she needed to move on. Which included getting out of his bathroom and his life. She swung the bathroom door open just as a shadow crossed the room.

"Crickets and rain!" Mara yelped, heart in her throat. When she could breathe again, she saw that Ethan stood framed in the doorway, swathed in the half-light. Realizing she sounded like a nervous schoolgirl in a haunted house, she forced a shaky chuckle. "Sorry for screaming. Thought you were a ghost."

"You're not that lucky, Mara." He briskly moved to the kitchen island. "I'm very much alive. Which is more than could have been said for you if I hadn't been up early yesterday."

Since she couldn't argue with the truth, she leaned against the door frame, as much for support as effect, content to watch him moving about the galley-style kitchen. Like her initial, hazy impressions, Ethan had indeed filled out. The romantic male beauty of his youth had hardened into planes and angles that demanded attention. And reaction. Forced to fill the silence, she hitched up the sliding sheet and offered, "Um, thanks. For the bandages and stuff. And for, uh, pulling me inside."

Ethan thought about what would have happened if he hadn't made it downstairs in time. Shell casings had littered the alleyway when he checked outside. Then, as now, terror, like a tidal wave, crashed into him again and he resented the hell out of the feeling. Coolly, he retorted, "I have first dibs on wringing your pretty neck, Mara. I couldn't very well let them kill you." Taking his mind off the dents he'd examined in the steel door, he lifted a can of vegetable soup. "This work for you?"

"Fine." Mara didn't dare leave her post at the door, which was doing a fine job of keeping her upright.

"Problem?"

"No." He'd probably poison the soup, she thought, but she'd take her chances. "I'm fine."

With a short nod, he reached inside a drawer—perhaps for a knife, Mara imagined fatalistically. When he came up holding a can opener, his expression bland, she exhaled softly. "How long was I out?"

"You've been in and out for an entire day." Interminable

hours while he sat at her side like a lovesick fool. But he wasn't. "Your fever broke and I went downstairs to work."

Mara tried not to pitch forward, hoping she'd make it to the bed before her legs gave out. Ethan had seen her weak and pitiful. She wouldn't offer him a second showing. Instead, she locked her knees and evened her voice over the cascade of nerves. "You did a nice job patching me up. Barely hurts."

"Liar."

She chuckled ruefully. "Okay, it burns like the devil. But I've had worse."

"Get shot often?" Damned crazy conversation, he thought. Chatting about bullet wounds when all he wanted to know was why she left him. But they were playing polite, so he queried, "Occupational hazard?"

"Now and again."

At the offhand response, Ethan wanted to snap. He'd forgotten how cavalier she was about her safety. He'd been the one who kept them out of trouble or talked her out of foolhardy escapades. Safe, dependable Ethan to her wild, capricious Mara. His temper, usually mild and unruffled, threatened to erupt, but he held it in check. With effort. No way he'd let her drag him back to before, when she was all that mattered and his role was to save her. Yet a concern he couldn't quell had him asking, "When did you last eat?"

Mara shrugged. "Don't remember." She pushed away from the door and carefully began to make her way to the bed. "If you'll let me fuel up, I'll be out of your way soon."

"You're not going anywhere, Mara. From the way you're swaying, I doubt you'd make it down the stairs."

She didn't disagree. Lowering herself tentatively, she commented, "I figured you'd want me out as soon as I was mobile."

"I'm not an ogre, Mara." He gave her a long, patient look. "Otherwise, I wouldn't have pulled you in."

"Why did you save me? You don't owe me anything."

Because the only answer he'd found during the night disturbed him deeply, he merely shrugged. "Old habits, I suppose."

"You've always been good at that. Saving me," she agreed dryly. "How are you?"

"Don't pretend to care." The cold flash in the dark brown eyes as Ethan looked up should have warned her. "Let's agree to not make small talk, okay? I'll feed you, give you time to recuperate, and then you can be on your way. Deal?"

Mara nodded. At a loss for words other than pleas for forgiveness—a rare occurrence for her—she was fine not having to cast about for what to say next. *Sorry about stealing everything you worked for. Didn't mean to break your heart.* She couldn't imagine that he wanted to hear that from her. That he'd believe it. So she'd do as he asked and keep her mouth shut. At least that was the plan until she felt her sheet slip again.

"Do you have clothes I could borrow? I don't mind the toga look, but my arm's getting tired and I can't use the other one." She wagged her left arm and shrieked at the surge of pain.

In seconds Ethan had rounded the island and was at her side. "For Pete's sake, Mara, you've got a freakin' hole in your arm.

I'm doing my damnedest to avoid taking you to the hospital, but you open up that wound and that's where we're headed." He nudged her to the futon and lightly pressed her down. "I'll get you a T-shirt and shorts. Just sit still."

He rummaged through the closet that opened up next to the head of the bed. Passing her the red shirt and plaid boxers, he glared at her. "Do you need help?"

Not if my arm falls off, she thought snippishly. Aloud, she answered, "I think I can manage." When Ethan continued to stare at her, she arched a brow. "A little privacy, please?"

With a grunt, Ethan turned away, but remained in place. Mara rolled her eyes at his broad back and let go of the sheet. The brushed cotton pooled in her lap and she bunched up the T-shirt in her right hand. She slipped the opening over her head and angled down to slide her right arm through the sleeve. Easing her left arm through by laying the shirt flat, she made it all the way to her elbow. Then she had to crook her injured bicep.

"Hexagonal hell!" she squealed. "Pas de deux!"

Ethan spun around and found her tangled in the shirt. One arm flailed uselessly, while the oversized red shirt bunched high above her naked breasts, the soft brown curves tipped by deeper peaks. In traitorous fashion, his body reacted like he hadn't seen a woman naked in years. But it was this woman, this body, that had tormented him for a decade. The more she struggled, the more she cursed and the more knotted the shirt became. Amusement warred with grim desire, and Ethan forced himself to push desire aside.

"Stop struggling, Mara," he cautioned, "You're just getting more tangled. Let me help."

"I can take care of myself," she huffed from beneath the shirt. More determined than before, she bent her arm to yank at the fabric. "Rat's toenails!"

Unable to stop himself, Ethan chuckled. What amused him more than the flailing was the variety of nonvulgar imprecations she chose. He'd forgotten that Mara rarely took the Lord's name in vain or preferred her own form of cursing to the four-letter words so common in modern speech. The commandments she could break, he thought, but cursing was more than even her flexible morals could stand.

Emitting a hushed laugh, he crossed to her side. "Here. Let's try something else." He batted her hands away and firmly gripped the bottom of the shirt.

With careful tugs he brought the material over her head and removed it. He strode to the closet and grabbed a denim button-down from a hanger. Ignoring her barely covered breasts, he quickly guided her injured arm through the hole, his knuckles brushing subtle shivers along her skin. She shoved her good arm through the other sleeve but fumbled at the buttons. Cursing beneath his breath, Ethan swiftly latched the slippery plastic disks, his hands barely steady.

As soon as he finished, Mara reared away and reached for the bottoms, prepared to dislocate her arm rather than have him touch her again. She gritted her teeth and prepared to endure.

Knowing the Mara he remembered would never ask, he

plucked the boxers from her fingers and tapped her foot. Defeated, she lifted her legs at his commands, standing when he lightly tapped her hip. Ethan carefully avoided his handiwork on her shin. At her waist, he flipped the waistband over to reach the drawstring inside. His knuckles grazed her stomach, and both of them inhaled sharply. Ethan pulled away as though stung and bounded to his feet.

"They're not so big," he muttered.

"No, they're fine." Mara yanked at the hem of the shirt once more, for good measure. "Thank you."

Ethan shrugged. "No problem." He returned to the kitchen and set to work opening a can of soup. While it warmed in the microwave, he retrieved a box of crackers from the cabinet. The timer beeped imperiously, and he absently reached for the serving bowl without an oven mitt. The ring of the phone trilled into the room, an unexpected interruption.

He dropped the serving bowl, cursing. Hot soup splattered across the counter, its droplets stinging his arm. He jerked his arm away and knocked over the open box of crackers. Soup dripped over the sides of the countertop, falling to the floor. And the phone continued to shrill for attention.

"Should I get it?" Mara ventured.

"The machine will pick up," he responded tersely. When she winced, he refused to feel guilty. Serves her right, he told himself. If he didn't trust her, that wasn't his fault. But he had to grit his teeth to stall the apology that sprang to his lips. No conversation, no recriminations, nothing that would show that he had ever cared. Stoic, distant politeness might protect him, he imagined, from slipping too easily into past patterns.

The ringing of the phone stopped and the machine picked up. "You've reached Dr. Ethan Stuart. Please leave a message at the tone."

Lesley's voice wound through the speakers. "Ethan? It's me. I suppose you're down in your lab, playing with your bodies. Enjoy yourself now, because I'm coming on Friday, ready or not. Remember, my flight arrives at six P.M. Make sure you've refrigerated your cadavers before I get there...I don't plan to share."

The machine beeped to signal the end of the message. Ethan busied himself mopping up the rest of the spilled soup. The silence lengthened, and again he found himself on the verge of an apology. But Mara had no rights in his life anymore. None. She had forfeited any claim to him ages ago. "Dinner will be ready in a second. Can you sit at the table, or do you need me to feed it to you?"

Deflated and unwilling to have him come that close, Mara hurriedly levered herself off the futon and made her way to the table. She pulled out one of the two ladder-backed chairs decorated in the same nickel plating as the nightstand and the table. "I can eat here."

"Water or juice?" Ethan held up a carton of orange juice. "You need fluids."

She nodded. Between her race through the city and the minor blood loss, she needed to drink as much as possible. According to the mysterious Lesley, she had to be in fighting form by Friday, if not before. "Both, if you don't mind."

"No, I don't mind." He placed the glasses and bowls and silverware on a tray and carried the lot to the table. With the effortlessness of one who'd waited a thousand tables in his youth, he served them both and returned to the kitchen to discard the tray.

They ate in tense silence, until Mara could feel her nerves tighten and fray. If she was going to be here for even a day, this couldn't continue. So she'd go first.

" 'Dr. Ethan Stuart'? So I did see dead bodies downstairs."

"Research." Ethan lifted his beer and drank deeply. His plan of absolute silence wasn't exactly practical, he decided. Grudgingly, he elaborated, "I'm a forensic anthropologist."

Nibbling at a cracker, Mara sensed a thaw and pressed a bit more. "I'm not sure I understand what that means. I thought anthropologists studied culture or something."

"We do. I study culture through the examination of dead bodies, usually to resolve legal matters or answer scientific queries. What caused their deaths? What were the communal illnesses and what do they tell us about life? What did a people look like, feel like? How did they act?"

"And Lesley? Is she an anthropologist too?"

Ethan lifted shaded eyes to meet hers. "No. A geology professor." He sipped at his soup, not wanting to continue the conversation about Lesley. The less he explained about his business in Kiev, the better. She'd be gone before Lesley arrived anyway.

Besides, he had his own questions that demanded answers. "Why were those men chasing you?"

Mara shrugged, as though being shot at was a routine part of her day. "I cheated the lead guy. I guess it's pique." She met his shocked gaze with a lazy smile. "You know I'm a thief and a liar, Ethan. Don't look so astonished."

"Is that what you do for a living? Cheat thugs and hide out from killers?" Embarrassed hurt clouded his baritone voice as he ground out the question that had preyed on him. "Was I your first victim or had you been doing this for a while?"

"You don't want to know."

"I don't ask idle questions, Mara." He took a deep draft from the bottle. She owed him this explanation, if nothing else. "Was being with me a game for you? Did I ever mean anything?"

"Ethan!" Abashed that he wondered, she stared at him. "How could you ask me that?"

"How could I not?" he countered evenly. "I thought about it afterward. Here I was, this geeky foster kid, and you were the mysterious urchin who'd do anything. You had your demons, and maybe I was simply a diversion."

"You weren't." Explanations crowded on her tongue, but before she could speak, he shrugged.

"Forget I asked."

"No. I'm sorry, Ethan." She offered the quiet apology without fanfare. Setting her spoon down beside her bowl, she clasped her hands together to stop herself from covering his. "I know saying it doesn't help. Meaning it won't make it better. But I am sorry for what I did to you."

"Which part?" he prodded.

"All of it. The lying. The stealing. Not saying good-bye." Her fingers clenched briefly as she thought about the why of it all. The part of the apology she could never give him. "You deserved better. You always had."

"I deserved you." Ethan pushed away from the table with a harsh shove. He gained his feet easily and paced over to the island with his bowl. Resentment steeped over a dozen years bubbled to the surface. He switched on the taps and began to scrub the bowl with a determined fury. "I woke up on the roof that morning and you weren't there. I even rode out to the church. I went to see your grandmother, but she wouldn't talk to me. Neither would your father."

At that news, Mara blanched. "You spoke to my father?"

"I didn't know what else to do. But he claimed that he hadn't seen you either." Ethan returned for her dishes, jerking them up from the table. He remembered the scene clearly, his frantic demand for answers on the porch of Mara's house. Reverend Reed's easy denials. The sight of the others peering out from behind tattered curtains and flimsy doorways. "I nearly believed him, but then I saw your shoe."

"What?"

"The shoes you were wearing that night. Those absurdly high heels with the gold buckle. I saw it at the edge of the yard and I knew you'd been there. But no one would tell me where you'd gone."

Trapped in that morning again, he twisted at the tap and angrily wiped his hands on his jeans. He hunched his shoulders, bracing for what had come next. "I woke that morning to find nothing of you left. Your clothes, your perfume. All gone. But even then I didn't think you'd stolen from me. I only noticed when I came back from the church because I wanted to use the money to try to find you."

"Ethan." Shame, sour and strong, choked her. Instinctively, she rubbed at her hip. "I'll pay you back."

The hushed offer forced a mirthless laugh from him. "You think I want the money? God, I never did know you, did I?" He shook his head, weary with resignation. "And you sure as hell never knew me."

Mara stared at his back as he walked to the door. He paused there, one hand braced against the wood.

"Stay up here. There's more pain medication in the bathroom. Take a couple of pills before you go to sleep."

She had to ask. "What are you going to do?"

He straightened but didn't turn around. "Get as far away from you as I possibly can. And wonder why in the hell I bothered to open the door."

"I DON'T KNOW what happened to her," Rabbe whined into the cell phone. "It's like she vanished into thin air."

"But we do know that magicks aren't real, don't we, Rabbe?" The calm question did not disguise the menace that lurked on the other end. "Are you sure she went down the alley?"

"Uh-huh. I saw her turn the corner. I had Guffin drive around the other side to block her in. There were only three streets, and I checked every one. But nothing."

"Did you search the buildings on those streets? Ask the patrons inside if they'd seen a young woman?"

Rabbe squirmed, but answered honestly. "Uh, no. It was pretty early in the morning, and I couldn't see as anything was open yet. I jerked on the door handles, but none of them budged."

"Then that poses a problem for you, doesn't it? Because you are quickly running out of time. And my patience is wearing quite thin." The soft voice carried quite well over the phone lines because Davis Conroy was a big man. He had topped six feet by the seventh grade, and continued to shoot up until he was nearly twenty. Built like a semi, he had never learned to allow others to have their way. There was no need.

He was also a rich man. Decades sweating out labor on oil rigs and hewing black gold from unyielding ground had given him an instinct for tapping undiscovered finds. If the wells he dug inched too close to legitimate claims, he consistently found a way to keep the disadvantaged quiet. These days, he left his settlement work to others.

But one grand pursuit had eluded him, until a recent discovery. One that Rabbe allowed to be stolen from him. Conroy fingered his father's key, the brass gleaming from its regular polish. "I've paid you well to bring me what I wanted, and I expect to receive it. Are we clear, Rabbe?"

The affirmation squeaked out. "Y-Yes."

When the call clicked off, Rabbe could feel his chest easing, his muscles relaxing. A tough guy all his life, few struck the fear of God into his jaded heart. The client on the phone was one of them. From a voice that sounded like an angel of death, to a supernatural way of knowing what was going on, it was fuckin' scary. Rabbe didn't believe the story Conroy had spun about a treasure map and millions in gold, but when he'd heard the bounty on Mara Reed's head, he couldn't resist.

The bitch had played him for a fool, which was bad enough. Worse, though, she'd stolen Conroy's property and a wad of cash from him, and for that she'd have to pay. If Conroy got what he needed from her, Rabbe would get his $50,000 and pocket another $250,000 that he'd split with Seth. Plus, he'd get back his pride. Conroy said nothing about bringing her in unused.

He'd use her, all right, he thought, rubbing himself through his pants. Might even give Guffin a ride on her. She was fine as well as sneaky, and she'd suckered him by promising to let him have a taste. But that too had been a lie.

So now he'd break her in and break her down, and then he'd deliver her to someone who wanted her badly enough to pay a king's ransom.

Mara Reed was gonna get hers coming and going. He guaranteed it.

CHAPTER 4

"MARA . . . MARA . . . MARA, WAKE UP." ETHAN SAT NEAR HER crooked knee, tapping her flannel-covered hip smartly. "It's time to take your antibiotics, Mara. Wake up right now or we do this the hard way."

He'd been nudging her toward wakefulness for nearly two minutes, and his patience was nearing the loose knot at the end of its tether. Years ago he'd have waited patiently for those huge cinnamon-colored eyes to blink sleepily and for that slow, satisfied smile to smirk across her face. Then, his life had revolved around her needs, had found its meaning in loving her.

He'd been a fool. A smitten, soulful fool. Honesty required that he admit his culpability. He'd fallen for her first because of her streak of exploration, and her fearlessness. How she relied on no more than her wit and guile. His exact opposite. He could blame her for leaving, but he should have known better. Now he did.

Ethan swatted at her butt again, eager to move on with his

day and away from her. Quickly. "Damnit, Mara. Sit up and take your medicine."

"Go away," she mumbled into the bunched down pillow she'd pulled over her face. "I'm not sick. I'm asleep. Take your own medicine."

The guttural growl that rumbled out of Ethan's throat would have terrified a lesser woman, but his intended victim failed to take note. With the soft, dark voice his students recognized as incipient fury, Ethan calmly threatened, "You can either drink the water, Mara, or you can wear it. Count of three." He pushed up from the futon and gained his feet lithely, cup at the ready.

"One…"

In silent response, Mara snuggled deeper into the pillow, unconcerned.

"Two…"

She reached behind with her good arm to tug the blanket over her head.

"Three."

With a swift, studied move, Ethan snapped the blanket free and tipped the cup. The cascade of ice-cold liquid drew an immediate response.

"You four-eyed son of a two-legged jackal!" Mara yelped as the water splashed in her face, soaking her hair and the pillow beneath. Instantly alert, she awkwardly levered herself into a sitting position. The stream of curses continued as water ran cool rivulets down the borrowed nightshirt and along her sleep-warmed skin. "I would have gotten up," she muttered crossly. "Five more minutes wouldn't have killed you."

"I'm not operating on your timetable." Ethan serenely returned to the refrigerator and refilled the empty glass. "As long as you're a fugitive in my home, you're on my schedule. Understand?" He offered her the refilled cup with one hand, and extended his open palm with two pale beige pills. When she reached for them, he closed his fist. "Understand?"

Mara pushed soggy curls back from her eyes and arched a single insolent brow. "Yes, I get it, Nurse Ratchett. Loud and clear. One more step out of line and it's the plank for me."

"You're mixing your metaphors," Ethan corrected mildly. When she poked her tongue out at him, he quickly dropped the pills on the healthy pink flesh. And thought heatedly of the feats he knew that tongue could do.

Memories, like his libido, were hard to suppress. Every look, every gesture she made, served as a searing reminder of a different time. His body cared nothing for resentment when she slept in a T-shirt and little else and looked soft from sleep. *Like she probably looked for all of her customers.* The thought settled into his gut like acid, and he jerkily extended the glass.

Mara took the water and gulped the pills down. "Why are you staring at me like that?"

"Like what?"

"Like I'm a specimen on a petri dish."

"You're imagining things."

"No, I'm not. I study people, Ethan, and you've got something on your mind. What is it?"

The question swirled in his thoughts, but he refused to give it voice. *Are you a prostitute? Is that what you're running from?* Yet when she poked her tongue out again in insolence, he didn't care if she traded sex for money. Enthralled, he leaned close and murmured, "Keep at it and I'll take you up on your offer. But I won't be the one to pay."

Mara swiftly closed her mouth, finding it suddenly difficult to swallow. An accusation pulsed inside the warning, but she couldn't fathom its meaning.

"Smart girl." He turned away from the futon, unable to see the sudden rise in color in her cheeks. Instead, he walked to the bathroom to grab a towel from the rack. Returning to the studio, he tossed the plush green fabric to her, and she snagged it in midair with her good arm. "Clean yourself up. I've got to go into town for supplies. Stay inside. Don't touch anything or answer the phone. And don't go down to the warehouse."

The orders were barked out while Ethan collected his wallet and a slip of paper scrawled with letters. Mara assumed the paper was his shopping list. Hopefully, she thought, it included an appointment to have his stick removed.

"Excuse me?"

Mara looked up to find Ethan glaring at her, and she realized she'd muttered her thoughts aloud. He'd been sniping at her for nearly forty-eight hours, and she was fed up. Never one to back down, she shrugged. "You've been in a pissy mood for two days now, Ethan. Either stop treating me like a rabid infection or send me on my way."

He fixed her with a narrow look and retorted caustically, "Where, exactly, would you go? The Lucky Lake Lodge? Or maybe the Starburst Motel? Or somewhere else where you can ply your trade? Kiev doesn't have a bordello in town, but I'm sure we can find you suitable employment, if that's what you want."

"Bordello?" Mara stared at him, incredulous. "What?"

"No need to act shocked, Mara. You seem to be unable to keep your own counsel awake or asleep. I know what you do for a living. And why that man is after you."

Mara cocked her head, wondering if she'd given herself a concussion somewhere along the way. "You know what I do? And you think that I'm a prostitute?" She spoke the words slowly, to be certain there was no room for misinterpretation.

Ethan gave a short nod. "I would have imagined call girl, but your choice of accommodations don't suggest that you fetch a high price."

"My accommodations? Oh, the Lucky Lake." Mara covered her mouth and closed her eyes. Then her shoulders began to tremble.

Seeing her reaction, Ethan cursed beneath his breath and crossed over to the bed. "Oh, damn Mara, I'm not judging you." Guilt slid beneath righteous indignation, and he uncomfortably patted at her shaking shoulders. He had no right to chastise her choices when his weren't above reproach. And if making her living on her back kept her alive, then he couldn't be angry. Casting about for soothing words, he murmured, "I'm sure you're doing what you think you need to do to get by. Ah, honey, don't cry."

Mara's head shot up, barely missing Ethan's chin. Looking down, he realized that it was laughter—not devastation—that shook her body. "What the hell?"

"You think I'm a prostitute? That some john is after me?" The question spilled out between peals of laughter.

For the second time that morning Ethan gained his feet and glared down at her. He was not amused. "Actually, I assumed it was your pimp."

"Don't know much about the trade, do you, professor?" Mara threw her head back and laughed harder. "A pimp wouldn't chase me to Kiev for his cut. It wouldn't be worth his investment. But it does explain why you've been such a prig for the last couple of days." She scooped back the damp locks that had fallen on her forehead and fixed him with a steady if not entirely sober gaze. "Look, Ethan, if you want to know about my checkered past, just ask. Stop speculating."

Sorely tempted, Ethan folded his arms and shrugged. "I could care less about how you spend your time, Mara."

Mara had the good sense not to laugh, but she couldn't restrain a grin. "Could have fooled me."

"Fine. You're right. I do care. Because until you're better, I'm stuck with you. Forgive me for being worried about who might want you dead. God knows I'm over it now." Livid at having shown any concern, Ethan turned away. "Since you're feeling so chipper, perhaps you'll be ready to leave on Friday. I've got a guest coming, and I'd prefer not to expose Lesley to your kind. Whatever that is."

"I'm not a whore, Ethan," Mara retorted stiffly. "I sell my services, not sex."

"But you can be bought." Ethan walked to the studio door and paused to look back at her, still seated on the rumpled bed. "Either way, looks the same to me."

When the door closed behind him, Mara blinked hard, refusing to admit that what burned so fiercely behind her eyes were tears. She didn't cry. Not ever. And certainly not because some stiff-necked prude called her a whore. She scrambled out of bed and stalked over to the closet. Her borrowed shirt was drenched, and she was tired of looking at it anyway.

"Always was self-righteous," she muttered darkly as she scavenged for clothes. With angry abandon she yanked the neatly hung oxfords from their wooden perches and tumbled stiffly pressed khakis to the closet floor. Petulant zeal had her crushing the precise creases beneath her bare feet as she reached to the shelves above for the boxer shorts he'd stored there. "He has no idea what I do for a living. And he has no right to judge me."

Paying scarce attention, she selected a red T-shirt and gray shorts. "I may not be a college professor, but I'm not trash. I've never been trash." She slammed open the bathroom door, ignoring the sound as the wood crashed against the wall. "I'm an entrepreneur. And I'm damned good at it." She yanked back the shower curtain and twisted the taps onto full. The burst of steam echoed her mood perfectly. "Last year I made a quarter of a million using my brain, not my body. And what did he do? Studied dead bodies for stodgy old men. Pervert."

Denim and cotton dropped to the bathroom floor, and Mara stomped into the shower. "He thinks I'm a tramp. Fine." She poured a pool of creamy green gel into her hand and lathered her skin with brisk, angry movements. "He thinks I don't have feelings. Who cares?" Ignoring the dull ache in her arm, she scrubbed at her skin, muttering constantly. "Arrogant prig. Moralistic jerk. Obsequious worm." Soon the narrow space smelled of cucumbers and forests. Out of insults, Mara inhaled deeply, and exhaled on a ragged breath. "Damned Ethan."

When her breath caught on a hiccup, she rinsed herself quickly and shut off the taps. She wrapped herself in one of his towels and braced herself on the lip of the washbowl.

Mara forced her eyes to her reflection in the mirror. She didn't lie to herself, believing that at least she should always know the truth. And the truth was, she was confused. She'd come back to Kiev for two reasons. One was to hide out from Rabbe and Guffin until she could use the journal to find the answer to a mystery that had haunted her since childhood. Millions in gold coins were hidden somewhere in Texas, and only five people in the world had ever known where.

If she could find the keys and the map, and find the money, she'd never have to work another day in her life. She'd buy an island off the coast of Martinique and live the life she'd always dreamed of. Because gold stolen more than seventy years ago was worth a king's ransom today.

She combed through wet curls, tousling them around her still too wan face. The other, more important reason she'd come back was to see her grandmother. The woman she'd left behind when she fled Kiev and her father's wrath. There was no map that could tell her how to fix that mistake.

Standing in the bathroom, staring in the mirror, she wondered again if the money would do everything she needed it to do. Pay for the lies and the heartbreak. Buy her another chance. The woman who stared back at her offered no response, and stiffly, she turned away. All she needed was information and time, she reminded herself tartly, then she would have everything she'd come to Kiev for. With a sharp pull she opened the bathroom door and inched into the studio.

Perilously close to wallowing, Mara decided to call for reinforcement. She tapped a damp foot imperiously as she waited for the call to connect.

"Caine."

"Hey, Sebastian." Mara barely resisted a sigh as she sank onto the chair near the phone. Clutching the armrest, she asked, "You able to find information for me?"

"Always straight to business with you, isn't it? No playful banter or naughty foreplay. Just wham, bam, where's my information?"

Grinning, she retorted, "I prefer to play in the shallow end of the pool, Sebastian. I try not to swim with sharks. Or toy with them."

"Bright lady." Sebastian rarely consorted with partners, given his line of work, but Mara Reed often made him want to reconsider his position. "Police don't have a clue about the woman's death. You've got my intel on Poncho and Guerva, but I'm still looking into the Reese name you found in the journal. The other two were easy to connect to your grandfather, but without a last name for Reese, it's hard to pin down."

"Okay." She hadn't expected much, but the disappointment struck hard. "Do you know who Rabbe and Guffin are working for?"

"Everyone in that circle is being very tight-lipped. Has to be a big player for that level of caution. These aren't choir boys."

"Know when you might hear something?"

"Another day or so. I'm cashing in a few favors for you, darling."

"Thanks so much. I owe you." Grateful, Mara relaxed in Ethan's office chair. "I'll call in on Friday. Assuming I don't get shot again."

"Mara!"

"I'm all right. Ethan saved me." The minute the words escaped, she could have bitten her tongue. "Don't start with me, Sebastian. For the love of whatever lower demon you worship, don't start."

"I was only going to ask if you're okay."

"I'm fine."

"No thoughts of unrequited love or heart-wrenching guilt?"

"None." *Liar.* Mara grimaced. "Ethan doesn't know what's going on. And, no, I didn't think he'd be here."

"But you hoped." Sebastian offered the observation quietly. "I didn't pour the ouzo down your throat, and a drunken confession is still a confession, Mara love."

"I'm no fool. Besides, he's dating now." Mara winced lightly. No, she wasn't a fool. Which is why she'd accept that Ethan had moved on with his life and so had she.

Liar.

On the other end she heard a knock. "My appointment is here, darling. Check in occasionally to let me know you remain among the living. I'll let you know if I learn more."

"Thanks, Sebastian."

She rang off, oddly deflated. Wandering to the futon, she folded her legs beneath her and tried to distract herself with television. A quick flip through the channels failed to catch her attention, and she opted instead to explore her cell. After interminable bed rest, she was restless and eager to move. To learn more about this new Ethan Stuart.

Though the studio had only four walls, the array of books that covered nearly every free surface should prove amusing, she decided. At random she lifted a tome near his computer. "*Sango, the Fourth Alafin of Oyo.* I didn't know he studied religion."

She scanned the spines of other books. The remaining volumes seemed to deal with his work as a forensic anthropologist. But when she moved to the stack on the lower shelf of the desk, her heart nearly stopped. With careful hands she reached for the books and read the titles aloud. *"Great Train Robberies of the 1930s. Methodology of Identification Analyzing Tattoos and Tattoo Pigments."* Beneath the books more titles had been stored, each with their pages heavily tabbed.

Mara reached for the textbook on tattoos with trepidation. It seemed that she and Ethan had something new to talk about.

"MARA, I'M BACK," Ethan warned as he turned the knob. He didn't want to spook her. Since her return, she'd been moody and jumpy, which he assumed should be expected from a woman with a bullet wound. However, his patience was wearing thin, and he would need answers soon. As the door swung wide, he found that he'd have them sooner than he expected. She sat on the futon, a book open in her lap. His boxer shorts had rarely had a higher purpose than framing the legs she'd stretched along the bed.

At the sound of his entrance, Mara prepared herself. Nonchalantly, she tipped the book up to display the title.

He stormed into the loft, door slamming closed behind him. "What the hell are you doing with my books?"

"I got bored." With interest, she watched his eyes widen in alarm when he recognized the binding. She moved her shoulders dismissively. "Just doing a little light reading." She tipped the book over to show him the title. *"Great Train Robberies?* Didn't realize you'd become a crime buff, Ethan."

Coming to a halt at the end of the futon, he saw up close the quirk of lips that signaled she was baiting him. "I've got several interests," he hedged.

"Like stolen gold?"

Ethan met her eyes again and recognized the gleam that made the brown sparkle with mischief. He scowled and dropped down on the edge of the futon. "How much do you know?"

"Quite a bit, I think." Mara stretched her legs out, easing the muscles that had become cramped from hours of reading. One calf brushed against Ethan's knuckle, and sensation zinged along nerve endings. It took all of her willpower not to recoil, or worse, to ease closer to the long, elegant fingers whose prowess her skin remembered. Craved.

Instead, she swallowed hard but deliberately relaxed. "In 1937 a Bostonian wildcatter named Saul Schultz struck gold in Longview, Texas. He decided he didn't trust Mr. Roosevelt any more than he trusted Herbert Hoover. Especially after Roosevelt outlawed the private ownership of gold in 1933. Schultz refused to put his wealth into worthless American cash. Instead, he made a deal with a Mexican *jéfe* who offered to convert the cash into Spanish gold. Coins cast by Queen Isabella herself."

Because he was caught, he picked up the story. "Schultz was more than a wildcatter, though. He fancied himself a history buff. He not only needed a place to hide his gold, but he'd come into possession of artifacts liberated from a museum. Schultz had to put them out of the sight of his soon-to-be ex-wife and nosy regulators. Lucky for him, new wealth brought power. And a friendship with a governor at the Federal Reserve."

Her voice husky and tense, Mara finished, rearranging her legs on the mattress. Suddenly, no pose was comfortable. "So Schultz makes arrangements to put his millions in gold coins on a train headed for Dallas. Only, along the way, the train is robbed from the inside. Thieves remove more than half his stash during a stop in San Antonio and disappear into the night."

"Reverend Micah Reed and his Traveling Missionaries." Ethan scooted closer, closing the distance she'd opened.

Mara didn't shift away. "I thought you didn't believe me. You used to laugh."

He grazed intense eyes over her, remembering their last conversation about the lost treasure. Too near his touch, her silken skin taunted, and he had to focus hard to reply. Reminding himself of the consequences of action, he murmured, "I used to do a lot of things, Mara. Including listen to you. A few years ago, I came across this story, and the pieces seemed to fit. I've been working on this ever since."

"You mentioned artifacts."

"Yes. A totem to the Yoruban god Shango and a manuscript written by a Shango priest." The knot of tension in his gut tightened and the stark hunger that had been with him since her return sharpened. "I've been searching for them since I read about them in grad school. My research led me to that train. The one your grandfather robbed."

"What's their value?" She bent toward him eagerly, but

stopped at his reaction. "I'm not asking about the money, Ethan. I simply want to know why you care." Incensed, she bent her knee to move away, accidentally pressing skin to skin. It galled that the lightest contact shot arrows of silvery pleasure straight through her. She edged away quickly, but not before Ethan noticed.

He lifted his hands to fold across his chest. "The manuscripts are priceless. According to my research, this priest had discovered a method of preserving the dead in a nearly mummified state, but without the normal embalming chemicals used by the Egyptians." Excitement at being able to share his findings bloomed and he forgot distance. Touching her knee, he explained, "If the priest did write down his methods, there is so much to learn about the history of Benin and Togo and Nigeria. And the contributions to my field could be incalculable. Chemical combinations modern science hasn't considered."

As he spoke he traced absent lines on her leg. Skeins of desire slithered along her skin and, finding her hand hovering above his errant fingers, she jerked away.

Ethan hadn't noticed his meandering until the silken warmth beneath his fingertips disappeared. Intrigued by her nervous reaction, he asked politely, "Is something wrong? You jumped like a scalded cat."

Embarrassed and aroused, Mara responded coolly, "Nothing." Nothing a cold shower and a reality check couldn't cure.

"Good." To tease, to test, he traced the bandage on her calf with a lazy grace, satisfied when he felt a shiver. "So what now?"

"I don't know. I didn't plan on sharing."

"And you will now?" Ethan lifted his hand, surprised. He hadn't expected it to be that easy. "Why?"

"Because you probably won't go away. You're stubborn, Ethan. I do remember that."

"And you don't play well with others. I remember that."

"I have my notes, that's about all." She saw no reason to mention the journal that lay in her knapsack. Ethan—smart, conscientious Ethan—had come on a quest for a statue and some papers. The gold to him was probably irrelevant, but she had debts and obligations. After those were settled, she'd happily share the wealth, but bringing Ethan into her world was out of the question. He wouldn't last five minutes against Rabbe and Guffin. Best course of action was to string him along until she learned what he knew, then located the gold on her own.

But one never told a dupe he was a dupe. A good con artist got what she needed without ever giving the mark reason to worry. Most likely, the clues she needed were at the Reed compound, buried beneath mounds of dirt and secrets the family was very good at keeping. Mustering a conciliatory half smile, she asked, "Where do we start?"

"Not at the church." As though he read her mind, Ethan said lightly, "If you're planning to go looking there for a map, don't bother."

She focused on him intently. "What? Why not?"

"There's nothing out there." Ethan got to his feet and wandered to the window. "I've been searching there for weeks. Haven't found anything."

The blow of disappointment was almost physical, and the stab of fear that followed jolted her. Without the money and the means to flee, she was a dead woman. Rabbe was too close, and she was running out of time. Finding her grandfather's stash was her last, desperate hope. A long shot, she realized, but it was better than the alternative. Having no hope left. "Are you sure?"

"Chi Development has been excavating the property next to it for nearly three months. They dug deep enough to discover there were already squatters on the land. Unidentified bodies, which did not sit well with the city council. It was a golden opportunity that I hadn't expected. No pun intended." Ethan drummed his fingers on the windowsill. "I've used my project to check every inch of the house and the property. Nothing."

"Then why are you still here?" Mara turned to watch him. Ethan knew something big. She could always tell. Poker with Ethan was a sucker's game because his tapping fingers were a certain tell. A tendril of hope unwound inside her, pushing up through the despair. "If there isn't a map, what's the point?"

Ethan debated how much to tell her, a woman he knew he couldn't trust. Yet, there were two mysteries here, three if he counted his inscrutable Mara, and he planned on solving at least one of them. "The map isn't there, but I think there may be clues hidden in other places. You might know where. As long as I help Chi, I've got complete access to the site."

"Convenient."

Ethan continued to tap softly and stare out the window. "Yes. The authorities have no record of many of the deaths, and they need to determine why these particular bodies were buried. The medical examiner believes all the deaths were from natural causes. My job is to determine who they were before they died. Chi Development is anxious to move on the project. Once we know who we've found."

Mara tensed but kept her tone level. There was no way he could know, she thought anxiously. After so many years, how could anyone know? But she had never been one to duck asking the question. "If you didn't find a map at the site, what did you find?"

"Just the fifty-six dead bodies so far." He turned to her then, grinning broadly, like a little boy with a prized frog. "Wanna see?"

CHAPTER 5

THE HUMAN BODY TOLD A STORY LONG AFTER THE SPIRIT HAD departed. Brittle bones whispered secrets, when the ear had been properly trained to hear the truth. His truth, Ethan thought as he and Mara descended to the bottom floor of the warehouse.

In the cold, shadowed cavern of space, he'd set up shop with fifty-six bodies recovered from unmarked graves on the outskirts of Kiev. He explained his project to Mara. "Chi Development purchased all the land just south of town. Had clear title, until the crew started digging to lay foundation. Then they found this." He pointed to the rows of human remains. "The property is adjacent to your father's church."

Ethan guided her down to the last couple of steps. Mara hesitated. He didn't press, and instead hit the landing and strode to the metal tables arrayed in precise rows. He gently motioned her forward, but she shook her head.

"Oh, no."

"Mara, come on. They're dead. They won't bite. And I have something to show you."

"I can see from here," she retorted, hanging back. Mara stared, transfixed by the gruesome sight and what she imagined he'd discovered. She shuddered and pushed away the threat of memory. He doesn't know yet, she reminded herself. He's guessing. With effort, she leveled her voice, erasing the currents of dread. "Can't you simply tell me? Why the show and tell?"

"Because we're partners."

The simple declaration held her still. "Just like that?"

"I don't play games, Mara. A deal is a deal. I'll show you what I've found, then you show me yours." With practiced motions he snapped on latex gloves and covered himself in a white lab coat. He held a bundle out to her, slightly out of reach. "Will you put this on? In case you decide to join me?" The urge to push surged strong, but Ethan realized that few shared his passion for the past in skeletal form. If they were going to be partners, she would have to join him willingly. If she chose not to, he'd know up front where he stood. After a few seconds' impasse, he set the coat and gloves on the table. He shook off the disappointment and, with a shrug, moved to the cadaver he'd been working on.

"Like I said, the developer broke ground, only to find an unregistered cemetery. The bodies were in boxes, but none had been embalmed. They searched county records, but nothing turned up. More than fifty people had been buried without identification—men, women, and children."

Mara inched closer to the bottom step. His disappointment pricked at her conscience, drew her closer. She knew what lay beneath the sheet at his hand, why the bodies he'd found had been buried so ignominiously. They were as familiar to her as her own family. Members of the church that had controlled her life for eighteen years. A past she had actually believed was buried. Apprehension warred with pride, and she settled on the bottom step, not yet ready to move forward. "Isn't it illegal to dig up corpses?"

Ethan noted her movement. To distract, he launched into explanation. "Yes. Particularly if they are from a tribal burial ground or an historical site. Normally, the project would be terminated when the bodies were discovered, but this is Texas. Chi worked out an arrangement with the county. If the remains didn't have historical significance, the company would pay for relocation to the Kiev cemetery. Since the graves were unmarked, the sheriff's office asked for help in identification. That's where I came in."

Mara swept a long look over him, from the white sheet to the smock. Partners, he'd said. For now. She took a short breath and it whispered out. "I need help putting this on." Still unable to bend her left arm without pain, she settled for cocking a fist on her right hip. "You've got thirty seconds to explain why I'm down here, or I'm gone."

The tone of bravado was undone by the faint quiver Ethan could hear in her voice. Stifling a grin, he crossed to the staircase and helped her into the smock. He waited until she'd put the gloves on and then he returned to his patient.

"Tattoos." He pulled back a white sheet to reveal a body. "I think these marks may be our clues." For the second time, he beckoned Mara forward, and she approached cautiously. Proud of her, he teased, "They're dead, Mara. The dead can't harm you."

"Of course they can." Unable to suppress her shudder, she eased forward, careful to give the body wide berth. When she shivered, she blamed it on the cold of the warehouse and not the preternatural trepidation that settled on her like a shroud. She already knew what he wanted to show her, knew it the moment he explained where the bodies had come from. The Second Church of the Spirit.

She glanced down at the uncovered body. "Show me."

"Look. Here," Ethan instructed as he tilted the body forward. "This is what I was hired to study."

Because he focused on the dead man, he failed to notice Mara's observation of him, the admiring look that stole into her widened eyes. He handled the remains delicately, she realized. Hands that could have coaxed music from a grand piano instead played along fragments of body, urging out tales about their time on earth. They arranged the cadaver to angle it into the light, and she braced herself.

On the aged skin, a symbol stood out in stark, black contrast.

Ethan focused on the strange shape of the Greek letter. "I've found Greek letters on all of the bodies," he murmured.

Mara stared at the ridge of flesh that had been burned and raised by scar tissue. Her father's doing. "These are brands. You mentioned tattoos."

He glanced at her. The flat tone showed no surprise at the marks, only at the method. "Yes, these are from a branding iron. The burns run deep and left shadows on the bone of the decomposed. I've also found trace ink stains on the bones of others."

"On the bones?"

Ethan nodded. "A scientist in London has a theory that the tattoo ink settles in the bone over time. You don't get a perfect image, more like a hazy reflection. But it's there." His eyes locked with Mara's. "On every body, I've found the same symbols. Greek letters. Branded. Except for two bodies. Those two have been tattooed with the letters."

Mara asked calmly, "What do you know about the marks?"

"It's peculiar. I haven't come close to the entire alphabet. Some letters are repeated on several bodies, while others occur sporadically. I've found most of the lesser-used graphs on the corpses of children." He draped the sheet over the deacon's face. "The marks are similar to the tattoos, but not the same."

"Do you know what it means?" Mara asked, playing for time. Bailey's journal recounted tattoos, but in garbled fashion. He'd even drawn crude pictures of his mark. In a moment, Ethan would ask a question she had been forbidden in childhood to answer. Prompting the confession, she asked, "Have you deter-mined what the markings say?"

"No." Because he knew the answer, he softened his voice to ask the next question. "Do you? Know what the letters mean?"

There it was. The first part of the reason she'd run away twelve years ago. This time she'd answer. "They aren't letters. It's a code. A holy code."

Something in her brisk delivery caught him off guard. "A holy code? Your father?"

Mara nodded, slipping away into a past she'd run miles to forget. "Christian numerology. My father was obsessed with it. When one of the church members died, he would mark the bodies with a holy number. So that God would know of their faithfulness on earth. Or their sin. As a child, I had to memo-rize the entire table."

Fascinated, Ethan gripped the edge of the gurney. "And Greek was one of the original languages of the Christian church. Your father spoke Greek?"

"No. He didn't know the language, but he understood the numbers."

"Numbers?" He pointed to the mark dubiously. Although he didn't speak the language either, he, like most college attendees, was familiar with the Greek alphabet. "Looks like the letters iota and epsilon to me. This is a number?"

Mara nodded absently. She couldn't seem to look away from the images that haunted her. "In Greek, letters and numbers are the same. One through ten are the same as the first nine letters of the modern alphabet plus diagamma." Anticipating his next question, she supplied, "Diagamma is an obsolete letter in the alphabet. But in numerics, it represents the number six. Twenty and higher are either combined like Roman numerals or they have their own letter. Like pi for eighty or rho for one hundred."

"I didn't think about that." Using his latex-covered index finger, he traced the ιδ on the man's hip. He'd noted Mara's reaction to the symbols; in particular, her absolute lack of reaction. His theory that the symbols on the dead bodies were connected to the church and to the gold and the artifacts shifted inexorably toward fact. Nonetheless, any good theory required confirmation. "Iota and delta. That would be..." He paused, running through the alphabet. "Fourteen, right?"

"Yes."

Her response promised more, and Ethan waited. And waited. "Mara? What is the importance of fourteen? Why tattoo it onto a man after death?"

"Not after. As he lay dying." Death and memory crawled across her skin once more, and she realized her most efficient tack for this scene was honesty. "It was a tribute. Like other evangelicals, my father felt that the presence of numbers in the Scriptures held holy meaning. Because Greek is considered one of the pure languages of the Bible, along with Hebrew and Aramaic, he relied on Greek numerals to do his work."

"His work?"

Mara's eyes flashed with a smoldering resentment. "It cer-

tainly wasn't divinely inspired, despite his lies to the flock."
Taking a deep breath, she continued harshly, "He subscribed to
a philosophy that spoke of bodies arriving at the pearly gates
unadorned and without clear direction for admittance to heaven.
According to him, St. Peter would get confused, I guess."

"Are you serious?" Ethan took a step toward her, but she
reared away. He didn't try again. "Why did he do that?"

The mirthless laugh echoed in the warehouse. Mara felt the
cold condense inside her, the shame of family secrets that she'd
prayed Ethan would never touch. "Dad was determined to be a
good help on earth. So he marked the bodies either before or
after death. The symbols marked their state before leaving this
mortal plane."

"And fourteen means..."

Like a teacher, she explained the twisted rubric. "In biblical
numerics, fourteen is the mark of deliverance. Salvation. This
must be Deacon Jessup. He lived a rather sinful life before
joining my father in his spiritual totalitarianism. I thought of
him as a cruel man with an empty soul. Dad found him to be
the perfect attendant."

Driven to soothe, Ethan closed the distance between them
again. "Did he hurt you?" He laid a gentle hand on her arm,
waiting for the recoil.

Mara shook her head once and wrapped her hand over his.
"Not now. Don't ask me now."

Seeing the woman who refused to back down from a fight
beg for respite spun an impotent anger through his blood.

Obadiah Reed had a lifetime of sin to answer for, but Ethan realized he would deal with that later. For now, perhaps, she needed to focus on the mystery.

Slowly, he led her to a table where a pile of photographs were spread out across the granite surface. Each photo held an image of a Greek symbol emblazoned on a hip or back. "Can you translate these for me?"

Mara set her shoulders and pushed off the lingering chill. "Of course. It's in my blood." She checked each picture, startled anew at her father's handiwork. On the slight bones of a child's body, she identified ε, the letter—and the number five. "Grace. This one means grace. Most of the children were converted young. When they died, he absolved them." She explained the kappa of twenty, which signaled redemption, and the β of the faithful witness. An automaton, she identified his entire catalogue, but at an image of Ϝ, the diagamma symbol, she stopped, aghast.

Standing behind her, Ethan didn't see the tears well. He reached past her to the photo. "I don't recognize this number. Is it the one you mentioned?"

"Uh, yes. Did you identify the body?" Her father saved this symbol for the wretched few who disobeyed.

"The autopsy and records we found identified her as a Ms. Kate Super. Did you know her?"

"She helped my mother escape." She remembered the branding, the screams from the shed. "This symbolizes the manifestation of sin. The evils of Satan. He was condemning her to hell."

"My God."

Mara offered a brittle, humorless smile. "That's the point, isn't it?" For most of her life, she'd lived with the perversion of religion. A despot of a father who controlled the souls of men and women too weak to defy him. Not quite a cult leader, but perilously close. Families crowded onto a compound, following a spiritual leader who accepted their paychecks and penance with equal sanguinity. Her father didn't demand that they believe in him, treat him as a messiah. Instead, he demanded obeisance to his twisted brand of Christianity, and heaven help those who rebelled.

Ethan wanted to press, but he had one more revelation to share. "Can you look at something else?"

"Why not?" Dutifully, she followed him to another room where refrigerated units hummed lightly. Ethan opened a compartment and pulled out a tray. He lifted the sheet to reveal a man's arm.

Mara jolted. "Is it a mummy?"

"Not quite." He pointed to the aged skin, which was yellowish-gray and waxy. "It's a phenomenon called 'adipocere.'" Ethan touched the preserved flesh. "Sometimes, when the dead are placed in wet areas immediately after death, a complex chemical reaction takes place that preserves the soft tissue. Adipocere is from Latin. It means fatty wax."

"Never heard of it."

"Most bodies are embalmed after a natural death. And state

law requires proper burial. Even if the body isn't embalmed, natural decomposition will erode the tissue and leave only a skeleton after time." He uncovered the body, down to the man's waist.

Mara froze.

Ethan looked up and caught her wide, fearful look. He deliberately continued to explain the science, giving her a moment to compose herself. "East Texas is humid almost year round. We get almost more than fifty-five inches of rainfall a year. With Kiev right on the Sabine River, the ground has a number of seeps and creeks. Whoever buried these bodies didn't dig very deep. There was an underground spring nearby, and the seeps bled into the graves. It was enough."

Unable to look away from the man who'd once bounced her on his knee, Mara whispered, "Enough for what?"

"Enough to preserve this on his corpse." Ethan reached out his free hand and tilted her chin up. "What?"

Mara jerked her face from his hand. "It's Poncho."

"You recognize him." It wasn't a question.

"He died when I was four or five." Taking a shallow breath, she steeled herself to look at the body without interest. "Of this disease?"

"Adipocere isn't a disease. It's a chemical reaction." He pushed the sheet lower. "And it preserved this on a body that died nearly thirty years ago. This tattoo is not like the others."

Like flame, suddenly the mark on her hip began to burn.

Spinning away, Mara headed for the steps. "Sorry. Lesson's over." She tossed the words over her shoulder as she rushed up the stairs.

In the loft, she stripped off the lab coat and the latex gloves, heart racing. Poncho's tattoo. Bailey's drawing. Her grandfather's marks. It all came back to the Second Church of the Spirit. Which is where she was headed.

Her first shoe was barely tied before Ethan burst through the door.

"Running again?"

Mara hunched over her sneaker and didn't look up. Meeting his eyes might make her stay. But he had figured out too much, and that would make him a target if she did stay. Coating her words in disdain, she scoffed, "I'm done here. Dead bodies marred by a religious zealot's decoder ring isn't the clue to a fortune. I thought you had more."

The rebuff stung and Ethan raised his hand in defense. Then dropped it. Stupid fool, he chided himself angrily. He should have known better than to trust. But he'd been rocked by the sight of her with his books. Not only by the fact that she'd discovered his plans, but that when he entered the apartment, the sight of her in his clothes, on his bed, seemed perfectly natural. *Perfectly right.* "Don't leave me, Mara. Not like this."

Summoning her best performance, she raised her head. "Like what, Ethan?" she scoffed lightly. "All you've got for me are corpses with my father's version of pin the sin on the donkey. I assumed from your notes that you knew more. You don't. So I'm gone."

Afraid he couldn't stop her, terrified that he needed to, he held out the one set of photos he hadn't shown her before. "Take a look at this, then. Before you run. Again."

Warily, Mara nipped the photos from his hand, careful not to make contact. The body on the slab was Poncho. She riffled through them, stopping at the fifth shot. Shooting him a look, she said, "I saw this downstairs. What's your point?"

"According to my research, Poncho had quite a history here in Kiev. Bar fights and nights in jail until your grandfather bailed him out. The story goes that when he got drunk, he'd drop his pants and show complete strangers his naked butt. He claimed it was one part of the key to a fortune in gold."

"I told you, the marks on the bodies were made by my father. Poncho was much older."

Undeterred, Ethan flipped to another photo. He pointed triumphantly to the shaded mark on the magnified photo. "These bones were found in the cemetery. I think it's your grandfather's body, Mara."

She jerked subtly, appalled. "My grandfather? You dug up his bones?"

"Unmarked graves, Mara. I didn't know whose bodies these were until I arrived. I've already made arrangements for them to be reinterred in the main cemetery. I'm sorry."

"No. No, you couldn't have known." Mara touched the photo

delicately, studying the image. Biblical numerics were specific, she knew. Only certain numbers had meanings. The symbols Ethan had photographed were spaced too closely to be specific digits and they did not form any words.

More numbers.

Insight coalesced and she understood where her next clue could be found. Casting her voice with disappointment, she shrugged at Ethan. "I can't decipher these for you."

Eyes narrowed and suspicious, Ethan prodded, "You can try."

"I can't. I won't." Mara leapt off the bed and resumed gathering her things hurriedly. She snatched up her duffel bag, mumbling, "If I were you, I'd drop this wild goose chase, Ethan. No good can come of it."

"Advice from you? How the hell do you expect me to trust anything you say?"

"I don't. But without my help, you've got no choice. Let it go."

"Will you?"

"Absolutely." Mara swung the strap across her shoulder. "Thanks for the hospitality and the patch job. But I need to move to safer territory as soon as possible. The men hunting me are bound to return. I'd prefer to not lead them to you. I owe you."

Owed him? The pithy phrase stung, like a kick to the gut. Not long ago there'd been more between them than a balance sheet. They'd been lovers. Partners, for an instant.

Fool me twice, he thought, and the blame's on me. To think he could rely on her had been his fault. She'd reminded him of who she was, and he would accept it. Again. Grimly, he left her side to jerk open his closet and grab a pair of khakis. Bunching them, he aimed for the spot on the bed near her, tempted to aim higher.

She ignored the pants and turned to the door.

"Put them on," he instructed brusquely. "You probably don't want to skulk out of here in boxer shorts."

Because he was correct, she set her bag down and shimmied into the pants. "I'll be out of your way in a minute."

Stifling a snarl, Ethan moved to the desk. "Take your time. I'm just grateful to have the warning this time," he sneered. "Should I check my wallet?"

At that, she simply met his burning eyes. Her voice, like her face, held no emotion. "Screw you, Ethan."

He sat on the corner of the broad desktop, bracing his leg on the floor. Folding his arms, he drawled, "As I recall, that's what you did before you took my money, darling. I'm not in the mood for a repeat performance." Even as he spoke the words, Ethan winced internally. Only Mara ever drove him to cheap shots and juvenile attacks. He'd forgotten that about them.

Before he could apologize, Mara had gained her feet. She reached for her backpack at the foot of the bed. Slinging it awkwardly over her shoulder, she headed for the door. She gripped the knob tightly, regulated the hitch in her breath. Four days. She'd had four days with him.

That was more than she'd expected. More than she deserved. "I'll send your clothes back when I get a chance."

"Don't bother." He firmed his mouth, biting off the question that unmanned him. Why did she keep leaving him?

Because the answer was clear, he said nothing. He hooked his fingers together, prepared for a wave of self-disgust. Years ago he'd found his answer. Mara required excitement, adventure. Traits he didn't possess. Twelve years ago he'd been too staid for her, and obviously that hadn't changed. He could pretend that playing with the dead held intrigue and danger, but in the safety of a laboratory the worst that would befall him was a rash. Mara recognized this before and she'd seen it again.

At least this time she was leaving before he fell too hard.

In the doorway, Mara looked over her shoulder to the only man she'd ever loved. His leg swung negligently, the heel tapping the desk's leg. The afternoon light burnished his dusky copper skin and the hauntingly handsome features were cast in relief. A firmly molded mouth that had crept into her dreams night after endless night, and eyes that could see through her.

In those eyes, she'd once been beautiful. Not a misfit or a mistake. Simply his. She looked her fill, knowing it would be her last. This time, when she left, she wouldn't be coming back.

No one would ever see her as he had, would love her as he had.

Dropping her bag, she spun on her heel and crossed the expanse between them in long, hurried strides. Ethan didn't move.

When she reached his side, she cupped his face in her hands, the fingers trembling with anticipation. "I missed you. I'm sorry."

Then she closed her lips over his and gave herself to one final kiss.

The moment her mouth touched his, Ethan felt the world slip away. Soundlessly. Completely. There was only the glide of Mara's lips against his. The insistent press that cajoled his mouth to open, to welcome her inside. Heat, like an inferno, blazed in his veins. Temptation, like a song, clouded in his mind. It demanded that he slide his arms around her, that he trail his hand along her spine to sink into the silken curls at her nape. He wanted to pull away, to resist the skeins that would bind his heart to her again, but he'd forgotten that she tasted of honeyed sweetness. Instead, he sank deeper, plumbing her mouth for secrets, for answers. For oblivion.

Mara moaned beneath the hungry kiss, wrapping herself against him, desperate to crawl inside. Their tongues tangled, danced, and she reveled in the movement. She splayed eager palms against his chest and tormented the flesh she found there. Too far away, she gripped his waist to pull him closer, until she stood cradled between his hard thighs.

Not close enough, Ethan thought hazily, and he surged forward until his leg slipped between hers, their mutual sighs rising into the air as their hips fit into one another. Tilting her chin, he changed the angle of the kiss, determined to taste every change, to find every memory. Licks of fire burned his skin where her tongue traced his mouth. He caressed the high, taut breasts that were naked beneath his borrowed shirt. When his fingers crested the first peak, she gasped into his mouth.

"More. More." She panted out the demand, fumbling at his buttons. Her body fairly vibrated with anticipation. It had been so long since he loved her. "Once more."

Drowning, he let sensations swamp him, filled his lungs with the scent of her. As passion submersed him, he thought dimly that he would never surface again. "No."

Ethan wrested his mouth free and quickly set her away from him. While Mara swayed in stunned reaction, he walked into the kitchen on legs that weren't at all steady. At the faucet, he fumbled to open the taps and poured a glass of water. Swallowing quickly, he refilled the glass. The cool liquid slid down his parched throat, but there wasn't enough water in the world to put out what Mara had begun.

He loathed that with a single kiss he'd forgotten his vows to himself. And his almost promises to Lesley. He despised that he'd been dragged—no, that he'd rushed—back for more. More heartache. More disappointment. More loving a woman who never understood what that meant. A woman he would never be daring enough to satisfy.

"I thought you were leaving," he rasped out, staring into the empty glass. If he met her eyes, he would beg. "If you need money—"

"N-No." Mara flushed with embarrassment, but she refused

to slink away. "I'm not a whore, Ethan. I can take care of myself."

"I didn't mean—"

"I know." Just as she knew that for a second he'd wanted her again. Needed her. With her body still pulsing, she resisted the urge to touch her mouth. To press the kiss against her lips so she would never lose the taste of Ethan's desire. Because she knew now he would never touch her again.

For the second time she went to the door, anxious to get outside and find a place to think. To process. "I'll send your stuff soon. Thanks."

She rushed out of the studio, willing herself to keep it together until she made it downstairs. Her thoughts swirled with confused longing, and she banged her arm against the railing. She made her way to the door, eyes away from the covered bodies. Clasping her throbbing arm, she levered the door open and emerged into the alleyway, head down. Straight into danger.

"Hi, Jennie." Rabbe's gravelly welcome was accompanied by strong, hurtful hands wrenching her wrists behind her. "Or do you prefer Mara?"

She tried to scream in agony but a wet, slippery palm covered her mouth before she could emit a sound.

"None of that, lady." Guffin pressed his hand tight, grinding her swollen lips against her teeth. "Don't want no one to come an' save you this time. Not till Mr. Conroy gets a look at you."

"Shut up, moron." Rabbe scowled at his partner, and Mara

kicked out at him. Her foot caught him in the solar plexus and he doubled over, out of breath.

Taking quick advantage, she jammed an elbow into Guffin's ribs, but the man moved quicker than she thought. He released her mouth and instead shifted into a chokehold. As the meaty arm tightened around her windpipe, Mara's struggles stilled. Black dots danced before her as she clawed at Guffin's forearm.

In response, he squeezed harder. From what seemed a million miles away she heard the dulcet voice explain, "I'm not like Rabbe, miss. I don't like hurtin' women, but I will." She felt the barrel of his silencer tracing her side. Nearly out of air, Mara stopped resisting. As soon as her legs stilled, the constriction eased. "Now, you just come along to the truck and we'll be on our way."

Mara stumbled forward, urged along by the cold press of metal at her side. Rabbe regained his breath and caught up with them. "Bitch, I'm gonna enjoy myself with you, ya hear? As soon as the boss gives the word, I'll make you wish you'd never met me." He reached for her breast, but Guffin shifted into his path.

"Don't. Mr. Conroy didn't say nothin' about you hurting the lady. He just said bring her to him."

"He won't care if I have a little taste, Seth. Now move out of my way."

Rabbe tried to reach for her again, but Guffin topped him by a good six inches. He stared down at his partner, the pale blue eyes soft but filled with warning. With Mara tucked by his side, he gestured with his pistol. "You focus on driving, Arthur. I'll take care of Ms. Reed." When Rabbe hesitated, Guffin pointed again. "Not gonna happen, Arthur."

Muttering beneath his breath, Rabbe circled around to the driver's side while Guffin put Mara in the rear and slid in beside her. She startled when he reached past her. "You need to wear your safety belt," he explained sweetly. "These SUVs have a habit of flipping over. I don't think they're safe, but Arthur likes the size, don't you, Arthur?"

"She's not some damned guest, Guffin! Stop treating her like the Queen of frickin' England."

"There's no call to be rude," countered Guffin mildly. "Or to be unsafe." With a satisfied smile, he clicked the lock into place. Of Mara, he asked, "Is it too tight?"

"It's fine," she answered dazedly. "Thank you."

Guffin grinned widely, displaying a dazzling array of gold and white teeth. "Common courtesy isn't nearly common enough." He leaned forward to tap Rabbe on the shoulder. "We can go see Mr. Conroy now."

CHAPTER 6

THE EXPEDITION CRAWLED ALONG SHAHAR, WEAVING INTO and out of viscous afternoon traffic. A high sun blistered the ground, and the pavement steamed beneath its rays. Because it was Texas, trucks, rather than cars, crowded the four-lane county road and forced the SUV into a modicum of conservative behavior. Rabbe cursed steadily as signal after signal stopped his momentum. The massive engine purred beneath his hands, begging to be released to roar.

"Podunk town," he muttered, blasting his horn at a red Dodge Ram that inched forward ahead of him at a snail's pace. Frustrated by Guffin's chivalry and everything keeping him from his revenge, he cracked the window enough to stick his head out. "Move that ancient piece of crap before I show you what a Ram is!" He nudged the Expedition closer and leaned on the horn again. "Come on, move it!"

Guffin frowned at the red light, then leaned forward. "Don't rile anyone, Arthur. We've got what we came for. No need to cause trouble." He thumped Rabbe on the arm. "Try them breathing exercises I showed you. In through the nose, out through the mouth."

"Up yours, Seth," Rabbe snorted. "I'm not doing any sissy meditation. Save that for your boyfriend."

Unperturbed, Guffin shrugged, pulling out his cell phone. "It will be your funeral when you die of a heart attack."

Mara listened to the bickering with half an ear and a pounding heart. Someone named Conroy demanded her presence, and she had no idea why. Given Rabbe's urgency to bring her, instead of giving vent to his expected murderous rage, she assumed Conroy had something to do with the journal and Mary Kay's death. His name tugged at her memory, but she couldn't place it.

"Ms. Reed, Mr. Conroy would like to speak to you." Guffin held the phone out and she accepted it warily.

"Hello, Ms. Reed."

"Mr. Conroy?" The smooth, cool voice held menace and power. She allowed her voice to tremble violently, thickened her words to sound teary. It wasn't difficult. "Please don't hurt me. I'm sorry I stole from you."

Conroy allowed the silence to lengthen. "Ms. Reed, I've gone to a great deal of trouble, almost for naught. But if you have my property in your possession, I think we can resolve this upon your arrival."

His journal. And he was the man responsible for Mary Kay's death. "Where am I going?"

"To meet me. And demonstrate that your penitence is real." Conroy fondled the key, imagining its mates. "You'll help me find the others and the gold, won't you?"

"I don't know where it is."

"Think harder." The growled threat made her tremor real. "I'll see you soon."

Rabbe glanced in the rearview mirror and saw her face pale. He grinned. "Conroy doesn't play nice. Hope you've got his property. Otherwise, I'll ask him to let me convince you to share. Like Cassandra."

Reports of what Rabbe had done to Cassandra, her partner in Detroit, had made the front page. The police hadn't known about Mary Kay. Slick, greasy shame roiled in her stomach. In a harsh whisper she murmured, "She didn't know about the scheme. Not all of it. Wasn't her fault."

"Hmm. Maybe I should have listened to her. But it was hard to hear her over the screams," he sniggered.

"Cut it out," Guffin commanded. He patted Mara's shoulder awkwardly. "Mr. Conroy does not appreciate tormenting women. Keep it up and I'll report you."

"Sissy." But Rabbe returned his attention to the road. They'd stopped at another traffic light, one of the gazillions in this rinky-dink town. "I can't wait to get the hell out of here."

"I find it charming," Guffin said. "Quaint. All the little shops nestled in their nooks and crannies." Pointing across the road, he exclaimed, "An old-fashioned soda shop! How lovely."

Mara caught the wistfulness and turned her attention to him, shaking off her horror. "Kiev is quaint. Built during the gold rush in the 1800s. Mrs. Kneller, who owns the shop, says it's been in the family for generations." She sent him a shy grin. "Makes the best orange crème you've ever tasted."

Seth preened under the attention. Given his height and girth, most ladies found him terrifying. "Might have to try it out. Next time you're in Brooklyn, try Mannie's in Dyker Heights. Amazing egg cream."

"I will." Mara tried to recall her last trip to New York. "Dyker Heights? Near Bay Ridge?"

"You know it?"

Adopting the patina of an accent, she launched into a description of her three weeks there. The scam had been an art swap at the Brooklyn Arts Academy. Soon, Seth was chortling in appreciation.

"Stop entertaining her, moron!" snapped Rabbe. The truck had come to another standstill at a red. The tinkling laughter that had filled his head now grated unbearably. Grinding his teeth, he warned, "Mr. Conroy warned us. She's trying to distract you."

Guffin bristled. "Keep your eyes on the road. Ms. Reed and I are enjoying our shop talk."

Rabbe wanted to argue, but above the red Ram the light changed to green. He punched the horn sharply; still, the truck idled at the light. On either side, traffic resumed its motion, but the truck did nothing. The truck's driver had his head down, and Rabbe could only see the outline of shoulders hunched over the passenger seat. Because he sat on the truck's bumper and the car behind him had drawn up close, he couldn't maneuver the oversized vehicle enough to cross lanes. Trapped, Rabbe snarled and jammed the horn again. Through the open window he hurled more invective, each word increasingly more graphic.

"Calm down, Arthur. You'll only piss him off."

"Like I give a shit."

Mara listened to the string of obscenities and plotted her move. Rabbe had a limited vocabulary but an inventive imagination, one that kept his attention averted. She watched Seth instead, tensing with anticipation when the truck's owner burst out of his vehicle, shotgun in tow. The grizzly bearded stranger tipped his hat low and trained both barrels on a suddenly quiet Rabbe.

"Told you to calm down," Guffin chided. He glanced out the passenger window and spied a sheriff's car at the next intersection. "There's police up ahead, Arthur. Be nice to the man or Mr. Conroy's going to be pissed. Apologize and let's be on our way."

In response, Rabbe reached for his Luger on the seat beside him. The chamber was loaded, he knew, and faster than a dead man's shotgun. "He should've stayed inside," Rabbe warned. "I ain't gonna be punked by a cowboy."

Recognizing the tone, Guffin pleaded, "Shoot him and we'll have to deal with the cops. Mr. Conroy won't take too kindly to that."

"This will only take a second," Rabbe promised tightly.

"Keep an eye on the girl." He swung the door open and leapt out, pistol at the ready.

Which was Mara's cue. Using the flat of her hand, she chopped Guffin in his throat and elbowed his gut. While he gurgled for breath, she released the seat belt and scrambled for the door lock. Guffin gasped for her to stop. Rabbe heard the back door open, but his eyes were glued on the angry cowboy.

"Get her, Guffin!" he yelled in strangled frustration. "Don't let her get away!"

Irritated, Guffin snatched up his gun and burst out the side door. Mara heard the metal creak with the force of his motion, and she ducked between two cars. Like Guffin, she'd seen the police car parked outside the luncheonette. Behind her the shotgun blasted its report and she could hear the shattering of glass. More ominous, though, was the thud of Guffin's feet as he chased her.

"Don't make me hurt you, Ms. Reed!"

Mara didn't bother to point out that he'd already shot her once. Instead, she focused on the dull tan and black paint of the Lorimar County Sheriff Department sedan. Plowing through the passersby on the walkway, she murmured her apologies, head down, legs churning.

Because God had not completely abandoned her, the glass door of the diner swung open to expel the sweetest sight Mara had ever seen. She skidded to a stop and threw her arms around her high school nemesis. "Linda DiSantis? It's so good to see you!" The pristine white uniform with its familiar shield signaled safety. As did the gun holstered at her hip. Mara had never been so happy to see a cop. Or two.

A short, squat man exited the restaurant behind Linda, a cigar chomped between his teeth and a gold star flashing on his lapel. He stared at the disheveled woman who had her arms wrapped around his wife. "Linda, honey? This a friend of yours?" Prepared for any answer, he inched his stubby fingers toward the gun that rode low on his hip.

Nonplussed, Linda took Mara's arms and gently pushed them away, then scanned the young woman, her eyes widening in recognition. "Mara Reed?"

Relief nearly collapsed Mara. "Yes. You remember me?"

"Of course." Linda nodded briskly. "How could I forget the girl who embarrassed me in front of the entire junior class?"

Oh, the devil. Mara was preparing a fulsome apology when she caught Guffin's reflection in the window. "Get down!" she shouted as she tackled Linda and bowled them both into the diner.

The sheriff jumped clear of the falling women. He jerked his firearm from its holster and leveled the weapon at the giant who came to a lumbering halt in front of him.

Guffin glared down at the little man, then swiveled his head to check on Rabbe. At the moment, the cowboy was busy braining Rabbe with the business end of the shotgun. Quicker than most gave him credit for, Guffin swiftly changed tactics. "Sheriff, there are two lunatics brawling down the street." He pointed to the intersection where Rabbe had regained some control and was systematically slamming the Expedition door into the man trapped inside its frame. "I think they're gonna kill each other."

The sheriff swore softly and reached for his radio. From her sprawl on the diner floor, Mara could hear the operator connect. "Donna, I've got a 245 in progress. Looks like Tyler Vines and an out-of-towner. Both damn fools have guns, but they're just beating each other senseless. Send Evan out here with the wagon." He disconnected and grabbed Guffin by the elbow. "You're a big man. Come be my deputy and help me break these fools up." Without waiting for a reply, he tugged Guffin, who followed meekly, but not without shooting Mara a silent warning.

"Sorry about that," Mara offered as she lithely gained her feet. She extended a hand to Linda, who reluctantly accepted the help. Assured that Linda was unhurt, Mara scanned the diner for a back exit. Spotting the swinging door leading to the kitchen, she flashed a rueful smile at Linda. "I'm also sorry about eleventh grade. I was insensitive."

"And I was a snot." Linda grinned. "I was sixteen and in love with Ethan. He was in love with you. We were bound to hate each other."

Mara laughed and angled her head to watch the sheriff and Guffin. She had precious few seconds to escape. "Well, I'm glad I had a chance to run into you. I'll see you later." She spun on her heel and headed for the door.

She didn't expect a sturdy, feminine hand to snag her arm.

Looking at the clear, unpolished nails, Mara mumbled, "I've got to be on my way, Linda."

The grip didn't loosen. Instead, her old classmate angled her head to catch Mara's eyes. "What did that man want with you, Mara?" She gestured out the window to the scene. Guffin had Rabbe in a headlock, and Mr. Vines was being handcuffed against his hood. A crowd had gathered, and all traffic on Shahar had come to a halt. "Did you have something to do with the car accident?"

"No. I'm just on my way out of town." Mara inched closer to the kitchen, only to be stopped by Linda again.

"My husband is the sheriff, Mara. But I'm the chief of police." Linda tightened her grip on Mara's arm and tapped her gold shield. "You pushed me into the diner because you saw that large man rushing at us. Want to tell me why he's still keeping an eye on you?"

Mara stared out the window, and sure enough, Guffin and Rabbe were both watching her through the glass front. A deputy had arrived on the scene, but she had no doubt Rabbe would smooth-talk his way out of handcuffs. Panic arced through her, and she tried a rusty trick her grandpa taught her. The truth. "Those two men kidnapped me and they plan to kill me. I need to get out of sight before they come back."

Linda DiSantis considered herself a fair judge of character. From her reading of Mara Reed, she was getting as close to the whole story as she was likely to. For now. "Fine. Go hide in the kitchen. I'll go out to Bob and tell him to place the whole lot of them under arrest. Then I'll meet you around back. Deal?"

"Deal." Mara lied without compunction. Honesty was a rare commodity in her world, and she felt it should be used sparingly. For dramatic effect, she allowed her eyes to well up, knowing how the amber magnified the tears. "I'm so afraid, Linda. Please help me."

Her voice quavered on the plea, which she considered a nice touch. Amateurs would have been tempted to emit a quiet sob, but a professional never overdid a bit. Blinking once, she squared her shoulders. "I'll wait in the kitchen." She paused near the doorway. "Thanks, Linda."

The police chief hurried out to help her husband. The instant she was out of sight, like a bullet, Mara shot through the kitchen, dodging waiters carrying laden trays. She skirted past a disgruntled chef and sprinted out into the alleyway. She could hear the shouting on the street and the strong alto of Chief DiSantis winding its way between the hostile male ones: Rabbe, demanding that he be released, and the twang of the innocent Mr. Vines in search of his purloined shotgun.

Mara ducked behind the restaurant Dumpster and cut through the shop next door. Soon she was away from the center of town. With nowhere to go. Obviously, she couldn't return to Ethan's place, not after that stupid kiss. Plus, Rabbe and Guffin, and their mysterious employer Conroy, knew about that hideout.

"Bullocks," she hissed. If the Bobbsey Twins found her there once, they'd probably try again. Only this time they'd encounter dependable, safe, law-abiding Ethan. The man she'd put into harm's way.

She needed to find a pay phone and warn him, Mara thought wildly. Once again she began to jog the streets of Kiev. At intersection after intersection she poked her head out in search of the once ubiquitous phones that had lined the city's streets. But there weren't any today. Not a single, solitary pay phone that could eat her money and refuse her call.

After ten minutes she slowed down to ease her labored breathing and rethought her strategy. In this day and age, even a hick town like Kiev was awash in cell phones, eliminating the need for phone booths.

Unless, Mara thought dully, a person didn't own a cell. Like friendships, cell phones required contracts and commitments and ties. And, she realized as the thought occurred to her, knowing a person's phone number.

She was losing her touch. Ten blocks before this lack of vital information occurred to her? Inexcusable. Mara hid beneath a massive orange awning promising pedicures in one hour. Hell, she didn't even know where he was working, and she doubted the phone at the loft was in his name.

There was nothing for it, except to go back and warn Ethan.

THE INSISTENT BUZZ of the doorbell yanked Ethan out of his reverie and into the present day. With a bitten-off oath, he pushed away from his laptop and jogged down the stairs. He had no idea how long the buzzer had been signaling him; he tended to become engrossed in his work. The mystery of the symbols he'd found seared into the flesh of some and tattooed onto other bodies had captured his imagination to the exclusion of all else.

Except the woman who stood at the door when he swung the metal frame open. "You're back."

Mara thrust Ethan inside and muscled the door closed behind her. Turning to him, she instructed, "You need to get out of here."

Ethan watched her closely—and tried to dampen the pleasure that welled up inside him. He hated the reflex, nearly as much as he wanted to hate her. Needed to hate her. "I don't take instructions from you. This is my place, not yours."

"In a few hours it will be your tomb if you don't listen to me." Mara surged past him and sailed up the stairs. "Do you have a car? Is it parked nearby? Where do you keep your suitcase?" She hurried to the closet, flinging open the doors. "Can you go anywhere besides Austin? That's the first place they'll look."

Grabbing the valise, she tossed it onto the futon and began gathering clothes. Lucky for her, Ethan was obsessively neat. No issues with color coordination here, she thought dryly as she stacked khakis with solid, printless shirts. His closet didn't contain a single frivolous item, except for a miniature tower of silly T-shirts. She lifted one and opened it fully to read aloud.

" 'No bones about it . . . Forensic Anthropology does a body good.'" Groaning, she peeked over at a flushing Ethan. "Tell me this was a gift."

"It was a gift," he mumbled, snatching the article from her. When she reached for another garment, he grabbed her hands to hold them still. "Hold on, damnit. What's going on here?"

"I told you. You need to get out of town. Fast." Mara tugged at her captive hands, but he didn't relent. "I can't pack if you don't let me go, Ethan."

"I don't want you to pack for me, seeing as how I don't plan on traveling today. Or anytime soon." He slid his hands along her arms to clasp her shoulders. For the second time in a week he found himself holding what he thought had been lost for good. His voice clouded with temper and a pounding relief. "You've been gone for hours, and now you show up out of the blue—again—and tell me that I have to leave. I need more."

Mara tried not to notice the warm weight or how her skin pulsed eagerly under his touch. Instead, she deliberated about how much to reveal. "When I left, Rabbe was waiting for me."

His grip tightened spasmodically. "Rabbe? The man trying to kill you?"

"One and the same. This time they caught me. Right outside the warehouse." Mara met Ethan's startled gaze. In for a penny, she decided. "They'll come back, and this time they won't stop until they get what they're after."

"You." It wasn't a question.

Mara nodded. "Yes, me."

"Which doesn't explain why I have to flee like a criminal."

She tried not to wince at the accurate description. Criminal. Con artist. Grifter. She'd been called worse. But to hear it from Ethan stung more than she would have expected. "I am a criminal, Ethan. And a liar. I told you that before."

"What do these men want?"

"Rabbe wants $50,000 that I stole from him a few weeks ago." *And a diary I stole.*

"Then give it to him."

"Can't." Mara thought about the hospital bills she'd paid off. The $18,000 for tests and treatment. Another $25,000 to pay up the bill at the nursing home for another quarter. And the $5,000 anonymous donation to the H. A. Brown Memorial United Methodist Church in Wiggins, Mississippi, where the good Reverend Abrams allowed her to camp out in her car last spring. She'd spent the rest of the money trying to escape Rabbe, but none of this was any of Ethan's business. "I spent it."

"You spent $50,000 in a month?"

"I'm a frivolous harlot, Ethan. Keep up."

"So because you're greedy, I'm in danger."

"You've got it. So believe me when I tell you to run." When Ethan merely stared at her, Mara recognized the expression. It was his *no way in hell* look. At this point, she reasoned, he had a right to know more. Not all, but more. She rolled her shoulders lightly, preparing for the explosion. "I also stole a journal."

"You're being hunted for a journal?" Ethan spoke softly, in a cool, faintly disgusted tone.

She'd heard it before. Generally, right after the look.

"Our lives are in danger over a journal?"

"That belonged to one of my grandfather's partners."

Ethan narrowed his eyes. "You told me all you had were notes. You lied to me."

"Hear me out." Mara held out her hands pleadingly. "I conned Rabbe into taking me to his room and showing me his stuff. His journal," she corrected quickly. "Actually, the journal of a man named Virgil Bailey. One of my grandfather's partners. Rabbe had been hired by someone to come to Detroit to find it. Probably heard the same stories I had. Diary of a man who claimed to have stolen gold coins in the 1930s."

"And you stole it from him. Why am I surprised?"

"Rabbe raped and killed the owner. Before I got to her to steal it." She screwed her eyes shut, the better to avoid the look of bitter disappointment sure to follow. Much harder to bear than the no way in hell face. "Inside the journal there were Greek symbols. Similar to the ones you found on the bodies. My grandfather and Poncho."

"You knew." His hand clamped around her collarbones, firm and unyielding. "And you ran."

Defensively, she countered, "I'm not sure what I know. But I am certain that you've got to get out of here. Rabbe has a bead on this location, and he'll be coming with reinforcements."

"If you're not here—"

"Then they'll kill you to keep you quiet. It will be my fault. I led him to you. To your home. I won't be responsible for you being hurt." With that she shrugged off his hard grip and reached into the closet. She snagged a set of shirts on hangers, all neatly pressed. Gesturing to the far side of the room, she told him, "You'll probably want your computer and your books. I don't know what to do about the morgue downstairs."

"Mara, stop it." Unwilling to touch her, Ethan stepped into her path. "Stop it. I'm not going anywhere."

"Because you want to die?"

"Because Lesley is coming in tomorrow. I can't slink out of town and leave her here alone."

Mara had forgotten all about Ethan's girlfriend. The woman he was willing to die to see. In stormy response, she stalked over to the telephone and yanked the receiver off the hook. Shoving it at him, she commanded, "Tell her not to get on the plane. If you care about her, you'll make her stay in Austin."

"I can't. She's on an overseas flight. There's no way to reach her." He took the phone and replaced it on the cradle. "This place is impenetrable. As long as we stay inside, your gun-toting friends won't be able to get to you. Or me."

"Do you plan to teleport your girlfriend inside?" Mara sneered. "Fancy trick, college boy. Rabbe and Guffin will stake this place out and they'll have your lady before she makes it to the front door."

Ethan said nothing for several seconds. Mara assumed his silence meant that she'd finally convinced him. She quickly returned to her furious packing, trying to outpace the guilt and fear. Once Ethan was safely on his way out of Kiev, she would still have to contend with the specter of Rabbe. Not to mention his employer, Conroy.

She'd never heard of him, but he was probably Arthur's silent partner who paid for Detroit. Maybe this Conroy was more amenable to a deal than Rabbe had proven to be. Perhaps she could bargain with him, or maybe get a job on his payroll. She was slick with numbers and cards, and she could do a long con with the best of them. She was nothing if not patient.

"We'll have the police bring Lesley here." Ethan folded his arms across his chest. "I'll call tomorrow and have the morgue van rendezvous with Lesley and transport her here in the truck."

"Which will require that you open the door."

"No, it won't. There's an underground passage that leads to the basement of the warehouse. Where deep cold storage units are kept. That's where I keep the bodies until I need them."

"And this tunnel isn't public?"

"No. The former owner of the warehouse sold bootleg whiskey during prohibition. The police have used the tunnel to deliver the bodies to me. Chief DiSantis can arrange it."

"You've been working with Linda?" Oh, the day kept getting better and better. "All right, Einstein. Set it up."

CHAPTER 7

THANKS, LINDA. I OWE YOU ONE." ETHAN REPLACED THE HAND-
set to the phone. He'd just lied to a cop. Him. He'd never
jaywalked, never gone more than a mile over the speed limit
without remorse. Yet he'd nonchalantly misled an officer of the
law. No, he hadn't any clue why those men were after Mara.
Absolutely, he'd let her know if he learned anything.

Beyond the windows, night had fallen, and street lamps flickered into action along Gaul Boulevard, floating orbs of half-
light that barely penetrated the inky dark. The town had settled
in for the evening. With its proximity to Caddo Lake, lush
dogwoods bloomed well into the summer, dusting Kiev with
white blossoms. Occasionally a semi truck rumbled beneath the
windows, but mainly silence reigned.

Mara wore another pair of his boxers that left her legs bare
and a white tank top she'd found tucked away in his closet. The
soft, worn cotton clung diligently to every curve. She stood at
the kitchen island making herself a sandwich the size of her

head. Bread, cheese, and the container of meat littered the counter, crumbs joined by discarded plastic wrap and soiled utensils.

Feeling the pained rumbling of his own empty stomach, he could have done what he used to do—filched half before she could drench the turkey in her favorite, repulsive concoction of mayonnaise and maple syrup. But instead, he moved to the refrigerator for leftover spaghetti from last night's dinner.

She'd settled easily into routines they once shared, a skill he'd never learned. To flow with the tide or roll with the punches or whatever the proper metaphor. Mara had always inserted herself seamlessly into a situation, molding it to her needs. He, on the other hand, stood awkwardly on the sidelines and waited for the proper moment, an invitation to join.

As teenagers, he'd been captivated by her refusal to allow the world to set the terms. Fascinated enough to overcome his natural reservation and invite her to a midnight marathon of *Indiana Jones* movies. He didn't know that she would be locked in her room for breaking curfew. That hadn't mattered to her. She'd reveled in the moment. Envy, now as then, lodged deep in him. She created a freedom for herself he couldn't emulate. Or touch.

While the microwave whirred, he offered, "The sheriff will pick Lesley up at the airport in the afternoon. They'll use the tunnels."

Mara looked up from her machinations, knife in hand. She'd willfully disobeyed a police order. Experience told her that cops didn't like unanswered questions. Her hands gripped the handle tightly. "Did she ask you about me? About them?"

"Of course she did, Mara. Not everyone is as gullible as I am." He jabbed the microwave panel and popped the door. That had been Linda DiSantis's second question. The first was how long Mara had been in town. He'd lied about both, too easily for his comfort. "I told her you were here with me and that you were scared that the men from the accident were stalking you."

"She knows that's not true." Reaching beneath the island, Mara scooted out a stool and perched on top. Her legs swung negligently, her heel scuffing the rungs. "I told her about Guffin."

Ethan set his lukewarm plate on the counter on the opposite side. He wasn't ready to sit too close. Instead, he twirled noodles around his fork. "Linda's a good cop. I don't doubt she realized there was more to your crafty lies the minute you snuck out of the diner."

"People believe what they want to believe, plausible or not. It's human nature." She nibbled at her sandwich, syrup oozing onto her fingers. "We are creatures of fantasy. The tooth fairy. The Easter Bunny. Winning the lottery. Human beings enjoy the art of the lie. We revel in holding off reality for another day. Pretending that what has to come can be put off if we don't admit the truth."

Like the fact that Lesley's arrival would force him to make a choice, Ethan conceded. He couldn't have Mara here if he truly sought to try a life with Lesley. He glanced up from his dinner to see Mara's dainty pink tongue licking the sticky syrup that had dribbled along her fingers. The unconsciously sensual movement shafted lightning into his belly.

Without a word to her, he dropped his fork, snagged his keys from the countertop, and opened the loft door. "I'm heading downstairs. Don't bother me." He didn't wait for a response. He rushed down the stairs and into the warehouse.

But even there he felt pursued. Tormented. Hell, he thought, he'd never expected a space so vast to suddenly feel like a prison. Then again, nothing about this project had gone as he expected.

He wandered over to the pallet where the body identified as Verna Bair had been placed. Setting out his instruments, he wondered how he'd managed to find himself exactly where he'd been a lifetime ago.

Returning to Kiev should have made him famous and freed him, all at once. His credentials and tenure had been built on less than a series of well-preserved bodies marked by a madman. If he found the Shango manuscripts, he'd be a legend.

Most of his colleagues saw him as fastidious, boring even. Straight-arrow Dr. Stuart, always willing to take on an extra class or pick up the most vacuous task. Finding a fortune in gold and an ancient African artifact would shock them all. He returned to Kiev to prove to himself and to others that he had a streak of adventure and a patina of recklessness. That Ethan Stuart could be dangerous.

And his return to Kiev had been Lesley's idea: Go home and

lay to rest all the ghosts that kept him isolated and that he refused to talk about. She'd given him three weeks. And he'd been
right on schedule.

Until Mara.

Now, despite his best-laid plans, the only two women he'd
ever cared for were about to meet face-to-face. He couldn't have
screwed up his life better if he'd tried.

Exasperated, Ethan returned to his examination of Ms. Bair.
The M.E. had identified her from dental records, courtesy of
the Lorimar Dental and Orthodontics Practice. Kiev, the
county seat, was the only town of any note in Lorimar County.
Population 18,742, according to the marker on Highway 7. As
such, it was the locus of all medical knowledge. Its environs
hosted two dental practices, a free clinic, and at least four GP
offices. The main hospital, in the center of town, boasted the
county's top orthopedist.

Lifting his tape recorder from the worktable near the gurney,
Ethan began to record his findings. "Specimen identified as
Ms. Bair, age forty-four. Resident of Kiev, Texas. Research indi-
cates that Ms. Bair sold insurance in the tricounty area until
1992. Investigations have not revealed any mention of her since
that time. Ms. Bair was unmarried, but she appears to have
borne children during her lifetime. Cause of death has been
determined to be cardiac arrest, but no foul play is suspected.
Like every body located in this area, the right hip has been tattooed with a symbol. To this researcher's eye, it appears to be
the Greek letter theta. Sources inform this researcher that the

symbol correlates to fruitfulness. Other bodies of child-bearing women share the same mark."

He set the recorder on pause and reached for the digital camera. Framing the shot, he captured the gauzy black ink that had drifted through dormant pores over the years. The circle with a single dash in the center resembled a doughnut with a misshapen hole.

"Are you hiding from me?" Mara draped her arms across the banister. The bullet wound was healing nicely, signaling its presence with a dull throb occasionally. A perfect complement, she imagined, to the ache in her chest.

She knew that Ethan couldn't stand to be in the same room with her, and tomorrow she'd have to pretend not to care that his girlfriend was in town. Any acting skills she claimed would certainly be put to use. No time like the present. "I'm not going to sleep quietly while you plan my fate. And I'm not going to let you hide from me, hoping I'll just disappear."

"I don't believe in miracles, Mara." Ethan pierced her with a quelling look. "You've never been one for doing what others expected. But you're not the center of my world, darling. I came down here because I wanted privacy."

"Playing with cadavers. I hate dead bodies." Mara treaded lightly on the steps. "However, since you refuse to leave, we probably need to decide on a plan. Which means you'll have to talk to me."

"Linda and I have a plan." Ethan flicked the white sheet to cover the supine Ms. Bair with the ease of practice. Bending down, he unlocked the wheels to prepare the gurney for transfer into cold storage. The other bodies that had not decayed to bone were held in the facility. Skeletal remains were stored in a separate area for study. The construction crew had uncovered several bone fragments that had the faded ink markings, markings that could lead to the gold and the artifacts or simply be a zealot's handiwork. Gold, adventure, bravado. Mara. *Careful what you wish for.* "Go to bed, Mara."

"I'm not a child, Ethan. I decide when I'm tired and when I'm ready to talk. Right now, I want to talk." This last emerged on a jaw-cracking yawn, which she tried vainly to hide.

Ethan smothered a laugh. He clasped the iron railings and shook his head. "I might be in the mood to have a civil conversation with you in the morning, but not tonight."

"You can't ignore me away, darling."

"No, but I *can* ignore you." With that satisfying shot, he tapped in the electric key combination, and the storage door slid open. Ethan guided the body inside the facility to the rows of storage lockers that had been converted for his use.

"You don't ask me any questions."

The quiet comment came from the doorway. He glanced over his shoulder. Mara propped herself against the concrete wall. His gaze took in her bare feet, and for an instant she reminded him of the young woman he'd once known. He'd had a million questions for her, an insatiable curiosity about her every thought. Who she was? Who did she want to become?

But this new creature, with the sharp edges that could slice him clean, this woman he was afraid to know. Afraid that the curiosity would return, and with it the myriad other habits he'd shed. Like waking up with her on his mind. Going to sleep dreaming of her and not Lesley. As he had since her return.

"I know everything I need to know about you, Mara. As I've known for some time, you're a liar and a thief. And you've explained that you're a cheat and con artist."

"I've made a good life for myself."

She is so blithe about it, he thought. So nonchalant about threats and danger and murder. As though this—this insanity were normal.

She sounded like his Mara, the soft, southern lilt glided over her words like sunlight. She looked the same, maybe thinner, the beauty refined by hard living and maturity. But she was not the girl he remembered. Still, the images of both collided, swirled in his thoughts. Two women, two memories, with only room for one truth. Certain his head would explode, he spun around to face his confusion. "Who the hell are you?"

"Do you want to know?"

"What I want is to have you gone. I want to go back to not knowing where you are. Not caring about what happens to you."

"I didn't come to you. You brought me inside. Your choice."

"I've never had a choice about you." He stopped himself, hearing the plea layered by distrust and tendrils of possibility that threatened to choke him. In vicious self-defense he countered, "Why did you come back?"

"To help you."

"Because of you, I'm now the target of gangsters—"

"Not gangsters. Hit men. There's a difference," she corrected wryly.

"Whatever. You brought these men to my door. These killers. Don't lecture me on the nuances of criminal behavior. To my mind, you're all alike."

Mara stared at him, stung, then stumbled away as if from a blow. "You don't mean that."

"Honey, it's just a matter of degrees." Ethan pushed past her to return to the warehouse and failed to see the slight color fade from her cheeks. Halting at the end of the workstation, he leaned heavily against the metal desk, hands splayed flat, dipped his head and sighed. It was all too much. "I don't know the rules in your world, Mara. I don't know if it's de rigueur to be shot at on Monday and kidnapped on Thursday. I'm not clever enough to make quips about having my life threatened and that of the woman I love."

"You love her?" Mara whispered the bitter question. She curled her fist tight, knuckles scraping against the crevices in the concrete, grateful for the pain. At least she had proof that life could carry on, even when her heart ceased to beat. "Lesley?"

Troubled by his betraying slip, by the fact that he wasn't sure of whom he spoke, Ethan squared his shoulders and lied without compunction. He still refused to look at her. "Yes. I do. And I don't want her exposed to your kind."

"My thieving, whoring kind?"

"Your words, again. Not mine." Ethan resisted the compulsion to turn to her and gather her close. To apologize. "I need you to leave, Mara. Tonight. I'll help you, but I can't work with you."

"I have nowhere else to go." She said it simply. "I've run out of places to hide, Ethan. This is it. Home." Though he couldn't see it, she shrugged, a weary shift of shoulder that told its own story. It was simpler to hold the truth inside, she decided. Easier for everyone. But she understood better than most that the truth had shades and layers and angles. That by sharing a sliver of honesty, few would seek more, sated by what they believed they comprehended. "The Reed fortune is what I came back for. I need the gold to stop Rabbe and Guffin. To save my life."

Ethan returned to her then. He stood in front of her and grasped her elbows, pulling her away from the wall. "Fine. So go and find it. Leave me out of it."

"I would, if I thought you'd let the mystery go." She tugged at her caged arms, but his grip held firm. "Admit it, Ethan. If I ran off and hunted for the treasure on my own, you'd chase after it."

"No, I wouldn't." Lying, wishing his words were true, he grated out, "I'd be willing to sacrifice finding the manuscript to have you out of my life again." He leaned his face in close, their breaths mingling. Her huge brown eyes filled his vision and her scent rose up to twine its skeins around him.

Baffled, he inhaled deeply, against his will. In rough tones he growled, "You disrupt everything, Mara. My thoughts. My work. Hell, I haven't slept in four days because of you." Unbidden, his thumb began to trace the silken skin at her elbow. The skin beneath trembled, and he reveled in her body's tiny betrayal. "I've spent a lifetime undoing the damage you caused before."

"Then why did you come back?" She echoed his question softly. Her brain was growing fuzzy, lulled by the shivers that danced along her captive flesh. "You could have turned the company down. You have a new life in Austin. A new love."

"To exorcise ghosts." Ethan freed one elbow to slide his hand along her arm, trailing fire. With a short step he erased what had remained of the distance between them. "To bury the dead, Mara. I needed to be here without you, to know that I could. I deserve a life that isn't clouded by you. By memories."

"Are they all so terrible, Ethan?" She lifted a questioning hand to rest on his shoulder. When her fingers curled around the nape of his neck, he tugged her closer yet. She moved into him willingly, eagerly. Fluorescent light gilded the room and a bulb flickered intermittently, drawing the room in guttered shadows. "Why can't you stay away?"

"Because you owe me." He stared at her mouth. The dark lips, wide and welcoming, taunted him. Tempted him. "By God, Mara, you owe me." In the next instant his mouth closed over hers.

Even as he tasted, the countless reasons why he should stop swirled in his hazed thoughts, but none seemed imperative. What mattered was how her mouth softened beneath his. How her lids drifted down and she arched effortlessly into his hungry body. That her high breasts, covered by his borrowed shirt, seemed to swell to fill the emptiness of his hands, that her arms wrapped him close, as though he belonged. All that counted was the glorious drowning, when memory submerged the present and they were again two people drawn together by an irrefutable desire. By a passion and a bond that would not be denied.

Mara gasped beneath the lips that seemed determined to devour her. In his hard, deliberate kiss she could taste the confusion, his resistance to the need that stretched taut between them. Logic demanded that she pull away and spare both of them the coming regret. But she hadn't expected a second chance to feel like this. Craved. Control slipped into the gray dimness of the warehouse and left only the compulsion to savor. She reveled in the slick glide of tongue, the subtle nip of teeth. The hard, lean body that had filled out over the years accepted every curve she offered, as though they'd never been apart.

CHAPTER 8

*B*UT THEY HAD, HISSED MARA'S RELUCTANT CONSCIENCE. AND he'd moved on with his life. Even as his beloved hands closed over her hips to drag her impossibly closer, the warning shrilled caution. She was not the woman he loved. Worse, if he betrayed Lesley, she'd be the one he'd blame.

Summoning a will she didn't realize she possessed, Mara flattened her palms against his chest. The heart beneath raced with a vital speed, and her resolve wavered. Fevered kisses snaked a chain along her throat, burning away reason.

"Ethan," she moaned into his ear, tracing the exotic whorls there. "Are you sure?"

In mute response, insistent hands anchored her thigh and hiked it near his hip. She could feel his hardened length, could remember its promise. Desperate now, she scrambled for buttons, loosening them from their moorings.

Ethan skimmed beneath the loose cotton to fasten his eager fingers around her naked breasts. With delicate savagery he toyed with the hard, sensitive tips and reveled in her abandoned cries. Determined to fend off caution, he dragged them both across the room to the laboratory table and lifted her up.

The cold marble at Mara's back shocked her senses and she reared up. "Ethan!"

He joined her, bearing her onto the surface. "I want you." He traced a line of wet fire along her collarbone, then dipped his tongue lower. "Should I stop?"

Mara grasped futilely for reason. Surely, she thought fuzzily, this was wrong. Because . . . because . . . The answer shone dimly, only to evaporate in the blaze as his mouth consumed her swollen flesh. Deeper and deeper he drew her in, and she had no reason except to bind him tighter. Legs tangled together. Hands clasped, fingers intertwined. Sibilant wishes drifted over skin and into the cool air that surrounded them.

A man's blue shirt fell to the floor, followed quickly by bunched white cotton. Soft yielded to hard, and angles sought the poetry of curves. Mara fumbled with the metal buckle at Ethan's waist, too consumed to remember good intentions or the vengeance of consequences. She couldn't recall not being with him, not needing him inside.

Ethan feasted and hungered for more. The piquant flavor of the satin beneath her breast. The robust spice hidden at the indentation of her waist. It had been too long, he thought, too long since he'd been sated. Too long since he'd let himself covet a woman's body, gorge on sensation alone. When she measured him, he shook with the force of need and delight. "Oh, Mara. What do you do to me?"

She bowed up to murmur the answer. "Anything. Everything." Smoky laughter echoed her promise. "Just let me love you."

Love you. Love you. The phrase reverberated in his head, churned his scattered thoughts. Words Mara had never spoken to him before, when they were all he'd ever yearned for.

Gently, Ethan reached between their linked forms to still her hands. "This isn't right." Shifting away, he clambered off the lab table and felt along the floor for his discarded shirt. He rose from the ground and draped the fabric over her. "We can't do this, Mara. I can't do this."

Shaken, mortified, Mara scooted into a sitting position. She slid off the table, leaving the width of it between them. Eyes flashing, she fumed, "You started it this time, bucko. Not me."

Her fingers trembled as she tried to adjust the bunched fabric. The difficult act was made all the harder because Ethan remained bare-chested, fly half open. Images flashed in her mind, and she blushed fiercely. The last time she'd made out with a man on a table, she and Ethan had been in study hall after school. Then, as now, she'd been left unsatisfied and aching. The pain riled her, made her livid. She lashed out, "Second time today, Ethan. Makes me wonder how much you actually love this other woman."

The whip-smart observation hit its mark. Ethan barely flinched, and bit out, "My relationship with Lesley is none of your business." More invective came to him, but he went silent. He recognized the look of shame on Mara's flushed face, felt the same greasy sensation in his gut. But Mara was right. This time had been all his fault. He exhaled slowly and shook his head. "I'm sorry," he offered softly. "I shouldn't have kissed you."

Because the kind apology was worse than the silence, Mara shot him a venomous look. She didn't need his pity, or anything else from him. "We're even now. One for one." With the tatters of her dignity drooping about her, she adjusted the waistband of her shorts and squared her shoulders. She quickly skirted the table with the length between them. "And you can have your privacy. I'm going to bed. To sleep."

"Fine," Ethan agreed shortly. "I'll bunk down here again." He let her make it halfway up the staircase before he warned, "Don't answer the phone, Mara. Or try to sneak out of here to-night. I won't come after you."

Mara scurried up the stairs and into the loft. Despite Ethan's admonition, she dragged her bag from beneath the bed. She grabbed the pile of clothes she'd unpacked earlier, tossing them inside the case with abandon. With each furious throw, she stewed. No way was she staying here, waiting for Dr. Lesley to make a house call. Not when she could still feel Ethan against her. Not when she could hear him saying he loved the brilliant professor.

She didn't stand a chance. She wasn't stupid, Mara reminded herself, storming into the bathroom for her loaned toothbrush. Her grandmother had drilled into her a decent vocabulary and respect for English, and because of her grandfather, she knew enough Greek to hang out in Crete for a month's hiatus. So what, she decided, if the bulk of her education had been self-taught? Perhaps she'd only seen the inside of a college once, when she was scamming a business school mark. The braggart had turned out to be a losing proposition, though she'd done quite well on her financial derivatives exam. Hell's bells, she'd get a 4.0 in the School of Flim-Flam.

None of which would impress Ethan or his professor in the least. Her exploits couldn't compare to the good doctor, not when her only claim to fame was a tattered old quilt and a family myth.

With that sobering thought, Mara stopped, turned, and collapsed onto the futon. Drained, she drew her knees up beneath her chin and wrapped her arms around them. Her heel bumped the backpack, which tumbled to the hardwood beneath.

She was way out of her league this time. Ethan wasn't a struggling kindred spirit anymore. He was a talented, successful academic who had found a new life. One that was arriving special delivery tomorrow afternoon.

Which meant she had to figure out her next move.

Taking a deep breath, Mara unfolded her legs and stood. She was done with moping and bemoaning her luck. Fists on her hips, arms akimbo, she surveyed the clothes that had spilled onto the floor. Running wasn't her way anymore, and neither was whining about poor choices. Her way, should she choose to remember, involved plans and projects and adrenaline. Independence gave no quarter for mistakes. Rule number seventeen. Make your bed, lie in it, and be sure it can fit in a duffel bag.

Mara chuckled ruefully. She'd obviously forgotten that one, she thought as she bent to retrieve her borrowed finery. The duffel bag and the air mattress had been abandoned in Louisiana, but what she did have with her would be sufficient. Mara Reed survived on her wits and her brain. Neither of which had been left in Alston.

She stacked the khakis from Ethan neatly on the hamper. Normally, she'd offer to wash, but she'd seen no signs of a washer in the warehouse, and a quick trip to the Laundromat was out of the question.

Briskly, she marched into the kitchen area. Plotting, she scraped Ethan's discarded plate of spaghetti into the trash. Find the gold. Pay off Rabbe, perhaps with interest and a handsome bonus for Guffin. Slip down to the nursing home to see Grandma Reed once more, then hop a plane first-class to the islands. She could easily envision herself stretched out on a beach with brilliant white sand and gorgeous men in loincloths.

Nice plan, she chided herself as she rinsed the dishes, but there remained the stumbling block of Mr. Conroy. His polite threat to her life wasn't idle. As she wiped the plates dry and arranged them in the cupboard, Mara wondered how exactly she intended to defy the Fates again. Clotho could spin as she willed, but she herself refused to be bound by others' plots for her destiny.

She'd simply have to return to the basics. Mara plopped onto a stool and filched a paper and pen from the drawer in the island. With quick, familiar motions she drew a table with three columns. Across the top, she scrawled *Problem, Solution, Resources.* Problem one had to be the $50,000 she owed to Rabbe and the journal she'd taken. If she found the gold, money problem solved. The journal fell under the undefined category of "Finder's Keepers."

And she'd use it to solve the next problem of locating the gold. Unfortunately, she mused, the solution seemed to involve Ethan. She penned his name beneath that column, accenting the script with a bold question mark. Right now her only resources were Greek numbers on dead bones, a journal, and the research she and Ethan had independently conducted. A whole heap of uncertainty.

But more than she had before.

Under the problem column she scribbled the name Conroy. Learning more about him was as good a place as any to begin. Mara nodded to herself. The most effective tool for a confidence woman wasn't weaponry or even her financial stake. It was research. To fool the smartest mark, the most excellent implement was to know more about him than he did. The advent of the Internet had simplified her job considerably.

Mara walked over to Ethan's laptop, its screen black. With a few keystrokes she'd brought the computer to life. Using the passwords she'd memorized by furtively watching him when he thought she slept, Mara logged onto the Net. She pulled up the Google site and typed in her search terms: *Arthur Rabbe* and *Conroy*. It was a long shot, but often the simplest route yielded the answers.

The screen flashed and the combination of names appeared in blue. After shuffling through the items, she realized the direct approach might not work. Instead, she tried the grouping of *Conroy* and *Seth Guffin*. According to her notes, Guffin operated strictly as muscle, never as the lead on an operation. Despite his gentility toward her, he was known for his facility with light arms and breaking human ones. The search yielded two hits.

Fingers almost unsteady, Mara clicked on the first link. The computer whirred into action, slowly downloading a newspaper article from Rockaway, New York. The grainy black and white photo showed a tall, broad-shouldered man standing outside a courthouse. Beside him, Seth Guffin smiled mildly for the cameras. The caption identified Seth Guffin as a former muscle for hire who worked for several New York crime families. He'd been accused of aggravated assault by a Long Island contractor who claimed Guffin had beaten him to a bloody pulp when the man refused to pay a fee to a real estate mogul.

The jury, according to the story, had believed Mr. Guffin's employer instead. Davis Conroy had testified that Mr. Guffin had merely acted to protect Conroy from a belligerent contractor who'd been terminated for shoddy workmanship. Mara skimmed the story, noting with interest that Guffin had been acquitted by a single juror vote. She clicked on the next item, an article that chronicled another run-in that Guffin had with the law. No mention of Conroy.

"What are you doing now?" Ethan spoke from behind her,

and to her credit, Mara merely gulped. He braced his hands on the back of the office chair and leaned close.

"I'm working. And you?" She tried to casually page down to the bottom of the story, but Ethan's hand swatted hers away from the mouse. "I thought you were going to bed."

"Couldn't sleep."

Mara could feel his breath tracing her cheek, and she forced herself to sit still. "Can I help you?" she asked, proud of the absence of tremulousness in her voice. Any second now he'd see the one line that would shoot his temper through the roof. Maybe he'd assume she was catching up on the news.

"Is this the guy chasing you?"

No such luck, she thought. *Thanks, again, Fates.*

Ethan reached past her to scroll the screen. Obsidian eyes quickly read the item, which gave Mara time to prepare. So she was ready when Ethan spun her chair around and caged her in by closing his hands over the arms. "For the love of God, Mara, you're running from the mob?"

"Now, don't overreact, Ethan."

"Overreact?" Ethan spoke softly, menacingly. "Exactly what constitutes an overreaction when you find out you're being hunted by mobsters?"

Mara shrank against the chair and kept her voice level. "Rabbe doesn't work for the mob, Ethan. He's a petty thief and thug."

"Who killed a woman and shot you."

"If they wanted to kill me, they would have. Rabbe doesn't have much patience."

"What about Guffin? Are you telling me he's not a gangster?"

Flummoxed by the unassailable article on the screen, she conceded, "Yes, he, um, is Rabbe's partner. But Guffin is strictly autonomous these days. If he still worked for the Family, I'd have heard about it before." Mara stroked the bunched knuckles on the armrest. "Relax. It's not the mob, I swear."

Unconvinced, Ethan bored his eyes into the pale brown ones that fairly sparkled with innocence. He didn't trust them for a minute. "What aren't you telling me?"

"I've told you what I know," Mara answered more or less truthfully. "Rabbe and Guffin aren't gangsters. They're hustlers who are after the journal I stole."

"Then why the article?"

"I've been running since I stole the map, and I haven't exactly had time to do my homework on Guffin. So I was conducting reconnaissance. To be prepared."

"I'm afraid to ask, but prepared for what?"

"If we're going after the gold, we need to know who'll be tracking us." Until she knew more about Conroy, there was little reason to mention his involvement. But she owed Ethan as much of the truth as she could. "Who knows about your interest in the gold?"

"No one. I keep my own counsel."

"No one? Not even Lesley?"

"Lesley knows I'm here to work on an identification project. Which I am. I saw no reason to tell her that I was fool enough to go hunting for a pot of gold."

"She wouldn't believe you?"

"Actually, she probably would. And she'd beg to come along."

"Don't want to share your wealth with her?"

"I want the manuscript, Mara. The money is yours. But I'm not convinced yet there will be anything to share."

"Have faith, Ethan."

For a second time that night Ethan caught her gaze. He watched her steadily, as though trying to read her mind, to ferret out every thought. Finally, he nodded once. "I'm trying, Mara. I truly am."

"EXPLAIN IT TO me again, Arthur." Conroy spoke in low tones into the telephone, forcing Rabbe to hold the receiver tight to his ear. On his end, a sleek silver headset cupped his ear gently, the microphone at his jaw. "I want to be certain I understand."

Rabbe shivered in the sultry heat. His hands and feet had numbed and his throat felt tighter than a virgin. "We picked her up outside the warehouse, in the alley where we'd been on Monday."

"The same alley where you lost her four days ago, you mean?"

"Uh, yes, sir. Mr. Conroy. I thought we should stake it out, see if she returned to the scene."

"Very clever of you. So she came out of the warehouse and you—"

"Guffin grabbed her from behind and I got us to the truck. We put her inside, and I drove for the meet point."

"I believe you left something out, Arthur."

The liquid vowels terrified Rabbe—especially when they coated his name with an edge of threat. Near panic, he clutched the phone more securely. "No sir, Mr. Conroy. We put her in the truck."

"But you didn't begin to drive until you'd secured her hands and feet. Surely, you gagged and blindfolded her, to be sure she couldn't recount her trail to the authorities. Assure me, Arthur, that you or Seth took those very rudimentary precautions after I spoke with her."

Rabbe started to respond, but Conroy interrupted. "And please don't lie to me, Arthur. It makes me quite cranky."

His teeth began to chatter, clicking against one another despite the tightening of his jaw. "Seth was responsible for securing the lady, Mr. Conroy."

"Which is why I'm paying him the lion's share of the compensation. Oh, no. He isn't the one who demanded seventy-five percent, is he, Arthur?"

"No, sir. I am."

"You are what?"

"Very sorry to have failed you, sir. Because I did not properly secure the prisoner, when the man blocked my truck, she was able to escape." Rabbe and Guffin had agreed earlier to keep the exact details to themselves. "Guffin pursued, but she received assistance from the local police."

"So a young woman who is barely five-seven, 150 pounds soaking wet, manages to outwit you and outbrawn Guffin? She eludes the authorities and goes underground. And you haven't picked up her track yet. Have I missed anything, Arthur?"

"No sir." Sweat beaded on Rabbe's upper lip and trickled along his temple. "That's what happened."

Davis Conroy tipped the Corinthian leather seat into a reclined position and sipped daintily from the glass of merlot. Beyond his vision starlight dusted the sky. When flying, he preferred to have the shutters drawn, which helped him pretend that he'd not left the ground. He had no love for flying or for the other pursuits that millionaires adored. Davis Conroy had one true love, and that was money. He reveled in the pursuit, lusted after the conquest, and basked in the spending. He'd never had enough. Like his father. A man too stupid to finish what he started.

And, thanks to incompetent staff, the treasure he'd dreamed about his entire life was slipping through his fingers.

When the stem of the glass snapped, Conroy allowed the rich red wine to soak his sleeve and spill onto the pristine white carpet. The stain deepened until it resembled nothing so much as blood.

"Arthur, are you listening to me?"

"Yes, sir."

"Listen carefully, as I intend to say this one time. Are you listening?"

"Y-Yes, sir. I'm paying attention."

"Mara Reed has something that belongs to me. To my family. I want it back." Conroy could hear his mother's harsh, rasping words as she recounted the thievery of the Reed clan. "You have two days to bring her to me, Arthur, or I will grow disenchanted with our arrangement. Do you understand me?"

"I do. Sir."

"Good."

"Um-um, Mr. Conroy?"

"What?"

"We think she's staying inside a warehouse. I've got Seth out doing some recon, to see if we can find out what's inside."

Conroy sat up and steepled his hands together. A slow, catlike grin curved his thin-lipped mouth. After nearly a year of searching, a petty criminal with a misogyny complex had led him to the rumored diary he'd hunted for decades. Luck had led him to Mr. Rabbe the first time, but had Destiny decided to take his cause up again? "What's the address of the warehouse, Mr. Rabbe?"

"Six fifty-three Shahar Boulevard, sir. It's a big warehouse, but the company that owns it went out of business, we've heard."

"Your information is half correct, as usual. The company was a meat-packing plant. I bought the company and the buildings last year."

Rabbe couldn't stop his jaw from falling. "You own the building? So you've got a key? Should I send Seth to come get it?"

"No, you nimrod," Conroy snapped, "I don't have a key. I don't need one. Christ, I hate working with amateurs."

"Sorry."

"Because I am a generous man, Arthur, I will forgive your sluggish wit." Conroy closed his eyes and leveled his breathing. The blood pulsing at his temple returned to an undetectable beat. "It seems the building in question is currently occupied by an employee of mine, a Dr. Ethan Stuart. He is working on a project for me, and should be on-site. My guess is that Dr. Stuart and Ms. Reed have a history, if he's willing to harbor her. You and Seth should find out exactly what that history is. Today."

"Absolutely, Mr. Conroy."

"Do not make another move on Ms. Reed, unless she appears to be leaving town. In fact, I want you to make your presence known, but do not approach her."

"You don't want us to bring her to you?"

"No. I don't." The steepled fingers wove together and clenched. "Keep an eye on her. And don't lose her, Arthur. If she eludes you again, I would advise you to run. Very, very fast."

CHAPTER 9

ETHAN SLEPT FITFULLY, HIS DREAMS FILLED WITH ROARING Twenties gangster mols bearing submachine guns, stolen kisses in the midst of gunfire, and frolicking cadavers showered in gold coins. By dawn he was eager to escape his tortured imagination and face his real nightmare.

He jackknifed into a sitting position, cursing the crick in his neck and the knot in his stiff back. No surprise, he conceded sleepily, considering the narrow gurney he'd converted into an awkward bed. A week of sleeping among the dead had him feeling their pain. Resignedly, he rubbed at swollen eyes and swung cramped legs over the side. Yet another perk of having Mara reenter his life.

After studying his feet for a moment, Ethan blinked at the murky sunlight filtered through the high slats of window near the ceiling. Lesley would arrive around six P.M., which left him only hours to come up with a plausible explanation for his ex-lover's presence, the charming police escort that would meet her at the airport, and the gunmen lurking out by the trash.

The thought nearly had him lying down again. But he was no coward, Ethan chided himself. If his world planned to collapse around him today, he'd be right in the thick of it. With a sigh, he swiftly sifted through the options. Sending Mara along with Linda made the most sense. The police could better protect her from Rabbe and would ensure that he and Lesley would be left in peace. The downside was that the only living clue he had to the treasure would leave with her.

The next best option was cooperation. Find out what Mara knew about her grandfather's heist and compare her information to his own. Ethan rolled his neck to ease the tension. He'd get the information, but he'd have to harbor Mara and entertain Lesley at the same time.

Well, he thought fatalistically, sailors had the devil and the deep blue sea. He merely had to contend with two beautiful women, each with her own special reason to hate him. Cheered by the dismal thought, Ethan trudged up the stairs.

Since Mara rarely surfaced without help, and never before nine, his first act of the day would be blasting her out of bed. As he ticked through his morning itinerary, the furrow in his brow grew deeper. Fifteen minutes of cajoling Mara to wakefulness, another ten arguing over who got the bathroom first. Then the inevitable fight over their next move. Pausing at the studio door, he kneaded the tense muscles in his neck. Perhaps Daniel was better off. Ethan ducked his head, and in a warning shot, tapped on the studio door and opened the door.

"Wake up, M—" Ethan froze in his tracks, then rubbed his eyes again. "Mara? What the hell happened here?"

"Good morning. Thought you'd be up soon. Breakfast is almost ready," she chirped from the kitchen, fully dressed and draped in a makeshift apron that closely resembled one of his lab smocks. "I don't remember. Do you like your eggs scrambled or over easy?"

"Scrambled," Ethan answered automatically. "You cook?"

"On occasion." She began to whisk eggs into the bowl with a competent hand. "Why don't you go wash up while I finish?"

"Am I awake?"

"Funny boy. Go get dressed."

Dazed, he rummaged through his closet for clothes and stumbled into the bathroom. To shock himself out of the obvious hallucination he was having, Ethan twisted the taps in the shower into full cold and stepped inside. The frigid blast forced a string of ribald curses, and accepting that he'd actually just witnessed Mara Reed making him breakfast, he adjusted the temperature and quickly showered.

When he emerged fifteen minutes later she waved him to a seat at the island, where she'd set out plates and utensils. And napkins. He didn't realize he *had* napkins.

"Made pancakes. I love syrup." With an expert flick of the wrist, Mara turned the browning disk in the air and caught it on the griddle easily. She caught Ethan's stupefied look and explained, "Waitressed at a dive in Tucson when I first left Kiev. You should see what I can do with a pizza crust." Transferring the pancakes to a platter, she asked, "Could you grab the juice from the refrigerator?"

"Sure." Ethan retrieved the carton and brought it to the counter. With a soft voice, attempting not to spook her, he inquired gently, "Did you get into the medicine cabinet, Mara? Some of those pills aren't for human consumption."

"Don't be a smart-ass."

"Definitely not dreaming." He sat, watching her for signs of a trick. But all he saw was genuine pleasure. "Are you okay, Mara? Seriously."

"I'm fine. You've seen me happy before," she scolded, carrying a platter covered with pancakes, bacon, and eggs to the counter. "And you've seen me cook."

Ethan nodded. Suddenly starved, he heaped his plate with food. "But I've never seen you willingly wake up on the correct side of dawn before. Usually, you're surly and nasty this early in the morning." He shoveled a forkful of eggs into his mouth. "These are good."

"Thanks." Mara poured juice into glasses. "Try the pancakes. You had some pecans in the cupboard. I hope you don't mind."

Shaking his head, he cut into the steaming golden pile that he'd slathered with butter. When the first forkful hit his tongue, he moaned in ecstasy. "Why have we been eating soup all week if you can cook like this?"

"I don't think you trusted me around your knives."

"Touché." Ethan smiled good-naturedly. "However, for the

record," he added, jabbing the air with his empty fork, "I would have risked it if I'd known you could do this with flour." Flashing a contented grin, he tucked into his meal. Maybe the devil was on holiday. After all, he'd been expecting a row over his edict that she stay inside, not a home-cooked meal and enjoyable company. The fatigue that had trailed him upstairs evaporated, and he reached for the mug of coffee she'd set by his glass. "Thanks, Mara. Really."

"You're welcome." She speared her eggs and chewed slowly. Swallowing, she said, "I've changed a lot, Ethan. More than you'd imagine."

"Twelve years is a long time, and I have a fairly healthy imagination." Sensing a truce, he asked, "What else has changed? I noticed you cut your hair."

Mara lifted a hand to the short bob of curls. "This is easier to manage. In my line of work, keeping salon appointments can be difficult."

"I guess." Ethan thought of her narrow escape yesterday. "Why do you do it, Mara? You're smart, talented. Resourceful. Why not do something else?"

"What else? I don't exactly have résumé skills. Short order cook. Computer hacker. Recovery specialist."

"Recovery specialist? Do I want to know?"

"Probably not." Mara refilled his cup to distract them both. Sebastian wouldn't take too well to her use of the phrase in polite company. "It's a family trait, Ethan. My grandfather was a train robber. My dad conned fragile souls out of their hard-earned paychecks. Even my mother did a stint as his evangelical sidekick before she ran off. Other than my grandmother, I haven't exactly had counterexamples to follow."

"That's bullshit. We grew up in the same town, Mara. Same lives. I didn't become a crook. I worked hard. Honestly."

"There isn't a dishonest bone in your body, Ethan. Besides, you were always destined for something better. Teachers knew it. Our classmates knew it. Even my father could see the potential. All you had to do was get away from here."

"I would have taken you with me." The words slipped out and hung between them. Too late to take them back, Ethan thought. Might as well finish it. "I thought we were leaving Kiev together. You and me against the big, bad world. We had plans, you and I. Real ones."

Mara stirred sugar into her coffee, thinking about the nights they'd plotted their escape. Ethan had been so certain hope lay around the bend or in the next town over. One of the many qualities she had adored in him was his sense of purpose. Of destiny. With Ethan, she could believe she'd been meant for more. For better. They would make love and fantasize the world they'd create together, and she had to believe.

The trouble came when she had to leave his arms and return to the real world. Try as he might, Ethan never understood the difference. "We had pipe dreams, love. I could sketch pictures, but I was never going to be a famous artist."

"Maybe not," Ethan protested, "but you had—have—other talents." As Mara pursed her lips in denial, he thought of other, heated expertise she possessed. Caught up in his imaginings, their fingers touched as they simultaneously reached for the cream. At the point of blistering contact, both snatched their hands away. "You could have become anything."

"My grades weren't going to get me a scholarship, and we both knew it. Only one of us was going to college, and the day your letter came—" She stopped, caught.

Ethan stared at her, stunned. "You read my acceptance letter?" One of his deepest regrets had been that she left before seeing their dreams come to fruition. But to hear that she'd known and left nevertheless was a fresh blow. "The night you left me."

Mara watched camaraderie fade into a flat, black look that had her searching for excuses, but none occurred. Nothing would suffice except for the truth, and she couldn't offer him that. "It came that afternoon. The envelope was pretty thick, Ethan. I knew what it meant."

"That you and I could leave town. Together. Like we'd planned." He pushed his plate away, his appetite gone.

"*Your* plans, Ethan." Mara thrust away from the table. "I didn't apply to college. If I'd come to Austin, I would have been dependent on you. That wasn't what I wanted." To become another anchor on his dreams had been unthinkable. Unbearable. Especially that night.

"We were a team. You and me against damned near everything else."

"But who was going to protect you from me?" Mara burst

out. She lifted her hands in mute entreaty. "You were so smart, so kind. Like some fairy-tale knight. Mean kids, nasty teachers, my ogre of a father. Ethan would fight every battle for me. And I let you. I allowed you to take care of me, and you never once asked for anything from me in return. Not even my love."

"Would asking have made a difference?"

"I don't know." She paced away from the kitchen over to the window. Wrapping her arms around her waist, she watched a flight of swallows winging north from the coast. The flock soared high, arrow-straight. Together. "Besides, you shouldn't have had to ask."

"That doesn't make sense. You left because I didn't beg you to love me?"

"No. Because you would have stayed whether I loved you or not." Mara shivered in the warm room, and Ethan joined her at the window.

"I deserved to make my own choice, Mara."

"Well, it's too late now." She shifted incrementally, leaving a gulf wide between them. Unwilling to look at him, she watched the sidewalk below. And hastily stumbled back, grabbing at Ethan's arm.

"What are you doing?" he demanded as he staggered into her. Quickly, he caught her up to steady them both. She splayed her hands flat against the solid muscle of his chest, tempted to curl her hands and hang on. Instead, she wriggled away, but he simply shifted his grasp to her elbows.

"Down there. I saw Rabbe and Guffin. They're standing in front of the building."

"Oh." Ethan relaxed his hold reluctantly and returned to the window.

Mara gasped and seized ahold of his shirt. "What are you doing? I just told you who's down there."

"And I want to see the men who are holding me hostage. Plus, the window is tinted from the outside. They can't see us." Ethan pressed against the tall pane and studied the men. "The one in the black suit?"

Relaxing slightly, but still on edge, Mara sidled up to him. "That's Guffin. He likes to dress like a Gambino. Thinks it makes him look professional."

"Nice suit." He cocked his head to focus on a smaller man wearing what he knew to be Armani. "That one's better."

"Arthur Rabbe. He considers himself a ladies' man. Makes a decent living running card scams in Detroit, Chicago, and Milwaukee. Businessmen who want a pretty lady on their arms and a stack of chips on the table. Rabbe supplies both and leaves with their cash."

As they watched, Rabbe motioned to Guffin, who waved his arms in the universal signal for *do it yourself*; however, Rabbe did not appear to concur. He latched onto Guffin's collar and jerked the big man down to put them at eye level. Soon Guffin was nodding quickly, and Rabbe released him.

"Can you figure out what's going on?" Ethan asked softly, as though they could be heard on the street below. "What's he saying?"

"I don't read lips, Ethan." She spoke sharply, frightened by the reminder of how she'd led the killers to him, then softened her tone. "But given the direction they're headed in, I'd say Rabbe wants to do some recon. Guffin doesn't want to desert his post, but Rabbe's in charge." She pointed to the ominous black SUV parked across the street. "Look, they're heading for the truck. That means we've got some time." The idea she'd mulled over since their encounter last night hardened into a plan. Neither she nor Ethan had enough information to lead them to the gold, and what she'd seen in his laboratory indicated that she might know more than she thought. Resolved, she tugged on Ethan's elbow. "Let's go."

Ethan resisted, his head still spinning from her earlier revelations and his first sighting of the men who wanted Mara dead. He looked at her when she yanked at his arm a second time. "Go where?"

"To the one place that may have some answers."

FADED YELLOW CLAPBOARD clung to the frame of the ramshackle ranch house, its paint peeled and chipped. Weeds had run amuck across the almost barren yard, and wiry chickens pecked at the green sprouts that dotted the ground. Mara waited for a wave of sorrow or disgust, some remnant of feeling for what had been her home.

She felt nothing.

The windows were thick with a coating of cobwebs and dust, mottled and graying. Screens lurched from their moorings, and doors hung loosely on rusted hinges. In the distance, bulldozers stood idle. Beyond their shovels, mounds of loamy black soil had been piled high.

Mara opened the car door, wincing as the heat surged inside. "Are those from the construction company? Chi Development?"

"Yes." Ethan watched her, her profile haunted and lovely. He waited for some sign that she needed comfort or to escape. But she merely lifted her jaw, as she had a million times in their past. The finely sculpted chin would angle in a second, he thought, indicating that she was ready for battle. Whether she knew whom she was fighting or not.

"Are they digging over here?"

"Not yet. They don't have permission to dig on your father's property. Apparently, the rightful heir hasn't responded to their queries."

"Dad passed away six years ago. I didn't bother to come home for the funeral. The court sent me some papers, but I didn't read them." He didn't need to know that she'd learned about her grandmother's failing health from a court clerk. He thought poorly of her as it was. No need to give him any more ammunition. "I couldn't care less about this place."

"Surprise, surprise."

"I don't need your approval, Ethan." Mara swept her arm wide. "But out of curiosity, how much would it cost to sell off the last of my family's lovely mark on this earth?"

Hearing what sounded like sorrow beneath the bluster, Ethan bit off his retort. Instead, he watched her closely, looking for a reaction, something that showed she cared. "I don't know. But no one would blame you if you sold out." He alighted from the car and circled the hood to help her out. Because she seemed to need it, or because he wanted to believe she did, he draped a comforting arm across her shoulders. "We don't have to do this now, Mara."

"Yes, we do." She inhaled deeply, taking in the scent of juniper and clay, the acrid smell of oil that hung over the entire town. "He was an evil man," she offered as she walked along the cracked sidewalk. Cobblestones had long since eroded into a treacherous path that made it simpler to walk on the dirt path that ran alongside. "He was a zealot. A preacher." She twisted the silver band she wore on her thumb. "Maybe God did tell him to do everything he did."

"God had nothing to do with what happened to those bodies," Ethan declared. Lifting a hand to shade his eyes, he watched her closely. "Your father put those marks on dead people. Not the hand of God."

Mara gave a short laugh. "Didn't you know? He was the hand of God. Every time I got a beating for running around or being out too late, I became quite familiar with God's palm print." Unconsciously, she lifted her fingers to her cheek, rubbing at a memory. "Sometimes, the good Lord needed help." She slipped from beneath Ethan's arm and moved slowly to an azalea bush that held soft pink blooms. "If Daddy was feeling extra spry, I'd have to come and pick a few branches for my punishment. Pick too small, and there'd be the devil to pay."

"Let's go, Mara. We'll come back later."

"We were lucky to sneak out this time. Rabbe is growing restless. If my grandfather left any information here about the gold, now is our chance to get it. So come on."

Before they moved, in the distance an aged white sign with black hand-lettering waved in the breeze of passing cars.

THE SECOND CHURCH OF THE HOLY SPIRIT.
OBADIAH REED, PASTOR.

εχομεν δε τον θησαυρον τουτον εν οστρακινοις σκευεσιν,
ινα η ηπερβολη της δυ
ναμεως η του θεου και μη εξ ημων.

"What does it say?" Ethan asked quietly. "It's in Greek, right?"

Mara stared at the sign, stunned that she'd forgotten. After a lifetime of watching that sign from her window or hiding behind its posts as she waited for a ride into town, she'd ceased to notice the phrase. To remember the words. She turned to Ethan, amber eyes narrowed in bemusement. "It's from Corinthians. Second Chapter. 'But we have this treasure in earthen vessels, that the excellency of the power may be of God, and not of us.'"

CHAPTER 10

'LL BE DAMNED." ETHAN GRABBED MARA'S HAND AND BROUGHT her over to the massive white and black billboard that swayed unsteadily on aging wooden posts. They came to a halt at the massive base. Up close the colors were more dingy gray and sooty black, mottled by the elements. The lettering seeped ink into the plywood, and the symbols beneath the words were, well, Greek to him. Turning to Mara, he caught her elbow to draw her closer. Pointing up at the twisted symbols, hope sprouted and he murmured, "Are you sure about what the words say? About treasure?"

Mara nodded slowly. She looked over at the ramshackle house, with its peeling white paint and busted windows. Inexorably, she followed the slope of the roof to the far west corner of the structure. For most of her life she'd been forced to look at the billboard from her bedroom window. Her father's idea of a joke, she'd assumed. When she grew older, she often hid behind its pillars as she waited for a passing truck to slow enough to hitch a ride into town.

She'd always found the swirling Greek script pretentious, an exotic lure for the uneducated and easily duped. The scriptural reference, like a thousand other passages from the Good Book, had been drilled into her head as a child. Memory verses, scripture readings, and Bible study lessons had conspired to crowd her thoughts with pithy phrases about virtue and goodness and salvation. Lies told by a man who hated his only child.

"Mara?" Ethan caught her hand. The slender fingers were like ice, despite the scorching heat. "Talk to me."

His words sounded as though they'd emerged from a tunnel, and Mara opened her mouth to respond but nothing emerged. She could hear the bellow of her father's sermons, the raucous tumult of the choir putting his exhortations to music. What had she been thinking, to imagine she was ready to be on this soil again? To be in his space? She'd never be ready.

Ethan chafed her cool flesh and searched the emotionless face for some clue to the churning thoughts he could almost hear. In contrast, she stood like a statue, frozen and immobile, glazed eyes fixed on the passage. Anyone else would have believed her tranquil, but he could tell that she was seeing something else. Something ugly and terrible. He held her hand more tightly, convinced if he didn't, she might slip away from him. Worriedly, he prompted, "Come on, honey, say something. Out loud."

Blinking dazedly, Mara watched the sign with a fixed fascination. That the words lost a great deal in the delivery from a ranting, livid man who seemed to only half believe in the God he espoused had sapped them of meaning. When one despised the messenger, she realized, the message meant nothing. "It's been here forever. And I never saw it before."

"Tell me about the passage, sweetheart. Who put it here?" Ethan's mind swiftly sifted through the possibilities. If her father was the origin of the obscure phrase, then their grand discovery could simply be a mocking coincidence. But if someone else had planted the clue...He squeezed her hand again, harder this time. "Mara, I need you to snap out of it. Tell me what you know."

With a shudder, she twisted to face an impatient Ethan. Her eyes closed, squinted tight against the sun's glare. "This one was put up by my father. But it's a replacement. My grandfather used to have a hand-painted sign planted here. There was a hurricane in 'seventy-nine, and the rain destroyed it. A week later my father had the parishioners out here putting up this monstrosity." She angled her head to examine the tall wooden stakes. "Made them carry the beams out of the woods. He told them they were creating a beacon to God's children."

"Did he say anything else? Did he mention the gold?"

Mara tugged free of Ethan's hold. "No, he didn't. Daddy never talked about Grandpa Reed. He considered him a heathen and a disgrace."

Like grandfather, like daughter, Ethan thought. Mara had rarely spoken of her family with him, always glibly changing topics when he probed too deeply. If the conversation revolved around the Reed gold, she was a fount of information, but let him ask anything remotely personal, and she shut down.

Then, he'd been willing to allow silence, since she typically kissed him into submission to aid her cause. But too much depended on what she knew. What her family knew. Still, given the grayish cast to her skin, he'd have to tread lightly. "But he was an evangelist too. Started the family business, right?"

Fisting her hands, Mara followed the path of a semi as it barreled along the two-lane road. Dust billowed in its wake, the plumes of reddish brown dancing on the motionless air. Answer the questions, she told herself, and change the subject. "Grandpa Reed didn't practice what he preached. He had two loyalties. Money and my grandmother. Religion was a means to a profitable end. The whole blind seer gimmick helped."

"Your grandfather was blind?"

"According to legend, he saw the light of God out here on the road, a modern-day Paul. Changed his life. He gave up his sinning ways and accepted the path of the Lord." Mara smiled grimly. "I remember seeing him preach once when I was younger. He wore these black glasses, but I swore he could see me sleeping."

Ethan chuckled. "Nice trick."

"Made sense at the time. Eyes of God and all that."

"Was he one of those fire and brimstone preachers?"

"Grandpa understood sinners, being a practicing reprobate himself. Plus, he didn't care for hypocrisy. I think the people enjoyed hearing about a kinder, gentler deity. The God he preached about didn't mind backsliding or mistakes, as long as you tried harder the next time. Feed the hungry, clothe the sick, and try not to stay too long at the juke joint. Make your best effort and help another along the way. That was Grandpa's complex, nuanced theology."

Didn't sound like the Reverend Reed he remembered, Ethan thought with a frown. The one time he'd heard Mara's father in the pulpit, he departed the tent revival depressed and certain a fanged, cloven-hooved Satan was primed to snatch his worthless soul from him. And that the exercise would be quite painful. He probed, "When did your father start leading the church?"

"After Grandpa Reed died. But when Daddy took over the church, he told the mindless flock that my grandfather had perverted God's teachings. That it was his duty to return them to the path."

"Is that when his religious art phase began?"

"He concocted that after he started siphoning off more than their ten percent. Dad laid into the hell and damnation rhetoric fairly heavily. A world full of hopeless sinners that only castigation and poverty could cleanse. When he started taking his work literally, Mom couldn't take any more." As she spoke, the soft amber eyes hardened, cold and bright. "He believed that the Church of the Holy Spirit was God's true family. None of the flock could ever leave."

"But your mother did." Ethan braced a hip against the pole, his gaze fixed on Mara. She rarely spoke of the woman who deserted her when she was a little girl. "You were only seven when she left?"

"Eight. She moved home to Mississippi, to be with her parents." In a flash Mara could see herself standing at a black wrought-iron fence, right below the sign as rain streamed down, screaming for her mother to take her too. For someone to save her. But no one listened, and she had learned. That was the day she made her first rule. She was her own salvation.

She shuddered, and Ethan took a step toward her. She seemed so fragile, he realized. He'd never noticed before how tightly she held herself. How she could be with him and so far away. Gently, he placed his hands on her shoulders, the bones delicate beneath his touch. With a finger, he tipped her chin so their eyes met. "I still don't understand why she didn't take you with her. What kind of mother leaves her daughter with a lunatic?"

Mara jerked once, then stilled. When she spoke, her voice was flat and resigned. "She wasn't strong enough, I guess. My father wouldn't have let me leave without a fight, and I don't think she had the will to challenge him."

"I suppose she gave all her courage to you. I've never known braver."

"Ethan." As a rule, she didn't talk about her family, didn't think about the two people who'd given her life. She swallowed hard, her throat gritty and dry. "I don't feel brave."

"Talk to me, Mara. For once."

Overhead, a hawk swooped low and released a keening cry.

She'd made that sound before. Mara rubbed at her chest, at the dull ache that throbbed near her heart when she let herself recall that afternoon. In low, uneven tones she described the day to him.

Once again the rail-thin woman with sunken cheeks and haunted eyes yanked open the door to the yellow taxi. She didn't look at Mara, didn't hug her close and whisper foolish promises. No, her mother had ignored the tugs on her dress, the frantic clutching at her suitcase.

Even as Mara chased the car, the big black tires spun in the mud, caking her in filth. Sinking into the muck, she'd wept for what seemed like hours until her grandmother found her.

"She was a coward." He spit out the word. "A spineless coward."

Mara responded by shaking her head. "She wasn't strong enough to do battle with Obadiah Reed. No one was."

"You did," he retorted, but his knuckles gently caressed her cheek. "You fought him."

Unaware, she nestled into the stroke against her skin, indulging. "I was stupid. And I paid for it. Over and over again."

Punishments she would never discuss with him. There hadn't been marks on her body, but he'd known there was more than just harsh words and groundings. Back then, though, he hadn't known what to look for. What to ask. But he'd ask questions now. "Why didn't your grandmother take you and leave? She had to know her son was a tyrant."

"Take me where?" Mara laughed tightly. "Nana was an

elderly woman whose career had been circus work. She had no money of her own and no family except my father and an eight-year-old whose own mother didn't want her. No judge would have given her custody, and my father would have retaliated."

"So she stayed here with you?"

"We just had each other. The Reed women stick together. Until I deserted her." Mara yanked herself free of Ethan's arms.

Reaching out, he tried to touch her arm, but she scrambled out of range. "You saved yourself, Mara. What happened between you and your grandmother or between you and me—"

"Makes me just like my mother!" Mara curled her lip, sneering. She pushed down the rise of bile, rummaging for the bravado that had always served her well. She wasn't going to allow the truth to slice too deep. Become too honest. Instead, she scrubbed at her face, at unshed tears, and tossed her head up. "I'm a product of my environment, Ethan."

"A truism, Mara. But we make our own lives, our own mistakes."

"Well, you've been warned about mine."

"Yes, I have. And I'm still here."

"Because you're a fool."

He cursed beneath his breath. She wasn't wrong. Thousands of questions lingered between them, ones he refused to ask because the answers might satisfy him. And the pain, the rage, were somehow preferable. But if he was going to stand by her, he needed resolution. Questions she'd have to answer at last. "Why did you leave, Mara? I know you're not a coward, and I could have sworn you loved me. If you're not like your mother, why in the hell did you desert me?"

Lies crowded on her tongue, eager to be told. Anything was better than the truth. "I wanted to go." She angled her head to watch him while she lied again. Sunshine gilded him in a halo and cast her face in shadow. Perfect. "I didn't want you anymore."

Ethan flinched at the cool delivery, the smooth rebuff. Too smooth. Too cool. "Liar." He stepped to her, crowding her against the pole. "Why did you leave me? Because I was too safe? Too simple?"

"No!" Startled by the question, she forgot to lie. "You raised yourself, without anyone to help. What greater risk could you take?"

"But I wasn't daring, like you. I calculated odds and you defied them."

"I ignored them. Until you got into college and I realized how little we had in common. College for you, parole for me. I didn't want to be in your way."

"Try again." Ethan set a hand near her ear, his face nearly against hers. Without the sun blinding him, he could see the widened black pupils, the fearful golden brown. The perpetual smirk faded into consternation, and whispery breath hitched in the slim column of her throat. There was something, he could sense it. See it. With the truth near, he pressed harder. "Why?"

"Okay, yes, I was tired of you." She feigned boredom, rolled her eyes. "You wanted Austin, I wanted New York."

"A minute ago, I would have believed that. But you're lying." His eyes gleamed with determination. He would have this mystery solved. "Why did you run away from me, Mara? When we were so close to having what we wanted, why throw it all away?"

"Because I had to!" The plaintive words burst out and she planted her hands on his chest and shoved. Ethan didn't budge. That she was grateful would occur to her later, when she wondered over the reasons she continued to speak. Her voice rose on a shout, loud enough to drown out the myriad excuses she'd used to punish herself for a decade.

Damn him, she decided wildly. If he wants honesty, by God, he'd have it. "I left for you. I got home that night and my father was waiting up for me. One of his followers had taken the job seriously. Deacon Bellamy, the man on your slab? He'd trailed me into town. Saw us at the movies and at your place. Reported to my father that I was no longer pure."

"He saw us?"

"Evidently. Because when I snuck into my room, Dad was waiting for me with Jessup and a few others." The story spilled out, played out in her mind's eye. "They were wearing white and one of them had a black box. I started to lie to my father, but he slapped me. I shut up."

"Bastard."

"Honey, that was just the warmup." The syrupy drawl she'd shed as a child returned, slowing her words, elongating the re-telling. "Daddy recited Matthew 5:29 in a litany. I'd never heard him sound like that before."

"Like what?"

Mara paused and looked at him. "Happy. Almost gleeful."

"What was he saying?"

" 'And if thy right eye causeth thee to stumble, pluck it out, and cast it from thee: for it is profitable for thee that one of thy members should perish, and not thy whole body be cast into hell.' "

"He was going to kill you?"

The laugh chilled Ethan. "No. I was just an unclean vessel, a woman betraying him like all women. But you were the eye that offended. You defiled his daughter, and they decided that you had to die."

"You aren't serious."

"Very serious." She wrapped her arms around her waist, a poor shield against memory. "They grabbed me and lashed me to the bed. Daddy kept ranting about purity and chastity. About salvation. He convinced himself that unless you were dead, you would continue to corrupt me and condemn the entire Second Church of the Spirit to hell." Caught up, she reached for the waistband of her borrowed khakis and snatched at the fabric.

Ethan tried to still her hands. "What are you doing?"

"Showing you who I am." Pushing his hand away, she shoved the fabric low on her hip to the ridged scar at her hip: Kα.

"Kappa. Alpha." He calculated swiftly, "Twenty-one? What was twenty-one?"

"Overwhelmed by sin. Lost to salvation. Basically, a vessel of evil."

"He burned that into you?" He trained his eyes on her, reading for the first time the shadows that lurked in corners. "You could have told me, Mara. We could have left together."

Eyes dry and burning, she retorted, "And go where? To Austin with you? I wasn't enough for you."

Ethan raised his hand to her face. To the stubborn chin and silken skin that captivated him. "You had no right to make the choice for me."

"I had to. Because unlike my mother, I gave a damn about someone other than myself for once. I was stronger than she was. Between my father and your chance at college, there wasn't really a choice. If you came with me, you'd lose your chance and he'd keep chasing us. But if he thought I'd deserted you, I'd be another faithless woman and you'd be an innocent victim. So I left to save you."

"Why didn't you write? Call? Something?"

"Because I wasn't good enough for you, Ethan. You were brilliant and noble, and you would have taken me with you. Or worse, you'd have come after me."

"Would that have been so bad?"

"Probably. The first time I stole, I was eleven. I swiped a pack of gum from the drugstore."

"Hooligan."

"I enjoyed it. The rush of taking what wasn't mine, of breaking the law. Mr. Harper had made fun of me, so I decided to show him. The next time it was a clock radio. By the time we were in high school I'd graduated to lifting wallets and sliding bills out of purses."

"I didn't know."

"Of course not. You could only see the good in me. I loved that about you. And I knew that one day you'd see the real me and hate me. Or worse, you'd be disappointed."

"So you left to save me and yourself."

"Yes."

"You're a fool, Mara. I never had any illusions about who you were." He walked toward the front porch with its sagging steps and sat down heavily, overwhelmed.

Mara remained by the sign, exhaustion wrestling with contempt. For years she'd told herself she'd left to save him. Had she simply used her father as a reason to do exactly what her mother had? To leave because staying was too difficult? Too honest?

She made her way to the stoop and leaned against a splintered railing. "I didn't mean to hurt you, Ethan. I swear I thought I was doing what was right. What was best."

"I'm sure you did. But you were wrong." Unable to find any words that would ease the sting, he pointed to the sign. "What about that? Do you have any idea why your grandfather put it up?"

Grateful for the reprieve, Mara latched onto the change in topic. "Bailey mentioned digging a hole to hide his key. That all of them did."

"Out in Austin, right?"

"Maybe. Maybe not." Mara stood abruptly and skirted the dilapidated building. Behind the low-slung ranch house a wooden structure lurched drunkenly, supported by rotting beams and worn timbers.

Ethan trailed at her heels. The abrupt transition from devastated to businesslike should have annoyed him. But Mara was a chameleon, and it wouldn't do to forget it. "What are we looking for?"

"The deacons kept tools in this shed. We need shovels." She jerked at the door, but a heavy aged lock secured the structure. It refused to budge. Kneeling, she squinted at the mechanism. Even if she had the right picks, rust had filled the slot. No makeshift key would penetrate. She rose and began to search the ground. "Look for a rock or something."

Willing to take orders, he quickly scanned the overgrown thicket near the shed. "You think there's something beneath the sign."

Mara inched along the side of the shed, eyes peeled. Careful not to stick her hands anywhere she couldn't see, she parted weeds and bramble. Thorns pricked at her fingers. She welcomed the distraction. "My grandfather wasn't a stupid man. And he was cunning. What better place to hide a sign than beneath one that few people could read?"

Because he agreed, Ethan merely nodded. According to his research, Micah Reed had been more clever by half than the men who followed him. Like grandfather, like daughter. Flat on his belly, he reached beneath the shed. He had no idea whom he resembled, in person or in spirit. Unlike the kids he'd grown up with in the orphanage, he had never really cared. To him, the only history that mattered came scribbled on parchment or lay in the silence of bones and sinew and science. Familial ties had never bound him.

Identity, he'd always believed, was a very personal creation. A man became what he wanted to be. Genetics may have given him true black eyes or the long, ropy muscles he'd worked hard to sculpt into strength, but the work he did, the way he behaved—that was his doing.

As he groped beneath the building blindly, he wondered how he had failed to realize that Mara held the opposite to be true. Father, grandfather, mother. She imagined that they had shaped her, made her who she was. The sins of the father, of a family, driving her further and further away from the woman she could be. Should have been.

In the dark he gripped an oblong shape, hard and cool to the touch. "I've found something!" Scooting out from beneath the building, shirt filthy from his efforts, he lifted the metal pipe triumphantly.

Mara skated around the corner of the shed, holding a rock. Seeing the pipe, she dropped the stone to the ground. "Good job. Let's see if it will break the lock." Together they approached the entry. Mara stood off to the side, giving Ethan room to work.

He swung at the lock, driving the metal down onto the hinge where the top looped through the door. Twice, three times, he struck the padlock. On the fourth swing the joint gave way. Quickly, he tossed the pipe aside and ripped off the lock. Mara jerked the door open and hurried into the musty interior.

"Here," she warned as she lobbed a shovel toward Ethan.

He snatched it from the air and waited for her to rejoin him. They raced to the sign, silently agreeing to dig on opposite sides of the post. The sun rose higher as the shovels bit into the packed ground, baked by summer. Soon, sweat slid down their faces in wet, dusty streaks. Ethan dug hole after hole, moving faster than Mara. Working counterclockwise, he excavated the area easily, after years of practice and training.

"Reminds me of a dig I went on in grad school," he muttered as his shovel hit a patch of rock.

Mara swiped at her damp brow. "Where were you?"

"Madagascar. Hot as Hades, with no air. We were out there digging for six days."

"Looking for what?"

"We were on the Tsaratanana Massif, a volcanic region of the island. They'd found bones near a volcano site from the 1800s. My team was invited to come and investigate whether the bodies had been the victims of the volcano or other causes."

"Couldn't they tell from the burn marks?" Intrigued, Mara propped her hands on the shovel. "Why would they need you?"

"Because I'm special, darling."

The hint of Texas drawl and the cozy grin skipped Mara's heart a few beats, and she was loath to disagree. "How do you fit a hat over that oversized head?"

With a long, serious look, he replied, "A good haberdasher."

Laughing, Mara smiled. "Seriously, what could you have told them that an autopsy wouldn't?"

"I learned from my examination that several of the bodies found had been buried before the volcano. Most had died of natural causes, including a form of influenza." At her quizzical glance, he explained, "Certain diseases affect bone mass, and the bacteria that cause the disease don't immediately die when the tissue does." He chattered on, explaining the methods of spotting causes of death, of mapping a human life from what remained after death.

"Fascinating."

Stung by the dry tone, Ethan ducked his head and began to dig again. For a moment he'd allowed himself to relax with her. To pretend they were here as friends, not as forced partners. "Didn't mean to bore you," he mumbled.

"You didn't," protested Mara, perplexed. "What did I do?" When he didn't respond, she dropped her shovel and crossed to him. Laying a hand over his, she stopped his motions. She waited until he lifted his eyes to hers. "Confound it, Ethan! Talk to me."

He pulled at his hands, but her surprisingly strong grip held him still. Unwilling to sink to a petty tug of war, he returned stiffly, "We're different people with very different lives. You race around the world stealing. I just study dead people. I realize it must be stultifying to listen to me ramble on about it."

"Ramble?" Genuinely confused now, she fumbled for an explanation for the sudden chill between them. "I asked you a question and you didn't treat me like an imbecile. You were explaining and I was listening. Then I said your work was fascinating. What did I miss?"

Feeling abruptly foolish, Ethan mumbled, "I thought you were being sarcastic."

"Dolt." She spat out the word, her temper flaring. How dare he think so little of her and himself. But she'd not given him any reason to expect more. Since her return she'd made such a point of protecting herself, she'd never told him what she thought of the man he'd become. Holding his gaze, she offered, "I'm proud of you, Ethan. You did exactly what you promised yourself you would. Became somebody. A smart, accomplished man who travels to war-torn countries to solve medical mysteries." She cupped his cheek. "I admire you. I always have. I've missed you."

In quiet tribute, she drew his mouth to hers. The meeting of lips was soft, almost delicate. Gently, reverently, the kiss offered apology and acceptance, penance and remorse. Too soon for both of them, Mara pulled away. "The sign."

They returned to their positions, each digging quickly, lost in jumbled thought. When Mara's shovel struck metal she nearly didn't notice. The second time the shovel vibrated from the contact she paid attention. "Ethan! I think I've found something." She scattered dirt in every direction and uncovered a compact box with a θ on the lid. The hand-painted letter quickened her breath and she sank to her knees.

Ethan dropped down beside her. "Open it. It's yours."

With unsteady hands she pried open the lid. A leather pouch lay inside, nestled beside a weathered roll of paper. She retrieved the pouch and poured a brass key into her lap. Etched into its handle was θησ.

"What does that say?"

"In numerics, it's 217. But there's no corresponding meaning." She lifted the paper. "Maybe this explains it."

Peering over her arm at the scrawled Greek, Ethan saw the black marks and agreed. "Can you translate?"

"Yes.

" 'Four gospels. Four winds. Four seasons. Four corners of the earth. But there is only a trinity for salvation. If you have found this, you are a step closer to a treasure I could not claim. I hope you are of my lineage, of my treasure. I pray you are not my son, but that you are braver and wiser than he. Keys to unlock our treasure. May God be with you.' "

"Four keys."

"Poncho. Bailey. Grandpa. Reese. And Guerva. According to Bailey, he hid the safe. He wouldn't have received a key."

Ethan stared at the page. "Only a trinity for salvation."

"Does he mean we only need three keys to open the safe?"

He concurred, having the same thought. "Possibly. But we don't have sufficient data. The symbols are different and now we have one key. I wish we had something more. Someone who could give us a place to start."

Absently, Mara rubbed at her hip. One last secret, but there was no point to sharing it now, she decided. "The symbols on my grandfather and Poncho aren't numerics. And they got their tattoos from another source." She closed her eyes, recalling the graceful strokes that twined the Greek symbols into a single work. "Those were drawn by an artist."

"Who?"

Mara tucked the paper inside and dropped the key next to it. Rising, she shook her head, startled that she hadn't put it together before. "The only Reed who's ever been worth a damn, probably because she didn't share the blood. My grandmother."

CHAPTER 11

ETHAN DROVE THE LONG, GREEN CONVERTIBLE WITH DETER-
mined precision. The summer storm began without warning, and rain pelted the windshield in fat, tumescent drops and
echoed against canvas. Gray clouds gathered in the corners of
the sky, framing a cerulean blue splayed against the horizon.
The contrast was stark and fit his mood perfectly. Relief and
rage in awkward concert.

Mara's bombshell continued to reverberate in his spinning
thoughts. She hadn't left because of him. Sneaking into the
night had been an act of foolish chivalry, not an indictment of
the boring, sensible young man who loved her. And in doing so,
she'd likely saved her own life in the bargain.

His conscience burned, though, because he'd never realized
how fine a line she'd walked to be with him. The whole town
laughed at the loony preacher and his followers, but Ethan had
not considered that Mara courted danger each time he cajoled
her into sneaking into town to see him. Silly teenage choices
could have cost her everything.

Still, he fumed, she hadn't trusted him enough to share that or anything else important with him. Not even her fear for him. Twelve years of agony explained away by a feeble attempt to protect his life. As though she had the right to make that kind of choice without him. How dare she pretend that she left because he'd be better off without her? They both knew the fact of the matter was that she'd been afraid to try. To be better than she was. To be with him.

He tightened his hold on the steering wheel, determined not to do what he so desperately yearned to—to stop the car and throttle the arrogant little coward.

Violence wasn't a part of his makeup, but Mara exposed facets of personality he'd prefer not to know. In fact, she seemed to revel in blithely exploding the careful myths he'd constructed to keep his sanity. Almost daily she'd rekindled another emotion he imagined seared away by neglect and regret. And she stoked fires he'd prayed were extinguished.

How was a man supposed to move on with his life when the past curled up on the bench next to him?

He shifted gears forcefully, metal scraping against metal. Beneath his hands the engine coughed in irritated response to the abuse of its transmission. The wave of angry nausea that had been chasing him since her announcement rose again, and in response he punched the accelerator. The vintage Plymouth he'd restored leapt at his command.

At least something in the world gave a damn about his wishes.

"I'm not in the mood to deal with the cops today," Mara offered helpfully from the passenger seat. "You drive any faster and you're gonna get a ticket."

"I'll pay for it." With a quick check of the speedometer, he shifted into fifth.

Mara heard the wind whip past the windshield, the sound a dull roar. Much like the headache building up at her temples. She'd always heard that confession was good for the soul. No one ever mentioned that it wreaked havoc on the nervous system. Ethan was wound tighter than a spring, but despite that, she felt compelled to taunt. She needed some reaction from him, something other than careening down a deserted highway in a freak storm. "I'd consider slowing down, dear. You passed the speed limit ten minutes ago. Around the time that cow went flying past the car."

Ethan spared her a hooded glimpse. "Cute. But if you're really worried about your safety, I'd suggest you buckle your seat belt."

"Buckle my seat belt," she mimicked snidely. "What's with the crash test dummy instructions lately? First my kidnapper solicitously harnesses me in, and now the man determined to break the sound barrier is concerned about me flying from the car." With a harrumph, Mara slid lower against the supple beige leather, arms folded across her chest. "I wouldn't need a seat belt if you'd drive the speed limit."

Ethan retorted mildly, "I'm over it by nine miles. The police won't care until I pass eighty-five." He looked over to the shoulder of the highway. The absence of police vehicles had him urging the needle up another notch. "Do you want to see your grandmother or not?"

"Not if it means I'll be in a companion gurney," muttered Mara. "Your girlfriend doesn't arrive for another few hours. We've got time."

Ethan reached out and twisted the knob on the radio. Peabo Bryson poured out, asking if anyone could stop the rain. He adjusted the volume and the speedometer inched up another notch.

Turning in her seat to face the window, Mara peered out into the driving rain. Streams of water slicked along the glass. Black topsoil drank in the water greedily, but there was too much to take it all in. Puddles formed on the surface and glistened beneath the scattered shards of light that pierced the clouds. Brown-eyed Susans and indigo horsemint lined the road, clinging to the welcome drops.

If the storm was an omen, she couldn't tell if it was good or bad. For better or worse, though, she was about to find out. Only two people in the world had real cause to despise her. One sat next to her, gunning the engine like an Indy racer, trying to outpace tomorrow. The other lived in a nursing home two towns over.

Following a drop as it slid along the clear pane, Mara tried to recall why breaking ties with her grandmother had made sense a dozen years ago. At eighteen, sore from her father's retribution, she'd thrown her belongings into an old army duffel bag and crawled out the broken window in the rarely used attic. She'd shimmied out on the roof and dropped down below, ready to dash for the highway.

Huddled behind the house, she was shocked to feel a hand close around her arm. When her grandmother silently pressed crumpled bills into her hand and kissed her forehead, the tears Mara hadn't shed since her mother's desertion fell onto a paper-thin cheek. In exchange for her freedom, her grandmother made one request.

"Write to me, my Mara. Don't forget."

But between stealing from Ethan and conning her way across the West, it got harder and harder to compose a letter that wouldn't reveal too much. That wouldn't disappoint. Soon the silence had stretched too long for a simple letter to suffice.

Moving Grandma Reed to a nursing home after her father's death had been the easiest solution. The probate attorney followed her instructions well, telling the elderly woman that the sale of the church had netted enough to settle her into Haven House. Mara found the name redundant and ridiculous, but the director agreed to take care of her and they accepted cashier's checks. No questions asked.

Life was much simpler when answers weren't necessary.

"Does Mrs. Reed even know you're in town?"

Apparently, Ethan didn't share her disdain for queries. But at least he was speaking to her. Flopping over to face him, she arched a sardonic brow. "What do you think?"

He didn't bother to respond. Instead, Ethan scanned the

rearview mirror, and seeing no traffic, shot across the lane to the exit for Shreveport, Louisiana. "What's the plan, then?"

"I don't know." She drummed her fingers against the dashboard, trying to ignore the knot in her throat. To distract, she glanced at her hand. Good gravy, she needed a manicure soon. Henri, her go-to guy in Atlanta, would be appalled. Ragged cuticles and broken tips. And not a lick of polish. "It's been a while since we spoke."

"How long a while, Mara?"

"Oh, a couple of years, give or take ten."

The easy answer stunned him. He'd expected a hint of remorse, some semblance of contrition. "Do you have any sense of loyalty? Any at all?"

Rounding on him as the indictment squarely hit its mark, Mara blustered, "I don't have to explain myself to you."

"Hell, Mara, the way you're going, you won't have anyone left who cares to hear the excuses anyway." He downshifted and coasted to a stop at the end of the ramp. Checking the dashboard clock, he saw that it was barely past eleven. It felt like an entire week had passed. Outside, the rain stopped as suddenly as it had started. He followed a road sign that indicated gas and food ahead. He'd refuel the car before they continued into Shreveport. Which raised the pertinent issue of where in Shreveport they were headed to. "Where is the nursing home, Mara?"

"Um, I don't know." Mara squirmed a bit, heat rising along her nape. "I didn't realize we were coming out here today. Didn't get directions."

Biting off an oath, Ethan asked softly, "Do you have a phone? Can we call?"

"No," was her mumbled response. "I don't own a cell."

"Of course you don't." Exhaling sharply, Ethan fished his phone out of his front pocket and dropped it into her lap. A lecture on preparedness struck him as a waste of breath. More than likely it would lead to another fruitless argument. "I'm going to pull into a service station for gas. Contact the nursing home to get directions. We're just off 173."

Mara picked up the phone and mocked him with a crisp salute. "Aye aye, *mon capitain.*" Ethan poked his tongue out, and the impudent gesture startled out a laugh. She shouldn't be surprised, though, she supposed. Beneath the layers of reliability and stolid commitment to principle, she remembered the streak of playfulness that emerged at the oddest moments.

He cut the engine and popped open the gas tank. Once the fuel started running, Ethan headed inside. Sighing gustily, Mara turned her attention to the task at hand. As she tapped in the number, she rehearsed her possible opening lines. *Hey, Grandma, long time no see.* Perhaps she could start with a joke. *A lawyer and a penguin were walking along a beach . . .* No, no jokes. The line trilled imperiously and she waited for the connection. Maybe she could throw herself on the bed and sob like she had as a kid. Back then, a well-timed waterfall was good for peppermint candy and a gumball or two.

"Haven House." The call connected abruptly and a chirpy receptionist greeted her. "How may we help you?"

She could remember the stroke of the delicate, lovely hand, wiping at a child's tears. How the hand smelled of powder. Her grandmother's scent. A real sob crowded Mara's throat, and she had to cough before she could reply. "Uh, I'm a relative of one of your residents. Mrs. Aiko Reed. Is she available to see visitors?"

There was a pause on the other end, then the woman hesitatingly repeated, "Mrs. Aiko Reed? Are you sure?"

Terror seized Mara and she gripped the phone hard. "Yes. Mrs. Aiko Reed. She's a resident of your facility. Mrs. Reed." She swallowed with difficulty. "I'd like to see her today."

The cheerful tones became suspicious. Her lilt vanished, replaced by clipped accusation. "Who did you say you were?"

"I didn't." Oh, God. Had she waited too long? "I'm her granddaughter. Mara Reed. I'm on her visitor list."

"Well, Ms. Reed, I must confess I'm shocked to hear from you. In the six years Mrs. Aiko has been a guest, she's not had a single caller. Not one."

Too relieved to be annoyed by the reprimand, Mara offered, "I don't live down South, Ms. . . . ?"

"Ms. Rao. Sangeetha Rao. I'm one of Mrs. Reed's caregivers."

The haughty Ms. Rao stopped speaking to Mara, and she could hear a hushed conversation on the other end. "Hello? Hello?"

"Just a moment, please."

Classical music poured through the cell phone's speakers. Placed on hold, Mara scrounged inside the glove compartment for a pen and a scrap of paper with her free hand. She'd need something to scribble directions on, and given the receptionist's snotty attitude, she'd better be able to write fast.

Bracing her foot against the dashboard, she propped a steno pad on her thigh and flipped open the pages. Ethan's scrawl marked several of the green sheets, unintelligible notes about lividity and autolysis and cranial fractures. She flipped past a decent sketch of a human skeleton. His attempts at drawing in high school had all resulted in an awkward, cartoonish stick figure. Mara riffled through more pages, humming along to Ravel's *Sonatine.*

More references to body parts and chemical compositions. There had to be a clean sheet in here. Turning the notebook over, her hands froze. Hurried black scrawl had etched a name and number into the cardboard. *Davis Conroy. Chi Development. 713-255-5555.* The man Guffin worked for in New York. The same man they'd tried to deliver her to yesterday. Unnoticed, the notebook tumbled from her lap to the car floor.

Cold sweat broke out on her brow as the implications set in. Ethan hadn't rescued her. He'd trapped her, tricked her into staying with him until he could collect the bounty himself. All along he'd been working with Rabbe and Guffin. And now she was leading her pursuers to the perfect target. Her grandmother.

"Ms. Reed?" Ms. Rao chose that moment to return to the line, her tone noticeably warmer. "I've been discussing your request with our director. We typically don't allow visitors on nonvisitor days, but Dr. Harding is willing to make an exception. Mrs. Reed is a dear lady, and we're sure she'll be excited to see you."

Shaken, Mara reached down to grab the pad. "Can you give me directions, please?" When her voice quivered, she willed it to steadiness. Panic could come later. "We're on 173."

"We? Is this another family member?"

Choking over the horrid lie, she replied, "It's my fiancé. Is that a problem?"

"Aww, I'm sure Mrs. Reed'll be glad to make his acquaintance. Let me tell you where we're located." The directions came as though through a wind tunnel, but Mara forced herself to focus. She copied them on the first sheet she got to, unconcerned about the information on the other side. Overlaying her writings, she could still see the image of Ethan's solid handwriting forming the name of Davis Conroy. The pen shook violently and she scratched the words onto the page.

"Thank you." She managed to ring off politely, proud of her performance. The cell phone dropped to her lap, her hands trembling too hard to hold it any longer. With effort, she evened out the hitch in her breathing, demanded that her brain focus on the matter at hand. If Ethan had betrayed her, freaking out about it would do her no good. She wouldn't give him the satisfaction. Hell's bells, she was a professional.

Mara checked the storefront. Truckers loitered at the counter, she could see, but no sign of him. First she needed to hide the evidence. Quickly, she ripped out the directions to the

nursing home and shoved the steno pad inside the compartment. Folding the paper, she tucked it into the pocket of her
borrowed khakis. Ethan wore an identical pair, but hers had
been cinched high at the waist. To think she'd been grateful for
the loaner clothes, and he was part of the reason she'd had to
ditch her favorite pair of jeans in Alston.

While she waited for her temper to cool, Mara rummaged
through the car for a makeshift weapon. She stuck the ballpoint
pen behind her back, cap off for easy use. Then she unlocked
the car door. Once, in Miami, she had to leap from a moving
van, and when that decision was made, it was best to leap before
you had the opportunity to look.

Preparations made, she released her seat belt and anticipated
Ethan's return. For most, she supposed, the realization that
your partner was working for the man trying to kill you would
lend itself to histrionics or melodrama. But not Mara Reed. No,
sir. She would be the model of self-possession until she had the
chance to confront the bastard who had the temerity to doubt
her ethics when he was nothing more than a hired gun.

Eyes narrowed by renewed fury, she glared through the
windshield at the traitor who ambled out of the gas station.
Long legs ate up the distance between the sliding glass doors
and the convertible. She had precious few seconds to decide
how to play this one. An amateur would try the circuitous
route, which was usually a bad play. Usually, when you tried to
trick a person into conversation, he'd get skittish and cover his
tracks.

The direct approach played well, especially with overconfident pricks like Ethan. Already he assumed she was easy prey. After all, she'd been so grateful at his rescue act, she'd broken a twelve-year silence. Nearly a week of self-flagellation for a slimy louse manipulating her guilt and shame into confessions. He wouldn't expect a confrontation.

By the time he yanked open the door, she'd balled her hands into fists to prevent herself from clawing his eyes out. It required a surfeit of acting talent and the driving fear that somehow Ethan already knew her grandmother's whereabouts to relax her hands onto her lap.

"Get the address?" He stuck the key into the ignition, turning the engine over. The resulting purr of the V-8 pleased him. Three years of nights had gone into restoring the clunker he'd rescued from a salvage yard in Austin. Between the now cloudless sky and Solomon Burke crooning over the stereo, his mood lightened. "It's close to noon. We'll have an hour to visit your grandmother, then we might have a chance to grab lunch before we need to head toward Kiev." He steered the car out onto the access road. "Which direction?"

"West," Mara said evenly. She gripped the door handle with one hand and clutched the pen with the other. "What's the hurry, Ethan? Lesley's not coming until six. Did your plans change?"

Ethan shot her a quizzical look. "No. Why?"

"Just wondering. Maybe Davis Conroy is expecting you to deliver me to him by lunchtime. Wouldn't want you to be late."

CHAPTER 12

WHAT DOES DAVIS CONROY HAVE TO DO WITH ANYTHING?" Ethan flicked off the radio with an audible sigh. Frowning, he looked at Mara again. The honey-colored eyes glowed hot, a sure sign of temper. He recognized the subtle flare of nostrils and the too-calm voice. "What's the deal, Mara? You owe Conroy money too?"

Mara studied him closely. Usually, scoundrels had a tell. A twitch of the eye, a curl to the lip. Perhaps he'd show his. "How much did he offer you, I wonder? Decipher the code on the bodies and, as a bonus, I'll help you avenge your broken heart by delivering your girlfriend to your door. A bit of a rip-off, if you ask me."

"Avenge? What?"

She could almost believe his confusion, but she was smarter than that. "Or maybe your role was to extract the diary from me and what I knew of the bodies, then slit my throat. More his style, I'd suspect."

"Christ!" Ethan swerved onto the shoulder of the road, barely avoiding a collision with a station wagon. The tires crunched on the gravel bed and the chassis rattled ominously. There were still some kinks in the body work he needed to address. Not unlike the bend that Mara had obviously decided to round. With a jerk, he thrust the gear into park and spun in his seat. Reaching out, he grabbed Mara's hunched shoulders. "What in the hell are you talking about?"

Mara quickly raised the pen clutched tight in her fist, its tip angled in warning. "Don't touch me, you liar! Move a muscle and I'll sever a vein."

"A Bic pen will probably do no more than give me blood poisoning." Muttering, he snared her wrist in a blur of movement and bore a squirming Mara down onto the passenger seat. With more effort than he'd have thought, he wrested the blue ink pen from her claws, barely managing to duck as she swiped at his eye. When a flailing knee came close to unmanning him, Ethan shifted to clamp her legs between his own. "Calm down, damnit!"

"Don't give me orders, Judas!" she spat, bucking beneath him. "How could you?"

Insane. Apparently the entire Reed clan suffered from genetic insanity. Ethan trapped her wrists with one hand and gripped her chin with the other. Holding her face still, he demanded, "How could I what? Accept a job from a construction company?"

"Betray me!" Mara bucked again, only to further entangle her legs with his. The movement forced her thigh into precarious contact with his belly, and she wriggled impotently.

"Cut it out, Mara. I'm at the end of my tether with you."

"And I expected more of you, Brutus."

"More what? Give me something to work with here." He rested his forehead on hers, panting at the exertion. "Pretend I don't have a clue about what just set you off. One minute you're calling the nursing home to get directions, and the next you're accusing me of trying to murder you. Are you on meds and forgot to take them?"

"Don't play dumb, Benedict Arnold."

"Cut out the traitor references and talk to me!" Mara aimed a lethal knee and Ethan trapped her against the seat. "Stop it! What the devil happened while I was gone?"

"I realized I know your boss!" Incensed, she tried to wrench free, but Ethan merely squeezed her captive wrists in warning. The hands that manacled her wrists were hard and strong, but not cruel. Which she'd use. Deciding to bide her time, she inhaled gustily and relaxed her body. Lull him into lowering his guard, she determined, then she'd attack. In the meantime she would get answers. "Davis Conroy wants my blood. Since he's the one who's put the bounty on my head. And it's damned convenient that I am *saved*," she spat out the word, "by another one of Conroy's lackeys."

"I'm nobody's lackey, you loon. Davis Conroy is a businessman, not a thug. I've told you why I'm here. Chi Development hired me to determine the historical significance of the bodies they found on the property next to the church. That's all."

"Bull hockey, Ethan. Neither of us go anywhere near Kiev for a decade, and then suddenly you're hired to work there at the precise moment I'm in danger."

He had to admit, she had a point. Being hired to examine the exhumed corpses wasn't outside the realm of normal, but it didn't happen every day. And he'd always felt uncomfortable while talking to Conroy, though he'd never been able to put his finger on the reason. But still, Mara had leapt to wild conclusions. "Okay, okay, the coincidences are sketchy. But I'm telling you the truth." Realizing that one of them had to make the first move, Ethan released Mara and pulled her upright. "Listen, I received a phone call six weeks ago, offering me this job."

She coiled away from him, tucking her legs beneath her. Gripping the door handle, prepared to bolt if necessary, she asked, "Why you? Of all the forensic anthropologists, why pick you?"

"Because I'm very good." He grinned broadly when Mara rolled her eyes. "Not to be immodest, but I enjoy a good reputation. I'm thorough. I'm smart and I can take off for months at a time to work. Most of my colleagues have families, commitments. I don't have any ties."

Before she could stop herself, Mara said, "There's the good doctor."

Looking away, Ethan rubbed at the back of his neck. "This isn't about her."

"Fine. Let's stick to the topic. You get a call from a construction company that wants to hire you to inspect fifty-year-old bones with strange markings. You're not suspicious."

"I'm a scientist. Markings, old bones. They're my thing. Like a guy asking you to steal a car."

"I don't do cars."

"Nice to know you have standards. Anyway, the request was vetted by the university and the authorities. Exceptionally well-preserved bodies and remains, given the burial conditions. In temperate regions like this, the decay of bodies varies. The coroner didn't believe there'd been foul play, but he wanted to be sure before they were moved to the county cemetery. The potential find and the chance to look for the Shango manuscript made it worth the investigation."

Grudgingly amused by the excitement she could hear, Mara shook her head. "As fascinating as that is, I'm more concerned about your employer and his connection to the thugs out to kill me."

"I'm not convinced by your premise, Mara. Why would Davis Conroy be connected to a card shark out of Detroit who bought a journal?"

She hadn't a clue. "All I know is that Rabbe was very eager to turn me over to a Mr. Conroy yesterday."

"Mr. Conroy? Not Davis Conroy?"

"Yes, Davis Conroy. I found an article on the Web. Guffin used to be one of his security guys."

"In New York?"

His arched brow spoke volumes. Mara frowned over the slim possibility that it wasn't the same man, but she had a gut feeling about this, and her instincts rarely failed her. "I know what I know."

"What you know is that a man named Davis Conroy in New York hired a couple of goons to snatch you. And that another man named Davis Conroy, a reputable developer, asked my university to loan me out for a major anthropological find." Yet even as he spun out the rationalization, Ethan doubted his own story. Convenience of evidence was a certain trap for scientists. Offer a person a trite but believable theory and they stopped thinking. Stopped searching for more.

Mara obviously concurred. "Another coincidence? Spare me. Davis Conroy is mnemonically significant, Doctor. Not too many of them floating around East Texas, I'd wager."

"But Chi Development is an outfit out of Austin." When her mouth gaped open, Ethan braced for the worst.

"Chi?" For the first time the name struck her. "Chi? As in the letter in the Greek alphabet?"

"Yes." Ethan tensed, the obvious smacking him squarely in the eyes. With a bemused groan, he spoke aloud what had already occurred to Mara. "Exactly like the letter. And like the tattoos on the dead bodies I was engaged to investigate. And the ones in Bailey's journal."

"Another coincidence?" Feeling confined, Mara swung open the door and leapt out of the car. Her feet sank into the wet grass and weeds tangled together on the shoulder. Absently, she scratched at her earlobes. Whenever she felt nervous, the skin there would itch maddeningly.

Ethan recognized the familiar tick, and he slid across the bench and jumped out to join her. "We appear to have a bona fide mystery on our hands," he offered quietly.

With a snort, Mara slanted him a look over her shoulder. "Ethan Stuart, master of the understatement. A mystery is who ate the last of the peanut butter or where I lost my wallet." Kicking at a discarded Coke can, she mumbled, "This isn't a mystery. It's a conspiracy."

Because he couldn't disagree, he walked past her to swipe at the crumpled metal. For several seconds neither spoke as he lobbed the can into the air and caught it on his knee. Adroitly, he danced the container in the air like a soccer ball, passing it from knee to knee. "Conspiracy. That's a good word. But who are the players? Conroy, who's a millionaire several times over?"

"Rabbe and Guffin are merely hired muscle."

"You and me. Ex-lovers drawn together by chance."

Mara hopped onto the hood, her legs dangling. She wasn't touching that one. "The common thread here is the gold and the manuscript."

"The gold, Mara. I'm the only one who cares about the manuscript." He launched the can with a solid kick and it soared into a ditch.

"You shouldn't litter," Mara admonished absently. "Bad for the environment."

"Thanks for the tip, Smokey." When she stared at him, eyes steady and censuring, he muttered beneath his breath about selective morals but stalked over to retrieve the trash. He returned to where she sat and propped his elbows near her leg. A gentle breeze drifted past, lazily pushing at the car's antenna. Welcoming the respite from the heat, Ethan turned his face up. "What do we know?"

"Davis Conroy is hunting for the Reed fortune. He knows about Bailey and about my grandfather. Probably about Poncho as well. Not sure about the sign at the church."

"As eerie as it is, I don't see how it connects. Or maybe we're missing something in the Christian numerology."

She slid off the hood, too restless to sit still. Images of her father and the other deacons sneaking into the night with another dead parishioner had been blocked out for a reason. Memory, she fervently believed, was highly overrated. "No connection. I can't see why they'd matter to Conroy. Christian numerology has its adherents, but no actual significance."

Ethan wanted to press, but he could see the edges of fatigue, the glassy look that had her eyes sparkling like gemstones. "Okay, we'll file that for now. What else have we got?"

"We know that Davis Conroy wants to kill me," supplied a grumpy Mara. "We know that."

"No, we don't." Sensing her disbelief, he added, "Think about it. If Conroy wanted you dead, why would they have kidnapped you? It would have been easier to shoot you in the alley and deliver your body to him. Conroy must think that you know something."

"Maybe. Rabbe can't wait to do the deed, but Guffin wouldn't let him hurt me." She touched the scar tissue that had formed over her bullet wound. "Much."

"I can't fathom that he knows we know each other. You did a fairly good job of hiding our relationship when we were younger."

"To protect you."

Ethan unbent himself to hold his hands up in defense. "That wasn't an accusation. Just a fact. The only people who knew about us were your grandmother, Linda, and eventually your father."

"Dad wouldn't tell the others that his daughter was a harlot. Except for Jessup and the other deacons."

"So it's likely that my rescuing you was actually a happy accident."

"Don't sound so pleased about it."

"Look, if you're planning to be touchy—"

Mara winced. "I'm sorry. I'm just afraid for my grandmother."

"Why?"

"If Conroy wants me, it's because he thinks I know something about the gold heist."

"And you'd only know it through your grandmother."

"Right. She's the only person who might actually have some information for Conroy. What if I've put her in danger by coming back here?"

"We're in Shreveport, not Kiev. How many people know that she lives here?"

"Only the staff."

"Then we'll take precautions and keep it that way."

Odds were that Conroy had no clue about Mrs. Reed's existence, let alone her whereabouts, Ethan thought. Nevertheless, any man powerful enough to track Mara across several states had resources he could scarcely fathom. Dropping a companionable arm across her shoulders, he steered her toward the door, held it open, and took a moment to peel down the ragtop and stow it. Rebuilding the Plymouth had been not only a labor of love but an experiment. Without an instruction manual, he'd challenged himself to follow logic and mechanics to its logical end. Like his car, scientific method required that once a hypothesis had been formulated, testing came next.

Revving the engine, he smiled encouragingly at a pensive Mara. "Let's go see your grandmother."

THE RECEPTION AREA gleamed with recently buffed black linoleum and polished glass tabletops. Roman shades floated above wide, sparkling windows and poured in pools of natural light. Shades of verdant green and the palest rose decorated the walls, and soft, comfortable sofas stretched along their expanse. No stiff, spindly chairs here.

The soothing ambience nearly masked the astringent smell of hospital care. Nearly. Mara swiveled her head as a pink-smocked nurse hurried past, pushing a cart loaded with meds. The casters swooshed along barely making a sound, much like the staff of Haven House. Upon their arrival, perky Ms. Rao had ushered them into the waiting area, where more of the classical music she'd heard while on hold piped through hidden speakers. From her seat she could watch the star-shaped fountain on the lawn spurt streams of water through a cherub's open mouth.

Cheesy, she thought, but nice. A nice, quiet place with friendly staff and expensive amenities. Exactly what she'd hoped for and paid for. She crossed her legs, tapping her heel against the chair, and her lids drifted down. A nice, quiet place to cater to her grandmother's every need.

A poor substitute for the affection of an adoring family, but Mara assumed no one in their clan had the right to such lofty expectations. Probably preferred it that way. After all, the woman had suffered through the death of her husband, the tyranny of her son, and the desertion of her granddaughter. Being whisked away to a place that promised its residents peace and tranquility couldn't be all bad. Had to be better than the alternative.

"Ms. Reed?" Mara's eyes popped open. Sparkling green eyes,

the color of the potted fern on the front desk, were level with her own. "Hi, I'm Sarah Kihneman. I take care of Mrs. Reed." Preternaturally white teeth spread into a welcoming smile. "Wanna follow me?"

Mara nodded and motioned to Ethan. Together they trailed after the young woman along a serpentine hallway that snaked the length of the building. In deference to the age of their residents, Mara supposed, shorter corridors branched off every few yards, like tree branches. At the fourth branch Sarah turned.

"She's right down here. Room 147. Sweetest woman." Sarah spoke in a singsong cadence, a high trill of sound. "I could just eat her up."

Was chirping a requirement for employment at Haven House? Mara wondered. "Does she know I'm coming?"

Sarah bobbed her head in the affirmative. "Told her as soon as you arrived." Her dark blond brows lowered sharply. "We don't like to surprise our residents. Your arrival would have been quite the shock, let me tell you. I'm still reeling."

Ethan could feel her hackles rise, and decided to save the young woman from herself. "Mara and I don't live in town. We've been overseas."

"Six years of traveling. That's a busy job."

"Now, look here—"

"Very busy," Ethan interjected, and squeezed Mara's elbow warningly. "My Mara hated to move to Burma with me, but it was a once in a lifetime opportunity. Helping quell a civil war isn't the easiest occupation."

Sarah's smile, if it were possible, glittered even brighter. The doll eyes fluttered thick lashes in a parody of flirtation. "You stop wars?"

"I'm simply a small cog in the works."

Mara almost choked with disgust.

For his part, Ethan preened under the admiration and kept Nurse Barbie well away from the prodigal child. "Even sending letters from the country was a trial. We couldn't be certain they wouldn't be intercepted."

"You're so brave," she gushed, covering Ethan's free hand. She didn't see a ring on it, so she stroked it lightly. "Mrs. Reed will be so happy to see you're safe. If you can wait a moment, I'll go let her know you're here."

"I'm going to retch," Mara announced as the woman moved away. She clutched her throat in pantomime, and Ethan snatched it down.

"Behave," he hissed. "She can hear you."

"I'll behave if you do. Stop flirting with the teenager."

"I was trying to help." Ethan tried to mask his delight and failed. "Jealous?"

"Of you and a teenybopper? Please," she huffed. She was spared a retort by Sarah's return.

The wooden door swung wide on silent hinges, and Sarah joined them in the hallway. "All set. Come on in. She's ready to see you. I'll be back in a few minutes to check on the reunion. Have fun," she added. She tapped on the next door and went inside.

In the corridor, Mara remained stock-still. Like a steep descent from the top of a skyscraper, she could feel her stomach lurch violently. The urge to bolt speared through her and she took a step away from the door. There was no apology sincere enough, no penance dear enough, to explain her actions. That she only showed up to take more churned acidly inside her, and she shook her head in denial. "I can't," she whispered to no one in particular.

"You have to, baby." Ethan curved an arm around her waist, as much in support as to stop her retreat. He tipped her face to catch her eyes, which shone with the mix of guilt and shame that had become familiar to him in the past week. Of her sins, this was the gravest and the hardest to repent. "You can't run away this time. She's waiting for you."

Mara wagged her head, unaccustomed to the surge of panic. "I failed her."

"Don't be such a ninny, Mara Elizabeth." The wispy command floated from inside the room and nearly buckled her knees. "Come inside and say hello. Bring your beau with you."

With stumbling, frantic steps, Mara rushed inside and, with a sob, launched herself at the figure lying against a pile of yellow pillows. "Oh, Nana. I've missed you."

CHAPTER 13

S TOP BLUBBERING ON ME, CHILD." AIKO PROPPED HERSELF UP on the sunshine pillows the nurses insisted on stashing in her room. She didn't particularly care for the cheery hues, but it made the staff happy, so she obliged. Life was entirely too confounded to pester about the insignificant details. Like the color of pillowcases or blame for making choices that ripped at the heart. Softly, she stroked at the bowed head that lay gently in her lap and thanked the Lord for the astonishing gift. "Mara, honey. You keep on weeping and they'll have to bring a mop in. Dry your eyes and introduce me to your fiancé. Sarah tells me you two are getting hitched."

Hiccuping, Mara shot her head up and offered a watery denial. "Not married, no. We just said it to get him in here." She waved to where Ethan remained in the doorway. "Ethan Stuart, you remember my grandmother, Mrs. Aiko Reed."

"Ethan? My goodness, let me get a look at you." Aiko reached for the spectacles she wore on a chunky gold chain around her neck. Given that she was forever misplacing the cursed things, it seemed the best thing to make in the tedious seniors' jewelry and craft class she took on Wednesday afternoons. "Well, boy, you did grow into a fine drink of lemonade, now didn't you?"

Flushing, Ethan shifted his feet and barely resisted the urge to mumble *Aw, shucks.* Instead, he cleared his throat and replied, "You're looking lovely yourself, Miss Reed. Haven't aged a day."

"You're a liar, boy, but silver-tongued devils are God's sweet reward for living right." She waved an imperious hand at him. "Stop holding up the door and come inside. The nosiest biddies live on this wing, and if they get a listen to that lumberjack voice of yours, I'll have to fake a heart attack to get them out."

"Wouldn't want to put you to any trouble." Pleased, he kicked the door closed behind him, not noticing a pair of curious on-lookers who'd paused in the hallway. "I appreciate you seeing us on such short notice."

"Not often I get gentleman callers, Ethan. And when they bring my baby home, I owe them a debt of gratitude."

"Coming to visit you was Mara's idea." He stopped near the bed and laid a soothing hand on Mara's shoulder. Rubbing his thumb along the wires of tension he could feel beneath, he continued, "She wouldn't take no for an answer."

Mara shot him a grateful look. All the speeches she'd planned over the years—with carefully crafted lies and elaborate explanations—vanished the moment she saw the beautiful, beloved woman responsible for a quarter of her genes. The almond-shaped eyes and their pale brown color, both legacies of Aiko's Japanese heritage. Exquisite creamy skin wore their eighty-six years with an effortless grace, and as she hungrily studied the beloved features, she catalogued their reflection in her own. The haughty cheekbones, a delicate mouth that pouted slightly, the elfin ears.

"I look like you."

"Better me than that pinched-faced woman who spawned you," Aiko affirmed. "Luckily, all you got from her was your nose. Mine would have been too small on that face."

Instinctively, Mara rubbed at the long bridge. "I guess you're right."

"Faces are maps, my dear. Tales of sorrow and triumph." Lightly, she traced Mara's brow. "Here, you've grown a few lines. Comes from thinking hard. But the furrows aren't deep, which means you're probably quick on your feet. Can't spend too long pondering when there's a decision to be made." The fingers trembled almost imperceptibly as they drew the curve of her chin, the sweep of her cheek. "You take care of your skin, use your beauty to your advantage. But you're not vain."

"How can you tell that?" Ethan ventured, mesmerized.

"Skin is soft, well-cared for, but not pampered. Mara has seen the world, carries part of it with her, but she knows when she needs to let go." The tender contact turned firm. "That day, honey, you had to let go. Obadiah didn't leave you any outs. I knew it then and I understood. I understand. So say your apologies once, for yourself, and let that be the end of it."

"I should have written."

"A letter or two might have been nice, but that father of yours probably would have burned it first. Or had one of those hellspawn deacons do it for him." Aiko shrugged negligently. "When it counted, baby, you took care of me. After Obadiah passed away, the church folk were simply lost. Deacon Cornelius tried to make a run at anointing himself, but even fools can see dross when they look closely enough."

"Eventually."

"But, now, how did you come to hear about your father?"

"The *Kiev Post*." At Ethan's puzzled look, she dipped her head, mortified. "I have a subscription," she muttered defensively. "People should read the news."

"Oh."

Aiko shared a knowing grin with Ethan over Mara's bent head. "That gorgeous lawyer you sent down told me you'd found this place for me. How is Mr. Caine?"

Ethan scowled at the name, but Mara didn't notice. "Sebastian is well." She decided not to mention that Sebastian's encounters with lawyers likely ended with him pleading no contest. Mara skimmed the room, for the first time taking in the pleated drapes adorned in a symphony of tulips, and the ornate oak bureau that stood sentinel against a buttercup yellow wall. The aged wood had a familiar veneer. "Is that the dresser Grandpa made for you?"

"Carved it himself. Feared he'd cut off his hands, but Micah could do more blind than most sighted men."

Taking advantage of the opening, Ethan asked lightly, "How did it happen? How'd he lose his sight?"

Aiko stiffened, the gracious smile fading. "Had an accident in 1937."

"What kind of accident?" Mara patted the hand that rested on her knee. "You'd never talk about it."

"What's past is past."

"Not if it's trying to hurt your granddaughter," hazarded Ethan. "Was he hurt during the robbery?"

Narrowed eyes focused on Ethan, then traveled to Mara's expectant look. With a deflated sigh, Aiko sank into the pillows at her back and shook her head wearily. "Old coot loved to tell this child stories. Would brag about his sins like they were badges of honor."

"He'd tell me about my legacy. Six bags of gold coins waiting for me to discover them. But you'd never let him finish."

Aiko gave a short chuckle. "Used to make him right mad. Biggest story of his life, and I wouldn't let him tell it."

"Tell me now."

Hesitant, Aiko cast a suspicious eye over Ethan. "Who's trying to hurt Mara? What does a seventy-year-old robbery have to do with anything?"

"A man named Davis Conroy is trying to grab her," Ethan said. "And he hired me to examine the remains from the cemetery next to the church." He watched her carefully for reaction, and he got one. "Found your husband's bones and Poncho's body. Mara has a journal belonging to Virgil Bailey. He mentions Poncho's brother Guerva and another man named Reese. What can you tell us about them?"

"Reese. Reese Conroy," she whispered, nightmare returning with a vengeance that shook her soul. The sins of the father.

"Conroy?" Ethan locked eyes with Mara. "Are you sure?"

Aiko bowed her head. "One doesn't forget men like him."

"Who is he, Nana?" Mara cupped Aiko's cheek, this time to soothe. Fear emanated in stunning waves, mixed with a rage that felt palpable.

"Reese Conroy took Guerva's life and your grandfather's sight." Years later the metallic taste of horror still lingered on her tongue. "Micah led a troop of evangelists. They were also bank robbers. It was a good cover. Negro preachers were a dime a dozen, and no one expected them to steal. Micah worked most of the Hill Country and West Texas before he learned about the greatest heist of his career."

"The train to the Dallas Fed." Ethan offered her a glass of water from the pitcher by her bed. "Micah's job."

"Slick as satin, he was. They dressed as porters and slipped off the train in San Antonio." She reached for the glass Ethan held toward her. Sipping slowly, she recounted how they'd come to her booth at the circus with their odd request. "Mortified me, I'll tell you. Living at a circus quiets most of a lady's inhibitions, but I'd never seen so many naked derrieres before. Micah had me tattoo these little pictures on the men's hips. Painful as all hell, because the needle kept striking bone."

"Greek symbols?" Mara posed the unnecessary question. "Like this?" She pulled Bailey's journal from her bag and spread it on Aiko's lap. A gnarled hand traced the swoops and swirls.

"Micah built a safe with four locks. Each man on the team had a key. After the robbery, the men had twenty-four hours to hide their keys and return to the rendezvous spot. Micah got the coordinates, and he translated them into Greek. That way, only he and his men would know the truth."

Ethan covered Aiko's hand gently. "If he had the coordinates, he could have dug up the keys himself without waiting on the others, right?"

"Not without a lot of work. The coordinates were imprecise. Follow them and you get to the general area, but you'd never know exactly where to look." With her free hand she toyed with the chain at her neck. After so long, she hadn't expected to ever tell the story again. To explain how the gold had been lost. The chain tangled around her fingers as she spoke. "Micah was smart and cautious. As a further precaution, he sent Guerva into the Hill Country with a wagon and the safe."

"So Grandpa knew the coordinates to the keys and where the safe was hidden?"

"No." She took another drink of the ice water. The cool relieved her parched throat, easing the story that she told. "Well, he would have, but Guerva never got the chance to tell him."

"Conroy." Ethan ground out the name. It was a guess, but given Aiko's reaction earlier, he figured he was right.

"He didn't trust Micah or his men. When Guerva returned,

Reese panicked. He assumed they were in cahoots and planned to leave him out." She remembered approaching the campsite, said, "It sounds silly, but I'd fallen in love with Micah in those moments at my tent. So I followed him to the meeting point. I stood in the shadows and overheard the argument. Then I saw Reese attack Guerva." Rubbing at legs that were no longer capable of such amazing feats, she described flying through the air to stop him. "I got the gun away from him and over to Micah."

"You can do that?" marveled Ethan.

"Could. Worked for the circus, didn't I?" Aiko managed a slight grin. "I was quite something in my day."

"Nana."

"Yes, well, I tossed Micah the gun, but Reese wasn't finished. He wrested Bailey's gun from him and fired. Micah—" Her voice broke over the name. "He pushed me aside. The gunpowder exploded." She gasped, reliving the moment. "Micah was blinded, permanently."

The worst told, she slipped her fingers free of Ethan's and reached for the pull of the nightstand drawer. "Guerva was dead. Poncho devastated. By the time the mess was sorted out, Reese had vanished."

"Why not recover the gold then?"

"Bailey believed the money was cursed, and the rest of them didn't disagree. They swore to leave it buried, to not tell a living soul where to find it."

"Did you know?"

"No, but I understood why they made their vow. Penance takes a lifetime, and your grandfather swore he would pay it." She rummaged inside and lifted out a miniature frame. Handing the photo to Mara, she pointed to the sepia images inside. Two men stood behind a young Aiko. "That night, your grandfather, Bailey, Poncho, and I buried Guerva in the hills. Poncho and I traveled with Micah for a time, but when your father was born, we moved to Kiev. Micah took up preaching for real."

"And the gold stayed hidden." Ethan wandered to the window. "Without Guerva, there was no way to find the safe even if you had the keys. No map, no safe."

While Ethan spoke, Mara watched her grandmother and saw the almost imperceptible flinch. "What, Nana?"

"That's not exactly accurate. Guerva didn't tell Micah where the gold was. But he did tell Poncho."

"You have a map?" Mara inhaled sharply. "All this time?"

"No, Mara. You have. Since you were five."

Five? A map? Tidbits of memory became certainty, and suddenly she knew. "Fool's Paradise. The map is Fool's Paradise!" Mara bounced off the bed, her head spinning. Why, the crafty old lady! She had the map. Had always had it.

Ethan frowned over the outburst. "Mara? Miss Reed?"

The Reed women stared at each other, both poorly restraining matching smirks. He slanted a confused look between the two. "Does somebody want to clue me in?"

Exuberant, Mara danced over to Ethan and threw her arms

around his neck. In reaction, he caught her around the waist to steady the excited movement.

"Stop writhing like a dance-hall lady and tell the boy what you know," Aiko instructed. The promise she'd made scratched at her conscience, but to her mind, if she didn't say it, she wasn't breaking her word. "Tell him."

"Ethan, I've got the map! When I was five, Nana made a quilt for me. It had these odd bumps and valleys. A desert bowl filled with wildflowers, perfect for a little girl's imagination." She pointed to Aiko, her heart beating fiercely. "Poncho had his brother's map. You made it into a quilt and called it Fool's Paradise."

"Go on," she replied, edging closer to the fine line.

"Poncho gave you his brother's map, and in order not to break your promise, you stitched it into a quilt. And gave it to me."

"Thought about giving it to Obadiah, but he was too mean." Another layer of guilt settled snugly, but she was determined to get it all out. "Micah tried to be a good father to the boy, but Obadiah was wild. Hard to control when you can't see him. Boy had his father's tongue, though. Could sweet-talk molasses."

Ethan shifted Mara to curl his arm around her waist, and she leaned into him. "Did Micah tell Obadiah about the gold?"

Aiko noticed the comfortable stance and approved. The boy had adored her Mara, and unless her old eyes deceived, he still did. "When Obie was still a child, Micah had me show him the numbers that I'd tattooed on the men. By then I'd learned Greek."

"How?" asked Ethan, fascinated. Greek was a difficult language under the best circumstances, but with a blind tutor?

"Micah was a good teacher. I'd describe the letters to him and he taught me the language. The man could teach anything."

"So Dad learned the numbers. Where did the numerology come in?

"College. Obie fell in with a religious crowd and they taught him some nonsense about sin and sacred numbers. By the time he came back, he was a monster. Headstrong and greedy for power. Took what his father taught him and perverted it."

"There was nothing you could have done, Nana. He was a grown man."

"In any event, I chose not to give the quilt to him. Or your mother. But when you came along, I decided you'd be the one who'd find the treasure, if it was God's will."

Ethan saw the woman's certainty, but didn't quite accept it. "And you believe it is? That God would want your granddaughter to find stolen gold and profit from it?"

"The Lord works in mysterious ways, Ethan. A cliché, but as good an explanation as any. Otherwise, why do you think you showed up again?"

Uncomfortable with religious metaphor and with the knowing look she slanted him, Ethan quickly returned the conversation to more secular ground. "So we have Reverend Reed's key, the map, and the symbols to find Bailey's key and Poncho's. But Reese's key is lost."

Mara searched in her bag for her grandfather's note. Placing the worn paper in her grandmother's hands, she asked, "Nana, have you seen this before?"

"Micah couldn't keep his word any better than I have." She reached out and linked hands with Ethan and Mara, the note on her lap. "Poncho told me that he had sought a resting place for his key."

Ethan creased his brow. "Resting place? Like a cemetery."

"Poncho did like cemeteries. Thought it was odd." Drifting and tired, she squeezed their hands, her eyes firm. One more clue, she thought, and the past would be done. "Listen to me carefully. It only takes three to complete this circle, children. Three. Godspeed."

THEY SPED ALONG the highway, each lost in thought. Mara considered the implications of her grandmother's story. Yes, they had the map, and half the coordinates. Bailey's from the map, Poncho and her grandfather from the bones. She knew they were closer to the gold, but it still felt miles away. Ethan had mumbled something about an idea, but when she pressed him, he demurred. Still, she couldn't muster irritation, given the annoying gratitude she felt.

Mara folded the note and tucked it into her pocket. If they were going to be hunting gold and artifacts together, she probably ought to clear the air, she thought. Make her amends and whatnot before they got back to the warehouse. She felt like an AA member starting her ninth step. Surely, she warned herself, apologizing and showing gratitude in the same day broke one of her own precious rules. But she couldn't think of one. Instead, she screwed her courage up and mumbled, "Look, I think I may owe you a thank-you."

Turning down the radio dial, Ethan glanced over at her and nearly laughed at the pained expression. "Don't gush, darling. I might get ideas."

"Shut up and let me finish." *Like a Band-Aid, Mara. Just rip it off.* "Okay, well, if you hadn't been spying on me and saved me and then lied to me about trying to find my family's treasure—"

"Stolen loot and priceless manuscript," he interjected. "And I thought this was a thank-you?"

"Hush." She turned in her seat to face him and leaned forward to plant a kiss on his cheek. "If you hadn't started me on this path, I wouldn't have gone to see my grandmother. Thank you."

"You would have. You love her."

"Shame is a powerful deterrent, Ethan. I abandoned her."

"You were just a kid. She understood. And you more than atoned by covering the cost of her swank accommodations."

"I'm not—that is, I don't—"

"That's what you did with the money, isn't it? You've been paying for her care."

"I owe her."

"There are cheaper ways to pay a debt, sweetheart." Ethan could hear the embarrassment, and he found it endearing. "You're a good person, Mara Elizabeth Reed."

"Only my grandma calls me that." Mara set her heels on the dashboard and lifted her hands into the wind. "We've still got a lot of problems, Ethan. Finding the other coordinates. Locating the keys. Not getting killed by Conroy and his goons."

"Don't worry, Mara Elizabeth. I've got a plan."

CHAPTER 14

Will you sit down?"

Turning away from the window, Mara directed a frustrated glare in Ethan's general direction. Anxious, uneasy, she couldn't still the racing of her mind. Her grandmother's revelations swirled with recollections and possibilities. Somewhere in the middle of Texas, her destiny lay buried. If she had her druthers, they'd be on the road, map in hand. But instead of hunting for it, she was trapped in a box with dead people and their overly vigilant keeper.

"I don't understand what we're waiting for. We could be halfway to Austin by now." She folded her arms mutinously. "Linda could have taken care of Lesley."

Ethan grimaced. They'd had this argument every six minutes since leaving Shreveport. Ms. Indiana Jones wanted to go dashing into the breach with a raggedy quilt, a set of blurry tattoos, and an old lady's recollections; and she was none too pleased by his demurral. "We need to do more research. With

Conroy and his goons on our tail, we'll have to be prepared for anything."

"Not if we do nothing. Which they know." She returned to the window and pointed across the street. "They've been sitting down there for hours," she grumbled. Rabbe and Guffin had taken up post directly across the street in the ubiquitous black SUV. Every hour one of them would emerge and amble down the sidewalk to the fast-food joint on the corner. Since their return a little after one, they'd traded places, consumed what appeared to be a gallon of coffee, and never stopped watching the warehouse. De rigueur for a stakeout, she knew, but unnerving when she was the prey.

"As long as they don't move, we know Conroy doesn't have the information," he retorted mildly.

Annoyed by the entirely reasonable logic, Mara decided to pass the time by pouting. "It's almost seven P.M. Linda and your girlfriend should have gotten here by now."

Girlfriend. The word, one that Mara seemed to relish wielding, wasn't entirely accurate. In fact, Lesley would be surprised to hear the term used so generously. He'd meant to call her and update her on his situation, but time had gotten away from him. An itch settled in the unreachable spot between his shoulders. "Um, I checked with the airline. Lesley's plane landed on schedule. They should be here soon."

Mara strode past him, her vigil at the window abandoned for pacing. "Does she know about me?"

"Not exactly." With a low, long breath Ethan settled on the

edge of the futon, near Mara's mincing steps. The restless gait showcased trim, toned legs that wore a cutoff pair of his khakis. He'd agreed to the decimation, in deference to the heat, but he was having second thoughts. And third. And none of them were appropriate when his could-be girlfriend was en route. "I think we need to lay some ground rules."

She'd been expecting the conversation since they left Shreveport. In her head the rehearsed lines about being partners and grown-ups and mature adults sounded perfect. Of course, in her head Ethan resembled one of the dusty, wrinkly cows she'd seen meandering along the highway. Reality, though, had shades of a beard beneath a single dimple and a mouth that could tempt a nun. "I don't plan to seduce you while she's here, if that's what you're concerned about. I got the message loud and clear, honey. You're a one-woman man and I'm not the girl."

Since her easy words were exactly what he wanted to hear, Ethan wondered why they irritated him. "Kissing you was as much my fault as yours."

"Actually, the first kiss was my doing. The grope downstairs was your handiwork."

Grope? He didn't grope. They'd nearly made love on a lab table, yes, but it wasn't a clumsy grope. Temper rising, he bit out, "The point is, I haven't mentioned you or us to Lesley."

"Right. She doesn't know I'm here."

"She doesn't know you exist."

Mara's steps faltered. She shouldn't be shocked that his new lover didn't know about a teenage affair. After all, few of her friends had any inkling about Ethan. That most of her friends didn't know her real name may have played a part.

"Mara, listen." Ethan motioned to the futon. When she reluctantly joined him, he immediately regretted the invitation. It seemed patently unfair that his soap would smell so wondrous on her. That her skin glowed like it was lit from within. That after a week with her, images of Lesley's strong, classic beauty dissolved into impish features that sent shivers through his belly. "I need to explain."

Grappling for equanimity, she pasted on an indulgent expression. One that didn't reflect the hurt that shimmered in her eyes. "You don't owe me an explanation. We've both moved on with our lives. I never expected you to keep a candle burning for me. Or a torch. You know what I mean." She cupped his cheek, trying to ignore the warmth that radiated along her skin, that tempted her to move closer. "I'm glad you've found someone to make you happy. You deserve it."

The itch that had taken up residence between his shoulder blades and the watermelon-sized knot of tension at his neck dueled for supremacy. Unaccustomed to unraveling lies, he cleared his throat with effort. "I may not have been entirely clear about my relationship with Lesley," he began. Feeling like a schoolboy in front of the principal, he mumbled, "We care for each other deeply, it's true. And we are attracted to one another—"

Mara bounced off the futon mid-sentence. Accepting that he

was in love with another woman did not mean she had to endure a true confessions moment. She stormed into the kitchen, her back to Ethan. Carefully, she swiped at the mist that gathered in her eyes. "I don't need the gory details. You like her. She likes you. I'm in the way. I get it."

"No, you don't." Conscience warred with confusion. Hell, he didn't get it. A week ago Lesley Baxter was the woman he thought he could plan a life with. Now all he could think about was a cheat and a liar who made his insides melt and his temper flare. "Listen—"

"No." Mara stopped and turned to face him, arms akimbo. "I've got enough on my plate without trying to become friends with you, Ethan. Because we're not. Friends."

"Then what are we?"

"Allies today. Colleagues tomorrow. And as soon as we find the gold, long-lost acquaintances who don't send each other Christmas cards." She didn't bother to sob or to plead. Choices stayed made, whether or not you cared for the consequences. Didn't matter if the deck had been stacked against you before you sat down to play. You choose either to stay or hit. Not that she cared for conceiving of her life as a blackjack metaphor, but there was no help for it. "I'm a big girl, Ethan. I can take it if she can."

Coward that he was, Ethan remained silent, offering only a short nod. He'd tried to tell her, he reasoned. Perhaps it was for the best. What he'd planned to say, he didn't have a clue. More staggering, he was at a loss for what he'd wanted to hear in return. Disturbed, antsy, he headed downstairs. "I'll let you know when they arrive."

In the warehouse, he moved easily around the room, clearing tools and storing equipment. Though they hadn't discussed it, once Lesley arrived, they'd need to move. Quickly. Ethan figured they'd take his car and aim for the Hill Country. The primary obstacle would be eluding their guards. He had a plan for that as well.

It was daring, dangerous, and likely to fail. It was also their best shot at escape. He'd run through the options on the drive to Kiev, but his way made the most sense and served two purposes. One, it would cover their getaway, and two, it would buy them time. Linda would have to agree to play her part; however, he was certain she would, once she had the facts.

By the time the tunnel light flashed gold, Ethan was prepared. His notes had been organized and neatly stacked on the lab table. The bones were in their reinforced-steel containers, and the refrigerated units had been sealed and locked. The digital clock on the wall read 6:38 P.M.

He crossed to the access panel and typed in the code. Down the tunnel, a series of iron grates lifted into the air, and the police vehicle wound through the blackened passage. The loading dock was half a flight higher than the warehouse, so he climbed up the rickety steps to greet them.

As soon as the car came to a halt, Lesley bounded out to join him. Before he could speak, she reached up and planted a lingering kiss on his startled mouth. She lingered over the welcome, then leaned against the arms that had risen to catch her unexpected launch. With a voice throaty with laughter, she said, "Full of surprises, aren't you, Doctor?"

Ethan shot a look at Linda, who raised her hands, palms out. The universal symbol for *you're on your own*. Cops, he thought balefully, no help when you really needed them. With a sheepish grin, he returned his attention to the woman in his arms. "I assume Linda filled you in?" he asked with fading hope.

"Told me you thought I'd be safer with her and that you'd bring me up to speed when I arrived." Turning, she hooked her arm in his and took her suitcase from Linda, who'd moved to join them. "Let's go upstairs so I can see what else you've got waiting for me."

Or who, mouthed Linda, eyes dancing.

Ethan led the women through the warehouse. Linda saw the spotless surfaces and quipped, "As obsessive compulsive as ever, E?"

"He's never been late to a faculty meeting. Not one," Lesley offered conspiratorially. "We call him Big Ben. Behind his back, of course."

"In high school we called him Kiss Ass. Much more colorful."

Ethan refused to dignify either comment. Instead, he stood on the bottom step and waved them up. "Come on."

The suspense was killing her, Mara thought as she peered down at the street. What would Lesley look like? Sound like? Was she tall and willowy or petite and curvy? Given her own very average height and average curves, she had no sense of Ethan's type. Even worrying about them was foreign to her. She was confident that men found her attractive, but beauty was a lure, not a hook.

A pleasant, feminist thought until you were faced with an unseen supermodel with legs from here to Tuesday, she reminded herself. One with a doctorate and an actual, paid, legal position.

She sighed lustily. "Face it, Mara. You're out of your league."

"What's the game?"

Mara stiffened, then turned, a noncommittal expression plastered on. "Basketball. Don't have a good jump shot." Moving forward, hand extended, she sized up the competition. From the season-ready maroon Blahniks to a perennially chic black Chanel suit that hit mid-thigh, Lesley Baxter exuded effortless class and comfort with wealth. Rubies winked at her ears, the stones a perfect match for the simple pendant at her long, elegant throat. Chestnut hair swung in a short, sophisticated bob above her shoulders, the style an excellent match for the cameo face and flawless mocha-colored skin.

If there was a competition, Mara thought, she'd just lost game, set, and match. Her stomach plummeting, she turned up the wattage on her smile. "You must be Dr. Baxter."

Hazel eyes framed by sable lashes that would shame a cow widened slightly. But good breeding showed. She returned the half smile and murmured, "Lesley, please." The crisp Boston tones oozed politeness and distant curiosity. "And you are?"

The nauseous plummet of her stomach was met with a strike-on kick from a pointed toe. *Ouch.* Ethan hadn't been kidding. His Lesley knew nothing about her, and if he'd had his druthers, probably never would. Because she owed him, she said quietly, "Mara Reed. I work with Ethan."

Lesley flicked an inquisitive glance at the man who hovered near the kitchen. When Ethan discovered the shiny patina on his loafers, she returned her attention to Mara. "I thought Ethan was working alone. He never mentioned a partner."

"I'm a consultant," Mara covered quickly. Apparently, Ethan planned to be of little help during the first round of the gauntlet. But she was up for it. Linking her fingers together, she explained, "For the symbols on the corpses."

The cool hazel eyes chilled another degree. "A fellow professor, I gather. I see he's calling in a great deal of support for his research."

"We have that in common," Mara supplied simply, eager to end her conversation. She was getting frostbite by proximity. "I have some experience in Christian numerics."

Lesley curved her lips into a gracious moue of interest. "Ethan described a fascinating set of Greek symbols. He didn't tell me they were religious in origin." The censure was light but unmistakable. "Where did you do your training, Dr. Reed?"

Unable to tell if there had been mockery in the question, Mara cocked her head slightly. Warningly. "Not Doctor, Miss."

Ethan caught Mara's narrowed look and hurried forward. "Mara studied with an old master. No one you know, Lesley."

Lesley arched a single ebony brow, a nifty trick Mara had never learned. "And you are an expert on my Rolodex?" she said to Ethan. "How interesting."

Amused by the show but aware of the danger camped on their front door, Linda decided to intervene. "Shop talk can wait, can't it? We have more pressing matters to discuss."

"Indeed," concurred Lesley, her tone mildly miffed. "Perhaps someone would care to explain the two men watching the building or the police escort?" At the shocked silence, she gestured to the unshaded windows behind Mara. "I may not have studied with masters, but I am observant."

Because the entire situation was mainly her fault, Mara spoke up. In her most businesslike fashion, she explained, "The men downstairs are hired killers who want to kidnap me and retrieve information I stole from their boss. Turns out Ethan has been working for their boss, unbeknownst to him. The dead bodies he was asked to examine contain clues to a fortune in gold that my grandfather stole, and that their boss thinks Ethan and I can help him find. Linda had to pick you up at the airport because it's too dangerous for us to be seen leaving the house.

"I'm a full-time confidence artist. Not a religious symbologist. I only know numerics because my father was obsessed with mysticism and he thought he could communicate with God by imprinting symbols on the bodies of his dead parishioners. Sort of a ticket into heaven. He got the idea from my grandfather, who was a thief and a traveling minister, but nothing like my dad." She shrugged, looking at Ethan, carefully avoiding Linda's slitted gaze. "Did I leave anything out?"

"No." Ethan scratched his chin. "I think you hit all the important points. Except for one."

"Oh, I can't wait to hear this." Linda spoke from the kitchen, reminding herself to run a sheet on Mara Reed as soon as she got back to the precinct. "This must be a doozy."

"It will be," promised Ethan. "And you'll be a central part of it."

"Part of what?" The cop pushed away from the island and joined the loose circle formed by a stunned Lesley, a defiant Mara, and a suspiciously pleased Ethan. "I'm the chief of police, Ethan. A favor like picking up your girlfriend or helping you hide your ex is one thing—"

"You're his ex?" Lesley spoke for the first time since Mara's revelations. "You're the ghost he's here to get rid of?"

I'm a dead man, Ethan accepted. "Lesley—"

"When I suggested you come here to exorcise your demons, I didn't expect you to be quite so diligent."

"I didn't know she'd be here."

"It was twelve years ago," clarified Mara. "We were in high school."

"We were kids then, Lesley." He fumbled for an excuse, reading the mood that swept across her face. Glaciers held more warmth. "Just kids. Doesn't mean anything now."

"Yet you didn't see fit to mention her to me when we spoke this week." Taking in the battered duffel at the foot of the bed, she gave Ethan an inquiring look. "She's staying here, isn't she?"

"Only since Monday, when I got shot," Mara offered helpfully, though the sight of Ethan's rapidly paling face was deeply gratifying. Didn't mean anything, her foot. "Ethan saved me and put me up here. In his bed."

"Stop helping me," he groaned dully. "Lesley, honey, listen. I meant to tell you when I picked you up from the airport."

"Which you couldn't do without fear of being shot." Lesley focused on Mara, who managed to disguise her pleasure at the growing hostility. "You seem to be the only one capable of honesty here. Is something going on between the two of you?"

Ethan watched Mara, torn between horror and bemusement. The thought of Mara as the crucible of truth was laughable, if it wasn't so damnably accurate. He waited for her to respond, not sure if he preferred truth or a lie.

Truth or lie. The options dueled for release, and Mara sensed opportunity. Say the words, and Lesley would demand to be returned to the airport. Posthaste. Competition eliminated, problem solved. Except out of the corner of her eye Mara could see emotion flash in Ethan's eyes, in sharp contrast to the stoic expression. He was braced, she realized, for betrayal. For her betrayal. Shaken, she couldn't fault him. Her track record was lousy. But rule number eleven was to seize opportunity, regardless of the cost. Advantage, Mara.

Not at all sure what she was about to say, Mara began to speak. "We're friends. That's it. And barely that. He helped me out of a jam and let me crash here until I could move on. Then we figured out our connections, and we've been working together ever since." She stopped speaking, and heard Ethan release a soft breath. In that moment her heart broke once more and she squared her shoulders, dignity intact.

"All right." Lesley nodded once, and focused her interest on Ethan. "You told me you were searching for adventure. Nice job so far. So, what other delightful surprises do you have in store?"

In for a penny, Ethan thought carelessly. "Well, we need to blow up the warehouse. Tonight."

CHAPTER 15

LINDA ERUPTED FIRST. "HELLO? COP. UNIFORM. BADGE. DUTY TO uphold the law?" Her voice rose several decibels, each one bolstered by astounded disbelief, morbid fascination, and stubborn responsibility. "Telling me she's a thief—"

"Con artist," Mara corrected. "Much more nuanced work."

A snarl stopped the ill-timed explanation. Linda's hand spasmodically gripped the butt of her weapon. The urge to release the holster and shoot blindly nearly overwhelmed. "I didn't question Mara because you asked me not to. I played taxi for your friend here, again, without probing too much."

"Thank you, by the way," Lesley inserted graciously.

"You're welcome." Aghast, flummoxed, Linda advanced to stand toe-to-toe with Ethan, her formidable height an asset. Her voice dropped low, almost pleading. "Friendship has its limits. I won't break the law for you. You can't ask me to."

"Normally, I wouldn't," he responded gently. Friendship did

have limits, he believed. However, when the cause was important, those bonds stretched to cover the worst transgressions.
Because true friendship demanded more. "Our lives are on the
line here. Mara's. Mine. And now Lesley."

Because she could feel herself waver, Linda barked, "Whose
fault is that?"

"The men downstairs. Look, I wish I could have gotten to
Lesley in time to stop her from coming, but I didn't understand
what we were up against. Mara tried to warn me, and I refused
to listen. I'm listening now, and I don't see many options." For
hours now he'd considered every possibility, but he could see no
other way out. No other recourse. "I won't ask you to participate, but I do need you to look the other way. And to make sure
a fire truck arrives on time."

"No. Absolutely not."

Ethan nudged Linda to the kitchen stool. Mara trailed after
him, with Lesley not far behind. "Just hear me out. Mara was
being honest when she explained the situation. Our best guess is
that Davis Conroy, who owns this building, has those men outside to watch us. See if we make a break for it."

"We've already eluded them once today." Mara understood
the pull of duty that cordoned off Linda from agreement. Ethics
couldn't be malleable, not if they meant anything. Sure, she ad-
hered to a different moral code, but a code was a code. "Why
not use the tunnels again, but don't come back?"

Ethan had contemplated the option and discarded it. "Because I doubt they'll be that patient. If we aren't seen for a couple of days, Conroy will come looking. I owe him a report on my findings by Monday."

Unfortunately, Mara agreed. She blew out a short, resigned breath. "You want them to think we're dead. And that all the evidence died with us."

"Exactly." Ethan shifted to encompass the three women in his sights. "If we blow up the warehouse, they'll spend weeks trying to unravel what happened. By then we're on our way to the treasure and Conroy is none the wiser."

"Arson, vandalism, obstruction of justice, aiding and abetting a fugitive," Linda muttered. "All felonies. And what about the dead bodies—the real ones?"

"That's where you come in. If the fire trucks get here soon enough, the storage units won't be damaged. I'm done with my investigation, so the bodies can be properly buried this time."

"Do we know where we're going?" The question came from a subdued Lesley, whose skin had blanched over the course of the discussion.

"Mara does. Or at least, the clues to it." Ethan planted his hands on the countertop, his voice brisk. "We need to act quickly. Linda, you should return to the police headquarters. I'll call your cell when we're ready."

"I haven't agreed, Ethan." But her resistance wavered. "I took an oath."

"I understand." He moved suddenly and tugged her to the windows. Rabbe was returning to the SUV, and Guffin ambled past him, to take his break. "These men shot Mara and they kidnapped her. Their boss won't hesitate to do something worse soon. All I'm asking for is a blind eye. For now."

A cocky grin spread across his face. "I have the chance of a lifetime here. No more Big Ben or Mr. Kiss Ass. For once, I'll take a risk. A huge risk, and damn the consequences."

"I could just haul your buddies in. A night in a holding cell and you'll have time to make your escape."

"Won't work," Mara interjected. "Davis Conroy has resources. If Rabbe and Guffin lose our trail, ten more will show up tomorrow. They chased me from Detroit to Louisiana, and I'm good. With two of us moving—"

"Three." Lesley corrected. "I can help you. And I'm not leaving you alone with him. Again."

"Fine, with three of us, we'll be a bright neon sign. Ethan's plan is crazy, but it will work." Reading Linda's mutinous expression, Mara crossed to join her. "Remember tenth grade, Linda? When the cheerleaders would taunt you for being so tall and Ethan charmed them into leaving you alone. Or the fights Ethan would break up for you?"

"Not the same, Mara. Not even close."

"No, but Ethan is a good man. He's like a Boy Scout without the ridiculous uniform. He's never broken a law in his life."

"Strange that he'd start only after you come back into it," Lesley murmured.

Direct hit. Mara smiled ruefully. "You've got a point. But here's another. We stay here much longer and Davis Conroy will send in his army to get his information. They come here and you'll have thugs and gangsters from around the country converging on Kiev like it was Mardi Gras. You don't have the manpower or the experience to handle his type. Or, if we sneak out, he'll find us and kill us. Then our deaths will be on your conscience." She paused, then finished. "A fire you can put out now or one that you can't control."

"If I lose my job over this, I will make your misery my personal mission in life." Linda brushed past her, aimed for the door. "Call 911 by ten-thirty. The first engines will arrive by 10:45. Leave a message for me at home when you've gotten out of Kiev. Ethan, come show me what you've planned." As she made for the door, she mumbled, "Good freaking luck."

Ethan jogged after her. Left behind in the studio, Mara and Lesley maintained their positions and a leaden silence. Mara, Lesley noted to herself, appeared to be dressed in borrowed finery. The mangled khakis that showcased showgirl-caliber legs had obviously once belonged to a man of Ethan's height and build. Riotous black curls that women like her admired, but never attempted, framed a triangular face with strong, eye-catching features. Exotic, yet gallingly wholesome. Free, if it were possible, of makeup or even a stitch of lipstick. Which meant the whiskey-colored eyes were natural, Lesley allowed grudgingly.

Swaying slightly, she sank onto the nearby futon, ignoring the shabby comfort of the navy duvet flung over the puny mattress. The spare accommodations Ethan had selected did not invite guests. Other than the office chair across the wide space, the prime seating appeared to be where she'd settled, leaving Mara to perch on one of the kitchen stools or to sit next to her.

For her part, Mara stared with fixed determination at the shadow of Ethan's departing form, despite the closed door. Certainly, he hadn't left her here, alone, with his girlfriend. Feeling gauche in her ragged cast-offs, she lifted a hand to the curled fright that passed as her hair. As she did once a week, she swore she'd let the natural strands grow long and force herself into a stylist's chair. The kinky, untamed curls were no match for the sleek, sophisticated elegance of the professor. Even her vaguely southern accent seemed unconscionably coarse in the face of such—and she had to admit it—such class. The one attribute she could never mimic.

Nevertheless, the lady was on her turf. Gamesmanship required that she maintain the upper hand, and cordiality often lulled the unsuspecting far better than direct assault. With an internal sigh, she turned. "So, um, have a good flight?"

"So so." Lesley accepted that this stranger, this interloper, sought to put her at ease. With a thin, brittle smile, she added, "Takeoff was fine, but landing has been a bitch."

The gutter phrase startled a laugh from Mara. "That's one way to put it." At a loss for her next words, she circled the counter island, tugged open the refrigerator and buried her head inside. Taking a quick survey, she asked, "Thirsty? We've got—I mean Ethan's got—juice, water . . . I think I saw a beer in here somewhere."

"Water would be fine." Lesley absently toed off Italian leather that cost a month's salary for most of her colleagues and wriggled her toes in emancipated bliss. "Oh, and one more thing?"

"Sure." Mara poked her head around the stainless steel door. Swigging from the last Coke in the box, she asked, "What can I do for you?"

"Tell me if you and Ethan are sleeping together or if it's just been adventitious foreplay."

Mara wheezed as soda slid down the wrong pipe and the can slipped gracelessly to the linoleum. "What?" she sputtered. "I'm not even sure what adventitious means."

"It means casual, almost accidental." Lesley pinned her with an appraising look. "I prefer to know where I stand at the outset. Obviously, you and Ethan have a history. One that still binds you together. Given that you are not unattractive and mortal danger can be sexy as hell, it's not out of the question."

Heat suffused Mara's skin, mortification and shock mingled into a nice burning sensation that portended hell. Desperately, she cast a glance at the door, which remained stubbornly closed. "Don't you think you should be asking Ethan these rather impertinent questions?" Impertinent was the right word, she thought worriedly.

"Ethan is conveniently absent. Otherwise, I would likely hold my tongue. But when opportunity presents itself . . ."

Mara nodded shortly. One of her personal credos. She couldn't fault the lady, probably would have taken the offensive herself, had she thought about it. She snagged a juice and a bottled water from the fridge and a can of chips from the pantry. Calmly, she stepped over the puddle of caffeine and sugar drying on the floor. Ethan could clean up the mess. Joining Lesley, she declined an invitation to sit, and handed her the water. "Here you go."

"You haven't answered my question, Mara." Lesley twisted the cap off the bottle and gingerly removed the blue ring that remained. Laying it beside the discarded cap, she explained, "I don't care for the thought of putting my mouth where another's hands have been. Quite apropos, don't you think?"

Smooth, Mara thought admiringly. Class and *cojones*. Devastating combination. But she hadn't seduced a prince by looks alone. "Absolutely. However, you may find it difficult to avoid the possibility." She sipped at her apple juice slowly, the tart bite strangely soothing. Charm and disarm, her approach with royalty. Should work on the haughty as well, she mused. Coolly, she explained, "I've known Ethan for a long time. In fact, I've been in love with him longer than I've not."

The pronouncement caught Lesley off guard. Before she could stop herself, she blurted out, "You love him?"

"Yes," Mara confirmed evenly. "Have since I was sixteen. Since the first time he saved me."

Regaining her composure, Lesley probed with a steely look she'd perfected over the years, "Do you make it a habit of needing rescue?"

Nice return, she thought. But too far off the mark to sting.

Her relationship with Ethan wasn't about saviors. It was about redemption. More information than Dr. Baxter was entitled to yet. "Not really. I'm remarkably self-sufficient. But when I need him, he's always there." Sociably, she offered the chips. When Lesley silently demurred, she removed a couple and nibbled, musing. "Ethan has a hero complex, I'd wager. So afraid he's destined to be boring, he hunts for excitement."

"Usually in the safest places possible," Lesley concurred.

"Until now." *Until me.*

Lesley heard the words, though they were unspoken. Doubt pricked at her ego, but the jealousy she would have expected failed to materialize. She was curious, though. Apparently, Ethan had a weakness for kleptomaniacal waifs.

Regret quickly transformed itself into indignation. *The nerve of the man, inviting her to Kiev under false pretenses.* She had traveled on a crop duster from Austin on the vain assumption that years of flirtation were about to result in a declarative statement. Only to be met by police officers and his paramour. A scream of annoyance rose in her throat, but she forced back the display. The Boston Baxters did not engage in emotional outbursts. Or in petty tantrums.

Deliberately, Lesley shifted to face Mara. "Since I'm joining the trio, why don't you fill me in?"

"All right." Mara munched on a chip, ordering her thoughts. Catching Lesley eyeing the can, she tipped it forward. "Sure you're not hungry?"

The scent of salt and fried potatoes drifted close, and Lesley damned her perpetual diet. She deserved a break. "God, Pringles. It's been years," she exclaimed as she dipped into the can greedily.

Ethan flung open the door, nearly panting. Given his druthers, Mara and Lesley wouldn't know each other's names, heaven forbid spend time alone together. He'd shown Linda the layout and where he intended to place the charges. After trying one final time to dissuade him, she'd reluctantly taken her leave. Then he rushed up the stairs, expecting chaos or worse.

He hadn't expected to hear them giggling over snack food.

"Oreos. Especially the new ones with the yellow cookies," Mara was saying. "Once, while I was casing a mark, I ate an entire bag in one sitting. Combined with chocolate milk, those cookies are lethal." She balanced on the arm of the futon, her bare feet propped up behind Lesley. Garish pink polish blazed beneath the fluorescent lights, particularly when she wiggled her toes.

Catching sight of Ethan, Lesley returned the red chip can to Mara. "The arsonist has returned."

"Hurrah." Mara swung her legs around and dropped onto an open space near Lesley. With a quick look of confirmation at Lesley, she announced, "We've got an idea."

Wary, almost frightened, Ethan cut his gaze between the two of them. Matching expressions of contrived innocence had his blood pressure rising. "I haven't been gone that long."

"Long enough," Lesley responded silkily. "Mara and I have had a chance to talk. She's filled me in on our friends downstairs and your visit this afternoon."

Ethan narrowed his eyes, the black pupils laser-sharp and focused. "I don't want you involved in this, Lesley. Once we get clear of the warehouse, you're on the next flight to Austin."

"Not if you want my help with the coordinates. Or the location of the safe." She reached behind her and pulled out Fool's Paradise and the sketch Mara had made of the coordinates. "Ingenious design, by the way. Weaving together history and topography into a quilt."

Mara preened. "My grandmother is a brilliant lady."

"I'd love to meet her. I participate in a quilt circle myself." At Mara's skeptical expression, she explained, "I find the sewing relaxing, and academically significant. The preservation of a cultural normative through the domestic arts."

Distracted, fascinated, Mara asked, "I thought you were a geologist?"

"I am. But I studied history in undergrad. A hobby of mine." Lesley smiled at a bewildered Ethan. "I do have layers, darling. Most women do."

"So I'm learning," grumbled Ethan. "But to return to the subject. We're not taking you with us on a harebrained expedition without any guarantee for your safety."

"I don't mind." Mara rose from the futon and began to collect their debris. "I'm okay with maps, but these coordinates are approximations. Without Lesley, we could lose time. And give Conroy a chance to catch up with us."

"Plus, you're not the only one who has a streak of adventure." Rising to her feet, Lesley continued, "I didn't become a geologist in order to while away my years in an ivory tower, reading about discovery. I came here to satisfy myself, and that will happen. One way or another."

Ethan didn't miss the admonition or the spark of temper. He'd definitely been in the warehouse too long. As a man well-versed in the study of culture, his training demanded that he accurately assess a community or a group. Based on his observations of the women in the room, he would hazard a guess that regardless of his intentions, he had no say in the matter any longer. Chauvinism urged him to continue his useless arguments, but time was fast slipping away.

"If you're a part of this expedition, so be it. It's your funeral."

Mara snorted inelegantly. "That's the spirit, O Fearless Leader."

The title brought a sly grin to his face and presented him with the best moment of the night. "No, no, Mara. After I get us on the road, this is your mission. O Fearless Leader."

Without waiting for her reaction, Ethan began to issue orders. "Lesley, you should change clothes now. Once we've set the charges, we'll need to move fast and be prepared for anything."

Mara hurried to the closet. "I'll get you packed up while you break down your equipment. Do you plan to bring everything?" Throwing open his suitcase on the bed, she haphazardly bundled pants and shirts and tossed them inside.

Ethan opened his mouth to caution her about wrinkles, until the absurdity struck him. He walked to the desk and disassembled the laptop and accessories, neatly placing each item inside its carrying case. He wouldn't chastise Mara, but sloppy packing just wasn't in him. "We'll take as much as we can fit into the car. The trunk is pretty roomy."

"You've got an extra passenger," she reminded him.

"She can ride up front. There's plenty of space."

Mara refrained from comment. Instead, she stuffed the rest of the contents of his closet into the green American Tourister and slammed the case shut. White T-shirts and blue oxfords spilled out of cracks. Vainly, she poked at the errant cloth, opening and reclosing the lid. Finally, she forced the top down and clambered atop. Grunting with the effort, she managed to latch the suitcase, despite the seeping clothes.

Ethan watched the spectacle with gruesome fascination. "Um, Mara? I'll take care of my books. Why don't you take the suitcase down to the car?" Otherwise, he thought grimly, Dickens would soon be shoved cheek by jowl with Sneed and Walker.

With a shrug, she agreed. "Suit yourself."

SOON, THE WAREHOUSE had been emptied of most of Ethan's belongings. Downstairs, charges were laid using his forensic equipment and two semesters of graduate chemistry. A delay had been set for the loudest of the miniexplosives, the one whose sound effects would add drama to the show and alert the men outside. An accelerant trail led up from the almost flame-retardant warehouse space to the more fire-friendly loft. Once the hungry flames reached the door he'd set ajar, it would devour the notes and papers, magazines and newspapers, strategically strewn across the living area. To feed the fire as it traveled and gutted the building.

Ethan leaned into the convertible at the driver's side, arms draped along the door frame, elbow on the hood. The white canvas top stretched taut overhead, containing the items there hadn't been time to pack. Lesley squeezed in on the long bench beside Mara, who sat behind the wheel. Ahead, the iron grate lifted slowly on a mechanical pulley. The tunnel would lead up and emerge onto a side street nearly a mile away, close to the lake. From there they'd hop onto the county road and aim west. Assuming the fire behaved as expected.

"All set?" Mara checked.

"Ready." Ethan gave the utility lighter a test, the flame shooting out strong and bright. "I'll ignite the leads I've put near the lab tables and watch from the tunnels to be sure they're working. The second lead will direct the fire to the loft."

"You're sure there's enough time to seal the tunnel and run?" Mara tore her eyes away from the vicious flame to catch Ethan's. Worry flickered and caught hold, but she saw no companion concern in the steady black depths. Which alarmed her even more. A good criminal maintained an edge of fear, a natural adrenaline to keep her on her guard. Alert, ready to move. Without it, she grew too comfortable and got sloppy. A fatal mistake. "We can still back out, Ethan. Call Linda and tell her the whole thing's off."

"Absolutely," Lesley joined, strain evident in the tight tones. "This is a felony. You—We—could go to prison."

"Or we could pretend to be dead and instead hunt for treasure." He exhaled a short, pent-up breath. "But say the word and I call it off."

Lesley hesitated, ready to quit. But Mara shoved the key in the ignition and slammed the car door with a determined thud. "Go."

With a cocksure grin, Ethan sprinted down the black tunnel. He dashed inside the entryway, moving to the first of the detonators. He flicked the lighter and set the flame against the accelerant. The intense burst of heat caught him off guard and he jerked away. Blue flame settled into a dull orange and ate across the cement floor in the direction of the far wall. Mesmerized, Ethan watched the glowing path.

He'd done it. Almost. Movements sharp and tense, he ignited the remaining charges and rushed to the tunnel exit. Once the fire began to lick across the stairs, feeding on debris left there for that purpose, Ethan rapidly punched buttons to seal the tunnel. He darted beneath the closing gate and sprinted for the car, ticking off the seconds. Ten . . . nine . . . eight . . . seven . . .

Boom! The first of the concussion charges exploded.

Six . . . five . . . four . . .

Boom! Ethan slid into the car and Mara jammed the stick into gear. The convertible sped into the pitch-black, guided only by the bouncing headlights.

Three . . . two . . . one . . .

Boom! Boom! Boom!

IN THE WAREHOUSE behind them, concussive shocks like massive firecrackers echoed in the cavernous space. Flames shot high, feeding on oxygen and heat. The loft glowed magenta in the darkness, and Rabbe elbowed Guffin, waking him. "Look!"

"Shit!" Guffin hurriedly straightened, befuddled by the sight before him. The bricked warehouse stood on the empty street, a macabre pumpkin with its windowed eyes awash in fire. He seized the cell phone laying on the dash. "I'll call 911!"

"Screw that!" shouted Rabbe, struggling to turn the engine over. Sweat beaded on his lip, pooled beneath his arms. "We're getting the hell out of here! Cops find us anywhere near the place, and we'll be in jail before we can say Miranda."

Because Guffin agreed, he dropped the phone without argument and latched his seat belt. The SUV peeled away from the curb, speeding along Gaul. As they careened onto Shahar, the first of the fire engines streamed past, sirens blaring. Like any good citizen, Rabbe swerved to the side of the road, giving the authorities wide berth. Then he swung the Expedition east and headed for the highway.

CHAPTER 16

"ETHAN, GRAB MARA'S BAG FOR ME. I NEED TO SEE HER NOTES on Bailey." Lesley marked the atlas splayed across her lap with a pink highlighter. Despite the predawn hour, she was wide-awake and eager to dig in. To do something that might break the tension. "And a bottle of water, if we've got any left."

Silently, Ethan reached into the backseat for the duffel bag wedged between his laptop and Lesley's Coach valise. The faded army green provided a stark contrast, one he was in no mood to ponder. Snapping off a plastic bottle, he dropped the bundle in her lap and shut his eyes. "Here."

Lesley noted the taciturn response but said nothing. For nearly six hours they'd been driving across the state, staying off major interstates. At Mara's suggestion, they stuck to county roads that twisted through piney woods thick with green, yielding to wide prairies dotted by interesting stuff. Waiting for her turn at the wheel, she'd nodded off in staring at a bewildered deer gamboling across the road, and awoken to a field of cows grazing in a nearby pasture.

Since speeding past Caldwell around three A.M., the speedometer had inched steadily higher and the taut silence had deepened. Though she wasn't trained as a psychologist, Lesley understood enough of human dynamics to stay out of the figurative middle, even if she was presently wedged in the literal center.

On the first leg out of Kiev, she'd attempted polite conversation, but terse monosyllabic responses led her to coldly requesting their notes on the treasure. The quick, almost relieved response from both had buried her in research and away from unwanted confrontation.

Even their research notes were almost confrontational when compared to one another. Mara recounted the history of the stolen gold in a lyrical, melismatic style reminiscent of a campsong legend. Ethan's notes lacked the artistic bent, reading, she noticed, as a set of ordered observations. No mentions of personality or passion, simply a recitation of dates and actions. Spare, unsentimental. Intentionally distant.

Together, the two sets of observations and assumptions painted an enthralling tale of cunning and guile, of derring-do and clever deception, with sufficient reality to bring the story to life. Add a quilt that resembled the nooks and crannies of Texas Hill Country, and Lesley was hooked.

"Mara?" When she received a nearly inaudible grunt, Lesley continued, "Are you sure these journal entries are Bailey's?"

Mara nodded in assent. "Rabbe killed Bailey's great-niece to get it. My grandmother verified that the symbols are identical to the ones she drew."

"This symbol here?" Lesley pointed to a circle with a short line extending down from the base. "I thought all the symbols were Greek letters?"

"They are." Mara swept a quick look down to the page Lesley held. "That's the Greek letter qoppa."

Ethan stirred. "Qoppa? I don't remember you mentioning that one yesterday." He too focused on the drawing, brow furrowed. The symbol appeared on Poncho and Reverend Reed as well. "I thought it was a common symbol, not a letter."

"It's obsolete. Hasn't been used in centuries, except for ordinals. It represents the number ninety." Mara added, "And zeta is seven, not six." Mouth open to query, Lesley was forestalled by explanation. "Six is another obsolete letter. Trust me."

Deciding to do just that, she scratched the numbers onto her grid pad. The blue lines crisscrossed the page, forming hundreds of perfect, tiny blue boxes. On the drawing, intersecting the η, two additional symbols swooped in bold ink. Lesley recognized kappa and a second zeta, and Mara confirmed that the combination represented the number twenty-seven. Surrounding the four numbers, a larger symbol dominated the page. The graceful circle had been accented by a sloping flag extending from the top of the curve. "Delta?" she mused aloud.

"The circle?" Mara checked the expanse of highway before

her, and seeing nothing, spared another look at the drawing. "I thought that it might be. If these are coordinates, then they are ninety-seven, twenty-seven. I vaguely remember high school geography, but that would be ninety-seven degrees latitude, twenty-seven degrees longitude, right."

"But if we add the five as a decimal point," gnawing the pencil eraser, Lesley indicated the atlas, "we leave Austin heading west. Which makes sense, given the railroad depot. According to Ethan's notes, the Missouri-Pacific rail ran north from San Antonio to Dallas after picking up cargo from horses traveling from Mexico."

"Which puts us where?"

"In one of several small towns outside Austin. And nowhere closer to the key."

Mara drummed on the steering wheel, a thought tickling her memory. "Lesley, flip to the entry dated September 1937."

"Got it." She began to read aloud.

Poncho headed east with the Reverend, but I'm in no mood for church. Don't believe the Lord would have me now anyways. I've ransomed my soul for pieces of gold, gold I may never see. For my betrayal, I descended into hell to hide my part. Probably will not return. With Guerva in the grave, don't reckon there's a point to it. It's fitting, I suppose, that I said my last prayer in a cathedral. I drank from a fountain and asked for blessings. But I forgot to be sanctified.

"He talks about descending into hell to hide his key, I think. Are there any places near Austin where a man could do that?"

At Mara's question, Ethan craned a look at the atlas. Tapping the star near Austin, he speculated, "They each took a key and headed out a day's ride from the meeting place. In 1937, the only options would be a horse or a rather slow car."

"How slow?" asked Mara.

"A horse that has to do a day's ride will probably canter at about five mph, six, if he's an Arabian or a mustang."

"At best," Mara calculated swiftly, "a man could theoretically travel 144 miles in a single day."

"But if he's only got twenty-four hours to go and turn around, that's immediately cut to seventy-two miles," added Lesley. "If he sleeps for even a couple of hours, he's down to sixty miles."

"What's out sixty miles from Austin, Lesley?" Ethan asked. "Or near the coordinates."

Following the line she drew on the web of highways, topographical markers, and the veins of waterways, her eyes lit upon the answer. "Caverns. Rocks." Rapidly, breathlessly, she leafed through the pages to the section on parks and natural scenery, certain of what she would find. The page fell open, and she smiled broadly in satisfaction. "Wonder Cave. It's in San Marcos, Texas. A straight descent with a well on the bottom level. Cave explorers used to drink from it for good luck. Called it the wishing well. And it lies at 97.52 degrees north, 27.56 degrees west."

"How far away is it?" Mara zipped the convertible around a crawling semi, excitement building. "How far?"

"Thirty miles, give or take. More than enough time for the average horse to make it there and back to Austin." Ethan extended his arm past Lesley, who bent low over the atlas to mark the coordinates. Needing to connect, he touched Mara's shoulder. He squeezed the rounded muscles gently, running his thumb along the smooth, luminous skin.

Pleased, she gave him a quick smile, filled with anticipation. "Well, partner, here we go."

LESLEY HIKED ALONG the trail to the gift shop, eager to be inside. They'd stopped for flashlights and other gear, which Ethan put in a backpack slung across his shoulders. She had insisted on the detour, given that she knew the area well. At her insistence, her students made a pilgrimage to the formation once a semester. The entire area was dotted with signs welcoming tourists to Wonder World and offering tours of the cave from eight A.M. to eight P.M. In her hands, she clutched the portfolio where she'd made her own notes about Bailey's possible hiding spot. "The cave is part of a tourist attraction. The only entry point is through the gift shop inside the amusement park."

"Amusement park? For a cave?" Mara scowled at the notion. "Seems a bit much for a bunch of rocks. No offense."

"None taken. The Wonder Cave is considered geologically significant because it is the only cave in America formed by an earthquake." Lesley tossed off the fact as she rushed along the patch. "This entire area lies on the Balcones Fault Zone, one of the longest in the nation. Almost 350 miles, from Waco to the Rio Grande." She added the last as she disappeared around a corner.

"We're on a fault line?" Astonished, Mara stumbled to a halt, and Ethan collided into her. Both teetered for balance, and he slid his arms around her waist to steady them both. The move pressed her against his chest, and she automatically braced flailing hands on rock-hard thighs. Warm breath whispered at her temple, and in sensory response her fingers clenched the muscled length. Harder.

He could feel the imprint of her touch through the worn cotton. Instinctively, he contracted his hold, and firm, high breasts pressed into his forearm. For an instant they hung together, awareness rippling across flesh and sinking into bone.

Mara sucked in a harsh breath. Being held by Ethan felt natural. Right. But Lesley was not more than ten feet ahead of them, and now was not the time for the thought and images shimmering in her mind. With difficulty, she broke contact and lurched away. "Thanks," she murmured, then hurried to catch up with Lesley.

Ethan followed, more slowly than the two. Confusion warred with frustration. Soon, he and Mara would have to discuss what was growing between them. And well before that, he owed Lesley clarity. As soon as he found it himself. While he'd made no promises to her, her presence pricked his conscience. She was now in harm's way because he had begged for her help. Moreover, he couldn't ignore the unspoken purpose of her visit, or at least, what he'd anticipated when he asked her to come. Light flirtation or serious intent. Like everything else in his life since Mara's arrival, he hadn't a clue.

"Stop dawdling, Ethan." At Lesley's shouted instructions, he quickened his pace. They approached the entrance to the caverns, a crack in the ground that descended for nearly thirty feet. Reading the signs, Ethan felt his stomach pitch with disappointment. "The caves don't open for hours. And if we have to go inside with a tour guide, we'll never find what we're looking for."

"I could distract the guards," Mara volunteered. There was something inside, something they were meant to find. The thrill of potential discovery had her insides quaking with expectation, which warred with the thought of missing the big find. But, she reminded herself glumly, none of it mattered if they couldn't go in. "I've got some experience with the classic bait and switch. Can you slip past them if I get them to leave their posts? You still need to get inside the gift shop, and they're not open yet."

"Don't have to. Remember, you brought me along for a reason." Lesley fished inside the neat leather portfolio and emerged with a laminated badge. "Presto!"

"What is it?" Mara peered at the card, then a broad grin spread. "You have permanent access to the caves? How? Why?"

The other woman smirked, delighted. "I'm a geologist employed by the largest university in the state. Plus, I bring my undergraduate classes here every semester. I'm a regular."

Mara released a breath that jittered in her throat. "What else do you know about the cave?"

"Texas has more than 3,800 caves, but only a hundred or so are paleontologically or archeologically significant. Like I said, Wonder Cave is the only earthquake-created cave in the U.S. Approximately sixty-five million years ago Austin and the rest of this part of Texas lay beneath a shallow sea. Then the earth began to move, an earthquake hit, and the cave was formed."

At the repeated mention of the fault line, Mara squirmed. She wished she'd paid better attention in high school. Having experienced a shaker in California, she was in no hurry to repeat the experience. "Is it safe? I mean, with the region on a fault line, are we just another San Francisco waiting to happen?"

"Not exactly," Lesley explained. "The Balcones Fault has rumbled from time to time, but the earthquakes in Texas tend to happen in El Paso or thereabouts. The fault isn't active, that is, there's no slip between the two sections of earth that are separated by the fault."

"That's almost reassuring," Mara mumbled.

"Don't worry. The Wonder Cave is accessible to people on a daily basis, and it's been determined architecturally sound. It's basically a fracture in a massive limestone formation. Water has worn down the walls over the centuries, and new fissures have emerged. Geologists typically study caves such as these for speleothems." Blank looks followed her explanation, and Lesley elaborated, as though lecturing a class. "Speleothems are a catch phrase. They describe features found in caverns, where the features occur after the underground chamber of the cave has been formed. A scientist would look for common types, like dripstone, which are calcium deposits that form stalactites or stalagmites."

"I can never remember which is which," complained Ethan.

"C for ceiling and G for ground," Mara offered. "Stalactites form on the ceilings and stalagmites form on the ground. Right?"

"You might have a future in spelunking ahead of you." They crested the trail and approached the guard standing duty. Sighing in relief, Lesley recognized the sturdily built woman who wore a pristine white uniform and a pleasant half smile. "Hello, Mrs. Howard."

"Why, Dr. Baxter!" Yvette Howard ambled forward to extend a hand. "What brings you here this time of the morning? It's barely past dawn."

"I'm working on a field project for the university, and I've got another engagement later this afternoon. Today's the last day I have to get my measurements. I spoke with the owners last week, and they said it would be okay to stop by." Behind her back, Lesley sheepishly crossed her fingers. "I have a couple of colleagues with me. We'll be down there for maybe an hour, two max."

Yvette reached for her clipboard, searching for mention of the doctor's visit. "I don't see your name on here, dearie. And I'm not supposed to open the gift shop without prior authorization. There've been some hooligans hanging around here lately. Can't be too careful."

Lesley shook her head in commiseration. "I understand. I think their older brothers are in my freshman intro class. Children these days—"

"Got two growing boys myself." The guard sighed gustily. "They're a handful, each of 'em. Never thought I'd be wishing so hard for them to move into adulthood. Can't keep a box of cereal in the house."

Giving an expected laugh, Lesley tried again. "Haven't had the pleasure of motherhood myself yet, but I might invest in Kellogg stock before I do."

The loud guffaw from Yvette was punctuated by a slap on Lesley's arm. The camaraderie stung, but she winced internally and kept her smile in place. "You'll do, Dr. Baxter. You'll do." Checking the clipboard once more, the guard used the attached pen to scribble a note on the page. "My shift ends at seven, Doctor. See if you can't be done with your work by then. Porter comes on after me, and he's a stickler for protocol." Turning, Yvette unlocked the gift shop doors and pushed them open.

Lesley motioned them forward, and soon they entered the cavern. Lanterns had been strung overhead. Inside, Yvette flipped them into operation and light flickered into the yawning space.

"Nice work, Doc." Mara had been impressed, despite herself. She waited for her eyes to adjust to the dim lighting. "Plausible cover, good recovery. You sure you haven't done this before?"

Offering a noncommittal smile, Lesley led them along the staircase that descended into the cave. "Watch your step. We have to go nearly twenty-five feet down before we reach the first room."

Ethan brought up the rear. "How many rooms are there?"

"Wonder Cave has six rooms on three levels."

"Six rooms?" Mara posed the question, which echoed eerily on walls of the vertical descent. Carefully, she picked her way down the stairs and imagined Bailey creeping in under cover of dark. The key to a fortune clenched tight in his fist, if he had the patience to hold on. Patience Reese Conroy lacked. "How long has this been a tourist attraction?" she asked.

"Excavating a cave is tricky and often useless. If the cavern isn't scientifically significant, a government could waste a great deal of money and potentially cause a collapse by disturbing the balance. Seventy years ago this cave was opened to the public for fifteen years, but the man who discovered it, Mark Bevers, had no interest in doing more than a basic survey. New owners bought it and made it part of a theme park. It was a commercial venture. No need to hunt for hidden tunnels and risk a discovery that could subject the cave to government oversight."

Ethan felt his pulse jump. Following close behind the women, he scanned the dim interior, listened to the cadence of water as it pattered against calcite formations. "So in 1937 a man could have crept inside and hidden a key without anyone the wiser."

They left the stairs and entered the first room. Scrambling along a shelf of rock, Lesley replied, "Back then, no one would have cared."

Mara mounted the rock shelf behind Lesley, and she could feel Ethan on her heels. "What is this place?"

"Mr. Bevers, the man who discovered it, called it the Poker Room. He used to bring his cronies down here for a game. Said he enjoyed the natural air-conditioning." Indeed, cool air circulated around the trio as they spread out. "Bailey may have left his key anywhere. I'd recommend we search each room together. We've got a couple of hours, but not much more. When the tourists start arriving, we'll lose our chance until nightfall."

"Gotcha." Ethan took the west wall, while Mara moved to the south. Lesley focused her attentions on the eastern section.

Ethan quartered his section and methodically searched every crevice and break in the brittle limestone. More than once his hands closed on slippery objects that had the shape and feel of a key, only to be rewarded with broken calcite formations. Holding impatience at bay, he crawled along the Poker Room floor determined to locate Bailey's key.

When he bumped into the curvature of the wall, he noticed

an opening. Checking around, he saw Lesley kneeling near a column formed by deposits. Mara, for her part, stood on her toes, shoving her hands behind protrusions in the rock, unconcerned about what cave dwellers might await her fingers.

She had no fear, he thought bemusedly, and yet she was terrified of everything. The contradiction disturbed him. Hypnotized him. Give her a task, and she attacked it with gusto. No whining about responsibilities or rewards. But offer her love, and she shrank from the possibility as though it might prove fatal. What had she said to him? That she was afraid he might actually love her.

How was it possible she didn't know he had no other choice?

The question burst in his mind, and he was rocked by the revelation. He loved her still. Always. He admired the way she charged at problems, never waiting for a savior. And he respected the choices she thought she had to make, doing what she thought necessary to take care of her family. Anger coursed through him when he thought of her father's brutality, of her mother's abandonment. Of how she hadn't let him inside. Let him help.

If he understood her—and he thought he did—she couldn't have. Not then. The Mara he loved as a young man believed that she bore the burdens of her life alone. In sharp contrast, the grown-up Mara had quietly agreed to share her information with Lesley and finally given him her trust. At least, a part of it.

Ethan slipped through the opening into the unlit cavern that Lesley had told them was the Crystal Room, but his thoughts remained on Mara. On the impossibility of a future together. Too much time and distance and lies separated them. She'd spent their time apart swindling men and women out of their possessions. He'd focused on learning and teaching. On solving crimes in his own, detached way.

Her penchant for illegal behavior nicked at his sense of right and wrong, but being a recent arsonist himself, he could comprehend the thrill of standing on the precipice of jeopardy—of flouting the rules just for the hell of it.

Then, of course, there was Lesley. If Mara's misdeeds jolted his conscience, it was Lesley and her sheer perfection that spoke to the man he thought he was. She was erudite, lovely, and bold. Flashing his light around the small crevice, Ethan saw wet formations that glittered in his low beam. Like the crystalline rocks, Lesley was strong and beautiful, unexpected and wholly right.

But wrong for him.

With Lesley, he was smart and witty and safe. Mara, on the other hand, made him furious and agitated and excited. She stirred him in a way Lesley didn't, couldn't. He snapped off his beam and reentered the Poker Room. Mara and Lesley stood near the stairs waiting. Watching him.

"Ready to move on?"

CHAPTER 17

SPECTACULAR THOUGH THE CHAMBER WAS, WITH MASSIVE boulders suspended as if by magic from the ceiling and dazzling crystals dotting the walkway, a thorough search of the second cave netted the discovery of a black and white salamander and little else.

Mara grimly admitted that prospects for locating the key in the crevices of ancient rock faded with each passing minute. Morning would bring dozens of sightseers and too many questions. If Bailey had secreted his key away in this hole in the ground, he'd done an excellent job. Too good.

They were shooting blind, she thought bleakly, crawling to another pile of rubble and limestone. Light bounced off sparkles of calcite, ersatz diamonds. Fake jewels, a false map, an old man's tattoo, and confessions scribbled onto a burlesque poster didn't add up to much.

For more than a week every choice she made seemed to lead to a similar result. The potential for discovery stymied by a spiteful fate. Darkly, she ticked off the items. She finds journal, stolen from a dead woman. She runs to the safety of her hometown and manages to be shot and cornered. And last, and certainly the most absurd, she escapes into the arms of the one man who had good reason to want her dead.

A man who owned her heart and had given his to another.

Mara blinked at the sting of tears, refusing to shed one. These were all her choices and her consequences. Crying would solve nothing, and they surely wouldn't erase the intervening years when Ethan found his match.

On the other side of the cave, Lesley and Ethan chattered amiably as they searched, but Mara caught only snatches of conversation. Despite the garbled words, she could hear the easy camaraderie, the casual intimacy she'd once known. That she longed to recapture. But he'd obviously moved on, and she couldn't blame him for it. Lesley fit the grown-up Ethan much better than she ever could. Same brilliance, same ambitions.

Smoky laughter trilled over the stillness of the cave, and Mara flinched. Against her better judgment, she checked their position. Her eyes stung again when she saw how Lesley leaned into Ethan, head on his shoulder. As she watched, his arm rose to anchor her while Lesley shook with mirth. The words they spoke were irrelevant, Mara realized. The picture was sufficient. Ethan beaming, Lesley giggling. They fit together, a perfect couple.

Acceptance cut deep, the wound bloodless but complete. She'd lost him. A nameless, faceless opponent she could fight.

Would battle endlessly for Ethan. But not a woman who made him happy. Who could understand him and love him and be what he needed. She could see the truth, no matter how badly she wanted to deny.

One more gamble lost, but at least this would only cost her heart.

Choosing San Marcos and the Wonder Cave was another gambit, with lethal odds. All the prep work, all the research, could come to naught, and she'd be left with another debt she couldn't repay. One that could cost her life.

For the first time, though, she wondered if it mattered.

With a shiver, Mara continued to sift through centuries of debris that had chipped off the limestone and settled in the caverns. Layer upon layer of silt and sediment, nearly too deep to burrow through. Like the chamber floor, her chits were adding up, and it terrified her that she was perilously close to not caring.

"Hey, Mara!" Ethan shouted her name and she lifted her head.

She focused dulled eyes on his position, where Lesley knelt beside him, hand braced on his knee. Biting off a snarl, she mustered a short, "Yeah?"

"Making any headway?"

More like falling into the abyss, she thought caustically. Rhodes Scholar Barbie has me beat fair and square. Aloud, she replied, "No. You?" When he shook his head, she motioned with her flashlight to the benches that lined the end of the chamber. Sinking down on the hard slab, she rubbed at the healed bullet wound, the muscles strained by stretching and groping for a phantom key.

Overhead, grayish rock glistened beneath the wet that seeped into every corner of the cavern. Lesley had described the rock as chert. To Mara's eyes it resembled flint, but the doctor was the expert. When the two joined her, she let out a silent snort of frustration. Here she was, whining and mewling like a nebbish. A cardinal sin. Squaring her shoulders, she rounded on Ethan and Lesley, jaw set, heartache ignored.

She'd lost the love of her life. She'd be damned if she was going to lose the gold.

"Let's regroup. We've been looking for over an hour and nothing yet. We're missing something. Bailey expected to return here, and his clue was designed to help his partners locate the key if he didn't survive the intervening years. Why give coordinates that don't narrow the location?"

Ethan set his foot on the bench, rested his hands on his knee. The same thought had occurred to him. "He mentioned a room filled with diamonds, a well, and a cathedral."

Chiming in, Lesley corrected, "Yes, but the rooms each have matching characteristics. In the first room, the stalactite and stalagmite formations create those columns, which also evoke the cathedral atmosphere. Remember, in 1937 he had no way of knowing what Mr. Bevers used the rooms for. And the room you searched is nicknamed the Crystal Room."

"But there are more crystals in the room we just searched."

Ethan hefted the backpack onto the bench. He drew out Bailey's notes. "Doesn't match up. There are two rooms filled with diamonds. Bailey doesn't mention more than one."

"What about the well? Which room is it in?" Mara rubbed at the tiredness in her shoulders, fatigue warring with determination. "Or is there another room with higher ceilings?"

Lesley recalled her previous visits to the caves and the lecture she'd heard from the tour guides. "The third room is sixty feet deep. If any room resembles a cathedral, the Dome Room does. And the fifth room has the wishing well."

"Fifth room?" A clue ghosted across Mara's thoughts, and she filched the poster from Ethan. Trying to summon the idea that hovered just beyond reach, she studied the symbols. Her thoughts were jumbled, and she sifted through them, trying to focus. Bailey wouldn't have been so clever, would he? Mara stood abruptly, hope spinning madly. "Fifth room. Five. As in delta."

"Delta," Ethan repeated. A grin spread swiftly, and he gleefully cursed the cunning Bailey. "Damnit, you're right. It's a double entendre, Mara. Bailey used five to not only represent the coordinates, but if he told your grandfather anything, it could be another clue. Delta. Water. Well."

"Come on," Mara demanded, moving for the passageway, poster still in hand. "It has to be in there!"

Lesley caught up to her and shifted into the lead. "I'll guide us to the chamber. The Dome Room is vented by a deep shaft to ease the relative humidity. Without the shaft, it would be almost one hundred percent. We'll have to take another staircase to the bypass hallway. It's pitch-black and you don't know the terrain. I do."

Mara reluctantly dropped back. She thought about arguing, but to what end? Never one to ignore the obvious, she had to admit Lesley was the superior guide. "Fine. I'll follow."

Hiking swiftly but carefully, Lesley toured them through the area she called the Coral Passage and into a room steeped in total darkness. Aptly named the Dark Room, their flashlights barely penetrated the murky deep. Light switches protruded from the walls, but she pointed out that if they turned the lights on, one of them would need to retrace their steps to shut the power.

"Instead, I'd advise that we hold onto each other until we make it across." Lesley paused, and Mara gingerly gripped a bunch of silken, expensive fabric.

"Gotcha."

Behind Mara, Ethan curled his hand against her skin, knuckles grazing the small of her back. Tendrils of heat radiated along her spine, and she attempted vainly to ignore the echoing shocks in her belly.

Unaware of her struggle, Ethan waged his own private war. The simplicity of touch held too much power, he realized. Mundane contact of skin to skin should be a nonevent, but instead it set off a cascade of reaction. Molten want pounded through him, flares of recognition that called to him, blood to blood.

Contact with Lesley elicited a pleasant desire, not a fiery urge to devour. To merge.

They picked their way slowly across phosphorescent rock that glowed faintly in the black. His fingers slid against the sleek, smooth skin, softer than air. Half a lifetime stretched between them, and it only took a touch to erase the distance. Foolishly, he had imagined there could be another woman for him, another heart that he wanted to capture. But it was only Mara. Always her.

Certainty settled into him like a revelation, and he tightened his hold. She would balk, he knew, if he told her. Would sneer at him, eyes biting and sarcastic. But he understood her better this time, and if he looked closely, he would see the fear swimming in the amber pools. If she wanted him.

She had to want him.

Anticipation rose, but he quelled it when his conscience pricked. A few paces ahead, Lesley moved sure-footedly across the uneven rocks, a player in a game he'd brought her into unwittingly.

Though they'd made no promises to one another, both understood the reason for his invitation to Kiev. He needed her expertise, yes, but between them had been the promise of more. Of him finally putting the past aside and trying again. Because without Mara in his life, Ethan believed he could have loved Lesley.

But Mara returned and everything changed.

Whether he and Mara worked, Lesley deserved more than a man who could offer a corner of his heart, a pale version of love. Their friendship demanded that he be honest, and his code of honor required nothing less.

Once they found the key, he'd tell her, Ethan promised himself. He climbed the stairs steadily, wondering how she would take the news. Lesley wasn't given to tantrums or dramatic outbursts. The few times he'd seen her livid, she'd sliced a man off with cool tones and brutal wit.

It had been painful to watch.

Ahead of him, Mara stumbled and his hand slid around her waist to steady her. The satin skin warmed beneath his splayed fingers. His grip tightened. "You okay?"

Breathless, she murmured, "I'm fine." She slipped her hand up to cover his beneath her T-shirt, pressing him closer. "Thanks."

Lesley noticed that Mara no longer held her and she paused on a step. Turning, she called, "You guys all right back there?"

Voice rough, Ethan replied, "We're okay. Mara tripped, but she's stable. Here we come."

With deliberate strokes Ethan slid his fingers across her waist to retake the wide band of fabric. Leaning close, he urged, "I'm ready, Mara. Whenever you are."

Mara didn't respond. Instead, she fell into shaky step behind Lesley, trying ever harder to ignore the slide of tantalizing fingers as they traveled deeper into the cavern's hold.

Eventually, Lesley led them to a corridor that declined in

steep descent. They released one another to take firm hold of the handrails. Down they traveled, farther into the heart of the caves. At the bottom of the stairs Lesley levered the door open and introduced them to the Well Room.

"This room is more than 150 feet below the surface. In fact, it's the reason Bevers discovered the cave." Showing them inside, she explained, "He was drilling and the drill bit fell. He and his wife searched for it and found these caverns instead. Later they built a well here. Below us there is an underground aquifer-fed lake that extends west to another cave. Ezell's Cave is the only surface entrance to the cave that contains the lake, but it's protected by guards due to the endangered Texas blind salamander. Of course, when Bailey was here, no one knew or cared about the salamander."

"Would the well have been here when Bailey was?" asked Ethan, turning to survey the cavern walls. To his right a high, broad rock face of limestone contained holes, cracks, and fissures—each of which may have been Bailey's hiding place.

Bailey would have tried to keep the key out of sight for five years. To Ethan's mind, tucking it into one of these breaks in the stone would have seemed a safe bet. Next to him, Mara followed the same train of thought.

Meeting her shuttered look, he could see her reaching the conclusion he had—that the key may have slipped into the ancient limestone and be beyond their reach. Compelled to soothe, he closed a firm hand over hers, feeling the fine tremble that skated along cool skin. "We'll find it, honey. I promise."

Lesley heard the hushed reassurance and inwardly winced. Resignedly, she let the last vestiges of hope slide away. Ethan had never looked at her with the same eyes, she realized, and he never would. With longing and devotion and need.

She may have been able to coax the first two, but the last couldn't be prompted. Clearing her suddenly choked throat, she began to lecture, an instinctive shield. "Bevers designed the well in the early 1920s, I believe. It would have been here. Regardless, this room has the best hope of being what we're looking for." Checking her watch, Lesley saw that seven A.M. was only minutes away. Thank heavens. She didn't think she could watch them not watching each other for another second. "I need to go back up and talk Yvette into giving us more time. Work fast, in case her replacement isn't so nice."

"Be careful," Ethan cautioned as Lesley headed toward the stairs. He tried to touch her shoulder, but she edged out of reach. Ethan let his hand drop but said nothing. Grateful, Lesley disappeared into the black.

Slowly, Ethan turned to Mara. "Why don't you take this section, and I'll work over there?"

"Good." Eyes intense, nerves taut, Mara focused on a formation of coral that again resembled diamonds. Flashing her light over the crystals, she noticed a dark pock where the beam failed to penetrate. She crouched low to examine the crystalline rocks. She shifted through mounds, anticipation singing in her veins. It was close, close enough to touch.

A pile of stones like the chert Lesley had shown her earlier caught her attention. Chert that had hung from the ceiling and walls of the other rooms and was present nowhere else in this room. Using hands steady as stone, she dug through the flint until her fingers felt cave rock. She shone her beam on the cleared area, and illumined a slight break in the stones. A break that curved up and around the stone.

Pulse thudding, breathing short, Mara demanded herself to calm down. Quickly, she grabbed a piece of the discarded flint and jammed the hard, unbreakable stone into the crevice. With effort, she leaned into the makeshift crowbar and moved it around the wedged stone. When the stone popped loose, she teetered slightly but regained her balance. Whispering a prayer, she stuck her hand, unprotected, into the narrow opening. And closed her fingers around a leather pouch.

"Ethan?" The clarion call emerged on a thread of sound and she cleared her throat. "Ethan!"

He lifted his head, and seeing her position, rushed to join her. Skidding to a stop, he knelt by her side. "Did you find something?"

"I believe so." She held up the pouch, its deep brown mottled by the elements but intact. "We found it, Ethan." Silently, she offered him the damp leather.

"Together."

Ethan held the pouch as Mara fumbled with the tightly knotted strings and worked them free. Then she tipped over the lip and a palm-sized brass key tumbled to the cavern floor, the sound echoing through the space. Her heart stopped, redoubled its frenetic beat.

Decades of stories, a lifetime of dreams, gleamed in a bright key. She lifted the key, clutching the cool metal fiercely. "It has more Greek. Omicron and sigma. I don't know what the letters mean, but we have definitely found Bailey's key. One more."

With a victorious whoop, she launched herself at Ethan and the two rolled along the cavern floor, laughing. Ethan stood, scooped her up into his arms. Whirling her giddily, he exclaimed, "I didn't believe. Even when your grandmother told us the story, I didn't believe." He slowed, pulled her close, searching her face in the shadows. His arms banded around her waist, holding her steady. "You did."

Suspended between present and past, between victory and the unknown, she framed his face gently. "Believing isn't enough." Skimming keen fingertips along the familiar planes of his face, she stroked the arch of brow, the hollow near his poet's mouth. Though she spoke the words, both knew she meant more than the lost treasure. "Believing isn't nearly enough."

"What else is there?" He breathed the question into her flesh, nuzzling at the fragrant spot where throat and collar met.

"Knowing."

He held her closer, until her body molded to his, fit into every empty space. "And what if you can't know? What if there are too many questions? Too much hidden from you?" Gently, he drifted a kiss across a mouth that trembled softly. "Do you try anyway?"

The shudder caught her, swept through her. Her lips parted and returned the inquisitive touch. Like lightning, her tongue traced the long, firm lines, tasted and reveled. "You could. But it's a gamble. And you don't enjoy risk, Ethan. That's all I've got. That's what I am."

"Maybe I'm ready for risk. Maybe I need it." For a third time their lips met, but Ethan cupped her head firmly. In slow, terrible forays, he seduced her mouth into opening, into baring its secrets. Sweeping inside, he challenged her slick, restive tongue to duel, to tangle.

When she joined, he sighed his delight and feasted. Cool, then hot, desire drove him to dare. Need coiled inside, straining against reason. Too long he had weighed odds, planned each moment down to the minutest measure. His return to Kiev was a new beginning, a plunge into danger. Nothing frightened him, threatened his peace of mind as much as the woman in his arms. Beneath his questing mouth.

Driven, he caught her lips, his mouth a mimicry of their dance. In. Out. In. Out. Undulating faster, diving deeper, he wrung breathless moans that spurred him to more. Deeper. Hotter. Faster. Every breath was Mara. Every taste, her. Even in the darkness the closeness, the scent and feel and taste, surrounded him. Consumed him. Turning, he fell back against the cavern wall and anchored her to him.

Mara felt the slick serration of rock beneath her palm, but the jagged edges barely penetrated the haze that caught her, held her in thrall. Inside her, around her, there was only Ethan. Only now. Past sins were forgiven. Future transgressions absolved. In this moment she could be true. Could stay and be loved.

Power sang through her veins and pulsed hot and strong. Only he could do this to her. Could make her forget and re-member and not give a damn. Could cajole her into wanting what she could not have.

Refusing to be seduced, she arched into him, wresting con-trol. Now it was she who fed. In strokes of heady torment, she explored the nuances of a kiss. Soft, then sultry. Frenetic, then meditative. A benediction and a spur to race, to conquer. Unsat-isfied, she lathed at the taut line of his neck, the strong muscles corded along his collar.

He caught her breast on the edge of his palm, grazed its tip in search of the firm, delicate flesh. Victory mingled with a crav-ing he hadn't known before and he murmured her name into the air. "Mara. My Mara."

As her named floated up the cavern's shaft, Mara bowed to give him greater access, her eyes wide with stunned pleasure. And she saw the flash of light at the top of the cavern before it gutted out. Lesley.

Mortified, she wriggled free and unhooked her legs, jumping away as though scalded. In a hushed breath she hissed, "Lesley. She's upstairs. Now." And Lesley had seen her wrapped around Ethan, taking what didn't belong. "Your girlfriend saw us." Remembering the hushed endearment, she derided fiercely, burning with embarrassed anger, "Your Lesley. Your Mara. Why don't you make up *your* damned mind?"

Off balance, Ethan checked the precipice and saw the shadow disappear into the dim. Cursing steadily, he waited for his ardor to subside. Damnit, he hadn't intended this—any of it. Not until he'd spoken with Lesley. He wasn't a kid any longer, unable to control his urges. He was a man with responsibilities, and he'd allowed himself to forget. As he habitually did when he was with Mara. The real world fell away, and she became all.

But his clumsiness wasn't anyone's fault but his own. At the least, he owed Lesley an explanation, certainly an apology. The latter, he realized, would be easier. But how could he explain what he barely understood himself. Reaching for Mara, another apology owed, he felt something in him break free. The last of his resistance to the truth. "We need to talk."

"No." Mara stepped away, out of reach. She didn't want to hear another speech about his affection for Lesley, about his antipathy toward her. Defenses down, she wasn't sure she could survive another barrage of *I want you, go away*. Sinking deeper into the cavern's protective shadows, she murmured, "That's the third time, Ethan. I can't do this again. I won't." A sob rose, but the barest of sound escaped.

The wisp of pain echoed, and appalled, Ethan stopped his pursuit. "I'm sorry. Truly." He snatched up the backpack and slung it onto his shoulder. When he turned, Mara still stood in the gloom, eyes downcast. Knowing he shouldn't, determined he would, he crossed to her and forced her to meet his gaze. The wounded tumult he read in the shaded depths shamed him.

And reminded him of the morning he awoke to find Mara gone.

"We're even now. I hurt you, and you've gotten your revenge. I want you and you belong to someone else. My fault. My mistake." Mara jerked at her captive chin. "Let me go."

"I can't." Tipping her mouth up, he kissed her quickly, hungrily. "Give me a few minutes, okay? I owe her an explanation."

Before Mara could respond, he raced to the stairs. At the opening to the cavern, Lesley waited, spine stiff and proud. The passageway was empty, and in the distance he could see the glass doors that opened into the gift shop. Shadows moved in the store, signs that the park was preparing to open. An unwitting audience to the maelstrom he was about to release.

Ethan approached her warily, uncertain of himself and her. If she decided to shove him down the vertical shaft, he wouldn't blame her. Although no declarations had been made between them, he owed her more than the viewing of an enthusiastic, wild grope with his ex-girlfriend.

Contrite, he laid a light hand on her arm, prepared for recoil. Instead, she gently lifted his hand from her skin then dropped it as though it were soiled. He half expected her to whip out a lace handkerchief and dab at the spot where he'd placed his soiled hands.

"Don't touch me, Ethan. Not just yet." The request was frostily polite, but a flush of temper crested her cheeks.

"All right." He held his hands aloft and stepped away. "May I talk to you?"

"Now that your mouth is free, I suppose so."

"I deserve that."

"You deserve a hell of a lot more, damn you. And I deserved better."

"You did. You do." Ethan shoved his hands into his pockets. "I should have told you sooner."

She fumed, annoyed that he defused justified agitation with his admission. But she wasn't satisfied yet. "Told me what? That you're in love with her?"

Ethan considered lying. Wanted to lie and wanted it to be the truth. "Yes. That I'm in love with her."

Hearing the anguish, the friend in her rose and Lesley muttered, "Why didn't you?"

"Because I didn't know. Not then. And I don't want to now. It makes no sense. She's unpredictable and unreliable. She'll lie and cheat and steal. Before breakfast." Ethan paced away, embittered and baffled. "You're incredible, Lesley. Brilliant, gorgeous. Honest. One of my best friends."

"Much like a golden retriever," she retorted mildly. "But Mara is audacious. Bold."

"Reckless. Impractical."

"Smart."

"Sly," Ethan countered. "With no capacity to follow the law."

"With a sense of honor that's all too rare," Lesley said softly. "You respect her."

"She's got this screwed-up code, this integrity that needs a translation dictionary. She'll steal, but won't litter. Fight, but won't curse. She'll stand up for the weakest person, but will run if she might get hurt."

"You admire her." Defeated, she tucked her arm into his and steered him to the gift shop. "I never knew you had a thing for the impish waif type."

Ethan exhaled glumly, relieved. "I'd hoped it was like the mumps, get it once and then you're immune. Mara is a virulent strain of malaria. Once bitten, she stays with you forever."

"Lucky man."

CHAPTER 18

OWN IN THE CAVERN, MARA PACED THE UNEVEN FLOOR, WAIT-ing for Ethan's return. Minutes passed and she could hear a smattering of voices filter through the shaft. A quick peek at her watch revealed that the Wonder Cave Amusement Park staff had likely begun to arrive.

Which begged the question of what she was doing in the belly of a cave, when she'd already gotten what she came for. More, in fact.

She shoved the key into the leather pouch and cinched it angrily. Once again she'd let herself go and found herself floundering alone. It helped to soothe the heat of temper when she thought of the verbal lashing Ethan was enjoying from Lesley. The pleasure dulled, however, as she thought of her complicity.

Like the kisses before, she'd been a willing participant. And the first time, she'd been the instigator. Kicking at a pile of loose stone, Mara cringed. Lesley had every reason to despise her too. Though Lesley would have to work hard to outdo the job she was doing on herself.

In spite of her relaxed moral code, she did have standards. Don't take from those who couldn't afford to lose it. Don't con the helpless. Take credit when it's due and blame where it's warranted. And never compromise your code for a man.

Even if the man in question was the love of your life, she chided herself.

Screwing her courage to the sticking place, Mara sucked in a badly needed fortifying breath and ambled to the staircase. Ethan wasn't the only one who owed Lesley an apology. As demeaning as it would be, she had no choice but to be a woman about it and face Lesley's wrath. Determinedly, she trudged up the steep exit, preparing her mea culpa. If the princess was so inclined, Mara decided she'd even allow the lady a swing without ducking. Or decking her in turn.

Prepared for anything, her mouth fell agape at the sight of Lesley and Ethan fawning over what appeared from a distance to be a crusty old slab of rock. Worse, Ethan seemed to have all of his teeth in place.

Son of a three-toed lily-livered sloth. How had he talked his way around what Lesley had seen? Around what she could still feel coursing through her in seismic bursts of awareness? Advancing, she stopped at the end of the glass counter. Beneath the petrified rock, other fossils had been tagged and placed on display. Unimpressed by the centuries of scientific history, she asked silkily of Lesley, "Why is he still vertical?"

"Because he grovels well and he's buying me this." She extended a jeweled hand to the calcified rock. "I've had my eye on it for months." Reading the banked distress, hidden by the fierce glitter of anger, Lesley tugged Mara away from the counter.

"What do you want?" Mara asked frostily, jerking her elbow free.

Possible answers snaked through Lesley's mind, including several that would have Mara squirming. But she recognized the look of resignation and the hopeless tone in the throaty voice. The sneak thief was braced for the worse, expected it. A deep, almost imperceptible hurt glittered behind the fierce stare, belying the belligerent set of her shoulders. Feeling generous, she relented. "The same thing you do."

Mara squared her shoulders. "What exactly is that?"

"Let's not play word games. Ethan told me everything, and I'm okay with it. We'll be fine."

"Fine?"

"You really did a number on him, Mara. For years no one has been able to get within striking distance. Friendship, sex, sure. But both with the same woman? Ethan wouldn't permit it. It took me years to get him to tell me what had ruined it for the rest of us."

"He told you about me?"

"Not exactly." Lesley chuckled lightly. "But sufficient detail to show me that you were my version of Excalibur. Prying the story of your teenage romance out of Ethan was damned near impossible. It was nothing compared to getting you out of his heart."

Mara had no retort. Or reaction. Surely, she thought dimly, having your heart ripped clean of your body would remove the possibility of sensation. Though she hadn't realized it until now, she thought his kiss downstairs had meant something. Had meant everything.

Refusing to collapse, she nodded once. Feigning humor, she managed tightly, "I'd make him throw in a snow globe or something." She clutched the leather pouch in one hand and fished the car keys out of her pocket with the other, numbed fingers. "While he finishes his penance, I'm going out to the car."

By the time she reached the sleek, green convertible, insentience had worn off, to be replaced by a shaking, driving fury. She jammed the car keys into the lock, ripped the door open. The kiss, the kisses, she fumed, had meant nothing to him. To either of them. Here she was, racked by guilt, and to Ethan and Lesley she was a means to an end, with side benefits for him.

A light touch landed on her shoulder, and she rounded on Ethan, fist cocked. "Don't you dare touch me. Never again."

"Mara?" Warily, he stepped away, hands raised. "What's wrong?"

"Better question is what in the name of Charles Dickens is wrong with you?" Holding Bailey's key like a talisman, she dangled the pouch between them. "Did you two plan this with Davis? Lure me here, seduce me into helping you find the keys?"

"Are you crazy?" Ethan searched her eyes, looking for signs

of trauma. Maybe she'd hit her head when he left her in the caverns. Once he'd spoken with Lesley, he intended to fetch Mara, but they'd been distracted by the shop owner and her fossil collection. Mara had joined them before he could break away. He'd followed her out to the car to explain, but now he was more concerned about the bloody murder he could read in the bitter amber depths.

Palms out, he explained slowly, "We've had this discussion once already, Mara. Davis is using us both. And Lesley came to help me. She had nothing to do with any of this until I asked for her help. You know this, Mara."

"I don't know anything," she countered. "I don't know why you kissed me, and I'm at a freakin' loss as to why I care. You are a two-timing slug who can't seem to remember which woman he's with. Even with the lights on."

Because she wasn't completely wrong, Ethan couldn't take offense. In the past week he'd taken advantage of Mara and of Lesley, and it chagrined him to acknowledge his cavalier actions. But in the dim of the caverns he'd found clarity. Light. He'd found Mara.

"I've made mistakes since you returned, yes. I've apologized to Lesley, and now I'm apologizing to you."

"For what? Kissing me or lying to her?"

"Both." Ethan eased closer, and Mara retreated. "Lesley and I are over. We're just friends."

Friends? Is that what Lesley meant? Afraid to believe, she

remained hidden behind the safety of the door. Sneering, she taunted, "What happened, darling? She refused to take you back?"

"I didn't ask her to." He leaned forward, caging her between the door with its lowered window and the car frame. A breeze drifted past, stirring the black curls that framed a face he'd never been able to forget. "I told her the truth. That I want you." Pausing, he searched for the right way to tell her the rest. That he loved her.

Mara went still, eyes narrowed. *Want.* So pallid a description for the storm that raged between them each time they touched. Nausea rose, a sickly surge. A week ago having Ethan want her again would have been more than she dared imagine. Was it too little for her to accept?

It was what she dreamed of on empty nights, sneaking from town to town. Someone to want her, to need her. For Ethan to forgive her and hold her close. Some days she had been willing to beg. But now she wanted more. Needed more. Would have more. Tone dry, she replied quizzically, "For how long? Until we find the gold?"

Disconcerted by her lackadaisical air, he replied, "Is that an offer?"

"Depends." Mara relaxed against the car, the metal warm from the risen sun. Over Ethan's shoulder she could see Lesley hovering near the entryway. "Where does she fit in?"

Ethan didn't ask whom. He tossed back, "We've reached an

understanding. She'll help us decipher the remaining clues on the way to the San Marcos airport. Lesley's taking a sabbatical for a while."

"Because of this?" She glanced at the key that hung from her fingers. "Is it safe?"

"I didn't tell Conroy she was coming, and Linda doesn't think she was followed. Her trip is merely a precaution." Ethan reached out to grip her shoulders, careful not to hurt. But it was imperative that she hear him. That he give her fair warning. "Lesley gets on that plane, and it's just you and me, Mara. Us. No one else between us—not your father or your grandfather or our past. Are you ready to deal with that? With us?"

Mara heard the words and the passion raging beneath. She lifted her hands to where his fingers dug into her skin and pried them away. "I've been running for twelve years, Ethan. From everyone and everything. And I'm tired." Unconsciously, she threaded their hands, palm to palm. "I ran because I was afraid for you. Afraid of what being with me could do to you."

"You didn't answer my question."

Flexing her hand, she measured the steel beneath his skin, the firm, solid strength of him. Ethan was strong. Resilient. So was she. Strong enough to stay. To fight. To win. She lifted his hand, brought it to her mouth. Pressing a kiss to the work-roughened skin, she swore an oath. "I'm not going any-where, Ethan. This time, you're stuck with me."

"Then let's go."

"**DESTROYED?**" **DAVIS CONROY** softly repeated the news delivered by Rabbe, who slowly shifted away from the glossy metallic desk with its polished surface. The explosion he expected would be more terrifying than the one that had ravaged the warehouse.

Coming to the headquarters in Austin hadn't been his choice. He'd left Guffin behind in Kiev to dig up what he could on the cause of the fire. Though *left* was a generous term. They'd flipped a coin and arm-wrestled for the privilege of hanging back rather than facing their employer's ire. Guffin, the bastard, managed to cheat him out of both tries.

"We were watching the place like you said to, Mr. Conroy. Twenty-four-hour surveillance." Hearing the nervous tremor in his words, he braced himself. " 'Round ten-thirty or so we heard a series of pops. Loud ones, like big firecrackers. We rushed the building, but by the time we made the door, flames were everywhere." He and Seth decided to omit the actual details. Like the fact that they'd initially fled the area, hightailing it toward Louisiana. Then Guffin reminded him of the reach Davis Conroy had. Convinced they could salvage the debacle if they brought him good information, they returned to Kiev, stashed the SUV in an alley, and crept back on foot to watch the drama.

Sirens had wailed on the street, too late to save the warehouse. Firefighters tarnished with blackened ash had stormed the facility, and when Rabbe—playing the innocent bystander— asked after the condition of the building, one grim-faced man explained it to him.

"Somehow, the fire started in the lab where Dr. Stuart was working. Seems his chemicals got mixed together and caught fire," Rabbe now repeated dutifully to Conroy. "One of the chemicals acted as an accelerant and the flames made their way up to the loft level."

"Stuart and Ms. Reed are dead?" Again the question was subdued, almost meditative.

"Yes, sir. I think so." As were his chances of making half a million dollars. "The fireman said no one could have survived."

"Did they carry anyone out? Any bodies?"

Rabbe nodded. "Two bags. Man said the heat was so intense, it must have incinerated the bodies."

Conroy perked up at the comment. "Incinerated? Why would he mention that?"

Shrugging, Rabbe explained, "Guy said the skeletons barely had flesh on them. Had to figure the heat and the chemicals burned it off."

"You idiot." The insult was mild, a stark contrast to the furiously hooded brows that seemed to measure Rabbe for his shroud. "I told you Stuart was conducting research for me. That he was a forensic anthropologist."

Unable to discern why a dead man's job mattered, Rabbe decided to play along. "Sure. He was a doctor of some kind."

"He studied dead bodies, fool. Skeletons. The kind you could plant in a room when you decide to set fire to a warehouse and fake your own death." If he hadn't been so livid, Conroy would have chuckled at the ingenuity. What better

way to buy time to hunt for his money than to convince everyone that you were dead?

"But, boss, we were watching the building. Ain't no way in or
out except through the loading dock in the alley."

"Are you sure?"

Shit, he had been until Conroy asked the question. "We
haven't seen anyone enter or leave any other way," he defended.

"You wouldn't, if they were using another exit." Agitated
now, Conroy seized the telephone that rested near his elbow.
When the call connected, he instructed tersely, "Bring me the
blueprints for the warehouse we purchased in Kiev, Texas."

Seconds later a pallid, anxious man hovered in the doorway,
red hair receding almost by the minute. "Here, sir. Anything
else, sir?" Setting the roll onto the desk, he tripped his way to
the door. Summonses from Conroy often led to menacing instructions and the vague, undeniable threat of his untimely
death. He danced nervously, wondering what mistake he may
have made today. The miniature steno pad that he habitually
carried was creased from his handwringing. The pencil tucked
behind his ear bobbled. "Did I do something wrong, sir?"

"Shut up, Nigel." The growl caused both employees to inch
farther away. Conroy didn't notice, his attention glued on the
tracery of white lines across the expanse of blue. The Chi Development warehouse had been purchased at his instructions,
based on Dr. Stuart's needs. A working space with coolers and
room for laboratory equipment. A loft area for living and re-
cording the doctor's findings. The former brewery had been a

terrific find, cheap and easily purchased. At the time, he had no reason to be concerned about exits and entries, before he learned of the connection between Stuart and Mara.

Tracking a shaded area in the warehouse, Conroy found what he feared. His fingers curled into a fist and he said, "Nigel, come here."

At his approach, Conroy stabbed the page. "What is this?" Willing himself to calm, to think, he resisted the primal urge to throttle the insipid clerk who managed his accounts. Nigel's only saving grace was a genius for numbers and a preternatural ability to avoid taxation.

Peering down through trifocals that slid precipitously toward the end of his beaked nose, Nigel hazarded, "A tunnel of some sort?"

"A tunnel. Yes. A goddamned secret tunnel that seems to lead out and up to the street." Conroy drew along the tunnel and up to the higher elevation map. "Join us, Arthur."

Rabbe, who had sidled to the doorway, cursed beneath his breath. He returned to the desk. "Sir?"

"Call Guffin. Tell him to go inside the warehouse. Check the cold storage area for a tunnel of some sort. See where it leads."

"You think they got out?" Rabbe muttered the question, but believed. Smart bitch, he wouldn't put it past her.

"I'm sure of it." Settling in, Conroy pondered their move. He ignored Nigel and focused his attention on Rabbe. So far the man had proven a dismal failure, and because Seth had vouched for him, both would suffer the consequences. But it was too late to bring in a new team. Rabbe had blood lust driving him, a primitive, powerful force. Like a dog, if he could scent the trail, Rabbe would fall on Mara Reed quickly enough.

"Ms. Reed and Dr. Stuart are probably in the area. Send out feelers looking for them." Conroy reached into a drawer and removed a file. STUART, ETHAN had been typed across in bold black letters. He read through the pages, and finding what he wanted, he nodded. "Nigel, call our friend at the Texas Rangers. Have him put out an APB on Dr. Stuart's mint-green 'sixty-seven Plymouth convertible."

"Radius, sir?"

From his father's stories, he knew they'd each traveled from Austin to hide the keys. The one he possessed had been found in Round Rock, less than fifteen miles from Austin. Not surprising, Conroy acknowledged, given the fact that his father had been a lazy son of a bitch. The more enterprising members of Reed's troupe had traveled farther, he imagined. But they would have moved by horse or estimably slower motor transport. "A radius of 150 miles. But tell them not to stop the car, just report back to you."

Swiveling in his prized chair, the leather a product of his own hands, he offered the muted warning to the man awaiting dismissal. "Stay in contact with Nigel. When he's found the car, you need to track them closely. Don't let them know you're there."

"Yes, sir."

"Arthur, this is your last chance. Very last one. See that you succeed, all right?"

CHAPTER 19

THE THROBBING HUM OF THE MOTOR AND THE RHYTHMIC SLAP of air against the windshield. A bluesy number soaring through the speakers, a quixotic rumination on love and loss. Grateful for the breaks in the awkward silence, Ethan drove the convertible at a steady pace, skimming below the speed limit. He longed to open the engine up, to blast down the empty highway, but caution reigned.

The same caution that held him silent.

The trio in the car had a million things to talk about, but for the life of him, he couldn't think of anything to say. He'd explained and apologized several times already that morning. After a while the most sincere contrition seemed trite.

Instead of repeating himself, he twisted the knob and music poured through louder. Checking his mirror, he zipped around a slow-moving RV and eased over into the right lane. Saturday morning in San Marcos yielded sparse traffic, except for the semis common to Texas. Other than the semis, an indiscriminate trail of SUVs, and the occasional family wagon, the roads were empty. He slid a glance along the front seat to verify that he still had passengers.

Beside him, Lesley peered through half-glasses and reviewed Mara's sheaf of notes. She handily balanced an atlas on one thigh, using Ethan's lap for overflow space. Though she'd forgiven his romantic clumsiness, the frosty politeness that confronted him when he dared ask a question kept him quiet. Perhaps he could have struck up conversation with Mara, but he had no idea what she'd say. And for him, ignorance was bliss.

Mara turned her face into the swift breeze whipping over the open car. She'd play the next few days out like a long con. Short-term goal—prove to Ethan and to herself that she could stick. But the big payoff, if she could pull it off, would be showing Ethan that he loved her too. That the years and the lies and people in between had never been more than an interruption. Lesley had a point. She lived in Ethan's heart.

She just had to show him where.

Turning on the leather bench, she queried, "Any progress, Lesley? Poncho wasn't one for journals or letters."

Lesley blew out a breath. "No, he wasn't. According to your notes, Poncho traveled with your grandfather until they settled down at the church. And you deciphered his symbol as qoppa diagamma and lambda. Ninety-six by thirty degrees. But I've detected a strange symmetry in the drawing you made of what you and Ethan found on the body. The symbol of ninety-six has been drawn together and then inverted inside itself. And inside the lambda there's a smaller letter. An *n*, I believe."

"Nu. The symbol for fifty." Mara tapped the atlas, thinking. "That's how we realized it wasn't like the others. Too many numbers."

"Do you know anything at all about his background before he hooked up with your grandfather? Any clue at all?"

Mara pursed her mouth thoughtfully. "My grandmother once told me that Poncho served as a scout with the army before joining up with my grandfather. He would have been very precise with his coordinates, more so because of his relationship with Micah." She traced the faint lines of the map. "Is there any place of importance at 96.69 and 30.50 degrees?"

Lesley tracked the coordinates and nodded. "Caldwell, Texas. Seventy-nine miles from Austin."

"A hard day's ride, but doable." Ethan gave the map a swift look. "What is it close to?"

Mara scanned the tiny dots on the map. Texas was a state of hundreds of miniature towns, closed enclaves born when gold or oil or war struck. She named several that were near Caldwell. "And a place called Santa Therese."

Lesley's head shot up. "There was a huge oil strike there in 1931," she supplied with a thread of excitement. "Old army scouts often got jobs searching for new loads back then. If Poncho was good at his job, he probably would have been a natural for one of the teams."

"Where would you hide a brass key in an oil strike?" asked Ethan.

"I wouldn't," Lesley replied. "Too many people moving around, digging for the next strike. Professionals know better, but amateur wildcatters swarm over a find and scavenge for the dregs. In the twenties, few would have had the equipment to dig carefully. If he returned to Santa Therese, he would have put it somewhere else. A place where it wouldn't be disturbed."

"A cemetery." Ethan and Lesley looked to Mara, who'd murmured the idea. She spoke meditatively. "Nana said he liked cemeteries."

Narrowing her eyes, Lesley concurred. "Could be. Santa Therese went dry in the late 1950s. Whole town moved out. But they left their dead behind. We should give the cemetery there a try." Beside her, she felt Mara stiffen, but she let the collective "we" linger. She might have conceded the war to the little thief, but she wasn't convinced Mara was good for Ethan. And while she could be gracious, she wasn't ready to assuage Mara's sensibilities and vanish just yet.

Ethan heard the slip too. "Lesley, have you changed—" Before he could finish, he noticed a black SUV dart out from behind the trailer and then slip out of sight. It was the third time he'd seen it peek out and hide. "Mara, check your mirror."

"What am I looking for?" She fixed her eyes on the glass, which was filled with the cab of the semi behind them.

"Wait for it." Timing his move, Ethan slowed up. The semi

honked at him imperiously, annoyed. When the horn sounded again, Ethan dodged out and into the left lane. "Now."

Immediately, the black SUV zoomed into the passing lane behind their convertible. Ethan gunned the engine. The rev of the engine barely masked Mara's response. "Catfish fries and toads! It's Rabbe and Guffin."

"They've been on our trail for a while." Ethan shifted the car into the right lane once more, giving the semi a wide berth. "I didn't notice at first, but they kept creeping up then hanging back. Caught my attention."

"Nice job." Quickly, Mara calculated their odds. The convertible was fast, but neither she nor Ethan was armed. The men chasing them definitely came with firepower. Right now, Conroy's goons had no reason to suspect that their prey knew they were being hunted. "How far away is the airport?"

"Five minutes out." Following her plan, Ethan spurred the car faster. "Lead them to the airport and then sneak out?"

"It's our best option. They'll track us inside, thinking we're trying to run. With security these days, we can have the cops on them in no time."

"Track us?" Lesley chimed in, voice dubious. "As in, we'll be bait?"

"I will be." Mara twisted in her seat to face Lesley and Ethan. "Drop me off in front of the terminal. Rabbe isn't a fool, but he's no genius. He'll probably drop Guffin off and keep following you. Which means you'll need to set Lesley out of the car too. With only two of them, they'll have to pick a target. You're a known quantity. She isn't. They'll pick you."

"How do you know?" Lesley folded her arms to stop the tremors of panic. She struggled to keep her voice level. "These are the same men that kidnapped you and shot you, aren't they? Why wouldn't he simply shoot me as collateral damage?"

"Because if they tracked us to the caves, they believe we know where the gold is. Conroy has probably given them instructions to capture but not harm us."

"Probably? That's the best you can do?"

Mara met the doubtful look with one of morbid comprehension, wishing she could offer more. She recognized the dilated pupils, the sudden pallor brought by unwelcome glimpses of mortality.

She'd seen the look in a dozen mirrors and learned to control the loss of color. But Lesley's shocked concern resonated. She was frightened, and she had reason to be. Rabbe and Guffin had gotten to her twice now. Regardless of how fast she ran, how cannily she hid, they scented her. This time she had two novices whose safety depended on how slyly skilled she really was. Brand new territory. Having partners. Having other lives depend on her actions.

Adrenaline, a shocky jolt to a system wired too tightly, careered through veins narrowed in taut reaction. Impatiently, insistently, Mara warded off the rush of nerves and tension, forcing her pulse to slow, her breath to even. She owed them a way out, and she'd find one. And honesty. "Probably. Maybe. Lesley, I can't give you guarantees. If I were alone, I'd know what to do. But I've got you two to worry about."

"We all have our talents, Mara." Ethan loosed his attention from the trailing SUV and shot her a steadying look. With a shrug, he pointed out wryly, "I found the bones. Lesley located the cave. Yes, you've found a couple of the keys, but you haven't earned your keep yet. But this is your territory. Being smart enough to survive. To take care of the ones who depend on you. You're the expert here, baby. You know what we need to do."

He believed in her, Mara realized, dazed by the easy support. She searched his words for hidden meaning, for subtle sarcasm, but could only find a trust that humbled her. Emboldened her.

Outside the car, the airport exit sign flashed past, warning them that they only had a quarter mile left to decide on a plan. Mara raced through the options. Something Lesley had said about collateral damage. The phrase rolled in her mind, churning fast. *Collateral damage.*

Then it hit her. "Ethan," she said, speaking hurriedly, a plan forming. "I need you to miss the exit."

Lesley frowned. "I thought we were going to the airport. That SUV can overtake us anytime it wants."

"I know. And we are. Going to the airport. But first we need to buy some time." She monitored the SUV while she explained. "Clear?"

"The exit is coming up. Lesley, get into position." Mara scrambled to store their notes and the atlas, securing the lot beneath the front seat. In a second everything not latched down would be airborne.

She watched the mirror closely, muttering to herself. "Sorry, Mr. Trucker. Collateral Damage. Hope you drive good." The exit lane veered off from the highway, and she commanded, "Now!"

At her command, Ethan spun the car out, tires skidding wildly. In pantomime of a blowout, he shot past the exit sign and bumped the convertible onto the shoulder. The tractor trailer, with its long, silver containers, laid on the horn and attempted to screech to a halt. The canisters streamed behind him like a banner, sliding across the asphalt.

"Look out!" Guffin yelled as the trailer swayed blindly. Unprepared for the sudden downshift in the semi's speed, Rabbe charged into the left lane, placing the truck between the SUV and the green convertible.

Cursing roundly, he demanded, "Did you see if they took the exit?" Without awaiting an answer, he gunned the engine and whizzed past the truck. Annoyed, the semi also picked up speed, shielding the shoulder of the road from view. "Damnit, I can't see a goddamned thing!" He jammed the gas and, as the speedometer hit one hundred, he left the truck in his wake. "See 'em?"

"How could I see anything? Stupid trucker nearly killed us both." Anxiously, Guffin studied the blacktop. He couldn't see much with the haze of oil rising in the heat obscuring all but the mirage of other vehicles. "We should go back and check the airport, Rabbe."

"We'll lose time that way. Mr. Conroy thought they'd move to another town to find the next key. That's where we're going."

"But which town?"

"I don't know." Rabbe recalled with a greasy horror their employer's icy reception an hour ago. Bastard hadn't been happy when they explained how they found the green convertible and the occupants. "He was good and pissed that they'd been in the caves for so long before we arrived. Conroy thinks they found something."

"And he didn't like us not knowing about the other woman." Guffin had interviewed the gift shop staff. "Ms. Howard said she's a regular. Teaches at UT with Dr. Stuart."

Which gave Rabbe pause. "What the hell do a geologist and a CSI guy have to do with Mr. Conroy's fortune? And what does that skirt have in common with either of them?"

Guffin had been puzzling over the same questions, though he hadn't thought of Ms. Reed so crudely. "The journal you found in Detroit for Mr. Conroy. You said it was some kind of treasure map."

"Sort of. Notes talked about a heist back in the 1930s. Mentioned Spanish gold. Conroy gave me $50,000 to pay for it, but I got it from the owner without having to spend a nickel." A nice profit, until the bitch stole his money. "Thought fifty large was a lot to pay for some old papers."

"Maybe she works for them. Got hired to steal the stuff from you." Secretly, Guffin held back a chuckle. The thought of his misogynistic partner being taken by Mara Reed tickled the dickens out of him. Rabbe reveled too much in the torment of the fairer sex, a practice Guffin abhorred. The job might dictate a bit of harm, he acknowledged, but gratuitous violence against women turned his stomach. "Guess stealing your fifty was a bonus."

Snarling, Rabbe pushed the SUV above 120, swearing to catch up with the green car. Now he had three enemies—the bitch, her boyfriend, and the other bitch. Maybe he'd do them both and have the nerd boy watch. Miles flew by as he followed the winding highway.

"Arthur?"

"What?"

Guffin moved his shoulders diffidently. "I think they may have taken the airport exit. We've gone nearly twenty miles, and I don't think an old Plymouth is that fast."

AT THE ARRIVAL terminal, Lesley stood on the curb while Ethan unloaded her bags. Mara leaned against the scorching hood, unable to figure out how to play this one. After all, what was the proper decorum when a woman stole another woman's almost lover? Despite all the roles she'd played before, this one was new.

"You don't have to say anything." Lesley advanced to stand

next to her, shoulder-to-shoulder. Versace sunglasses reflected the bright rays, while Mara squinted against the glare. Together, silently, they watched passengers being unloaded and luggage pile up along the curb. "Ethan is afraid of you."

The comment startled Mara, but she merely replied, "Why? I'm no threat to him."

Laughing softly, Lesley corrected, "You're a threat to everything." Feeling magnanimous, she patted the younger woman's arm. "Ethan is a good, solid man who desperately wishes he weren't. He pays his tickets on the last day they're due, but he pays them. And I realize he was attracted to me because I'm a good, solid woman who speaks her mind and is just a little out of the ordinary. Growing up as I did, I had the freedom to be singular, but he didn't."

Mara stiffened. "I know. I've known him longer than you have."

"Don't get your hackles up, Mara. Let me finish my good deed for the day." Lesley faced her, tipped the glasses up, and locked their eyes. "Once in his life has Ethan done exactly what he wanted and damn the consequences. When he fell in love with you. That act of derring-do earned him an empty wallet and a broken heart. A dozen years wasted, pining for the one that got away. For some reason, probably testosterone poisoning, he wants to try it again. But he is convinced that if he does, you'll disappear. Again."

"I love him," Mara protested. "I don't want to hurt him."

"Forgive the amateur psychology, but you loved him before.

And you sacrificed your happiness together to save him. From your father or yourself. Doesn't really matter. Until you're ready to stand for him, you've already got one foot out the door. And this time, Mara, if you let him go, I won't give up so easily." Seeing Ethan moving toward them, she reached into the front seat and slung the strap of her black Coach bag over her shoulder. "My last bit of advice. Don't wait for him to see that you've changed. Show him. He's a scientist for a reason. He only believes in what he can see."

"Ready?" Ethan offered his arm gallantly, and Lesley slid her hand through.

Tossing a conspiratorial grin over her shoulder, Lesley finished, "Take care, Mara. Good luck with your treasure hunt. Be sure you know what you're looking for. As the expression says, you just might get your heart's desire."

CHAPTER 20

WE OUGHT TO FIND A MOTEL AND CAMP FOR THE NIGHT." Mara twisted to face Ethan, eyes shuttered against the afternoon glare. Dusk would be coming soon, and because they were avoiding major roadways, a two and a half hour trip had stretched inexorably into four. Fatigue deadened her eyelids and she blinked sleepily.

Too much had happened in the past week, too much for her system to process. Her exhaustion was mirrored in the slump to Ethan's shoulders, the lethargic glaze over black irises. "You're on your last legs, and it's an amateur mistake not to refuel when you've gotten the advantage. We won't have it for long," she warned. "Rabbe will be looking for us."

"He'll have to be damned good to find us out here." Ethan peered out at the rutted farm road, lined by sun-scorched grass tendrils that begged for rain. Though he'd grown up in an eerily similar town, the likeness jarred. Made him think of a time when he had rumbled along a country road, Mara tucked beneath his arm. "Where exactly will we find a motel around here? I only have credit cards with me, and I've watched plenty of movies where they use credit card receipts to track you."

"Good point. I don't have much cash." But they couldn't stay on the road, and with all of Ethan's belongings strewn across the backseat, they couldn't camp out in the car. Only one man she knew could help them out. Assuming he was available and amenable. Mara stuck out her hand. "Let me use your cell phone."

Ethan fumbled in his pocket and dropped the device into her outstretched hand. "Why don't you have a phone?"

"Too easy to triangulate locations these days. Plus, a good sound man can tap into a conversation and you're toast." That she'd used both techniques herself wasn't worth mentioning, she decided. "But cell towers are so sparse out here, they'll have a hard time pinning down a location for us," she explained breezily.

"Reassuring."

Ignoring the dry comment, Mara tapped in a phone number. After a brief pause, the call connected. "Sebastian? Hey, you."

"Find your pot of gold, darling?" Standing in the shadows of a bank, tropical breeze wafting past, waiting impatiently for the clerks to tack up the Closed sign, Sebastian welcomed the distraction. "Or other, more tempting prizes?"

"Getting close," she responded, deliberately vague. She had no intention of discussing Ethan with a smug Sebastian. The man already thought too highly of his insight. "But I'm in a bit of a jam. Conroy has been able to track us down, and now Rabbe's got us hiding out in cattle country. I need a motel. Paid in full before my arrival. Can you help?"

Sebastian heard the thread of exhaustion in the lovely southern lilt that he adored. Once again he regretted not being able to join her on her expedition, but Mara had been determined to make her own way. Stubborn lady. "Are you certain you wouldn't prefer more plush digs? It continues to disturb me how cavalier you are with your accommodations."

"No time for snobbery." They had this argument each time they worked together. Of course, Sebastian's only dependents were himself and his ego; while she had more pressing demands on her earnings. "We need a place fast and one that won't ask for identification." She quickly gave him an approximation of their location. "Cheap and seedy."

With a sigh, he lowered his phone and engaged another program. Seconds later he located a suitable hovel. "In a town fifteen miles away. The Renegade Saloon and Motel. I've arranged for the room, but I would expect you'll need quarters for the bed."

"Funny." Mara grabbed a pen and pad. "Where is it?"

Sebastian rattled off the directions, and after another caustic lament about her lack of taste, rang off. Mara scribbled the last of the information. "We've got a place to stay."

"Exactly who in the hell is Sebastian?"

Mara swiveled her head, startled. In profile, Ethan resembled nothing so much as an angry god about to smite a hapless peon.

The change in countenance was instructive. His long, sensuous mouth had thinned ominously in unexpected reaction. Nostrils flared and the black eyes went flat. Slowly, guardedly, she answered, "A friend."

His voice lowered the temperature in the car by several degrees. "Is he a close friend?"

"Best friend." Aware she tempted fate, Mara nevertheless smiled at the memory of how she and Sebastian first met. Two enraged men who blamed her for their losses at the track had planned to exact their pound of flesh literally. Sebastian made the first of many well-timed appearances, and Mara learned a nifty way of laying a man out flat. "I've known him for a long time. He's also a colleague."

Colleague. The same meaningless description he'd used for Lesley, Ethan realized. But with Mara, relationships appeared fluid, easily disrupted by the moment's impulse. Betrayingly, terribly, it occurred to him that he might simply be a pastime for her, something to do in Texas while hunting for treasure. They hadn't discussed tomorrow or whether she had any plans.

A dull ache settled around his chest, rawed his throat as he remembered her promise. *No more running.* Which didn't mean she wouldn't walk away. After all, if they were successful, she'd have more gold than Midas. Exactly what she'd searched for her entire life.

How foolish of him to imagine, for even a second, that he might mean more than money. More than excitement and danger and the art of the deal.

Especially if she had a partner willing to skirt the law with her. A man who brought a secretive smile to her face and was used to paying for her motel rooms.

Deliberately, Ethan squeezed the steering wheel, trying to level his tone, still his harshly thudding pulse. He had no right to interrogate her, no expectation that she'd been alone all these years. That she didn't have someone waiting for her wherever she called home. But jealousy and logic were poor bedfellows. He asked tightly, "Does he often make hotel reservations for you?"

"When I need help, yes." Mara clasped her hands beneath her chin, trying to fathom what she could hear beneath his words. Anger wound through his short, terse questions, buttressed by what sounded distinctly like jealousy. There was something else, but the description eluded her.

"Is he your lover?" The bald question tore out of him, and Ethan fixed his eyes on the road. Throat rough with confused frustration, he asked grittily, "Does he know you're with me?"

Puzzled by the accusation, especially when she recalled their earlier passenger, Mara retorted, "We're friends. Like you and Lesley."

In response, the convertible's engine roared as Ethan streaked forward. He shot her a narrow look. "I told you about Lesley the day you arrived."

"Actually, I heard her on the answering machine."

"The point is, you knew about her. Why haven't you mentioned him?" *And what the hell does he mean to you?* He'd cut out his own tongue before he asked, though.

"Sebastian doesn't really care to have his name bandied

about." Mara slid low on the seat, propped her feet on the dashboard. Guilt bumped into smug pleasure as she unraveled what was eating at Ethan. Fear. Of her and the life she led. She should tell him the whole truth, she thought.

"Is he as slimy as Rabbe or do you have better decision-making skills when it comes to picking bedmates?"

"Careful, Ethan."

"I'm just asking questions. If he's important to you, I'd like to know."

"He prefers to keep a low profile."

"Avoiding the cops?" Ethan notched the speedometer higher. Because he wanted to beg for an explanation, he sneered, "Sounds like a winner."

"Sebastian is a unique man. Very good at what he does." She permitted the innuendo to drift between them, enjoying the reversal. Watching Lesley and Ethan together had been hell. Ethan could rely on his imagination until he bothered to ask for the truth. Before he could respond, flat prairie yielded to more civilization. Mara glanced at her notes and instructed, "Take Route 21. The motel isn't far."

"I will pay him back." Hating the thought of indebtedness, Ethan scowled. "Call him and tell him I'll pay him back."

"I will not." Mara suppressed a chuckle, knowing it would only lead to an explosion. "He's not paying for your room. He's paying for mine. If you'd like to share it with me, you're welcome to do so. Then you can pay me and salve your ego at the same time."

"This isn't about ego," Ethan muttered. Driven, he edged the car faster. "I simply don't like owing someone I don't know."

"Liar."

He eased off the gas. Wearily, he swiped at his face, tired of trying to guess what lay ahead of him. In a sea of unsolved mysteries and hidden sins, her answer at this moment was the only one that mattered. Pride lost, he repeated on a desperate whisper, "Are you lovers?"

Mara thought of how she could use this, the whispered question that hung between them. Knots of tension tightened her gut, lodged in her throat. She understood the power of jealousy, how it could evoke passions and promises that would undo a lifetime of regret. A week ago, even five days ago, she would have told him yes and used his reaction to goad. The Mara she'd been would have lied to him without remorse and used his emotions to her ends. Would have stoked them until he told her anything she desired to hear.

"No. Sebastian and I are just friends. Only. Ever."

Ethan slanted her a solemn look. "You were about to lie to me, weren't you?"

With a wicked slash of a grin, she admitted, "Thought about it. Men do stupid things when they're jealous." She sobered abruptly. "I won't lie to you, Ethan. Not again."

He didn't bother to protest that he wasn't jealous, not with the surge of relief he'd felt. More, he was intrigued by her oath. "Why not?"

Why not? indeed. Mara stared at the blacktop, the slender

white lines flashing past in rapid succession. A pattern repeated so often that it became truth. Like lying and wishing, like wanting without expecting to have. Like being so close to Ethan that he found it impossible to ever let her go. In her mind the white lines faded into images. His mouth on hers. Bodies fused. Heat and need and yearning wrapped around them. Binding them. Her skin shivered in reaction as she decided.

"Because I don't want lies between us tonight. Especially not tonight." She slid across the bench, the motion sinuous and threatening. Remembering Lesley's admonition about initiative, she curled her hand around lean muscle, daring him to look. Mara nipped at his ear, her words a wisp of sensation and sound.

"Tonight, we both come clean, Ethan. No Lesley. No Sebastian. No twelve-year-old lies. Just you and me." Tracing the line of his jaw, feeling his body stir so near her fingers, her voice grew husky as she seduced. And let herself believe. "Drive fast."

THE CAR STOOD idle in the lot, its dimmed lights facing Room 152. Beyond the flimsy blue door, a honeymoon suite had been decked out in a wide, king-sized bed draped in gaudy red and gold. Ornate scrolls and tacky cupids hung on the walls, decorated the single bureau that languished in a corner of the motley room.

Mara stood on threadbare maroon carpet and waited. It seemed forever that she'd waited. Tonight she'd come full circle.

No more running. The oath sang in her head, in her blood. Ethan—brilliant, steady, courageous Ethan—would be hers once more.

Crimson danced around her in sunset. Ethan watched, determined to memorize every detail, every second. How the silky black curls slid luxuriously against his fingers. How amber eyes heated as he stroked the creamy skin at her temple.

Because he was a scientist, he felt compelled to question. To understand where this experiment would lead. "What are we doing here, Mara?"

She lifted her hand to capture his, dragging the strong, callused fingers to the place where her heart beat the strongest. Proudly, she fastened his touch there, shivered in reaction. Lost, she studied the bold sweep of brow, the beautiful features carved from stone and her most secret dreams. "I want you. Only you. Now. Tonight. Let me have you."

"And tomorrow?" He skimmed his free hand along the subtle curve of her throat. The skin there was a cool satin, strong and smooth. She watched him, her breathtaking face an enigma that dared him to know its secrets. "What happens tomorrow?"

Because she was a gambler, she felt compelled to hedge. To not put a name to what had not been decided. "Anything we want."

Reaching up, she anchored herself and let herself dream. In delicious exploration, she sampled the fullness of his bottom lip. With deliberate, wet forays, she traced the firm curve, licked at the seam that kept his mouth closed. On an ardent gasp, she snuck her way inside. Lips pressed close, she allowed her tongue to explore the dark, dangerous recesses. The serration of teeth, the slick caverns, the flavors of cool mint and Ethan. If she wasn't careful, she imagined dreamily, she could be caught here.

Ethan welcomed the uninhibited exploration, fire building. When the quick, agile tongue slid against his, he trembled with restraint. Mara tasted him as though searching, and the hunt tempted him. But this too was her journey, what she found in him her discovery.

The urge to plunge tore through him, but he settled for easing her closer, molding her body to his. While their mouths danced at her lead, Ethan reveled in the yield of curve to plane, of soft to hard. He clutched at writhing hips, guiding their motion. Memory and desire demanded that he act, but he could not. Would not. Tonight, he would take no more than was offered, would give only what was asked.

As though she could hear his thoughts, Mara broke the kiss. Leaning back, she searched the shadowed room, met his eyes. Black fire burned, and she shivered. "Kiss me, Ethan."

Unerringly, he captured her mouth, eager to devour. Inside, he thought, he too would find answers. Inside, he sought the firm, damp underside of her tongue, determined to leave no part of her mouth untasted. Sensations overwhelmed, every new touch revealing her, revealing him. Sweet, edged by bitter. Sharp, softened by warmth. Paradox and paradise, a banquet of contradiction that commanded he seek more. Driven, he plummeted deep, stroking and tangling with her in the sultry heat.

"More."

The demand rose between them, and he could not have said who spoke. Blindly, he slid one arm beneath her hips, lifted her up and into his hold. Desperately, he begged, repeating her words, "Let me have you."

At the stark plea, Mara gripped the placket of buttons and yanked hard. Bared to her, his chest rose with ragged breaths, and she exulted. She pressed fevered kisses to the smooth, hardened flesh. Intoxicated, she drew wet lines across slashes of muscle, reveling when he arched in pleasure. Enchanted, she nipped at the flat disk, and sighed when he trembled. Amazed that he thought he had to ask, she promised, "You do. Have me."

He broke then, fervent hands snaking beneath the thin layer of cotton to capture the fascinating globes of her lush breasts. He ignored the covering of lace, too impatient to release the catch. Seduced by the restless twisting of his hand, he crimped and tugged at the swollen flesh. Beneath his ministrations she stiffened into two hard peaks. He flattened his hands, letting her nipples pierce his palms as he soothed the ache he'd created. Tearing his mouth free, he feasted at her nape. "I don't want anyone else to feel this with you. To be with you."

Mindless, she pushed his shirt free, fixed her hands at his buckle. Then she raised her head to hold his keen gaze. "No one else, Ethan. I tried, but there is no one else." She slid the leather free, their eyes locked. Hunger raged inside her, demanding to be sated. Wicked thumbs teased her too sensitive flesh and stole her breath. But it would mean nothing if he didn't understand. "You are all I've ever wanted."

Ethan froze, stunned and humbled. He kissed her then, slowly, tenderly, a benediction and a beginning. Murmured into her mouth, into the night, "I've only ever been yours."

In hushed sounds he stripped away the red cotton, the black lace and lingering doubt. When the khaki shorts fell between them, he marveled at the slender lines, the strength and delicacy of her body. He brushed the sweep of taut, golden breasts, crested by a deeper hue that entreated he taste. That he feast.

Turning her, he skimmed moist trails along the arch of spine and dipped lower. She cried out, and he pushed her higher. He knelt beside her, strumming nerves and silken flesh into marvelous agony. Carefully, he traced the scarred flesh and its obscene pattern, the mark that had taken her away from him. He slipped lower, exciting and tormenting with equal measure. When he felt her first delirious release, he rose and swept her into his arms.

They fell onto the bed, a twine of limbs, a tangle of need. Refusing to be taken, Mara ranged over him, body pulsing with aftershocks. She stripped him and fed. At the concave of his stomach, she sampled and teased. Steel stirred near her touch, but she refused succor. Instead, she let herself wander, reclaiming what she'd abandoned. Heat here, power there. In her head, on her tongue, Ethan consumed her and she reveled in the destruction.

Panting, quivering, overwhelmed, they gorged on the piquancy of flesh, on the glide of skin to skin. Tumbling, he caught her and lathed at dips and hollows that remembered his touch. Rising, she streamed over him, mouth and teeth and fingertips wanton.

Cupping his buttocks, she dragged him up to meet her. Anchoring her shoulders, he surged inside to find her.

Free, restless, in love, she took him and gave him reign. She sank into him, nails and hips, taunting him to give her more, to take more than he expected.

Captive, he forced her to set the pace, to rock against him until her blood sang and her body bowed with exquisite distress. He fused their mouths, molded her to him, refusing to take, determined only to yield.

Higher and higher. Deeper and deeper. More and more. She flew above him, arched beneath him. He danced inside her, surrounded her.

Together, they crested the terrible wave, the ecstasy too much. Love, desire, passion burst inside. Holding onto Ethan, Mara accepted the next pleasured rush, fought to stay with him. Consumed by Mara, Ethan dived into rapture, determined to never surface.

Shattered, they rocketed together, neither sure of beginnings or endings, of themselves or each other. But in the dim shadows of night, with forever between them, neither thought of yesterday. Only tomorrow.

CHAPTER 21

SHADOWS LENGTHENED, BROKEN BY THE FLASHING GOLD OF neon lights welcoming comers to the Renegade Saloon. Mara stirred and enjoyed the subtle ache, the pleasant fatigue of skin and bone. In the dark, she sought the reassuring warmth of Ethan's skin, the settled thud of his heartbeat against her palm. Beneath her touch, muscles shifted, and gently, a larger hand covered hers beneath the sheet he'd drawn over their cooling bodies.

As though trying to erase the years, they'd sated themselves for hours. Again and again she'd coaxed him into loveplay, trying to say with caresses and the union of flesh what she could not put into words. That she hadn't known how hollow the emptiness had been until he filled her. Loved her. That lying with him, feeling him move and sink inside, felt like a haven. *Like home.*

And, heaven help her, she didn't know if she could leave if he told her to go. So she seduced and cajoled, praying the heat and speed would convince him to stay. In silent rejection of the inevitable, she ranged closer, pressing her body tight to his length. No, she determined, sliding wearily into sleep, she wouldn't go without a fight. *Not again.*

Ethan turned to rest his forehead against hers. He did not open his eyes, not yet ready to read what might lay in the amber depths. He barely understood the emotions tumbling through him. Want, need, desire, he'd expected. Craving, yearning, obsession—even that he'd accepted. Love too had found a place and burrowed deep. But the astonishing revelation that continued to ricochet through him was the longing—no—the compulsion to tenderness.

To savor and soothe, to worship and adore.

But each time he tried, she would wrest control from him and urge him into the tempestuous duel that left him spent and shaken. Not once during the long, passionate night had she allowed him to lead. To take her slowly and gently as he had when they'd been young and in love.

Instead, each time had an edge of frenzy, a sheen of desperation that seemed to hint at good-bye. She'd promised not to run, but Mara had not said that she would stay with him. Her life demanded a freedom he couldn't accept. An autonomy of action, one that permitted subterfuge and coercion. A liberty of the heart a permanent relationship could not sustain.

Yet, in the days since her return, Ethan had come to understand that he would compromise almost everything to keep her near. He squeezed lightly at the slender fingers curled against his heart. Was it possible she didn't know it already belonged to her? Always had?

Terrifyingly, he knew, she now also owned his soul. He'd forsake his code, his honor, all to be with her and damn the consequences. If she would let him. For her, he would uproot his life and follow her path. Because without her he might survive, possibly thrive, but would move in twilight. Of, but not belonging. In, but not a part. He would be complete, but not nearly the man he became with Mara.

With Mara. Softly, he drifted kisses across the brow wrinkled in restless sleep, along the slant of bone covered by perfect skin. Inexorably, he luxuriated in the brush of lips, in the quiet yielding when her mouth opened in sleep to admit his quest. In low, murmured tones he praised the slope of high, firm breasts, the mellifluous curve at her waist. With canny fingertips he strummed desire not into a conflagration, but a slow-burning flame that lit the night.

Silvery words shot through Mara's dreams, calling her into liquid pleasure, full and rich and waiting. When her eyes drifted open, he suckled at one rigid peak, the languorous pull more thrilling than she could have imagined. At her throaty moan, he captured her gaze, demanded her attention.

Watch me love you, he commanded silently. *Know that I will always be a part of you.*

By design, he flowed over every inch of gossamer skin in voracious, tender assault.

By turns he stole at her soul, destroying her with a generosity she scarcely understood.

Mara arched into him, unwilling to accept without giving. Understanding, he lay beneath her mouth, willing himself into stillness while she tested his endurance.

When he could take no more, when she tasted of him, he slid inside in a long, endless thrust that shattered them both. Sighs and pleas and moans mingled in enthralled chorus. Before they were ready, too steeped in the passion of tenderness to stop the night, oblivion broke over them, around them, through them. Limbs entwined, hearts beating in wondered unison, Ethan wrapped her to him and, at last, they slept.

"MR. CAINE?" THE ham-fisted knock sounded on the door a second time, and Ethan groggily lifted his head.

"Go away. You've got the wrong room." He grunted at the intruder and tucked Mara closer. The snatches of sleep they'd managed between midnight and dawn had been useless in the face of their intervening activities.

Mara blinked at him sleepily, and he felt himself harden impossibly. He hadn't realized how resilient the human body could be after years of drought. "Go back to sleep."

"Can't," she mumbled grouchily. "Crazy man banging on the window." She pointed drowsily to the wide, pale face she could see peeking through the break in the curtains. Luckily, one of them had the foresight to drag a sheet up after their last session. Probably wasn't her, she decided. "What does he want?"

"He's looking for a Mr. Caine. Told the lunatic he has the wrong room." Ethan shut his eyes, prepared to sleep just long enough to put his new verve to use.

"Caine?" Mara repeated the name, then cursed beneath her breath. With an agility he'd benefited from around two A.M., she vaulted over him, heading for the door. When she saw a single milky blue eye widen in appreciation, she turned, yanked the sheet from Ethan and twisted it into a sarong.

She raced to the door and jerked it open on the chain. The pallid, pie-faced teenager gawked at the glimpses of creamy brown breast she hadn't managed to cover adequately. Mara noticed the distraction and rearranged her makeshift drape. Drawing his attention upward, she encouraged, "You've got a message for Mr. Caine?"

"Um, yes, ma'am," the boy stammered. He'd seen more skin on the strippers who danced in the saloon, but somehow this was different. The quick look at the lady's breast had him counting the money in his wallet. Maybe today he'd buy himself an hour with one of the working girls. Dreaming of what he'd only seen in movies or through keyholes, he stared in fascination at Mara.

"The message—" Mara glanced at the gold nameplate pinned to his shoulder. "Roger? You said you had a message for Mr. Caine?"

Snapping to attention, Roger shifted on his feet guiltily. "Yes, ma'am. Mr. Caine left strict instructions to be notified if anyone called the motel describing you and him."

The boy stopped speaking. Mara waited, until she realized he wouldn't continue without prompting. "Roger, did someone call?"

"Oh, yeah. A few minutes ago. Asking for a guest registered under the name Mara Reed or Ethan Stuart. Told him we had no such guests by that name. Of course, most of our guests don't use their real names, you know what I mean?"

Roger chuckled at his innuendo, and she laughed lightly. He obviously wasn't a challenge to any high-level thinker, but he had information she needed. She resisted the urge to check the bed and see if Ethan was listening in. Hopefully, he was already up and packing.

"I get you. So, what did he say when you told him no?" In a show of trust, Mara released the latch and opened the door slightly wider. "Did you do as Mr. Caine asked, Roger?"

Bobbing his head rapidly, he explained, "I asked him for a description of the guests, and he described you and Mr. Caine. I said I didn't recollect any lady as pretty as you checking in, but that I'd be happy to take a message."

Mara patted Roger's suddenly sweaty hand in praise. "We're very grateful, Roger. My ex-husband is a mean man, and he'll do anything to get me back."

"Ex-husband?"

With a practiced sob, Mara swung easily into her explanation. "Arthur Rabbe. About five-eleven, sandy blond hair, slick look in his eyes. He likes to hit me when he's been drinking."

"Sonofabitch." Filled with chivalry, Roger clasped her hand between his damp palms. "Is Mr. Caine your boyfriend?"

"No, he's my fiancé. Arthur is determined for me to not be happy, so he's been tracking us across the state." Mara allowed her eyes to fill, the golden depths limpid and sorrowful. "If he finds me, I don't know what he'll do to me."

Roger squared his shoulders and lifted the pimpled chin in preparation for battle. "Don't you worry none, ma'am. I don't take kindly to bullies, especially the kind who'll beat on a defenseless woman."

"You won't tell him we were here?" Gratitude, as real as the tears were false, lightened Mara's voice.

"No, ma'am. I promise." Roger lifted her hand into an awkward kiss, and Mara smiled.

Leaning forward, she pressed her lips to his cheek. "Thank you, Roger."

Stammering, stumbling, he nodded and hurried back to the front desk. Mara turned to find the bed empty and the shower running. Moving fast, she rummaged through her bag for a change of clothes.

She didn't like deceiving the kid, but too much was at stake for an attack of conscience. Rabbe and Guffin had tracked them to this hovel in the outskirts. That meant she and Ethan were running out of time. They had to find the third key before Conroy caught up with them—or found the safe first. He only had one key, but if he didn't care about the artifacts, he might risk blowing the entire safe to get to the gold, regardless of Bailey's aqua regia concoction. She refused to let that happen. Ethan would have his glory and she would have her gold.

"Ethan!" she shouted at the bathroom door, which stood ajar. "Rabbe will probably be here within the hour. We've got to get moving."

He appeared at the door, measly towel riding low on his lean hips. "So I gathered. Did you tell him to warn us?"

"No." Mara selected a tank top that Lesley had loaned her, and the well-worn khaki shorts discarded by the bed. "Sebastian is good about things like that. But I should have thought about it. I'm slipping."

"Maybe you're starting to shed bad habits." Ethan moved around her to his suitcase, careful not to make contact. The frigidly cold shower he'd endured had done little to ease his ardor. Simply being in the room with Mara had a torpid effect on his body. However, the pieces of conversation he'd caught before he realized they needed to run had quashed thoughts of a repeat performance. "Not everyone lives like their lives are on the line. Perhaps you're unlearning."

"You'd better hope not," Mara cautioned. Ignoring his censure, she explained, "Conroy must realize we've found two of the keys. He may know that the safe is rigged to open without the fourth one. If we find the third one before he does, we might win. Which means he has to get us soon or risk losing everything."

"Go shower." Ethan conceded the point and began to gather their belongings. "I'll pack the car."

"Gimme five minutes." Grateful he hadn't pressed the issue, Mara hurried into the bathroom. As fragrant steam filled the air, scented by Ethan, she dropped her sheet and jumped beneath the scalding spray. Were Rabbe not en route, she'd tempt Ethan to join her. But cavorting in the shower would have to wait until they could drench themselves in gold coins.

Ducking her head beneath the torrent, she lathered quickly. More than once she scrubbed at sore points and grinned at the memory. Soon, she thought, they'd find the gold and they'd beat Conroy.

Again. Like grandfather, like daughter.

Excited to move, she finished quickly and, covering herself with the remaining towel, returned to the main room to dress.

Ethan stood in the doorway, staring at a departing Roger. Concerned, she crossed to him and touched his shoulder. "Honey, what's wrong?"

"Rabbe sent a message to Mr. Stuart." The low voice, raspy from lack of sleep, growled over the words. Turning, black points burned hotly with banked rage. "The message was to tell Mr. Stuart that Dr. Lesley Baxter didn't make it home last night. Until we arrive with the keys and the map to the safe, she won't be either."

CHAPTER 22

AT MIDDAY ETHAN JOGGED THE CONVERTIBLE INTO A MAKE-shift parking spot on the narrow rutted lane at Cementerio a Santa Therese. Mourners marched in stiff procession around the oval path that descended to the gravesite. On the air, wails rose in bereavement, and a priest moved among the grieving to offer comfort.

"I thought the cemetery would be deserted." Mara riffled through the guidebook they'd purchased on the road. In hushed tones, despite the fact no one could hear them, she whispered, "The population of Santa Therese is 307. Must be the whole town down there."

"Almost." Ethan peered at the clock. Finding the town had taken more time than he'd planned. Like many villages and hamlets in Texas, the only connection between point A and point B was an unpaved county road used decades before to drive cattle. The resulting surface refused speed, jarring the unwary traveler with potholes as deep as wells. Twice they'd been forced to scare stray cows and nudge them onto the closest pasture.

He climbed out of the car and braced his hands on the hood, immune to the pouring heat. Tension knotted his neck, coiled on his shoulders. Concern for Lesley collided with the tumble of emotions his night with Mara had wrought, and he couldn't find his balance. "He's got her, Mara. Somewhere, he's hurting her because of this. Because of us."

"She's fine, Ethan." Mara slide across the front seat and emerged on his side of the car. Ducking beneath his arm, she anchored her arms around his waist and hung back to catch his hooded gaze. "Look at me, Ethan. This is my territory. And I promise you, Conroy has no reason to harm her unless we fail him. Which we won't."

"We could." He lowered his forehead to hers, eyes closed. "All of this for a sheaf of paper and a sack of gold. Her life is worth more."

Mara hugged him tighter and kneaded at the rigid muscles at his back. "Yes, it is. Conroy knows it too. And he needs us. Without our help, he's got a single key and no clue where the safe is. When we find the key and the safe, as I'm sure we will, we bargain for Lesley."

"And if he doesn't go for it?" Ethan broke her hold but held her hands tight. "Or what if he decides he can find it without us?"

"Listen to me. This is my area of expertise. Men like Conroy live for the hunt and the reward. Plus, he's obviously a manipulative bastard who enjoys watching us scurry to do his bidding." She turned her hands beneath his to mesh their fingers. "That's why he paid for your research after that first find. And that's why he's had Rabbe tracking me without killing me. He's pragmatic and slick, and he thinks he's smarter than us both."

"He's not." Ethan murmured the words, trying to be convinced.

"No, he's not." Mara grinned suddenly and tugged free to encircle his neck. "Trust me one more time, love. We'll get Lesley back, find your manuscript and totem, and claim my grandfather's gold. It's in the bag." Covering her angst with a bright smile, she pulled him down into a bracing kiss. Over his shoulder, when her eyes finally fluttered open, she saw a dark line winding through the cemetery gates. "The procession is clearing out. Let's go."

Two hours later Ethan clipped at another tangle of overgrown vines that obscured the name of the interred body. He couldn't shake an eerie sense of familiarity; impossible, since he'd eschewed small western towns. In the far south corner of the cemetery, clumps of graves had been dug cheek by jowl. Apparently, burial maintenance was not a requisite for the cemetery. Blackberry bushes grew in scattered clusters, and thick, ropy weeds had reclaimed the wooden identification markers.

Down a row, Mara swore crossly. "Cremate me. When I die, I want my body burned and my ashes scattered. Don't shove me underground."

He repeated obediently, "Note to self, burn Mara."

"After I'm gone," she warned. She swiped at the rivulets of sweat trickling along parched skin. Grave-robbing was macabre at the best of times, but in the heat of a summer day, it was also positively ghastly. The act of hacking away at mischievous vines that seemed to procreate in droves had worn her patience thin. "Remind me what we're looking for again."

"I'm not sure. But my research on Poncho indicated a fascination with cemeteries. Perhaps he had a relative buried here. Or a good friend."

"How would we know?" Mara swatted at a bee the size of her thumb. "I didn't find any record of his friends other than my grandfather. And he was buried in Kiev."

"I'm assuming it will be under the name Alvarado, like him. His clue to your grandmother mentioned a final resting place." Ethan snipped at a wrist-sized vine. Across the swath of green, plain crosses dotted the landscape, mixed indiscriminately with marble headstones and tall statues to fallen soldiers.

Because Santa Therese had been settled during an oil rush, its topography offered few amenities beyond the thick sludge that had surged beneath the rock. The arid land enjoyed rare visits from rainclouds, making the soil unsuitable for farming. Cowboys had tried their hand at cattle, with poor results. Mangy heifers straggled across the sweep of occasional verdant ground, but boxed in by hills to the north and east and scorched earth elsewhere, Santa Therese had perished decades before.

He studied the dip of a short row of hills, and the image tickled his memory, something vital. Pausing, he set down the shears and rested on his haunches. "Mara, hand me the quilt."

She removed the tattered cloth from her bag, puzzled by the request. "What are you looking for? This is the map to the safe."

Nodding, Ethan agreed. "But look here." He pointed to a rise that Lesley had corresponded to a range of hills that had no connection to the rest of the region. "Stand up."

Confused but game, Mara lithely gained her feet and turned to stand shoulder-to-shoulder with Ethan. Holding the quilt aloft, he gestured to the hills. "Now, look at the quilt."

Mara scanned the distant vista and checked the quilt. "Okay. Hills out there and hills on here. But this is the Texas Hill Country," she reminded him quietly.

Excitement growing, Ethan jabbed a finger at the vibrant blue patches sewn into the fabric. "Bluebells. Yellow primrose." He circled the array of yellow. "Your grandmother told you that Poncho described his brother's map as a desert bowl filled with blues and yellows and greens."

"Which Lesley determined was a ravine of some sort."

"Not a ravine. A town. A small town built in the valley between three hills. One with bluebells, yellow primrose, and cacti. With a limestone shelf that eventually leads to an oil rush."

"An exact description of where we are, but not where Guerva hid the gold."

"Maybe it is." Ethan's smile widened, white flashing in the sunlight. "Think like the hustler you are, Mara. No offense."

Though she narrowed her eyes, she conceded, "None taken. Your point?"

"Five men join up for the heist of their careers. Reese is a loose cannon and a hothead, but you need him. Bailey has a talent for chemicals, but he's a scoundrel and a rake. Rarely stays still for long. Poncho and Guerva, brothers who've never been apart. Guerva is a deaf-mute who trusts only one man other than his brother."

"My grandfather." Mara stared at the quilt in disbelief. It couldn't be so simple, could it? Clutching his arm tightly, she murmured, "Here? Guerva hid the safe here?"

"Why not? Poncho and Guerva were inseparable. Each man had one day to hide his key or the safe and they were sent in different directions. Five men, four cardinal directions. Poncho and Guerva head out and meet up once they're out of sight of the others."

"Which explains why Poncho was so determined to give the map to my grandmother." She bent down, taking the quilt with her. Brushing aside a clear spot on the baked earth, she angled the quilt to reflect the terrain.

Ethan joined her, excitement bubbling. "According to the quilt, this ridge of hills should have a mirror set to the south." Twisting, he verified the locale.

"There's the monument." Mara poked at the knotted gray

fabric that rose nearly an inch above the quilt. Around the cemetery, matching gray statuary stared blankly at the vivid blue horizon. "The denizens of Santa Therese appear to like statues to the dead. Nana didn't add any clues."

"The answers must be in the quilt. Poncho helped her make it. For a reason." Pensive, he glared at the enigmatic coverlet. "It must be staring us in the face."

Mara crawled closer and patted the hand he'd fisted on the ground. "You're the sleuth, Ethan. How do you solve a forensic mystery?"

Breathing slowly, he ran through the steps in his mind, repeating them to Mara. "Start with observation."

"All right. We've got a quilt that looks identical to the town of Santa Therese. In general. The three clusters of hills. The wildflowers in the ravine. And not much detail except for the statue in the center of the quilt."

"Next, we create a hypothesis." Ethan shut his eyes, letting the scene play in his head. Like the reconstruction of the life of the dead, he counted on imagination to begin his inquiry. Random data collapsing into a theory. Aiko's quilt sketched the town clearly, but abruptly limited the scope to one area of town. One area with a gray statue. "We assume Guerva and his brother chose this town because of Poncho's work here. And when we blend that with his affinity for cemeteries, it makes sense that the statue is here."

"Okay, okay. We assume the statue is where the gold is hidden and we search here." Mara scrambled to her feet. "I'll take that side," she announced and turned to the far end of the cemetery.

"Wait. Part of testing a hypothesis is disproving all other available theorem. Such as the existence of other monuments in town."

"Look around, Ethan. Not much else is here." She elbowed his ribs gently. "Let go of the scientist now. This part requires intuition. Gut instinct."

"Gut instinct?" Ethan exhaled slowly, scanned the vista. The monument stood ruler straight, a beacon. Beyond it, a patch of grass had grown wild with weeds. No stone markers or wooden placards. Nothing to mark the grave except its presence in a cemetery. "Gut instinct. Come on!"

He dragged her past the rows of graves, across the expanse of the cemetery. Tools clanked noisily as he brought them to a halt. "Here!" Ethan speared the ground with his shovel. "The safe is under here."

Catching her breath, Mara stared at him, wondering if he'd lost his mind. "The monument is on the map, Ethan."

"Yes, it is. But look at it again and tell me what's not on there." He laid the quilt on the bed of weeds and jabbed at the area where they stood. "This patch of land is covered in red flowers. See any flowers here?"

Mara studied the quilt and the only spot of red on the quilt. "You're brilliant, Dr. Stuart."

"Instinct, honey." With a flourish, he scooped her to her feet and presented the second shovel. "Now start digging."

The pungent aroma of turned earth filled the air and a faint breeze wisped past, but neither noticed. Minutes turned into an hour, and Mara felt her confidence wane. "Ethan, it's not here. We've nearly hit China."

"It has to be here," he insisted, swiping at his brow. "I know it's here."

Mara heard the despondency creeping into his words and she set her shoulders. "Then it's here. Let's move over to that section."

"Thank you." Ethan shifted the shovel to one hand and stroked a thumb along her cheek. The streak of brown that appeared in its wake joined other stains on her skin. "If I forget to tell you later, Mara, I'm proud of you."

"For what?" she murmured, moved. "I haven't done anything."

"I know you now, Mara Elizabeth. I've seen you this time— and I know you. You're kind and brave and determined."

"I'm a thief and a liar," she corrected shakily. "That's what you know."

"No, this time I'm trusting my instincts. And they tell me I'm right about you." Ethan pressed a hard kiss to her surprised mouth and swatted her butt. "Start digging."

Shovels bit into earth once more and clouds gathered overhead. Fat drops of rain began to fall, mixing the dirt into mud. Ready to give up, Ethan jammed the metal into the ground. The vibrations sang up the pole and across his arms. "Mara! Come here."

She rushed to join him. "Did you find it?"

"I found something." Pointing to the hole he'd dug, he instructed, "Dig there." Soon the mud and debris had been moved to the side, leaving a trench nearly three feet across and six feet deep. Water pelted the chasm, swirling away to reveal the muted luster of brass. Kneeling, Ethan and Mara grasped the leather straps that crossed the sides. In unison they squatted on either side, prepared to lift.

"On three," Ethan shouted above the storm. "One . . . two . . . three."

With a great heave the safe broke free of the earth. Overbalanced, Mara slipped, dropping her end. Ethan tipped backward and tumbled the safe to the ground. Mara lay on her back, winded. Overhead, the rain sputtered to a stop.

"The aqua regia!" Mara panted out the warning, but it was too late to run. They waited for the explosion, but none came.

Relieved, Ethan crawled to her side. "You okay?"

"Yes," she managed. "I guess a fall wouldn't break Bailey's booby trap."

"Unless there's a delayed reaction."

Mara glared at him, but checked the safe for good measure. It lay on its side, and she pointed to the base. "Look!" Fastened to it was a key, identical to the ones in her knapsack. Suddenly refreshed, she and Ethan scrambled in the mud to the safe. With his pocketknife, Ethan pried the key from its moorings. Letters had been carved into the handle, just like the first two: αυρ.

"Alpha. Upsilon. Rho." Mara murmured the letters. "Eight letters. Omicron. Theta. Sigma twice. Eta. Doesn't make sense."

"Hand me the keys." Ethan righted the safe while she removed the two pouches they'd found. The lock had four slots with corresponding symbols. Carefully, she passed him the keys, but they didn't fit. "I don't understand. We've got the three keys."

"Hold on," Mara mumbled. She'd worked a safe like this before. One built before tumblers and combination locks. "It's a sequence."

"Hmm?"

"We can't put the keys in together. They have to go in order."

"Like one, two, three?"

Mara stared at the keys in Ethan's palm. "Sequence. A code." She grabbed the knapsack and removed her grandfather's note. "Here."

"What?" He studied the parchment, not sure of what he was supposed to see. "I can't read Greek, Mara."

Four gospels. Four winds. Four seasons. Four corners of the earth. But there is only a trinity for salvation. If you have found this, you are a step closer to a treasure I could not claim. I hope you are of my lineage, of my treasure. I pray you are not my son, but that you are braver and wiser than he. Keys to unlock our treasure. May God be with you.

"You don't have to. Just look for the pattern." She tapped the page in three places, where θησαυρός had been scripted into the text. "This is the Greek spelling of treasure. Repeated three times. And if we rearrange our keys…" Mara laid the keys on the sodden ground, the letters in order. "Voilà!"

"Brilliant." Lifting the first key, he placed the cold, wet brass in her palm. "Ladies first."

Mara inserted the key and turned slowly, fighting back impatience. The lock gave way and the slot shifted down. Then she handed Ethan the second key. With grave care, he pushed it into place and twisted the key. For the second time the keyhole moved. Mara took the third key and nudged it into place. Turning to Ethan, she laid his hand on hers and together they turned the last key.

A tumbler clicked.

Mara reached from the handle, her hand still joined with his. When the door opened, he pressed their hands palm-to-palm in victory. "Go on, touch it."

Inside the safe six satchels rested side by side. Mara tugged at the front bag, unprepared for its weight. With fingers that shook, she opened the top and dipped her hand inside. Gold pieces filled her cupped hands. In the light, the carved gold shone with a ferocity that rivaled the sun.

The past fell away and returned in a liquid rush that sang in her blood. "It's real, Ethan. And it's ours." Laughing, she dripped the coins into her lap, unable to comprehend that she'd found it. That they'd found it. "The Reed fortune."

"Yes, baby, you found it." He noticed a satchel that bulged more than the others and reached inside. His pulse thrummed with expectation, the potential for discovery at his fingertips. "May I?"

Mara nodded eagerly. "It's yours."

He dragged the heavy bag into his lap and yanked at the strings. The polished wood lay atop the mounds of gold, but he had no eyes for anything else. Wiping his hands on his shirt, he lightly traced the figures in the totem, brushed at the leather binding. "The Shango manuscript."

"We've won, Ethan." But even as the words escaped, she remembered what they stood to lose.

"Lesley." Ethan felt a wash of shame that he'd forgotten her, even for a moment. "We should let him know we've found it."

"Not everything." Mara reached for the bag he held.

Disgust reared but immediately dissipated. "Mara, no."

"This is yours. You've earned it." She removed the manuscript and the statue and tucked them into her bag. "He knows about the gold. Not about the artifacts. I don't mind losing one, but not both."

"Mara."

"I know." Mara poured the coins from her lap into the satchel and bound it tight. "Save it for later. I don't intend to lose without a fight, if you're willing."

"Anything."

"Good. Then Davis Conroy will get what he's bargained for."

CHAPTER 23

CHI DEVELOPMENT OCCUPIED A LAVISH ROW OF TOWERS whose footprint covered half a city block. Spires of chrome and glass rose above a ring of fountains, where nymphs and mermaids glistened in the crystalline spray. The lush green of the landscape elicited thoughts of meadows and open spaces, exactly as the designer intended.

Mara stared longingly at the rush of water, wishing they'd had time to do more than bathe in a gas station bathroom. She'd managed to clean most of the mud away, but only just. The image of her rose hip and lavender bath swept across her thoughts and she sighed.

"Ready?" Ethan prodded.

"Yes. We're to meet him on the fiftieth floor." Leaving her elusive scented bath, Mara checked the perimeter of the building, noting the discreet but heavily armed guards that stood post. "He's got tight security."

"Which will go off like a five-alarm fire when we try to bring this inside." Ethan stood behind her. He tilted the trolley on its two wheels. "The safe is solid brass. The metal detector will love it."

"So we'll have to go around it." Mara sent him an encouraging grin. "I told you. This is my turf. Trust me."

"I do."

The solemn response quickened her heartbeat with pleasure. Firmly, Mara faced the revolving glass doors and the flanking double panels that would admit them. Her plan, her choice. "We have an appointment."

Ethan followed tight on her heels, rolling the safe behind him. Doubt kept his muscles bunched, his eyes narrowed in search of trouble. The scheme Mara had hatched sounded deadly and impossible. And brilliant.

"Excuse me, sir." A harried desk clerk rushed over to his side. "You will have to take this to the service entry for inspection."

Ethan scanned the name tag pinned to his lapel. "Harold, is it?"

"Yes, sir." The teenager bobbed his head. "That's my name."

"Harold, please give Mr. Conroy a call. He's expecting us." Ethan jerked his head toward the radio on Harold's hip. "I don't think he wants me to use the service entrance."

"But it's Mr. Conroy's policy," the boy insisted. "All deliveries through the front entrance are forbidden and must be immediately directed to the service entry on the south face of the building," he recited from memory. He steadied his voice and urged, "You have to go around."

Having a security team attempt to open the safe would ruin everything. Mara caught Ethan's look of concern and swooped into action. She beckoned to Harold, who crossed to her. Despite the unsatisfying bath, she had come prepared. Perfume wafted up in the cramped space she left between her body and Harold's. She outlined the metal badge and lightly touched his thin shoulders. "Davis is expecting us, Harold, and he will be very displeased if we're delayed any longer. I'd hate to tell him you made me late."

"But, Miss—"

"Ms. Reed. Mara. I'm a close, personal friend of Davis's and this is my guard, Ethan." She waved behind her. "Say hello, Ethan."

Gritting his teeth, Ethan muttered, "Hello."

"I have a present for Davis, and I'm sure you know he absolutely despises it when others touch his playthings." As she spoke she caught Harold's sweaty palm and drew their hands up to her chin. The motion brought him closer, and his Adam's apple bobbed convulsively. "Wand Ethan, Harold, and I promise you won't find anything amiss. When you finish with him, you can do me."

"O-Okay." When he agreed, Mara dropped his hand, which gratefully grazed a breast. Emboldened, he gripped the wand that rested in his utility belt and approached Ethan. He ignored the man's greater height and forced steel into his tenor. "Spread your legs, sir."

After a thorough, nearly obscene wanding of both Mara and

Ethan, Harold admitted them to the bank of elevators. With a swipe of his security card, he released the elevator to travel to the top floor. Flushed, he stammered out instructions. "I'll let Mr. Conroy's staff know you're on your way."

Feeling generous, Mara planted a feathery kiss on his mottled cheek. "You've been a doll, Harold. I'll tell Davis how lovely."

"Thank you, ma'am." He stumbled out of the elevator. "Enjoy your visit."

The metal and glass doors slid shut and Ethan grinned. "Mara Reed, femme fatale. Who'd of guessed?"

Mara merely smiled. Then she turned grim. In a matter of minutes their lives would change. Forever. She was prepared, but Ethan wasn't her kind. "It's not too late, Ethan. We have other options."

"I'm fine, Mara. I can handle this if you can." He reached for her hand, linking them. "I wanted adventure and excitement. Now I want what's mine." With a shrug, he added, "He'll make his own choice."

Soon, the elevator buzzed and the car stopped. The doors opened and he released her.

She alighted from it and walked past the two men standing sentry. Ethan joined her, balancing the trolley. "Armed escorts?" Mara held her hands aloft. "Take me to your leader."

"You're not funny, bitch." Behind her, Rabbe strolled into the marble lobby, feet echoing on the tiles. "Mr. Conroy won't be amused by you."

"You're such a killjoy, Arthur." She lowered her hands and folded them at her waist, resisting the urge to leap forward and claw at his smug face. Adrenaline began to flow. Yes, this was her turf. "Where's your smarter, less savage half?"

Rabbe frowned at the insult. "I'm gonna enjoy doing you," he announced, advancing on her. Before he could wrap his hands around her throat, Ethan was between them.

He covered one fist with his own and contracted his grip. He stopped Rabbe's attempted jab and neatly twisted his hand, yanking the thug's arm high behind his back. Rabbe yelped in pain and the guards raised their guns. Ethan watched them calmly. "No need to shoot. I'm just giving your comrade a warning. Touch Mara and I'll kill you."

"Didn't know you were a fighter, Dr. Stuart." Davis Conroy appeared, flanked by Seth and a slight middle-aged man who seemed on the verge of collapse. "Rabbe, once again, you disappoint me. Handled by a scientist. You're a disgrace to your craft."

"Mr. Conroy—" The plaintive wail came as much from the vicious pain in his arm as the look Conroy gave the behemoths guarding the elevator. "I got them here, like you wanted."

Conroy sniffed. "I wanted what Dr. Stuart has brought to me. You gave me nothing." He motioned to one of the guards, who seemed prepared for the signal. "Please escort Mr. Rabbe to his car. Personally."

Whimpering, Rabbe broke free of Ethan's hold and tried to

dash to the stairwell. The titan stepped into his path and caught him by the throat. "The parking garage is this way."

"Seth! Seth, help me!" Rabbe pleaded as he was bustled into the car. "Fuck you, Seth! Fuck you, Conroy!"

The doors closed over his piteous threats, and Mara and Ethan exchanged a look. "Mr. Conroy, we brought the safe and the keys. We would like Dr. Baxter."

"Tut tut." Conroy contemplated the duo and their gift to him. In the squat metal box between them, his destiny waited. He would accomplish what his father failed to do. But he would do so with dignity. And without witnesses. "I don't conduct business in the hallway, Ms. Reed. Please, join me in my office. Our family connections warrant that, at least."

Mara and Ethan walked behind him, with Seth and the other man beside them. The office, if it could be termed such, ran along the entire phalanx of windows that faced the north. Deep crimson carpet gave beneath their feet, masking sound. "Seth, wait outside. Nigel, please have the safe set up on its table."

She watched intently as Nigel and the guard wheeled the safe to a pedestal. The lock faced the doorway, so the person opening it would have his back to the outer chamber. Pleased by the arrangement, Mara released a pent-up breath silently. So far, so good.

A gracious host, Conroy made his way to the bar. "Drinks?"

Ethan began to respond, but Mara cautioned him with a restrainng hand. "A glass of white wine would be lovely."

"And for you, Dr. Stuart?"

"Scotch. Neat."

Conroy nodded approvingly. "Is there any other way?" He lifted a decanter and poured. "I admire what you've made of your life, Ethan. May I call you Ethan?"

"Of course."

"From an orphan to a tenured professor. Quite renowned in your field. But I had no idea of your connection to Ms. Reed when I hired you. The turns of Fate." He returned to where they stood and indicated a black leather sofa. "Please sit."

Ethan led Mara to the sofa, settling her on the end and placing himself between her and Conroy, who delivered their drinks with a flourish and took a high-backed chair across from them.

"How gallant, Ethan. Protecting the woman you once loved. But I fear you misunderstand me. I simply wanted the safe and the keys to it." Conroy smiled easily, and reclined against the supple leather. Having achieved his ends, magnanimity flowed. "Would you like to see the contents?"

"I'd prefer to see that Lesley is unharmed," Ethan countered smoothly. "Please."

The smile broadened. "Once I have the keys."

Mara smiled more broadly, a brittle counterpoint to the temper she tried to dampen. The smug, superior countenance ground on nerves already shredded with exhaustion. Beside her, Ethan had a death grip on his glass, so tight she feared it would shatter. Niceties done, she joined the conversation. "Mr. Conroy, we both know that's not the way. Dr. Stuart is a novice here, but I am not. I learned at my grandfather's knee. First you produce Dr. Baxter, then I hand you the keys. After the exchange, Lesley comes with us and you keep the safe and its contents. Deal?" She sipped from her glass and watched him over the rim.

"My dossier on you did you precious little justice, Mara. From my research, I expected a cheap, blousy con artist who relied on questionable feminine wiles to fell her victims."

"And now?"

"I dare say, you're quite charming, if impertinent." The smile faded, replaced by a steely stare. "This is not a negotiation, my dear. It is a surrender. You used my bodies to find my keys and my safe. The operative word here is *my*." He rested a Waterford tumbler on one knee, the amber sloshing delicately at the sides. "Tell me, Ethan, how did you find the keys?"

"I didn't." Ethan inclined his head toward Mara. "The bodies you uncovered were a start, but she was the one who figured out that the marks were coordinates. Reverend Reed was quite clever."

The scotch in Conroy's glass sloshed higher. "The heist was my father's idea," he corrected bitterly. "Her grandfather appropriated his idea and turned the other men against him."

"Reese Conroy killed his partner and tried to kill my grandfather," Mara protested before she caught herself.

"A pity his shot missed. I understand that was your grandmother's fault."

Ethan restrained her retort with a gentle squeeze of her leg.

Conroy followed the movement and the generous smile returned. "Glad to see that you've taught her to obey you this time around. I didn't think you had the *cojones*, Doctor."

Because she could feel the tension in his grip, Mara spoke quickly. "Aren't you eager to see your prize, Mr. Conroy?"

"Davis."

"Davis," she repeated in mock meekness. "After seventy years, I admire your restraint. Millions in gold at your elbow, and you sit making idle chatter with a thief and a teacher. Interesting choice."

The urchin had a point, Conroy allowed. He'd waited a lifetime to avenge his father and to claim the treasure that should have been his at birth. He set the tumbler on a low table near his knee and stood. "Join me."

Ethan gained his feet and leaned in to assist Mara. In a whisper, he asked, "When is he coming?"

"Soon," she hissed. "Be patient. He likes to make an entrance."

"Ethan, Mara. My keys." Conroy extended a callused hand. "Now, my dear."

Mara politely declined, placing the pouch behind her back. "Lesley, first. I insist."

Aware that their combined fates had been sealed when they learned of his existence, Conroy felt charitable. He depressed the intercom once. "Nigel, please bring Dr. Baxter in."

Seconds later Nigel escorted Lesley into the room. She entered, head high, lip swollen from Conroy's ring. The creamy skin had grown wan, accenting the livid red mark near her mouth. "I told you, I won't help you find them," she began as soon as she entered the office. "I hope—"

"Lesley." Ethan cut off the tirade with a single word.

On a sob, she rushed over to him, into his embrace. "I didn't tell him anything!"

He wrapped her against him, and pressing her head into his shoulder, stroked the mass of dark hair tenderly. "We came to him. To get you."

Lesley lifted her head, eyes bright. "Mara?"

"Millions in gold for your safe return. Seemed a fair trade." Mara shrugged. "One good turn, and all that."

Conroy cleared his throat. "Touching reunion, but I'm a bit anxious to fulfill my destiny here. So, the keys?" He reached out for the pouch, and a second time Mara demurred.

Time was passing quickly and the most important part of their plan hadn't arrived. To buy time, she asked, "May I see your key, Mr. Conroy? Out of curiosity."

Narrowing his eyes, Conroy considered her request. With the guards posted outside and Nigel standing watch, the opportunity for ambush was nonexistent. He could indulge a lovely woman for a moment longer. "Certainly." He snapped his fingers once, and Nigel scurried to the desk on the far side of the room.

The velvet box was presented with an obsequious flourish that had Mara mortified on the man's behalf. She passed the leather pouch to Ethan and accepted the box. Opening it, she saw a key identical to the three she and Ethan had discovered. On its base, more Greek script had been engraved: παραδιδομι. Mara skimmed her stunned eyes over the text a second time, verifying her translation. "Have you had the inscription translated?"

"Of course. It says *'deliver.'* The Greek word *paradidomi.*" Conroy ran a quick hand over the surface of the safe. "Apropos, wouldn't you agree?"

Mara returned the key to his waiting grasp. "Absolutely." Out of excuses, she retrieved the pouch from Ethan. "These are yours, I believe."

Used to obeisance from his staff, Conroy didn't question her capitulation. He took the pouch and emptied the contents onto the safe, where it perched on the marble pedestal he'd purchased for the occasion. Curious, he searched the other handles for engravings. "Did you translate these, Mara?"

Praying he could not read the language, she replied, "It's a phrase. 'Unto us, deliver all.' All four keys must be read together. In order." She caught a movement in the hallway, heard a muffled pop that was music to her ears. "Do you need any help?"

At the offer, Conroy whipped his head around. "This is mine, Ms. Reed. Do not interrupt." Nigel stood behind him, blocking his view of the exterior room.

Mara sidled away from Lesley and Ethan, motioning them to remain still. Conroy inserted the first key. Her grandfather's key. The tumbler fell.

Hands sweaty, he reached for the second key and it slipped to the carpet. Mara checked the hallway, where another guard slid bonelessly to the marble. She rushed forward to help. "Allow me," she offered.

Nigel shooed her away, and Mara nimbly blocked his view of the outside. "I've got it, Ms. Reed. Please move."

Heart racing, she returned to her position. The second key, Poncho's key, turned easily in the lock. Her cue.

Opening her mouth, she released a bloodcurdling scream. Startled, Conroy spun around, only to find himself receiving a sharp, deliberate blow from Ethan's fist. The older man swayed tipsily. "Nigel?"

Lesley dove into action, ramming the manservant in the midsection with her shoulder. The impact sent them both rolling across the carpet. Mara leapt over the tumbled bodies and aimed for the door. The burly guard had finally processed the commotion and, with a muted roar, he charged. Like a bull moose he ambled forward faster than she would have imagined, but years of practice had her diving between his parted legs. Before he could turn, she jackknifed up and aimed high. He fell like an oak. "Lesley! Ethan! Come on!"

The glass doors swung open and Sebastian waved them forward. "Hey, gorgeous. Get a move on."

Mara flashed a grin and skidded to a stop at his side. Lesley ran past, with Ethan dead on her heels. As the two exited the room, Mara slammed the doors shut. They crowded into the elevator Sebastian had waiting and plummeted fifty floors.

When they reached the ground floor, the quartet raced past a bemused Harold, who watched open-mouthed. Mara hung back and grabbed his arm. "Harold, do me a favor!"

"Sure," he stammered. "Mara."

"I need you to call Mr. Conroy and tell him to not open the safe. Tell him it's rigged to explode. Then I want you to take this and run." She pressed two coins into his cold palm. "This is real gold, Harold. Don't spend it all in one place."

Eyes wider than the coins, Harold hurried to his post. A groggy Nigel answered the phone on the first ring. "Where are they?" he demanded.

"Gone." Harold started to apologize, but realized he wouldn't be an employee much longer. "Ms. Reed told me to give you a message. She said to not open the safe. That it was rigged."

In the suite, Nigel turned to his boss. "Mr. Conroy, no!" The older man jammed his father's key into the slot and turned it hard.

Nigel waited anxiously for an explosion, but nothing happened. Laughing wildly, Conroy inserted the final key and lifted the lever.

Until he died, Nigel would recall the spray of acid and the agonizing screams that reverberated through the office. Flesh melted like wax, burning the carpet and the floor beneath. Conroy collapsed, cursing his father and Mara Reed.

IN THE SLEEK Mercedes that Sebastian drove, Mara sank into the seat and shut her eyes wearily. "Another second and we'd have been goners, Caine."

"I like to make an entrance, darling." Sebastian winked at her in the rearview mirror, and catching Ethan's dark look, added, "I'm always pleased to save your pretty ass in the nick of time."

Lesley twisted on the front seat to examine Mara and Ethan. "What happened? Was that really the safe? Did you actually exchange millions in gold for my safety?"

Mara lifted one heavy eyelid. "Not exactly."

"What then, exactly?" huffed Lesley. "Was I in danger?"

Ethan answered before Mara could respond. "Mara figured out the key sequence when we found the safe. We removed the gold and the artifacts and gave them to Sebastian for safekeeping. Then he drove us to Chi Development. He had instructions to deliver the gold if our plan didn't work."

"Which was?"

Mara kept her eyes shut but explained. "My grandfather didn't trust Reese, or anyone else for that matter. So he had Bailey rig the safe to spew acid if it was opened the wrong way. After we opened it, I realized Conroy had no way of knowing that it only required three keys."

"And if you were wrong?"

"I wasn't. I knew it as soon as I read his key." Mara peeled open her eyes to meet Ethan's. "He was right about the word but wrong about the translation. *Paradidomi* means deliver up, yes. However, in John 12, the Greeks use the word in reference to Judas. To mean betray—or to deliver up to the authorities."

"Incredible." Lesley gave Mara an appreciative tap on the knee. "Very clever, Mara. Very clever."

But Mara heard nothing, sliding into sleep.

CHAPTER 24

TIME TO GO, MARA." ETHAN JOSTLED HER LIGHTLY. "WAKE UP."

"Where are we?" She snuggled deeper into the warmth beneath her cheek, abruptly realizing her pillow was his thigh. Nearly alert, she sat up and looked around. The car had stopped in front of the Austin Ritz Carlton. "Sebastian's choice, I take it."

Ethan nodded. "He and Lesley have already gone inside to check in. And you need an actual bed." Moving swiftly, he bundled her out of the car and steered her to the foyer.

"Mmm-kay." She trailed behind him, admiring the tuck and curve of denim as he booked their room. Still caught between sleep and waking, she didn't comment when he received one key and passed it to the steward.

The hotel room, in comparison to their earlier accommodations, was palatial. But Mara could only focus on the king-sized bed that consumed the space. She fidgeted uneasily as Ethan tipped the bellhop.

Seeing her discomfiture, Ethan sighed. "I can call him back. Get you your own room."

"No. No. This is fine." She scrubbed her hands over her eyes and blinked owlishly. "This is fine." Except she had no idea how to play the coming moments. Ethan stood near the window, framed by a setting sun. Instead of exhausted and worn-out, he was stunning and handsome and perfect. Everything she had ever searched for. It should have amused her, she thought sullenly, that a woman with a thousand roles to her credit couldn't figure out how to tell the man she loved that she wanted to be with him. Only him. "Shall we see what Sebastian and Lesley want to do for dinner?"

"Sure." He clasped his hands behind his back, not facing her. Despite the knowledge that it would come, he hadn't yet prepared himself for the good-bye. Vainly, foolishly, he'd hoped that she'd forget to leave him, that if he pretended they were together again, it would be true. But he'd gotten his one miracle and he didn't expect another. "But I thought you'd want to sit on the bed and count your gold."

"Count my gold." Mara managed a harsh laugh, remembering. "Of course. A thief revels in her possessions. And I got what I came to Kiev for. Enough money to leave this state and never return."

"I assumed as much."

At the cold pronouncement, Mara stalked over to the bags where they'd hidden the satchels. Dropping to her knees, she fumbled with the zipper and ripped at the drawstrings. The bag fell open, gold shining in the dimly lit room. "All the money in the world."

"Millions. You can go anywhere you want. Be anyone you wish." Ethan gripped the windowsill and stared into the empty dark. He understood then what every day of his life would be from that moment forward. Swallowing hard, he muttered, "Why don't I get you that separate room?"

The first coin grazed his temple. The second nicked his lip and skated off his nose. "What the hell?" Ethan spun toward Mara, agape. In steady, unyielding succession, gold coins pelted him. When one caught him squarely in the forehead, he reached her side in three strides. "Cut that out!"

"You think I want the money?" She scrabbled away, tossing coins like confetti. "You think I'm so soulless that I could walk away from you? Again. God, you know nothing about me!"

Warding off the rain of gold, Ethan chased her until her back rammed into the bed. Then he sank beside her and covered her hands. A vicious, terrible hope fluttered inside him, and he pulled the long, elegant fingers to his chest. "What do you want, Mara?" Another coin fell between them, and he whispered, "I thought this was it."

Beneath his hand, Mara splayed her hand against the rapid beat at his chest. "Not gold, Ethan." She covered his heart. "This is it."

"Tell me, Mara." Ethan tipped her chin, forcing her amber eyes to his. "For once, please tell me."

"I love you." The words floated between them, around them. "I love your courage and your tenacity. Your thoughtfulness and your ferocity." Unable to finish, she shook her head. "But I don't expect you to feel the same. Not again."

"Why not?"

"Because I don't understand how you could. Not after everything."

"Because I have faith in you."

Mara shook her head once more, afraid to trust. "I don't understand why."

Shaking his head, Ethan murmured, "Despite your upbringing, you don't really get this faith idea, do you?" He laughed softly, heart soaring. "Faith isn't about what I know of you. It's about what I believe lies within you. I know you have a good heart. That you'll face down hell itself for your friends. That you'd give your life for someone you loved."

Desperate to believe, she held his cheek. "How can that be enough? After all of the wrong I've done. The sins I've committed."

"I learned this from you, Mara. Redemption, faith. Love. They aren't prizes to be won or free gifts with purchase. Faith is looking at a sinner and seeing the potential of a saint. And redemption is what you find—what you've earned—when you finally stop punishing yourself for the sins of your father and see yourself. As I see you."

"Ethan." Trembling, triumphant, she drew his mouth to hers. For hours, for seconds. Forever.

She rested her forehead against his, grateful for second chances. And thirds. "I love you. Always."

"My angel. Mara, my lovely angel. You can't change this or con your way out of it. I have faith in you. I believe in you. And I love you too."

AUTHOR'S NOTE

Dear Readers:

Hidden Sins finds its start in a dusty little town, but quickly moves into a world as big as Texas. I hope you enjoyed Mara and Ethan and their search for love and forgiveness—and a wealth beyond measure.

Happy reading,
Selena Montgomery

ACKNOWLEDGMENTS

April 2006

Tremendous gratitude to Andrea Abrams, for the cultural tutelage; Robert Abrams, for his arcane knowledge; Carolyn Abrams, for the theological tuition; Damon Avent, for motor history; Brandon McLean, for a lovely site; Mirtha Estrada and Kate Super, for bolstering confidence; Marc Gerald, my excellent agent; and Selina McLemore, my terrific editor. And with abiding love for and appreciation to Leslie Abrams, my lodestar and finest critic.

ACKNOWLEDGMENTS

ABOUT THE AUTHOR

SELENA MONTGOMERY is the nom de plume of Stacey Abrams. After serving for eleven years in the Georgia House of Representatives, she became the first Black woman to run as the gubernatorial nominee for a major party in the United States, and was the first Black woman and first Georgian to deliver a Response to the State of the Union. In 2021, she received the inaugural Social Justice Impact Award from the NAACP Image Awards.

Stacey is an avid fan of television and movies, with a penchant for sci-fi, car chases, and heists. A bibliophile, her recent favorites range from Colson Whitehead, Robert Caro, and Nora Roberts to N. K. Jemisin, Rebecca Roanhorse, and Haruki Murakami.

As Selena Montgomery, she is an award-winning author of eight romantic suspense novels.